BUGZ
:contact

Published by Art-Amis
The Stables, Delamere House, Great Wymondley,
Hitchin, Hertfordshire, SG4 7ER

Copyright © David Jackson 2008
First Edition

ISBN 0-9554214 -1-1
ISBN 978-0-9554214-1-9

Printed in The United Arab Emirates
Printed using lithography on wood free paper

This book is dedicated to

Jennifer and Valerie

Thanks to Monica French, who travelled down from Scotland many times to help with the writing of the book. Also my wife Victoria, who had to juggle the editing of the book with the running of a small art business. Ross and Elspeth, along with a great bunch of friends who gathered in Castelfranco on New Year 2006, provided inspiration for some of the characters. These people, along with visits to CERN, Cambridge and Syracuse provided some of the reality in the story recounted by Elsie.

Illustrations provided by the marvellous Malcolm Fryer, whose evocative work can be viewed on www.art-amis.co.uk
Inspirational cover artwork and book design by Adrian Fuller.

As you may guess, Book Zero is only the beginning of the story.
That simple, dangerous number gives a clue to the future.

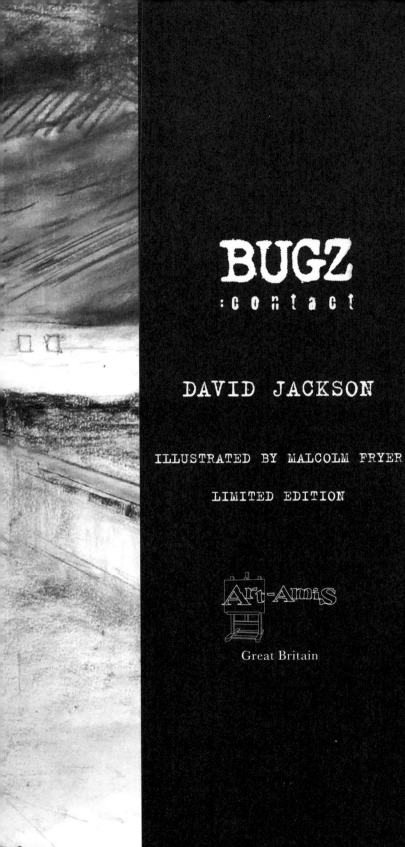

BUGZ
:contact

DAVID JACKSON

ILLUSTRATED BY MALCOLM FRYER

LIMITED EDITION

Art-Amis

Great Britain

'The
vacuum
of
quantum
field
theory
is
an
agitated
broth
in which
many
kinds
of
virtual
particles
wink
in and out
of
existence.'

Gordon Fraser (ed.),
*The New Physics for
the 21st Century.*

OUR REALITY TODAY

We are familiar with the world around us. Our senses, especially our eyes, inform us that everything has size, weight, colour, temperature, surface area and motion. Everything appears to enjoy an independent existence, something which Einstein termed an 'objective reality'. Such is our everyday experience.

It is harder to conceive of the scale of the cosmos, the fact that the farthest known edge of the universe is 13.73 billion light years away, and the fact that only 4% of our universe consists of ordinary matter.

It is harder still, to conceive of the scale of the microscopic and therefore generally invisible. By way of example, if you take a deep breath, you will have more molecules of air in your lungs than there are stars in all the galaxies in the visible universe put together. How then is it possible to imagine even smaller entities, for example, the neutrino, one of many types of subatomic particles known to exist and which has, for all we know zero mass, travels at the speed of light, and consists of nothing much except energy and spin? And who is to say that particles even smaller than the neutrino may not be discovered?

The Ancient Greeks contributed to the search for human origins by identifying atoms as the indivisible building blocks of our universe, differing in size and shape, moving aimlessly through space, colliding and deflecting like billiard balls or interlocking to build clusters. This mechanistic view of nature was quickly superseded by those of contemporary philosophers uncomfortable with the idea that everything, including human existence, was no more than the result of random atom collisions.

Understanding the way the world worked was not an end in itself. Understanding its purpose was what mattered, and that purpose lay elsewhere, such as in human's free will or in the meddling of the gods – not, at any rate, in the nature of atoms.

Having decided that small things such as atoms were simply there, and nothing more than motes in a sunbeam, humans looked away and focused on a subject of far greater interest; namely themselves, their place in the world and their purpose within it. They focused on the visible: the appearance of the solar system, the nature of movement, light and colour, the conversion of metals. Whether atoms were hard specks zipping about in space or squishy things packed closely together did not really matter. Absolute certainties and established rules did.

However, in 1900 the German physicist Max Planck opened the door to a new world, that of a tiny thing which obeyed the laws not of absolute certainty, but of probability. He observed that under ideal conditions the radiant heat energy from a hot body emitted itself in a jerky manner, in discrete packets or individual amounts, which he called quanta. In 1905 this quantum hypothesis was supported by Albert Einstein, who proposed that light was made up of distinct particles (photons) and not a continuous wave, such as had been believed throughout the nineteenth century. In 1913 the Danish physicist Niels Bohr proposed in turn that atomic electrons were also 'quantised', in that they jumped between fixed energy levels. This jumping of energy, a wave like fuzziness, made it impossible to measure precisely and at the same time the position and momentum of quanta subatomic particles. As a result, by the mid 1920s the new theory of quantum mechanics had been developed to take account of this wave particle duality and its probable behaviour.

The discovery was thrilling. It was also disconcerting. Humans had now to contemplate the rather 'unscientific' fact that the building blocks of their universe were not wholly predictable and therefore not under their control. Quantum particles do not travel along well-defined paths in space; they are directed only by the 'law of averages' and, moreover, seem to cooperate with each other as though possessing a form of consciousness at the individual level. Bohr believed that the uncertainty of their behaviour is something we should accept. Einstein, in contrast, refused to accept the notion of what he called 'ghostly action at a distance'; for all his modernist thinking he clung to the classical view that cause and effect underlay this world the way it underlay our own. However, it has since been generally accepted that the quantum world is not like our 'objective reality'. Subatomic particles seem almost to have a life of their own, neither good nor bad, and the humans are now back at the drawing board again to see what these little things whizzing around in space actually do, and what they perhaps think, if they are in some way conscious.

The study of this subject incorporates both hard science and philosophy, physics and metaphysics. The quantum physicist Richard Feynman remarked, 'I think I can safely say that nobody understands quantum mechanics.'

Let's meet these particles in their habitat. We can't see them but we can try anyway. Their properties can include mass, charge, position, velocity and spin (state of rotation) and they interact with each other. Imagine a pot of strawberry jam represents 'empty space'. If the bits of strawberry in it represent subatomic particles, the binding agent they float in represents one of the four fundamental forces in our universe: the weak, the strong, the electromagnetic, and gravity. These forces are made up of interacting particles through which the actor particles communicate, and the lumpy nature of the jam represents the particles' behaviour.

Particle accelerators such as the Large Hadron Collider at CERN in Switzerland create our windows into this world. By smashing particles together at close to the speed of light in order to study the results of their collisions, we can recreate to some extent the conditions of the very early universe to try to understand the fundamental nature of matter.

How, for example, can something be created from nothing? How do particles acquire mass? One theory suggesting an answer is the Higgs mechanism, whereby a zero energy, zero spin, unstable, quickly decaying and therefore hidden boson (interacting particle) moves through our pot of space jam and creates a drag on other particles, that is it provides the viscosity, creates the bits of fruit, gives surrounding particles their mass.

The Large Hadron Collider, scheduled to start up in 2008, may throw light on the Higgs boson's existence and the question of mass. The International Linear Collider, which may be up and running in the late 2010s, may do the same. It is only huge particle accelerators such as these that can track the transient phenomena existing within us and around us and making us what we are: curious and individual clusters of cosmic dust. They may even track what our souls are.

We might then really meet the subatomic particles within us; we might then really meet ourselves.

BUGZ
:contact

Dear Reader,

This is the greatest story never told, about the biggest subject ever described. It is a story that in part I lived, and it is also one that was imparted to me.

As we look out on our universe and its existence of over thirteen billion years, we may wonder where we fit into it. After all, out of the hundred billion suns or more and their satellites that populate it, our planet is but a grain of sand on a cosmic beach that slides off the far dune, beyond the reach of the most powerful scientific instruments imaginable. All this matter and antimatter with it that make up every particle, was once at the beginning of time compressed into the tiniest of pinpricks. It exploded and expanded, a single event known as the Big Bang and set the clock of our universe ticking. This commonly accepted fact is fantastical and reasonable at the same time. At our birth we were ripped from the underbelly of nothingness.

We face a conundrum. Does everything we see around us come from nothing? If so, how could it happen, was it by mistake or design? In either case, will everything remain preserved on a course set all those years back? Was it somehow planned, can it be altered?

We, as Homo sapiens, appear at best to have been around for only the last two million years, yet even during this brief existence changes are afoot. Why did the helix of DNA chemicals enclosed in each of these carbon bipeds evolve? Are the physical world around us and the human

1

stuff of which we are made the only things responsible for creating the phenomena we often contemplate and experience – dreams, ghosts, past life experiences?

We hear a lot about the human soul but we really don't know a lot about it. It is, should we say, an idea which is convenient for us to think of little, yet we probably all hope it might exist and goes to some after-life. We cannot explain everything around us with our current under-standing of science, although we will seek to understand what makes our universe tick (so to speak). If humans views their development as a voyage of exploration, they should know that this is not their odyssey alone. Stages of the voyage seem to be missing, not logged, and these are commonly accounted for by religious beliefs. But there has at times been a hand at the tiller that we couldn't see even if we tried, or at least couldn't until now.

The set of events related here involves life forms so small that atoms appear enormous in comparison. Consider this. The width of the human finger is 0.1×10cm. That of a virus is 1×10^{-5}cm (that is 0.00001 cm or 0.01 mm). That of an atomic nucleus is 1×10^{-14}cm. The size of the hand occasionally at our tiller is 1×10^{-32} cm (in other words, one hundred thousand billion billion billionths of a centimetre). Small in terms of size, then. But not power, for their power in relation to that of a super-nova would easily equal the power of a supernova to that of a storm in a teacup. The infinitely small holds the infinitely great in its grasp. We should not think of great green monsters from outer space but some-thing closer to home, maybe even existing among us.

I know this, for I was part of the story all those years ago in the sum-mer of 2042, when the world was a very different place. Humankind was more concerned with looking outward at the ills of the planet and global warming than looking inward at the greater conflict raging unnoticed in its midst: the conflict in equating logic and pure scientific thought with sacrifice and love. We were looking for something out there when all the time there were those looking out at us and, dare I say, influencing us like the gods of classical civilisation.

In my advanced state of bodily decay here in Earth time, I often think of those summer days, a time when the world had not even heard of Bugz, a world I understood. A time when time itself was black and white and had rules we obeyed, although the tiny hand at the tiller sometimes did not. I think of my family, especially my brothers, one of whom I have lost and one who is greatly changed. We were fresh-faced students back then, carefree and optimistic. After that summer the world changed forever, and I guess you make your own view if it was for the better or for worse, or if we could have done better.

I owe it to the Ashcroft name and especially the younger of my brothers to tell this story, much of which is contained on old data chips from my faithful IDO given to me by an unlikely hero called Blipp. My cleaning robot nearly carted it all out to the waste unit the other day. I may be in my nineties now but you should have seen me shift – and when I say I did so in two zicroseconds flat, I mean it.

I dedicate this work to the real architect whose legend will live on always – Zareth. I can only apologise to him in advance for having to use my simple cranky English terms in place of his far advanced and burnished messenger Bugz.

Elsie Ashcroft
Haslingdene Vicarage, Cambridge, 29 November 2116

1.ZYBERIA
Another universe in another time

In the beginning there was nothing.

And just after the beginning there were the Bugz,

powerful subatomic particles, that had spilled out in their zillions on the orderly plains and folds of the expanding fabric of their universe and carved out from nothing a multidimensional Zyberian empire extending to the neatly tucked edges of their universe.

A Bugz-eye view of an atom was to see it as planet-like in scale. Not that this dwarfed the Bugz, for what these minute building blocks of life lacked in mass they more than made up for in energy and power. They held sway over all things we might call 'atomic'. They shaped the pearl* topography of their own existence, the black and white plains and folds of the harmony and disharmony of their history and the zyberleagues of space around them.

Woven into a near seamless existence of calm logic and efficient function were two pure silken threads of ancient lineage, as black and white as the pearls, intricately spun from the noble signatures and complex equations of Superbugz. The black and white of clarity and balance provided the smooth symmetric pattern of Bugz society while hemming in and stitching up if not annihilating the motley and undesirable tufts of greyness and blur. All was clear-cut and hierarchical and regulated. As smooth as clockwork. Routine and predictable to the point of being dull, one might say if one were not Bugz. Giving the Bugz a sense of superiority that induced a sense of complacency, one might add. But

4

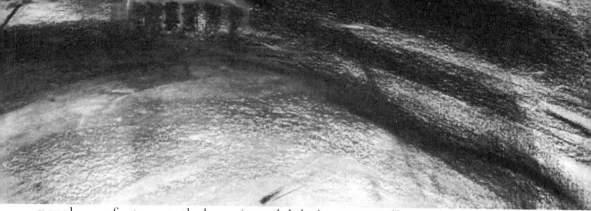

nearly perfect nonetheless, 'nearly' being a small word but vitally important to our story.

The stable nucleus at the centre of this pearlscape provided the structures and pillars and concourses of Bugz society for promoting concensus and civility in imitation of the all but forgotten golden age that had preceded it. This had been a time of pure harmony, the classical age of Zytopia, when cause and effect were in perfect alignment and the capital Zytop radiated peace. The Zyberian capital built several billennia later on the duzz-covered ruins of Old Zytop was but its pale shadow – not that many movers and shakers in the Zyberian ruling elite were aware of this, because they spent the bulk of their energy in debate over the means of achieving even greater harmony and devoting themselves to the nitpicking detail of measuring and honing existing equations*. A frequent saying in learned circles was that, for all their smoothness and clarity of thought, only Bugz could create conflict about the means of achieving harmony.

As a result, nearly all Bugz sensors were fixed on their point of destination, while almost none looked back to their point of origin and its rich heritage. The past was an obscure domain, left to the small clusters of teachers and Bugzhist monks who served the superparticle elite in the Council of the Apex and were generally regarded as mere fossil hunters and performers of rites.

The tenets that underpinned Zyberian society, to calculate the best way to take that tiny final step to a state of perfection, held true in every regard except one. As the great teacher and philosopher Zim observed to his noble Bugzhist associate Zein, how could Bugz return to the state of perfection they knew had once existed if they couldn't actually remember what it was? And as Zein for his part observed to Zim, what

5

did a state of perfection actually mean? The sterility of a clinical black and white order and nothing more? The strange cyphers and references spelt out in the Library's ancient records maybe suggested otherwise, but even the great Zein had not summoned up the energy to break the mould and take action to lay a new foundation.

ZARETH

The ancient records made mention of Zareth, a shadowy figure whose leadership had defined the age of Zytopia, a superparticle of another dimension, so legend had it. His signature track did not accurately resemble that of pure Bugz, and the power he possessed was neither light nor dark but rather a hybrid of the two. He had merged with the mass in his wanderings, his energy and spin attracting and exciting many of the Bugz he encountered in each locality, black and white, and even those further afield. The path he selected led, he claimed, to unity.

Such a path countered plain logic, however. How could one merge black and white if not to make wishy-washy and undesirable grey? It was said that Zareth had originally fused the two black and white pendulums of social order into one, but something had later caused them to slip out of sync. Like all items of balance, only a zicroscopic amount of mass added to or taken away from one side was needed to create great discord.

It seemed as though Zareth had been the harbinger of the great age of black Bugz domination and not the saviour many hoped for.

THE QUAKE: A TIME BEFORE ZYBERIA

The long and harmonious age of Zytopia came to an end when a strange and devastating Quake washed in from the furthest edges of the universe, sucking the charge from the outlying nuclei, and levelling the great civilisation of Bugz in layers of duzz*. The dark energy of this wave crashed through the three energy rings of Zytop, toppling its building blocks, filling each nook and cranny within, uprooting the capital's foun-

8

dations and unplugging the great energy viaduct that fed the labyrinth of conduits beneath Zytop. It initiated a chaotic phase of decaying structures and erratic cross currents, and led to the irregular clumping of negatively charged antiparticles in close-packed and secretive nuclei. In no time, it seemed, the behaviour of rogue particles and their accomplices brought about Zytopia's collapse and a power vacuum developed.

The white Bugz of advanced equations, who maintained a strict observance of the conditions of mutual dependence and equal function with their mirror black Bugz, found themselves quickly displaced and vastly outnumbered. Their counterparts wasted no time in amassing to form a powerful but unstable entity. The negative black Bugz charge trickled and crept along the passageways; it neutralised and snuffed out one by one the glowing lights of Old Zytop until only one speck remained, one which flickered unsteadily and secretly in the city's inner sanctum, the Great Library, the repository of all records known to Bugz.

The Library, buttressed as it was by the vast and unadulterated energy of past Bugz equations contained within its walls, was one of the few monuments to survive the Quake. Even so, the finesse of its intricate structures and the minutiae of its rich deposits were now tarnished and rubbed away. The Library's fabled light could no longer be seen with the passing of Zytopia, and its remaining structures sank under the drifts of duzz. Several billennia were to pass through the aeons of the black phases before Bugz society set ticking again its twin pendulum-like existence of power sharing.

There marched forth from the city's newly hatched laboratories, columns of replicate Bugz calculated to fill the gap, to tunnel through the duzz and stimulate activity. Not that quantity could make up for quality. Possessing equations that were shiny but without depth, and crude serial stamps in place of lavish signatures, this new generation was automatically denied the wisdom, heritage and uniqueness of the old order.

The new age Zyberia with its reconstructed nucleus, now had a new group of particles and superparticles that were starting to question the need to share power. Such questioning, some said, stemmed from ignorance and fear of the past; others said they were simply weary of constantly fine tuning the social equilibrium and pointed instead to the untapped riches of pure white and pure black.

9

Whatever the prevailing mood, the whole Zyberian universe was metaphorically tipped on its head the day that Zein received out of the blue a fat bundle of TT* Bugz. It was stuffed into his analytical units in such a way that the contents could only be unravelled theoretically by one Bugz, one special message for one special reader. The message it carried was odd, for it provided Zein with the answer to a question he didn't know, an answer that would lead to 'first contact'.

2. ICE CREAM AND ASSASSIN

Svetlana licked on a melting liquorice ice cream and gazed down at the water swirling below. Gone were the days when tourists flocked to the Plaza del Duomo and strolled up and down the waterfront. The water level had risen too high for safety, and Venice was crumbling at an accelerating rate. Shabby chic was becoming just plain shabby. Svetlana remembered its heyday and was relieved it wouldn't be long before she left.

She saw the greenish water wash over the cobbles and curl in long thin crests of scum, and how algae and sodden rubbish collected in corners and old doorways, along street channels and over the steps in front of the water gates. A gondola glided past, its occupants entwined in an embrace as though sensing the magic was about to run out. Of course, with the flexing of just one of the energy rings of the particle nestling within her, Svetlana could raise the very rock Venice stood on, but she liked to see the humans toiling at their self preservation. It was so pointless and so human.

It was time to hurry Marco along. He had just parked his Alfa Romeo, crossed the causeway, and was now walking purposefully along, but she still put an extra spring in his step, and lined up a Vaporetto, which glided alongside him and picked him up before he was sidetracked by the prostitutes who frequented this area. It delivered him straight to the water gate at the foot of her palazzo just a few metres from the Bridge of Sighs, and that was where she now headed.

11

She greeted him as he took the steps two at a time up to the Piano Nobile with its exuberant carved interior and thick bordello red rugs. He leaned forward for the anticipated warm kiss, but Svetlana turned away with a pout and dipped into her lilac leather handbag for the goodies he was expecting. He wasn't even being invited to join her on the sofa on this occasion. She handed him a pair of virtual Gogspecs and motioned for him to sit down in front of her on the divan. Slotting into the side of the gogs a hypo capsule which pricked Marco's temple, she waited for the drug to take effect before flicking on the virtual switch that would project a 3D image before his eyes.

The image floated in front of him.

CERN: The home of world particle science.
A virtual tour with commentary by Icarus Ashcroft.

'Look and learn,' she said, in a husky voice. 'The narcotic will help you navigate your way round the corridors of CERN in Geneva and then it will imprint it on your synaptic nerves as if you had designed and built the place yourself.'

'Really? Where did you get this little toy then, my angel?' Marco quizzed.

'It's something Henri, my good friend the Director General at CERN has been working on with the US military. He didn't know that the testing we've been doing would afford us a detailed 3D model of his own little empire. I think the US require it for briefing their special forces on the layout of potential terrorist targets and hide-outs round the world.'

'So you get on well with this Henri then?'

Svetlana smiled. 'I love powerful men. And you could say that he amuses me'.

'I'm drifting, Sveti,' Marco murmured, sinking back. 'You always have this effect on me anyway, and this time you're just taunting me. So sexy like a Russian princessssssss.'

'Yes, my little assassin, this time you're to lie back and think of CERN.'

Marco awoke some time later, to find Svetlana straddling him, removing the gogs and peering into his eyes.

12

'Now that's more like it, Sveti,' he smirked. 'Something tells me I won't need glasses for the next part of the briefing – ah!'

Grabbing Marco through his designer chinos and squeezing hard, Svetlana demanded, 'Tell me, how many security men are posted at the back entries of the amphitheatre?'

'Ah… two.'

'What colour are the chairs in the amphitheatre?'

'Turquoise.'

'And how long do you think it would take for you to get along the old ALICE tunnel to make your escape?'

'Five minutes, jogging. Damn you, Sveti, let go of my – '

'OK, so you know the place as well as you know the most intimate parts of your body now,' Svetlana said, releasing her grip and easing her athletically toned body off him. 'Now, Marco, here is an IDO chip showing a 3D layout of the amphitheatre, in case you need a hard copy for backup. And here is the encrypted key to the locker at the Maglev station where you will find a bag with the necessary Heckler and Koch firearm, made specially for CERN security. It will be loaded with four special bullets only. No more, no less. Be smart Marco, this gun wasn't easy to get and will add to the effect I need. You must not miss under any circumstances. Make your aim true.'

'This wasn't the kind of reception I was expecting when I came here,' Marco moaned, feeling his groin.

'Maybe not, but work comes first, don't you agree?' Svetlana said lightly, pouring him a coffee and sloshing some grappa in.

'You need not question my professionalism, Svetlana. I just wish sometimes that you put your hair in curlers and padded about in misshapen old slippers like my mama sometimes.'

'Talking of relatives, you come highly recommended to me by Papa, and the fact that your services are not exactly the cheapest, I take as proof of your professionalism. Study the info here and have your new friends in position.'

'All three of them,' Marco assured her. 'I've been the ideal recruit. Their little cell has proved very cosy indeed these last few months. While they've been dreaming about their peaceful protest, I've been dreaming about what I'm about to get from you, Svetlana.'

13

'What you're going to get from Papa,' Svetlana corrected him.

'We both know I'm getting it from you. Both that and the money.'

'Which you'll receive at four o'clock on the 12th of June, at the Beau Rivage in Lausanne. I'll be in my usual suite. Dump your vehicle well beforehand, remember. Leave nothing to chance.'

A flicker of anger crossed Marco's near lidless eyes, but he leaned forward with lips pursed for a kiss. 'I know best what I do, and what I do I do best.'

Svetlana sighed with pleasure. 'Then we are so alike, it seems.'

'Although fortunately not in every way, it has to be said.'

'No, not in every way. I'm so very grateful for that,' Svetlana said, pulling the long nail of her index finger down his pursed lips.

'Ouch, that hurt.'

'Arrivederci' my princess,' Marco thought. He would give her pain of a different sort when this job was over he thought, a nice bonus.

Marco made his way gingerly out through the front entrance. This lady was exciting, but dangerous. He didn't like it when he was not in control. However, the adrenalin rush he had felt on absorbing the information on CERN's layout made him itch to get on with the job.

In the meantime he would pay for some urgent relief of another sort across the grand canal after the rousing welcome he had just had. He could possibly put it on the tab, given the payout he was expecting in the near future.

3. GENEVA AIRPORT

Jonathan Stein felt his heart pumping and the sweat prickling as he collapsed in the driving seat, gripped the wheel and watched Geneva's airport terminal lurch away in the head-up display on his Chromathene* windscreen. For the past year he had lived with the knowledge that he had been one of only four people found alive out of hundreds killed after the crash of a C980 a mile away from Newark Airport's runway. He had been lying half-conscious and deaf on scorched grass when he had seen the flicker of garish-coloured fragments approaching him through the clogging smoke. They had materialised into fire tunics, badges and deft arms, silent shapes mouthing silent roars that had borne him up and away through a broken world to a cluster of flashing orange lights, in the middle of nowhere. That was before the thick band of night had choked out a good month of his life, before he understood that you could experience Armageddon and actually survive it.

The silver strands he saw flecking his hair in the mirror were a testament to this. He was only thirty-three, after all. 'Youthfully distinguished' was how he now described his appearance.The press had described as a miracle not only the four's sheer survival but also their extraordinarily quick recovery. They had, in fact, become unwilling minor celebrities in their various countries for a time.

This evening Stein had been thinking of those same figures silhouetted against the orange lights as his plane cruised to the gate in the darkness and waited for the air bridges while a crew of fluorescent jackets and

15

auxiliary vehicles teemed below on the wet synthetic runway. It had been a smooth landing, the most natural thing in the world, no fuss. His sigh of relief had made the passenger in the next seat look round at him. He punched his integrated booking reference number into the rental car's touch screen mounted on the driver's Chromathene screen, and drove off through torrential rain with the laser wipers steaming the screen free of droplets. He switched on some music classics from the 2020s and relaxed back in his seat as he passed a series of modern capsule apartments, an eco top-up station, and also the ultra-modern headquarters of Blipp, the nano communications industry brand leader whose multi-media devices had flooded the world. Stein recognised the sign bearing the familiar flattened cone- shaped characters of the Blipp Corporation's logo. It oozed its way into every area of public consciousness. It was Blipp this, Blipp that; it almost sounded like a term of censorship. Stein had succeeded in the past few years in getting his foot through the door to meet its chairperson, Bertholdt Lipp, not just once but on a number of social occasions and in the way of work. He had always found the man to be pleasant, unlike the grinning cartoon character image peddled in the media. The seemingly insincere smile and the detached, almost unhuman manner was simply because the man was focused.

Tomorrow would be a scoop for Stein: his first official interview with the man who had a huge vested interest in ensuring the smooth functioning of the nanoputers and virtual communications network at CERN, the European Centre for Nuclear Research. The day after that would be the big day for the many people whose lives revolved around CERN: with the official start up of its new and completely revolutionary particle accelerator.

Stein would want to despatch his report straight away after the interview. He imagined all those Americans hunched over their newspapers and screens, drinking in the usual speculation about Blipp's ambitions and demons, about the larger-than-life showman figure directing his empire from the nerve centre of his swish offices in Geneva. Stein knew the reality was that most people, focused as they often were on the more trivial and sensational, could not grasp the wider and more sober implications of the science that Blipp devoted himself to and the potential it had to transform their lives. If only they did...

16

The suburbs he passed through were neat and completely nonde-script. However, tucked away here and there on the odd corner he saw the shutters and long steep gables of a different time, a sort of make-believe world he had always carried within him, first on the streets of weatherboard houses in New Jersey, then along the whitewashed corri-dors of the Massachusetts Institute of Technology (MIT), and nowadays on the sidewalks of Manhattan. These old chalets were kind of familiar and had a 'human' feel. The crisp mountain air was familiar too, but it was becoming intolerably thin, to the extent that the UV fibre hats and the highest factor sunscreen had become government regulation wear.

Stein had been over here many times before. One of his girlfriends had abandoned him for the designer boutiques once she discovered he was only interested in exploring one alpine village after another.

'Get a life, can't you, and take the reality tablets,' she'd said with a tone of pity. He seemed to be rooted in the distant past, as though seek-ing some link of his own there, and he couldn't define it.

Stein considered himself to be the one rooted in reality; it was the rest of the world that needed to wake up. The whole planet was hurtling onwards ever faster with too many variables and too many dangers. Action was needed, but how he could have an effect was the perplexing issue. He could communicate the solutions in his editorial and try to influence others in this way.

He had gleaned snippets about his stunted family tree over the years, including an account of a teenage girl from a small Swiss community putting a baby up for adoption in 1903. From there the thin trail went to Eastern Europe and then the States and the Midwest before ending with the birth of Jonathan Stein Whistler, born 2009.

He hadn't made the grade as a world-class physicist at MIT, despite showing great potential; he'd found his niche instead on the well-regarded student newscast, spreading the word about the cutting edge of science. He'd found the cutting edge here, at the European Centre for Nuclear Research, just outside Geneva, in the early summer of 2042. 'The gateway to the stars', the papers liked to put it, but he'd pen some-thing more original.

Having checked in at the hotel he scanned the chip in the back of his hand across the door lock.

The door swung open and a voice declared in staccato European tones, 'Good evening, Mr Stein, I hope your journey was pleasant. A full

17

range of movelets are available. The troposphere restaurant is on the eighteenth floor and the cabaret has another hour or so to run this evening if you're in the mood.' Stein threw his wet jacket on the hydrogel chair with mock leather coverings, spread his arms wide and fell straight back into the cocoon of pillows on the bed. He was shattered. He spent all of ten seconds gazing up at the virtual sky on the bedroom ceiling, counting the stars and imagining the coming interview with the gregarious Blipp. A scoop indeed, but nothing like the scale of the one that would follow the day after when the window to a new universe would be opened. Zzzzzzz.

4. TRANQUILLITY IN CAMBRIDGE

Brooke Ashcroft smoothed out the checked picnic cloth, secured it on the grass with two china plates, tucked linen napkins under these and produced pieces of cold roast chicken and a bowl of salad from the depths of her hamper. She held out two fluted glasses for her husband to pour the champagne. It was as though the clock had been turned back a hundred, even two hundred, years or so before; there was nothing more idyllic than a sunny June day in Cambridge.

'To Sir Isaac,' her husband smiled at her, by way of a toast. 'To the four hundredth anniversary of his birth and his achievements. Who knows? Maybe in another hundred years someone will be sitting right on this spot, enjoying the river, enjoying May Week, and celebrating the centenary of what might well be called the Ashcroft detector – why not?'

'It's about time you got the recognition you deserve,' Brooke answered. 'And I say let's toast the two of us, not Newton. Newton's being done to death at present.'

'Yes, of course, to the two of us, darling, and to the Ashcroft name that it might have star billing for a change.'

'And to Lycian for coping so well with his illness. He could surprise us all yet with a first. He's putting in the hard graft, I'm sure of it, but it isn't easy.'

'Absolutely not. The boy's got hidden depths. But then I expect no less,' Ashcroft smiled.

They turned their heads as the sound of madrigal singing drifted up

19

the Backs from the Cam. A group of students floated by on the water, slumped back with the ubiquitous fibre sun hats pulled over their eyes, trailing hands in the water.

'Aren't we lucky, Icarus? It's great to be back, even if only for a long weekend. I refuse to believe tomorrow will happen, or the day after, whether it's your big day or not. The future simply doesn't exist, you know. I've frozen it in time, so we can stay here.'

Her husband stroked her cheek. 'I have to go, I'm sorry, but I promised my tutorial group I would have a big surprise for them, and I've thought about it and intend to give them the full story even before the press. I am going to ask our lot to see if they want to come along also it would be nice for them to know why they haven't seen me all these years. I know they know you are busy and they can talk with you, I don't think you have shut them out at all.'

'Come on Carus, they love you.'

'Ouch, that hurt!'

'You mean the truth of how close we are?'

'Just bringing you back to Earth, darling, like I usually have to. You're not to lord it over your minions too much. Remember, they like you and your odd ways and that's why you will trust them, and have got CERN to pay for their flights to help you in the past.'

Icarus brushed his lips on her cheek. 'I want you to know, darling, that without you and the family all this would mean nothing to me, nothing.'

'Well, that's our little secret,' Brooke smiled.

The contents of the picnic basket soon consumed, Brooke knew her husband only too well to expect him to linger with her in the early afternoon sun. He was keen to get home to the vicarage and spend time going over both the notes for his landmark speech at CERN, and the precursor meeting with his tutorial group at the Centre for Mathematical Studies up the road. He and Brooke enjoyed the brisk walk home – it was always a brisk walk, given Icarus' long legs. Their arrival at Haslingdene was the usual type of arrival, with Icarus marching ahead through the front porch, making a beeline for the study, and leaving Brooke to greet Mrs Nimmo for the usual friendly natter in the kitchen.

Icarus looked out of the French windows and thought of the hours of study and preparation leading up to today and what the next forty-eight hours would bring. The anticipation was palpable and the excitement made his heart flutter even in the calm isolation of his family home. The old redbrick vicarage sat forlornly at the end of a waterlogged drive, hidden from view by a high weathered wall. The unseasonal early summer gales had collected leaves around the bases of the pruned trees in the grounds, the weather was all over the place and the Cam had flooded twice in the last five years causing havoc in the village and nearby roads.

Joan Nimmo, the faithful housekeeper, had carried out her usual full-scale invasion, opening the sash windows to let in a fresh breeze that coursed through the house, banging doors and shaking papers piled high on the Prof's desk. She barged her way through everything, airing the bedding and thrusting the nozzle of the ionic fluxer round the tightest of corners to eliminate the tiniest particles of dust. Her ham-like arms and heavy-duty gloves were an industrial force to be reckoned with. Icarus knew her husband was an ex-boxer. He wondered, not for the first time, if the story was true that they staged regular arm wrestling contests over their kitchen table, contests she regularly won.

5. TWO DIFFERENT WORLDS

The crumbling capsule of faded gentility that was Haslingdene Vicarage stood in stark contrast to that of the workaday world of CERN with its curious blend of the futuristic and sparse and the colourful and rather eccentric. It was Ashcroft's other world.

Despite theoretically running their lives along the lines of customary clinical Swiss efficiency, the CERN personnel had still developed their own idiosyncracies and traditions. Streamlined and space-efficient state-of-the-art infrastructure jostled with bulky scientific instruments dating back to the 1990s and earlier, artifacts described as retro at best and junk at worst. The narrow grey and beige corridors within its buildings were lined with postbox red filing cabinets whose overflowing drawers squealed open and shut on rusting and skewed runners. Antiquated letter racks and filofaxes shared office space with multi-million Euro hi-tech pico laser scanners, Blipp nanoputers, and of course the banks and monitors of the colossal Grid facility, which wormed its tendrils round CERN and the entire world. When asked why envelopes and dog-eared calendars were still used here thirty years after such things had died out, the answer came that CERN wasn't actually Earth and normal human living, you know; next question?

Mountains of empty packaging stood in front of the lifts, the gents', the drinks dispensers and the gantries on the experiment sites. Cell-like offices led off the corridors on both sides and housed only plain desks, shelving and pinned-up family snaps; the equally plain windows looked out on the grassed stretches and pathways of the campus-like confines of CERN. The austerity of the workplace begged the question that humans and their needs were probably an afterthought in the creation of an environment that demanded long hours and the ultimate in personal endeavour.

The employees exercised the more latent sides of their brains by scrawling chalk on blackboards and amusing themselves with quirky games and competitions of their own devising. It allegedly helped to stop everyone from going totally mad in the hothouse of logic and grey matter.

The 'robotic cat', which roamed the corridors and was jokingly alleged to have cost more than the new accelerators, was but one product of a non-scientific and most satisfying staff competition that had passed into legend.

This simple device for trapping mice in a humane manner in order to repatriate them to the outside world was, however, an important one; after all, a short length of chewed wire embedded in a magnet might set the organisation back, a not inconsiderable ten thousand euros.

A bronze statue stood on the competition winner's desk, the figure of an exultant grinning mouse thrusting two irreverent fingers in the air. It had received the title of the mouse equivalent of a Nobel Peace Prize and the winner was remembered on every birthday after that with a card from the 'CERN Union of Mice'.

The route to Ashcroft's exalted position at CERN had been strewn with the best of credentials: a first-class BSc from Cambridge followed by lauded papers on the irregular properties of solitons and new applications in the field of magneto electronics. After a stint as visiting professor at MIT, he embarked on further postdoctoral studies for five years up to his high profile promotion at the age of thirty-one to the post of Lucasian Professor of Mathematics, taking the chair once occupied by Newton and Hawking.

From this position, and whilst retaining many of his teaching commitments, it was a short step to gaining the prestigious post of senior assistant to CERN's Chief Scientific Officer in 2026. He had been promoted to his superior's job seven years later, and now, nearly a decade on at the age of fifty-two, had been and still was a regular commuter to Switzerland.

Everyone agreed that Icarus Ashcroft had risen far – in fact some went further in saying that his head was stuck so high in the clouds that he had left the mere mortals below him. The only question voiced now with a tinge of jealousy was how much further he would need to go to satisfy his insatiable appetite for recognition.

Icarus had certainly kept his feet on the ground in terms of his home life, what with his social circuit in academe and family. On the death of his uncle, the Reverend Socrates Ashcroft twenty-five years earlier, he had inherited Haslingdene Vicarage in the southwest corner of Cambridge, a four-hundred-year-old redbrick building that creaked under the weight of family heirlooms and books. The vicarage had been in the Ashcroft family since the late seventeenth century, when a certain remarkable forebear, Icarus William Ashcroft the elder, had served as an assistant to Sir Isaac Newton in helping set up and collaborate on a range of scientific experiments. In this welcome retreat Icarus had been able to embrace Cambridge life wholeheartedly and bury himself away in exercises of the mind, studying and comparing notes with his peers.

He had met Brooke when she was a twenty-one- year-old graduate, at a Trinity College formal during a period of helping to tutor joint degree students. He was recently back from his stint at MIT† and that little American twang he had acquired reminded her of home. She was a major in languages and maths, a rare and classy Ivy League import in the Cambridge world, and her sharp mind and vivacity had enticed him out of the stuffy nooks of the library at home, the laboratory at work and the riverside local. As the daughter of

a Princeton professor she understood his world completely; as a social creature she showed him there was more to life than theorems and equations.

His convincing Brooke to stay on in Cambridge after completing her studies ensured that they made a good pairing. Most considered him to be the powerful intellect, but those well acquainted with the couple knew Brooke to be his equal in many ways and certainly the rock to his crashing waves. Brooke was the perfect influence in his life for opening up the vicarage to the fresh joys of family life and a circle of good friends, as well as mixing work and pleasure with trips to Princeton.

The children came along in quick succession: Scamander (Sam), Lycian and Electra (Elsie). Like their father and their Great Uncle Socrates whose home they had grown up in, they were named in the eccentric Ashcroft tradition of choosing Greek forenames that stretched back to the earliest parish records and maybe further. These names had often been abbreviated or adapted in order to avoid ridicule or confusion, but the christening practice had stuck.

The two boys looked set to follow in their father's footsteps. Both had physics as their first love. Sam had enrolled at Churchill, and Lycian was continuing the Ashcroft tradition by studying at Pembroke. Elsie preferred the classics, and she was in her first year at King's. Brooke's love of history had been passed on to Elsie, and the girl enjoyed the burgeoning science of decoding ancient text using maths, very much in the way

25

HERE LIETH

ICARUS WILLIAM
ASHCROFT
1651~1723

BLOVD HUSBAND
OF

MARGARET ANN
1665~1744

AND
DEVOTED FATHER
OF

HECTOR WILLIAM
TYDEUS EDWARD
OPHION JAMES
PITTEUS EDWARD
PHOEBE ANN

"FROM THE TINIEST
FLECK ON A WAVE
HEd FASHION THE
FULLER OF TIDES"

that cryptographers sought out patterns in cyphers. Icarus Ashcroft had enough air under his wings to see out his days. He'd had a key role in the momentous step taken to build the test facility for the new Parallel Beam Collider* at CERN and pave the way for its future site there, and he'd had a say in the unprecedented amount of resources allocated to it.

The scale of scientific breakthrough achieved in the lab from his first day there was matched by the gargantuan appetite of CERN's global data intensive super Grid* and its nanoputing applications, while Blipp's name was synonymous with hi-tech communications in the spin-off commercial sphere, emblazoned as it was on many leading communications products including the IDO* (Inform-ion Data Organiser).From lab to computer network to company, CERN's achievements were coming so thick and fast that even tight-fisted governments could not seize on the obvious political and economic opportunities fast enough.

CERN's Director General Henri le Baut had only to lap it up. His external relations officer Gayle Richter selectively blocked, chopped, manipulated and eked out all the goodies before they hit his desk in order for him to dispense, on her advice, grants and licenses, like a potentate seeking favours in return. Spin-off enterprises born of CERN research were being snapped up by all areas of industry: the military, pharmaceutics, communications. Gayle was expert at keeping everyone happy – VIPs, the world press, every member of personnel down to the errand boy. Invitations to the launch of the most powerful atom smasher ever built were like gold dust, given the modest size and strictly limited number of seats in both the new conference amphitheatre and the main arena of the PBC* experiment site.

Icarus's notes and picoputer lay on his desk, but that was not the first thing to draw his attention when he stepped into the study after the picnic with his wife. It was instead a medieval oak chest sitting on a baroque pedestal table near the bookcases behind his desk; a chest about sixty centimetres wide, carved with Doric columns and a panel of scrolling acanthus, and fitted with a sturdy iron handle and lock. Icarus removed a bundle of files and some odds and ends of electrical equipment which had been dumped on top of it, and placed his hands on its surfaces as though warming himself over a fire. He stood motionless for a few moments and stared out of the window, unseeing as though mesmerised.

28

There was a discreet knock at the door, and Mrs Nimmo looked in. 'I'm off, Icarus. Good luck with your talk at CERN, is it going to be on a live telecast?'

Icarus beckoned her in, keeping his hands on the chest, half gripping it as though seeking strength. 'Just one moment, Joan. You know what this means to me, after all these years of burning the midnight oil?'

'Indeed I do. I mean, I know it must be something very special.'

'It's not really about the Collider, whatever everyone else thinks. Even Brooke thinks it's that, I know. And over the years everyone has thought it was all about me, just me, and my wonderful detector. But I want you to know it's about the others and this world we live in, not my own little exploits. I'm thinking of all those scientists before me, the unsung heroes like old I Will Ashcroft who chose to live in Newton's shadow and have pursued the same dream, the same idea.'

Mrs Nimmo nodded. 'I know, Icarus. You've taken a lot of stick on behalf of your predecessors.'

'I don't want to be another nobody. I wouldn't lie about that. It's true that I don't just want to be that clever old Prof with a few well- received papers under his belt. However, I have a name that is not mine alone, and I want that to be a future rallying point. I want to give credit to I Will Ashcroft above all for my breakthrough. This step really is bigger than any individual can be, because in my heart I believe that even I Will, for all his ambition, did not want personal recognition. He was working towards some breakthrough in human understanding. For an appreciation of just how special these scientists were you just need to look in this chest; you will realise he was not alone.'

'No doubt we're about to find that out, Icarus.'

Icarus smiled. 'There are unsung heroes in this world, and Brooke and I know you are one of them.'

'Not just the cleaner with the de-ioniser, then?'

'I think, Joan, that I can only sum you up as a life-giving force, the one who nurtures and keeps the family together, the one who's no less than a second mother to the fearsome threesome. I don't know what we'd have done without you, given all the strain with Lycian's MS and hospital trips. And well, I know I get those moods of mine at times.'

'You don't need to say any more, we've had good times,' Mrs Nimmo said softly.

6. DANGEROUS PURSUITS
11 June

While his parents were picnicking Sam was making the most of his time after all the hard graft. He and his siblings had received a rare invitation to their Dad's high-powered tutorial group the following morning, and they knew that he was itching to reveal some new breakthrough he had been working on. It must be important to set a special time when he was so busy.

Sam and the other two would be staying put in Cambridge, making the most of the last few days with friends, the open air theatre, rowing races and May Ball before everyone parted company for the summer holidays. Sam had other ideas in mind too, the kind that involved putting his athletic skills to the test. He enjoyed a particular kind of challenge, one peculiar to Cambridge, one that was an illicit activity but had flourished for a century and a half. Nothing was more fun than climbing over bridges and buildings at night with no aids except hand and footholds – the more dangerous the better.

While Icarus was putting the finishing touches to his landmark speech, and Elsie was at an end of term garden party, the two brothers and some friends were fooling about on the Cam.

Sam was too impatient to wait for dark, the punt under his feet was slowing on its approach to Clare Bridge in order for him to indulge in a spot of daytime bridge climbing. Lycian was in his usual position at the rear, standing with pole in hand, while Sam was poised at the helm with his hands raised in readiness. With a light spring his hands caught hold of the ledge passing above and he hauled himself up the side of the lime-stone structure, his feet swinging easily over the balustrade at the top. He bounded over to the far wall to swing himself over and down once more. The large stone balls on the bridge's parapets always intrigued him.

There were fourteen of them, one of which had a clean one-eighth segment missing. One story went that the builder had deliberately left the job undone for not being paid his full due; another said that a wedge of stone cemented into the ball as part of a repair job had become loose and fallen out. Nobody knew for certain. Sam's feet dropped below the archway of the bridge and he glanced down to aim with accustomed ease for the flat bottom of the punt below him – except it wasn't there.

'Lycian!' he yelled, his eyes fixed on the dancing lights below him, the brighter of them gathering in streaked lines across the dark blue reflection of the bridge. During the long seconds that Sam remained dangling, he saw how the weaker lights seemed also to pull in from the murky surface around them; they were fusing with the brighter ones, they were forming the jagged shape of a 'Z'. He blinked hard and looked up to see what it could be mirroring, but nothing was there save a young onlooker with an icecream and a balloon. Sam's fingertips were burning. On looking down again he saw the punt glide into view, perfectly aligned, its occupants bracing themselves in expectation of his jumping in among them.

'Where were you?' Sam demanded, releasing his hold, just as the punt jerked unexpectedly away from him to shrieks of laughter, and Sam sportingly feigned a belly flop to amuse his audience as he plunged straight into the Cam.

'Bastards!' he yelled as he came up for air, spitting out the detritus from the river and wading after the punt. He was after revenge; he'd be letting the side down if he didn't make the effort. This sort of tomfoolery was a tradition, to be played out for the students and tourists on the banks.

Tomorrow night's climbing activities would go unnoticed, however. After the May Ball Sam would be donning his old jacket and climbing shoes and taking on one of the best challenges Cambridge had to offer with his climbing partner Christian.

Lycian had never been strong and athletic enough to get into the climbing, but he was happy enough to tag along on most things and assist his madcap brother. The warm clothing was essential. In the early hours, even in summer, you could feel you were dying of exposure if you ended up stranded a hundred feet above ground on a tiled slope with the rain or wind lashing round you, with only gargoyles and spires for company. He didn't believe in taking a rope. Having a safeguard was copping out; it did nothing to improve one's moral fibre. He and Christian had their IDOs, clipped on either wrists or collars as was convenient; these were enough for communicating and assisting.If they got caught – well, they couldn't get sent down now. The next time Sam would be climbing would be a long way off, in the Alps. There were new and exciting climbs opening up thanks to the retreating snow line.

7. ASHCROFT'S LITTLE SECRET

Ashcroft was sipping a glass of iced water and struggling to open the window wider, as the seminar room was stiflingly hot even at this early hour.

The cream-coloured pavilion-style buildings of the Centre for Mathematical Sciences off Wilberforce Road might have had its face-lift, and the campus may have at long last got its underground pedestrian link with the city centre, but the aged air-conditioning system was not coping with the muggy summer heat. Air-conditioning was now needed for much of the year. The growl it sent rumbling through the very fabric of the building made more noise than an old-fashioned electric fan. Ashcroft had no more faith in the likes of solar panels and bio-fuelled appliances than he had in burning gas and oil. It seemed that the more ecological the measures taken by man, the more of a problem each in turn proved to be, for it took heat to counteract heat and more energy to save energy.

Ashcroft was expecting his three progeny. Apart from them there would only be his exclusive, handpicked group of ten tutorial students, jokingly known on campus as the 'Prof's boffs'. He was already fidgeting with impatience when they gradually filed in, switched off their IDOs and signed a form that had been pushed under their noses as Ashcroft gesticulated with his bony forefinger. No words were exchanged; the Prof always gave the impression of assuming that this class simply absorbed his thoughts, that mind reading was in fact in order for the

33

most cerebral of this crop of young mathematicians. As they exchanged some banter, permitted amongst themselves, he looked on them protectively the way an eagle owl views its chicks in the nest. He was about to feed them the main course of his life's work.

What he had to impart indicated not only confidence in them on his part but also strict obedience on their part, on pain of something that would go far beyond their professional relationship. For if physicists were Spartan warriors, these were the king's bodyguard who would defend their ruler's ideas to the death while serving unquestioningly as his sounding board for future concepts and activities.

A few of the group were staying in academia, but most were set to go into related businesses or industries in such areas as quantum sensor technology and nano communications. They were all focused and driven and they bounced off the Prof's irreverent manner in class. He wasn't a dry old stick in their eyes; it was just that lesser minds couldn't understand the fires burning in his mind.

Prof and his boffs hadn't had really close and regular contact, of course, since he could only make occasional lectures and dinners in Cambridge, but they were a breath of fresh air to him. Five of them had made visits to Geneva to collaborate on his test facility at CERN, while the others were all being encouraged to pursue PhDs alongside work experience where possible.

He shuffled his notes, banged the bottom edges of the pages on his podium to form a neat block, and drummed the top edges with his fingers while he looked round.

The door opened again and a ragged mop of hair appeared round the crack. 'Sorry we're late, Elsie waited for us. My alarm didn't go off and Lycian's – well, you know. Actually, he's really rough.'

Ashcroft's drumming fingers signalled displeasure as he flicked them, without pleasantries, in the direction of their seats. His introduction was as brief as possible, outlining the specification of the ground-breaking multi-TeV* Parallel Beam Collider whose start up was imminent, and he handed round some glossy brochures plus information chips for installing in the students' IDOs. The students were familiar enough with the PBC and in particular Ashcroft's pet project, even if they could barely fathom the man's own inner workings.

Ashcroft's research, both theoretical and practical, in the area of two beam acceleration technology over the past fifteen years had made him the prime candidate for project leader. He had been in the enviable position of having the political and economic clout to test out his own avenues of theoretical research. The PBC was the new generation and all eyes were upon it. It would not only do what other accelerators had been doing, but would also complement them, and it would do so built to a novel design with particle collisions that would prove ten thousand times more powerful than any previously seen.

This new technology was eagerly awaited. Despite fresh fields of research opening up, there were still the same old questions demanding the usual answers about life, the world and the universe. Despite the technological progress and the new challenges laid down by climate change and the consequent social upheaval, there had been nothing like the breakthrough in quantum physics in the last century. The smallest of the small building blocks of life were clearly not giving up their secrets so easily.

Ashcroft had turned up at CERN when the PBC was no more than an experiment site consisting of a drive-beam accelerator, delay loop and combiner ring. He assembled a first-class international team and juggled the work in progress there with the teaching commitments he kept on back home. The job of Chief Scientific Officer was an extra string to his bow.

'Are we studying Bugzs, Prof?' Christian asked.

The Prof had rattled through a series of diagrams and photographs of complex machinery, and the screen was filled with three beetle-like shapes, a small black one, a bigger black one and a blue one.

'My artwork,' Ashcroft said. 'I trust you admire it. You all know the first two here, the big one and the little one. They're shy creatures, yet they act like big stars at a party; they attract others around them in a cluster as they move through the crowd. If they stop moving, the others surrounding them stop moving too. They're particles which, when they move, give mass to other particles. And they move incredibly fast; they're like butterflies that slip through our hi-tech cylindrical nets.

'That little black one you see is a devil. I'm sure you remember, the story about the Large Electron Positron Collider at CERN, and how just before its decommissioning in 2000 this tiny mite flashed past everyone and disappeared before you could say 'Peter Higgs'. There was no time to take notes or verify exactly what it was, but it was thought it might be . the Higgs boson, of course. Then history repeated itself twenty-two years later, when it paid a return visit to the Large Hadron Collider* just as that was about to be decommissioned. Same story. More guessing.

'Then in 2026 it was a case of third time lucky. This elusive particle, which was indeed a Higgs, the 137 GeV* Higgs as you know, was caught in the act of whizzing past just as the International Linear Collider was being bedded down for the winter. Its signature track was confirmed by subsequent observations. The God particle had been found! The light God particle, that is. Lots of data, lots of research, intriguing findings, so lots of funding too. Great stuff. If Peter Higgs' theory had not become a reality we could still be grubbing around the way we were doing a century back.

'So to the big black one, the Higgs' heavy relation, our friend the Curry boson. It zipped by four years later in the ILC as well, and weighed in at 500 GeV, named after my poor friend James Curry who choked on his lunchtime sandwich from the shock when he saw it. But he couldn't make its acquaintance properly. And you know the problem this time: no, the ILC was not about to be decommissioned, and no, it was not being bedded down for the winter. It was just not up to the task of producing it properly, for all its sophistication and high-level precision monitoring equipment. It got only a tantalising glimpse and couldn't substantiate it.

'Cue the go ahead for a multi-TeV accelerator. The PBC was at last being given the green light beyond the baseline programme and test facility stage. It was simply waiting for technology to catch up, and now here it was. I can tell you that the champagne corks and flash bulbs were popping at CERN that night.'

Ashcroft smiled at the memory. Even before the thirty-kilometre tunnel had been dug and the state-of-the-art components put in place, Ashcroft's detector was picking up the signature tracks confirming the existence of the Curry boson and, more importantly, the trails of a particle up to that point known only to him. He braced himself.

'So what's the pretty blue Bugz, Prof?' someone asked.

Ashcroft reached into his briefcase and pulled out another wad of notes, yellowed and crumpled like the last of the autumn's leaves, and placed in an old leather folder tied with cord.

'When I was a student I found it crawling around in this bundle, metaphorically speaking. We're all being reminded of Newton's achievements this year, but here's something that's not mentioned so much in history books. Newton spent a great deal of time in private study, down the road here in Cambridge as well as in London, leaving behind on his death a large body of unpublished work that he'd hidden away and that was in fact deemed "Unfit to Print" because of its controversial nature. For a good many years he also employed an assistant who was an ancestor of mine – my namesake, in fact. This Icarus William Ashcroft was apparently known in social circles as I Will because of his stubborn and obsessive nature traits, which I'm sure none of you see in me, of course. For those of you who've set foot in the vicarage – and I'm addressing those of you apart from our three stragglers today, can see his ugly mug on a muddy oil painting hanging over the fireplace in the dining room. Again, I'm sure you find no resemblance to me there. Anyway, I Will's job was to help conduct experiments and record the findings.

'Shortly after I turned twenty-seven, a relative passed on to me several bundles of papers together with the portable oak chest they had lain in for years. Some of these were remnants of Newton's "classical scholia", and I found the ones I have with me today tucked amongst these. The language is rather flowery at times, but they are based on careful consideration. And there aren't just papers. The chest was actually designed to hold what was once thought to be an astrolabe – but I see that in fact it's what I like to call an inner sphere, as it refers to particles rather than planets. You may recall Elsie, given you're a classicist, that around 1910 a similar item was discovered in the sea off Greece. I can't tell whether this is a copy or the actual original. I Will mentions a series of elaborate experiments he'd conducted on a favourite study of Newton's: particles of light and the measurable patterns in the phenomenon of colour. He describes the mantle of sky above us as being formed by the stitching of blue corpuscles, such fine stitching that it far surpassed the endeavours of the most highly skilled Spitalfields seamstresses and perhaps smaller even than the atom. He uses pretty vague language at times, perhaps on the instructions of Newton whose keen interest in the unorthodox and controversial meant he preferred to keep some things under wraps.

I Will says that, despite rigorous checking, some of his measurements do not tally with the forces of nature as he understands them. Some of these corpuscles, if they are particles of light he cannot tell, seem to move and even reproduce themselves of their own free will. They seem to be living, seem able to rend or mend the fabric of the sky through no obvious and normal external stimuli such as atmospheric conditions. He believes, of course, that this must be some divine act, that what appears to be free will is in fact the hand of God. He and Newton were all fired up in the spring of 1678 to examine further the behaviour of the blue corpuscles of water and green corpuscles of plants, and even make a start on the flesh-coloured corpuscles of human skin. There is a jotting in the middle of I Will's calculations that looks like an extraordinary tiered equation. It's written with a shaking hand, as though the man himself could hardly believe what he was taking down. This equation anticipates the splitting of the atom and suggests particles far smaller than the ones we've yet picked up at CERN. How he could possibly have carried out experiments that helped him formulate such an amazing equation and hypothesis I have no idea, but his workings appear to hold up. I invite you all to see this equation for yourselves at your leisure, and I've got with me a digital copy.'

Icarus lit up the plasma screen behind him, 'But a glance like this is not enough to get a feel for what it means. As you can imagine, I'm itching to study these findings more closely. Icarus William Ashcroft was not simply an assistant, that much is clear. He was an equal collaborator in Newton's work. He would not have broadcast any of this, of course. His claims would have sounded outrageous and there is no way he could have explained the equation even had he understood it himself. Remember, guys, that people had, until not so long beforehand, been tortured or burned at the stake for less. These writings were never intended to be read in his or Newton's lifetime. The document was therefore tied with a ribbon, sealed and stuffed inside other even more ancient papers in the oak chest. It's almost as if this particular chest were being used and handed down for a purpose. It dates much further back than the seventeenth century, I'm sure, even if some of the carvings are from Newton's time.'

'The chest which has always been in your study, the one I spilt some orange juice on?' came a voice from the back. 'The one you polish so lovingly when you think no one's looking?' 'Thank you, Sam – yes, that chest. It does contain very important items after all, from what I've examined during the past quarter century. Quite frankly, I don't understand all of its contents, and some of them I might even hand over to you lot for study after the start up if you're lucky!'

Ashcroft took a deep breath and paused as he looked round at his students. 'Now, I know I'm stretching your credibility when you hear what I'm about to say next, but the fact is that my choice of postdoctoral research and my success is in a large part due to I Will. His comments and hypothesis have inspired me, even though I have so far chosen only to rely on and quote from other confirmed sources. Perhaps, like him, I haven't dared to air his findings—not these far fetched ones. However, I believe I've now found evidence of these living particles on the readouts from my detector.

'What do I mean by 'living' particles? These particles seem to have independent action, constrained by no experiment. They are there, but they seem to follow no natural laws or any consistent pattern. There's enough work there to fill not only your lifetimes but those who come after you.'

Ashcroft scanned the wide-eyed expressions before him. He felt almost drugged with elation. He thought about the detector simulations, the recent test runs, the preparation of experiments and analysis of anticipated data. He recalled the endless small quantity tasks, the painstaking process of applying fiddly but essential little touches, such as internal silver coating for tubes, the way an artist applies the finishing touches to his masterpiece. He remembered the early hours of morning he'd spent pawing over the readouts spewed out by the dedicated processors, which in turn fed the myriad nanoputer clusters of the Grid. The events recorded by the readouts showed not just the familiar fountains of curls but also strange and jagged tracery. Many of the curls had looped round the zigzags until they converged like sunbursts. The zigzagging particles seemed to thread through the trails as though picking individual ones out and even, so it seemed, either consuming or cloning them. Ashcroft had been down on his hands and knees on the floor with the printed images spread round him, at first unable to grasp the full significance, and then he slowly began piecing together the evidence with the obscure references listed in the oak chest.

He stabbed at the blue Bugz on the screen. 'This particle, this ultimate quark, heralds a new world, it requires a new leap in our thinking. It inhabits a subgroup of particles that are a million, perhaps ten million, times smaller than the Higgs boson, smaller than any quark yet known,' he continued, 'and, well, it's conscious, guys. It's a conscious particle that moves through and accretes to it unconscious particles. It can assess the state of these other particles and bend them to its own will – even change them completely, perform alchemy, in fact.'

'Dad,' three voices said nervously and in unison on the back row.

'Hear me out. If we manage to control them, and if we get to understand their behaviours, we could develop applications so far undreamed of and who knows? – heal the skin of our entire ecosystem. We could not only stop greenhouse emissions but also reverse global warming. We could produce and reproduce living tissue all the more easily and in next to no time, such as growing new rainforests or treating human disease. We could, in effect reverse many of the ills on our planet and create our own Eden. Such riches can be ours! And they can all be provided by one tiny, tiny speck of life.' He tapped the blue Bugz. 'I've christened it the Midas particle.

'Yes, it seems we can play God. I'm not getting into the morality argument here – that's for others. I'm just a scientist after all. I look at what's in front of me and identify it. There's obviously a lot about this particle I don't yet know. But this is the future, it's your future. This is the biggest scientific discovery of our lifetime, and you're in on the sneak preview. So what do you say?'

Ashcroft beamed round at his shell-shocked audience. There had been one or two gasps and protests but nothing more. 'Okay, I'm a madman, I can see that my children certainly think I am. Tomorrow, just after eleven in the morning, when all the cameras at CERN are trained on me, they will know what we know, and only then we'll find out if there'll be a global stampede to have me locked away. But the truth will be out one day regardless. You must understand the difficult position I've been in. I couldn't publish this as a paper without it being shot down in flames for being such an outrageous concept.

40

I know there can be no sensible discussion about it until the proof is clear in front of our eyes when the PBC is fired up. Still, I just wanted you to know now, and to share this private moment with me. There's so much riding on this, and if anything should happen to me – well, the main thing is that you know about it. And if any of you are brave enough to suspend your disbelief and join me on my quest to find this little blue chap or maybe the other particles that perform other such tricks, I'd love the company. I could call this a continuation of our existing journey into small particles and call it a super quark, but it is my belief that we have gone to a new level of discovery and the rules will be different. In the detector we will herald a new era of nuantum physics, and while Midas may be the king of the moment we will find others. What I mean by this is a new chapter in our understanding of the physical world that fills in the missing pieces in all of our theorising over the last one hundred years. You are welcome to ride on my coat tails to further your own careers. On the other hand, if I'm proved wrong and end up vilified with my career in tatters around me, I've got plenty of work cut out back at the vicarage, all bundled in that old oak chest and just begging to be decyphered.

'Anyway, watch this space, or should I say inner space? You don't know what might zoom by in it. Could it be the Midas particle in glorious technicolour? Or could it be my once glittering career in flames?' He laughed nervously. 'I need a close knit young team, the best brains, those of you who will join my team at CERN, even if just during the summer, but I'm really talking several years. I need help so I can write papers just begging to be written. And then I need to launch my best-selling autobiography. Only joking, guys,' he said winking.

Ashcroft spread his hands in appeal, and shrugged when no answer was forthcoming. The students glanced at each other and clapped half heartedly. They remained where they sat. The Prof surely had a lot more explaining to do, but he had that familiar closed look on his face; he was gathering his things, smiling with triumph yet taut with tension. Lycian was flushed with embarrassment. Another scientist came to his mind, one who had also tried to create life. Would this Midas particle prove to be another Frankenstein's monster?

Sam and Elsie exchanged looks as tears welled up in Elsie's eyes. 'This is what dad has worked on for all these years,' she whispered. 'It's a dream come true, it's the ultimate dream.'

41

'Or the ultimate nightmare,' whispered Lycian.

'There's no need to pile on the doom and gloom,' she answered. 'Dad wouldn't call us in if he weren't pretty sure of his facts.'

'And that is what's so scary.'

Christian raised his hand and avoided the others' looks. 'Count me in, Prof.'

The students shuffled awkwardly, rose and left the seminar room in a stunned silence. They couldn't tell whether this talk had proven to be a climax or an anticlimax. They emerged from the building with no thought in mind as to what they'd been planning to rush off and do. They had also forgotten to wish their Prof well at the PBC start up – whatever 'well' meant now. Some checked what time it was, others could only think of the Prof's words still ringing in their heads.

Ashcroft had unpicked a minute stitching of the sky and was set to unravel the lot. Even if he was mad, there would be others who would take his place to unravel it. Whatever the students had got lined up for themselves now, it would be happening in a new world of Ashcroft's devising.

Sam listened to Lycian and Elsie speculating on what their father was embarking upon, what it was that made him tick, what would happen to him now. Sam ventured no opinion. There was no point having the pot call the kettle black. After all, he was remembering only too clearly the 'Z' in the water and wondering if all the recent partying had addled his brain.

Elsie pinched Lycian's arm. 'Did you feel that?' she asked.

'Course I did, you sadist,' Lycian winced.

'Just checking,' she said, but without her usual teasing smile, 'because it seems we're not living on Earth any longer. We're living in the world of the – what was it Dad called it? The nuantum world.'

8. AN INTERVIEW WITH A DIFFERENCE Same day

The secretary who swiped Jonathan Stein's press pass and checked his personal details on her nanoputer was struck by how deceptive appearances can be. The youngish man opposite her with cool grey eyes and a very loose checked shirt looked like a lumberjack who had fallen on hard times. It appeared as if he'd wandered out of the forest, pulled in his belt and needed several square meals. How this unprepossessing young journalist could have acquired an advanced physics degree and connections with people such as the tycoon Bertholdt Lipp was anything but obvious, but the back of hand implant did match the DNA scan of the person they were expecting.

Bertholdt Lipp gave interviews but only rarely, and when he did he was sparing with his time. However, remarkably, the whole of today had been put aside for this meeting.

Stein was escorted into the beam elevator which rose on ultra-fine metallic threads up to Blipp's fishbowl-like office with its tremendous view of the Jura mountains and also CERN, two kilometres away.

'Thank you, Julie,' a large voice boomed from behind a desk the size of a

No 201 JUNE 2042

ION-INFO
LEADING DIGIMAG OF THE ION-AGE

Bertholdt Lipp
Extrovert Billionaire

CERN Launch
P.B.C to come on line to unravel secrets of universe

New Plankto
200% more protein from seas riches

HYPERFUEL
Hydrogen cells mean new cleaner engines

43

dining table for state functions. 'Nice to meet you again, Mr Stein.'

On shaking hands, Blipp was momentarily surprised at the strength of the young man's grip, but then he smiled. It was only to be expected.

'Call me Jonathan if you want,' Stein said eagerly.

'Fine, just fine.'

'Your lunch will be brought at thirteen hundred hours sir,' Julie interjected, 'will Mr Stein be dining with you?'

'Of course.' Blipp graciously directed his guest to an armchair that enveloped his frame. 'Make sure there are plenty of treats, my dear. Our friend here looks decidedly undernourished.'

'I can tell you, Mr Lipp,' said Stein, sinking into the hydrogel folds and almost disappearing from Blipp's view, 'that the fat police* in the States are taking their job all too seriously.'

'I'm well aware of it, I've heard about the obesity laws and the food stores rumpus over there, but I doubt this is affecting you, Jonathan?'

'It isn't directly. At least I was allowed on to the plane - you know they're restricting travel if you don't fit within the biomedical limits set out by the fat directives, although these differ between states.'

'Still, now here you're here in a rather more civilised country, where I happen to own a small nutri-organic company – Plankto – you may have heard of it? It's set up for processing, ah… let's say, unusual food sources from the sea, to help tackle the global situation.'

'Most enterprising and forward-looking and beneficial, Mr Lipp,' Stein said brightly, thinking of the gunk he had digested on the plane over from the States whilst getting out his digibook and pressing the record scanner button on his IDO. 'Now, shall we go with the flow of the interview? Would you like the informal bit first?'

'Call me Blipp if you like, Jonathan. I've grown quite fond of my new name since so many people use it now anyway, thanks to the Blipp logo being such a big part of everyday life.'

'It certainly is. Now, to kick off with my first question…'

Blipp's nearly two-metre frame sank back in his equally vast hydrogel chair, and he viewed his visitor in the manner of an advanced scanner taking in every heat change and palpitation of its subject, to judge the effect his words might have.

'Jonathan, you know you're the right man, in the right place, at the

right time,' he observed. 'And more than that: although you may be, for-give me, a small man in terms of status and career, may I say you are not small in terms of importance. You are literally a one-off, so to speak.'
'Er, well, that's nice of you to say so, sir.'

'What I am going to tell you now will in many ways shock you,' Blipp went on, ignoring Stein's IDO scanner and pending question. 'It may even appear so incredible that you will be unable to grasp it just yet. I am going to tell you a little story that goes back over two thousand years, and you can pay particular attention as we come forward in time, to a century and a half back in a small Swiss town.'

Blipp clapped his hands as he spoke, and a gloom descended on the Chromathene plastic domed window, obscuring the view outside. He smiled at Jonathan and indicated the effect around them with a flourish of his hand. 'You've probably heard of this day and night simulation tech-nology; the CERN amphitheatre was the first to have it installed. This, however, is the really advanced version.'

Stein felt the perspiration on his forehead and a flutter in his stomach as the office viewer flickered to life on a virtua 3D display. 'My interview sir, I mean, Blipp.'

'Do not concern yourself with that, Jonathan. We have more important matters to attend to, which will help you see by the end of the day that I'm not only a useful professional contact for you – a prize catch I know, but also a friend to you. I say this advisedly, because you will see there are forces out there that would do us both harm. Sitting comfortably?'

Blipp had noticed that Stein's heart rate was increasing and his body was perspiring more, causing little peaks in the red colour spectrum he was monitoring.

'Now do not be alarmed Jonathan', Blipp reassured.

'There are two versions of this story. One is for personal consumption, between you and me, and the other is something I simply concocted for you, based on hard fact of course, to edit a bit and send to your boss back home. Yes, it's a sop, and a very convincing one, I'm good at persuading people, you see. Here, take it right now; it's on this IDO chip; look at it tonight and then send it on its way, so you can keep your editor happy. Now listen carefully, this is the important bit.

47

'Let me show you a bit of history. What you see here are real events from the actual time segment; I must apologise for the fact that the images only start in 250BC. Our zectroscope was damaged en-route and can't track back any further.'

Stein coughed nervously. 'You are having a little joke at my expense, Mr Lipp—Blipp.'

'No, Jonathan, I'm actually very serious indeed. I'll come on to zectroscopes and what you call my little joke when we have a chat after the show. Time is a relative thing, to quote our friend Einstein but it also has other facets which I can't give detail on now, but believe me, some of the images you're about to see are disturbing and deadly serious. I like it no more than you, but then this is humanity in all its glory.'

As the hours of virtua historical panorama unfolded and the conversation passed back and forth, Julie announced that lunch was ready in another smaller fishbowl room that led off from the first. The whole effect of the clear Chromathene plastic reminded Stein of some great experimental apparatus hanging in the sky. It was disconcerting in every sense because it seemed as if he was a part of the experiment. Blipp became increasingly earnest about the events being portrayed in virtua in front of them.

'Now, look at Archimedes here, Jonathan: a fine fellow close to my Earth heart and possessing a shining equation. And here we have Galileo, Newton and of course Einstein. I have interspersed the narrative about the great and the good with some of the less-exalted members of the human species. This Nero fellow, and Attila here, were not exactly paragons of virtue, and neither were Lucretia Borgia or Rasputin.

'So far so good,' he continued, as the zectroscope came right up to the present and showed Stein entering the Blipp Corporation's foyer. 'And here's the tricky history lesson you haven't learned until now, Jonathan.'

Blipp switched off the viewer, clicked his fingers and made the room flood with light once more. `You see, these scenes have not exactly been recorded but our viewer allows us to slip into parts of history. Now as you imagine this kind of technology isn't readily available to your everyday human, and this is where the big crunch comes...`

We come from another universe and we have been tweaking human development just here and there for the last two thousand years or so. Believe me Jonathan, I can tell your heart is racing, take a deep breath and just stay calm.'

A two-minute silence followed as Blipp viewed the stunned Jonathan Stein, who simply put his head in his hands and then stared blankly out of the window.

'It had to come some time, you couldn't believe that only you exist in this whole place with nobody else.' Blipp said, almost apologetically.

'Putting it like you do, in a matter of fact manner, I guess it makes sense, but I never thought I would meet, well, Aliens,' Stein said.

'Well, we don't see ourselves as aliens because you are very similar to us but just different, still you just don't communicate very well with what is inside you. You're either in trauma or aren't tuned in, but all you talk of is some idea of the soul.' Blipp continued, 'We think of souls as mathematical equations with an actual physical form and in our world you might use the term Bugz. Bugz are the equivalent of what you call souls and you currently can't make contact with Bugz because you are not scientifically advanced enough. We want to go back to our world and are trying to influence your development so maybe you can help us. Our leader, whose name is Zein – notice the similarity to your own name – worked out the probabilities of humans helping us. This is all part of a strategy put in place years back. We have been trying to help you advance so we can talk and you may help us answer some of our questions.

'This all appears one-sided, but we may be somehow related in some past, it is not clear,' Blipp said apologetically.

Stein had gone quiet. His appetite had long since vanished. He glanced at his coffee and wished he had something stronger. He looked about him and wondered if the circular lift door was locked.

Blipp was speaking with ease as though everything made complete sense, as though he were merely ticking off the history of his commercial empire. Einstein, he was now saying, had been connected to the Manhattan Project and the development of the atomic bomb during the Second World War. Einstein was a very special case and even the Bugz had not found it necessary to influence development because it was happening unaided.

49

The Bugz had over the centuries influenced certain very special human beings, and their contact with them had been predetermined and involved linking with these individuals' own equations or souls – getting inside them and somehow controlling them, influencing them. Stein drained his coffee, on the verge of making his excuses and departing.

'Two groups of human beings have been affected, one directly and the other indirectly,' Blipp continued. 'The first group of human beings we located, those capable of linking directly with the Bugz' equations were so called key hosts who could absorb and pass on information. Jonathan, you are such an example.'

Stein jumped. He thought he might retch, and yet somehow – incredibly – Blipp was making every word sound like common sense.

'Jonathan, I am talking of your equation of particles, the soul that exists within you that Zein will link so well with. He sees this linking as important – this equation match appears near perfect and cannot be ignored. If you are amenable to it, you will be following in a distinguished line down through the ages.'

Blipp tried to clarify what equations were; it seemed they could only be equated with man's soul. He added that Bugz could not understand why humans seemed to appreciate so little their own equations within them. They had spirituality and religion, and yet knew nothing of the science of the soul.

'But a soul is not a tangible thing,' said Stein, the scientist.

'That is where we may have to disagree: the fact is that humans have not been able to discover its physical attributes. We believe you knew of your souls, but had lost the ability to understand them. Bugz are not experts on everything human, but we are a different strand of what you call your soul.'

'Then there's the second group of human beings,' Blipp continued, 'who work with the key hosts and transmit the information they receive to other humans in order to disseminate it. We call them assistants, Jonathan. Zein has always maintained that assistants were essential for the spread of information here on Earth, like the stone thrown into a pond causes a ripple. Think of Zein's plan as some ancient armillary clock with the cogs moving slowly and irresistibly toward a plan conceived all those years back.

50

We are hoping that our opposite opponents led by a powerful negative force have not appreciated that the human equation may be the deciding factor in finding what salvation means and getting back to Zyberia. My Bugz name is Zim and I influenced the man you know as Archimedes. I am Bertholdt Blipp, but I am also Zim.'

Stein sat amazed and hopelessly out of his depth.

'Focus on what you have just seen, Jonathan. Look, you can see for yourself with the time segment on the screen.'

'So these weren't just actors playing out roles?'

'No. These are zectroscope time segments of what took place. For instance, you remember the dingy study with its heavy oak furniture and candles: it was in Trinity College, Cambridge. The two men in conversation are the real Isaac Newton and his assistant Icarus Ashroft – the first Icarus Ashcroft. We will see his descendant tomorrow giving a speech at CERN. Newton was influenced by a good friend of mine called Zon.'

'How do I know these aren't just actors?' Stein persisted.

Blipp shrugged. 'What do you think this is, Jonathan? A movelet of an extraordinary epic that just never received publicity so you missed it? Come on. Anyway, even with all the resources and power at my disposal I could not flip images quite like that. Newton, being born not long after Galileo dies. You saw old Galileo here passing away. Those men around him were the guards; he was under house arrest to stop the spread of scientific progress, but Zleo, with whom I am acquainted, ensured that his assistant spirited away his papers and instruments before they got their hands on them. Ziel, I will talk of her counter influence later, has not realised the effect of Zein's assistants through time. When Archimedes was killed, I was killed, his papers and inner sphere were taken from his home in Syracuse by a very brave female assistant. When Newton died he made sure his assistant then took the same papers and instruments into his own safekeeping. If Professor Ashcroft but knew it, he could trace his DNA lineage back all those years to these assistants.'

'You mean Ashcroft, the nuclear physicist, who is at Cambridge?'

'Yes, and I know you have heard of him because he is also running the PBC project at CERN. Something tells me you need a large shot of cold Geneva, my friend.' Blipp rose and poured out a glass of ultra cold steaming Geneva from a flask. It truly looked like something from the laboratory of a crazed professor, and what better setting could there be to imbibe it?

There was a pause as Stein downed the glass. He tried to gather his thoughts as he gasped from the cold.

'Think about the effort and sacrifice taken to get humans as far as this,' Blipp said. 'Think about the war-ravaged Europe of the 1950s. Think about CERN's manifold contributions, the Grid, and now the Supergrid and super g-mail, the arteries of human's lifeblood today that spread the pride and joy of his knowledge. The Blipp Corporation controls super g-mail, my friend. I am everywhere, and need to be too. My organisation's prime purpose is to provide us with information and to advance humankind's development.' He smiled at the stunned reporter.

'My office does not overlook CERN by chance, you know. This meeting is not by chance either; this isn't a case of you getting a lucky scoop. This is, in fact, where you come into it. You see, the atomic bomb on Hiroshima was a small step compared to the chain of events being set in motion at CERN tomorrow.'

Blipp paused, pressed his fingertips together and scrutinised Stein's face. 'Of course, none of this can be told to the outside world because the Bugz are no more infallible than humans are, and despite our working out probabilities and outcomes we know full well that this world of yours has that little element of uncertainty. Anyhow, even if you did tell the world, would the world believe you, Jonathan?'

'Do I need to answer that?' Stein asked, wearily.

'You now know there are white and black Bugz. Let me explain a bit more about the black Bugz whom, by the way, are headed by Ziel, who I mentioned earlier, or to give her real title 'Black Queen Zielzub.' Now, you survived a plane crash against all the odds a year ago, I happen to know.'

'I live with the thought of it every day. A sheer miracle.'

'The carnage that resulted from it is evidence of the lengths the black Bugz are prepared to go to to annihilate you and others. Your survival was not a miracle, my friend; it was sanctioned by us – an irregular and unprecedented move on our part, and only on the basis that we preserve the remarkable equation within you. A move which marked the beginning of open hostilities between us and those who are led by Ziel.'

Stein sank his head in his hands and breathed heavily. 'What about the other crash survivors? Was there a purpose with them too?'

'They are all special in their own way. You remember their names, I'm sure. Joan Nimmo, for instance. And do you know where she lives?'

'Somewhere near London, I think.'

'Cambridge, to be precise. Working for the Ashcrofts. And there's the lovely Gayle Richter, I know that the two of you have contact and that you've heard from her very recently. Gayle is influenced by Zag, who is one of us'.

'She's doing all the liaising for the press conference and start up at CERN tomorrow,' Stein said.

'A coincidence, would you not say? You all survived at our hands, including that Italian guy Enrico Raviele with his murky connections, who is now is in Ziel's employment. She didn't count on our sparing him while saving those who are important to us, but you could say we needed to keep her sweet to avoid further escalation of hostilities where possible. You see, humankind and this planet are no more than a stepping stone for her, simply part of the bridge over which she can get home. What we need are human equations like yours to help prevent the most likely outcome if the black Bugz have their way: outright extinction of part, if not all, of this planet.'

'I see,' Stein said slowly, still not able to make up his mind whether he was having a real life conversation or hallucinating from a Zapper overdose. 'You want me to save the world.' He nearly laughed. Yes, he must be hallucinating.

'Well, not quite, my friend, but you are an important part of it. You know, I can have you placed on some desert island when you've played your part and ensure you have your every need catered for. Money is no object to us. Think about it: time's running out anyway. You see for yourself the damage of climate change. Add to this an overwhelmingly powerful force that has scant regard for this little blue planet, and you know where all this will end up: a nice... round... zero.'

Stein got up and paced across the goldfish bowl Chromathene floor, considering the long drop below. The easy way out, he thought.

'OK, so this is an offer I can't refuse,' he sighed, 'and if any weird stuff starts happening, I know what that will actually be, not just me going mad.'

'I'm sorry, Jonathan, but you can rest assured there will be, should we say, a 'high occurrence of unusual phenomena'. Well, unusual to the

53

human mind, that is. And we need to have an understanding. You must realise that you are probably the most important human being on this planet, bar one other – but I'll tell you more about her at our next meeting, and therefore you must act accordingly.'

Stein threw his arms wide in despair. 'Any guidelines you can give me, Mr Lipp? I mean, Blipp? Preparation for the job? On top of the job I already do, which my boss thinks I'm attending to this very minute? Somehow I think it would take me the rest of my lifetime to get to grips with the stuff you're talking about.'

'I'm sorry,' Blipp repeated, 'but this is how it is. We can't just will it away; not even the Bugz have the power to do that. All I can say is that, in just the way you survived that plane crash, we may all of us have found ourselves in this situation not by accident but by design. We have probably been directed here by some other entity.'

'Oh, God,' Stein said. 'Please.'

'Well, you might call him God, sorry, you're probably just using a figure of speech, and he isn't god, but I can see how you think he could be. Anyway, I can't get into all that, but yes, maybe if this entity can be contacted, we can find out why we are here, and it might be the nearest thing we have to a kind of God here on Earth. I mentioned 'Salvation' and this is the word that drew us to this place.'

Blipp paused, and knocked back a long drink of mineral water. He was starting to tie his own Bugz-induced brain in knots with the God comment. 'Well, my friend, I can see it's too much for you today to take more of this in, but you'll manage it as the days pass. Anyway, after the information overload you've received you should sleep well tonight. You might also have powerful dreams, just be warned. Those receptors on your equation are now being triggered. Your little introduction to Zein.' Blipp chuckled. 'And you and I will be what you might call Bugz brothers. Bugz brothers – that has a nice ring to it don't you think?'

'I'm flattered,' Stein said, without sounding convinced. He was starting to feel odd sensations and waves of elation and fear all at the same time. And he hadn't digitised a jot on the planned interview. He fumbled with his IDO and looked awkward. 'Anyway, back to business, Blipp,' he said, scrambling to retrieve a sense of normality. 'You were kindly going to provide me with some feedback on your involvement in and reaction to the CERN launch tomorrow.'

54

Blipp beamed and waved at the IDO chip he'd handed Stein at the start of the meeting. 'It's all there, my friend. Your bedtime viewing before that powerful sleep you're going to have, so you know the same story as your editor boss.'

Stein staggered out of Blipp's headquarters, dazed and unseeing. He looked at the data chip clutched in his hand. It was amusingly shaped like a sphere with a bullet head. It had the orange, yellow and black colours of the Blipp Corporation logo plastered over it. He smiled; his editor would appreciate it. As for the bombshell dumped on him that afternoon – God, he needed his bed.

He saw things while driving back to his hotel. He saw himself in a Blipp superman outfit zipping across space. He saw himself back on Earth: it was on the brink of an unforeseen deluge, and he had the lead part of Noah. He saw a swarm of Bugz whizzing round his head. He would have gone off the road if the auto navigation hadn't been driving the vehicle.

He'd got himself a story, and what a story. What's more, he knew it wasn't fiction, and that was what was so scary about all this. He wouldn't be woken by the hotel comfort programme. He wouldn't hear himself saying, 'Oh, that was only a dream.' Instead it would be rise and shine the next morning feeling like a new person, literally.

When he went to bed a short time later, having felt so distracted that he'd failed to call room service for a night-time feast, he imagined what might be going on inside his head in the small hours. Tendril-like microscopic male and female plugs locking together in a snug fit that was 99.999999999999999998% perfect.

He sighed. What would his status be in this Zyberia? A superparticle, no less. Incredible. Except he knew it wasn't.

He couldn't get off to sleep. Once he succeeded, that would be that. And he had real reservations. He dozed fitfully, and after finally landing at one point face down on the floor next to his bed he crawled back under the electrostatic heat sheet to feel a calm seep through him. It might be three in the morning, but he had never felt such clarity of thought in his life. And this was because the carbon and hydrogen body was asleep but the powerful Superbugz called Zein was feeling its way round its new home, viewing the world now from a part-human perspective.

55

ZIM PROVIDES THE AFFIRMATIVE

Blipp took the voice link from Julie.

'Is that all for today, sir? Because I intend to get home if that's OK.'

'Yes, do go, and have a nice evening.'

Zim had been directing the development of Blipp's equation, and what better haul of treasures did he now have at his disposal than the global fishnet of Super-G* communication?*

His analytical units had worked overtime since latching on, and he had provided Zein with evidence that in the last few months there had been an outpouring of data from Svetlana Grigoriya's private address to an unidentifiable site in Venice and another in St Petersburg, also to a basket weaver's workshop in Bavaria, to the DG's office at CERN, and to a SISI technician with no obvious connections to the PBC project. The g-mail traffic had been heavily encrypted.

This heightened activity on the part of Ziel in the form of Svetlana had forced Zein to make the linkage with Stein finally. The less dangerous way of achieving this was to let Stein know the truth about the events unfolding the way they had and to ask for his cooperation. Zim knew that this day of asking for human sacrifice would come. Such was the power of Stein's equation that the linkage could not occur without his acquiesence. Zein knew that the better the equation fit, the more danger there was in the human equation taking control.

Zim confirmed during the day that the meeting with Stein was positive and that the joining could commence. Hence the sensations Stein was feeling.

The significance of the confluence of events would not be lost on Ziel, and he was sure the Super-G activity was the forerunner of the anticipated storm. Ziel was probably very confident that they would not crack the encryption. The information was fragmentary and needed analysing before appropriate action could be taken.

Zag, the powerful code-breaking particle who had co-opted Gayle Richter, was unable to make sense of the Super-G mail emanating from Svetlana's IDO. To the Bugz' way of thinking the human transmission index was akin to Stone Age scratchings on a cave wall, so why Zag couldn't break the encryption was a mystery, one which heightened the uncertainty.

9. THE LAUNCH

13 June 2042

There wasn't any obvious gateway, just hi-tech white and silver and narrow entries for service personnel and the odd hydrogen* bus stand. Stein had slowed his rental eco car to a crawl along the Meyrin road, peering through the side window, ignoring the driver behind him who e-honked* in annoyance at the virtual image of Stein's car on his dashboard screen and obliterated it. Noise pollution had reached such levels on crowded roads that, given the government ban on real horns, some enterprising gamer had invented the Road Rage (Not) programme. Stein had run an article on the whole topic where a driver in Buenos Aires had fitted a real rocket to his car and fired it at an offending car, killing the driver.

Pulling into the CERN entry lane, Stein found everything to be very low key. 'Am I missing something?' he called to the guard, whose scanner flashed across the encoded strip on the car's identification disc while two other guards scanned the car thoroughly for explosives before the plain CERN barrier went up. 'Isn't this supposed to be an important event? The place looks like it's hosting a funeral.'

The expressionless guard stepped back and waved him through. While the CERN site might have appeared sober and dry, you certainly couldn't call any interview with the chairman of the Blipp Corporation the same. And certainly not the surreal interview Stein had had with him the previous day. Apart from talk of Bugz and saving the planet, the man was simply brimming with enthusiasm. Stein had been one of the first in line to hear the pronouncements from the lips of the great man himself, plus the real lowdown on epoch-making happenings at CERN.

He edged round a crowd of people milling outside the reception building, most of them in sober suits or retro pencil skirts, sporting IDOs and donning various styles of UV fibre hats and queuing to get into the press conference. A patrol guard approached him and stabbed his finger at a bay nearby for the carlift for underground parking.

Stein climbed out, watched the car sink from view and plunged into the crowd at the entrance. He was famished. A coffee and croissant were not a great way to start the day when you had to fight through the Geneva traffic and then get hounded in the mass transit lane after giving up crawling and sitting at never changing lights designed to disadvantage the private car owner.

At reception, each visitor swiped the back of one hand on the reader for it to register their implanted identity chip and check the access code for this event. Stein's stomach needed lining with a stack of pancakes sloshed in syrup. Quantities of fat and carbohydrates didn't seem to push up his weight, so he'd never suffered the misfortune of being paid a visit by the fat police* back home to fine him. However, food purchases pushed up the electronic kilojoulemeter on his grocery card, and that meant facing starvation rations once it reached its limit unless he could trade points off the card of a sickly friend or stick-like neighbour. But that was a tedious affair, deliberately so, which ran the risk of being logged on the notorious fat police register. Food and now fresh water rationing might be global issues, and it was no wonder that the environmental lobbyists were gaining ground in the developed world. Flavourless GM foods in regulated quantities, designed to stem where possible the flow of energy-inefficient food transports, hit everyone where it hurt the most: their stomachs.

Stein saw the slightly stooping lean figure of a man he recognised from his year spent at Cambridge. Professor Icarus Ashcroft, the Chief Scientific Officer, was emerging from a taxi with a woman who was presumably his wife. She paused to push her soft brown hair away from her eyes and adjust a grip in it before they filtered in with the others. She must have said something amusing as she clasped Ashcroft's hand to be led in, for he smiled down at her. A couple of yards behind them a group of men were exchanging glances. One was dressed in a well-cut Italian suit; he hung back with an easy stride and kept checking his watch. He was tanned and lean built, his forehead receding above a prominent nose, which gave the effect of pulling the skin back from his nearly unblinking eyes. His three companions were plainly dressed in casual jackets over open top shirts. One had premature worry lines across his brow and a goatee beard; another was adjusting loose-fitting trousers over his thin frame. They were pushing ahead, silently and purposefully, each receiving without much interest one of the launch programmes being handed out complete with attached IDO chips.

A basket of day-limited throwaway IDOs stood in a corner, protected CERN property made available to the inevitable sprinkling of guests who came empty-handed or whose own IDO was faulty.

A UV eco LandWagon was discharging a large man in a linen suit, Bertholdt Lipp. His broad smile and ample frame would undoubtedly feature in headline news this coming week. He would be plastered over *The New York Times* at any rate, because Stein had stayed up late the previous night honing his copy from the IDO chip that Blipp had given him with the headline 'Blipp at Forefront of Landmark Technology'. A mock-up picture of the white-haired Blipp with half profile in a futuristic space suit in shiny orange, yellow and black was shot against the background of the Jura and its blue sky. The Blipp logo flew on a pennant in a sort of mock homage to man landing on Mars in the mid 2030s. The article praised Blipp's generous donation of two hundred thousand IDOs and IDO software to a South American country to aid its struggling telecommunications.

Stein crossed the reception, homed in on the nearest coffee machine and felt the caffeine straighten out every fibre and nerve ending. He had a couple of energy booster tablets in his pocket to keep him going too. Still, breakfast or no breakfast, there wasn't a more fantastic assignment than one that had to do with giant atom smashers, cutting-edge machinery used for working out what made the universe tick.

The visitors were now heading inside and up the escalator and steps to CERN's new amphitheatre, reputed to have state-of-the-art facilities housed under a semi-circular glass dome with its own renowned view over the Jura mountains. Stein followed them with a spring in his step.

60

He recognised the glass from Blipp's office, the same light-sensitive Chromathene plastic containing a unique filter. Its tinting effect by day had given rise to such sobriquets as 'the only building to wear shades' and 'the Ray Ban Building'.

At night its lower sides blocked out the glare of Geneva's lights whilst preserving overhead the magnificent clarity of the night sky, transforming the chamber into a planetarium. Within this sphere dawn rose and twilight fell. This microcosm of light and dark was no less than a coup de théâtre befitting a high-profile international scientific community, and the launch of CERN's new Parallel Beam Collider seemed a fitting occasion to inaugurate it.

This assignment sure beat what had once been the usual for Stein, rooting around for some impoverished hospital trust's shady bank details, bracing himself for a tirade from some animal rights activist, or sitting bleary eyed in a smoky police station, one of the last remaining refuges for nicotine addicts, when what he'd really needed was his bed. And that had been the exciting stuff, the daily bread for a novice hack on *The New York Times*.

When Stein dropped out from MIT he could have taken a worthy job elsewhere, a sub-editor on a science journal perhaps, but that didn't offer the pizzazz of working on the broadsheet that covered life at the heart of both the Big Apple and the scientific community at large. And covering that life was just great. There'd been the excitement over the Silver Spring pharmaceuticals scandal, followed by the furore over the new nerve-disabling chip introduced in security devices for tagging unstable individuals.

The science editor had got so sick of Stein's badgering for the big stories that he'd almost pushed this particular assignment in Stein's face while placing in his palm the coveted New York Times press pass. The man couldn't deny that Stein, with his European links and cosmopolitan ways, as well as that brain of his, was building up an A-list of connections and getting some key interviewees these days. Anyhow, the order that Stein should cover the launch had come from the top.

After all his days of grabbing, things were now falling into his lap. His connection with Gayle Richter, CERN's chief liaison officer and personal assistant to the DG, might have had an unusual and hardly pleasant beginning on that Newark runway, but it came in handy for regular informal briefings and networking. She had assured him that a number of their mutual acquaintances would be happy to meet up for a couple of drinks at the end of the event. There she was now, at her post on the dais at the centre of the amphitheatre, ready to meet and greet in her full regalia: snappy suit, clicking heels, immaculate hairdo and prominent silver insignia on lapel. She was advising and pointing in all directions for the benefit of her charges, when her eyes fell on the press stand, up at the back. She recognised her fellow plane crash survivor with his wide and indomitable grin, his full head of hair and well-built shoulders on a slim frame. He returned the brief wave she gave him. Invitations for the launch of the most powerful atom smasher ever built were thin on the ground, and it was important to make sure that the VIPs were selected carefully, as well as the members of the world press.

On the morning of the PBC start up Gayle Richter was in the CERN amphitheatre early. It was her job to co-ordinate the event, and as head of external relations, she was in a powerful position to advise the Director General which governments were interested in which new developments. It was not commonly known that the spin-off developments of CERN technology were coming thick and fast and being bought by the military, communications, pharma and agri industries. Gayle occupied a position of covert power while the Director General Henri Le Baut levered his own position like some potentate offering out bits of the kingdom for favours in return.

Stein glanced once more through the CERN programme and the info he'd received in advance. He tried checking his IDO messages, but the virtual earphones emitted some irritating buzz in his ear, so he switched them off. There was Ashcroft again. He was standing in the aisle shaking hands warmly with his colleagues from the PBC design team. He and his wife were also talking to friends and former colleagues from Cambridge.

Stein sighed, focused on his homework and rummaged through some of the background material on CERN. He could still add to his copy from Blipp's IDO chip, the odd truly personal touch to give that sense of immediacy to his editor.

For some time now, ever since the heyday of its giant ring accelerator, the Large Hadron Collider, the organisation had been flexing its muscles in a new role that took it beyond the confines of its Vatican-like borders. When CERN received the go-ahead to build the new Parallel Beam Collider on the site of the old LHC tunnel, Ashcroft's team members and their associates soon found themselves unpopular among large segments of the world's high energy physics community. The global funding for other older generation accelerators had been slashed in order to inject even more colossal sums into CERN's latest flagship.

The Americans were pleased with the go-ahead for the PBC, however. Stein remembered it well. Snubbed when the PBC's predecessor was sited in Japan and not Illinois as hoped, and still languishing out in the cold politically after a long period of entanglements abroad, the US administration found here an opportunity to save face. True, the PBC was not being built on American soil either, but this time the Americans wasted no time in signing up for full member status at CERN and donating both generous funding and some of its top scientists, including two Nobel prize winners. If you can't beat 'em, join 'em. Of course, you could also copy and enhance your own version later was the pragmatic view.

Marco Bergamasco loosened his collar and stretched out his legs as he viewed the assembled crowd in the amphitheatre. He was sitting well away from the three men he had arrived with. Unlike many of those around him, he was not admiring the clear dome or the view of the Jura. He was comparing the layout with his own implanted memory of the auditorium, with its spacious rows of rest stations leading down to the central dais. The hydrogel seating, turquoise in colour, was fashioned throughout like the one he was sprawled on, the smooth contours designed to mould round and support the individual body shape. He made mental notes of the identical tiered seating on the dais. Each rest station was complete with virtual nanophones, touch screens, blank sheets of paper, retro CERN inner space pens, and bottles of chilled, sparkling Jura water, all neatly arranged. He saw the rest station with the sign denoting the Director General's seat. The Senior Financial Officer and Senior Scientific Officer would be flanking him on both sides, with the speaker of the Swiss National Council and members of the CERN Council placed on either side of them. A handful of international political dignitaries and distinguished professors would be seated on the lower tier before them.

Marco's gaze travelled along the line of thirty-two flags of its member countries ranged round the chamber in order of magnitude, reflecting the contribution each one had made to the organisation out of its own gross national product. The vast 3D screen curving round the back of the tiers displayed the simple CERN logo of sky blue lines and rings on a white background. His gaze noted the exits. Ridiculously few for such a safety-conscious organisation.

Marco also noted Brooke Ashcroft's chic linen suit and soft bobbed hair, her confident smile and clear eyes. She had strolled down one of the aisles and had been looking, like her observer, at the tiered seating and nanophones. She looked radiant. Her husband would soon be up there fulfilling the dream of a lifetime. She turned as someone touched her shoulder from behind, and despite the distance she happened to glance straight at Marco. He flushed, but then smiled easily, too easily and in too familiar a way perhaps, for a quizzical look crossed her face before she focused on the person next to her. Marco then tried to make eye contact with Svetlana, but she blanked him entirely.

Several rows behind Brooke, a long haired postgraduate was shuffling along to fill the space next to a blonde, who was smartly dressed, peering at her touch screen and jabbing at it with flame red nails. The postgraduate beamed at her. 'May I?'

Svetlana pouted and removed her bag from his seat, placing it under her own.

'Thanks. I've come from CalTech,' the young man said eagerly. 'Boy, this accelerator will sure take some beating. We're working hard on our own version in Alaska, you know the one? Tiny, but specialised for the purpose; it's way off yet but it's leading edge stuff. Some of us lucky ones are over here to see the competition and pick up what we can, now this one's up and running. You can see my buddies there, four rows down.'

'Alaska's very cold,' Svetlana said. 'Russia's very cold too. Geneva's better.'

'Oh, sure. I'm taking in all the sights while I'm here: the chalets, the chocolate shops, and all those watches. Take a look at our itinerary, sorry, it's a bit crumpled. Your husband working here?'

'Are you going to talk talk?' Svetlana asked. 'I know all about Geneva already. I know all about Swiss watches. I know all about your dinky machine that has many many problems. But I don't know anything about these stupid virtual earphones and I already have a massive headache. So if you'll excuse me.'

The auditorium was nearly full. Gayle was shepherding her VIPs to their various places on the dais. Ashcroft had joined a couple of his colleagues on the upper tier. His wife had placed herself near the front of the auditorium amongst her fellow expatriates who were smiling or exchanging jokes as though it were graduation day.

Marco remained well behind his party, completely motionless in his seat, still observing her. Late comers wandered up and down the aisles to find seats, and the volume of chatter in different tongues reached uncomfortable levels as academics, engineers, technicians and members of CERN's observer states struggled to make themselves heard. Stein reflected on his talk with Blipp, he did feel different and in a better way. Everything seemed in clear focus. He could appreciate the complications in the levels of structure in everything around him

Svetlana had her virtual earphones on; she was rubbing her forehead, still jabbing the touchscreen in front of her and growling, 'Stupid, stupid.'

'Want some help?' the postgraduate ventured.

'There's some interference, some loud crackling, I don't know what. I always have problems, problems with electrical things. This is crazy. Lots of buzzing noises. My head hurts.'

She invited him to inch closer in on her and study the IDO connection supplied in her rest station. 'I want Russian. Everything sounds best in Russian.'

The student listened in, winced and nodded. 'Something wrong there. But hang on – ' He reached over Svetlana's superstructure and slid his fingertip over the screen. 'Oh, that's it: just some glitch, I'd say. You've got it now, ma'am. Well, I guess it's Russian.'

'I'm stupid, you're clever,' Svetlana sighed, digging in her bag for a Zapper, popping the pep-mint between ample parted lips and scrunching the firecracker wrapper back in her bag.

'I wouldn't say that,' the student assured her, indulgently.

Svetlana exhaled the glacier force of her Zapper into the boy's face. 'I'm only clever with big things. I like big things, you understand, not little things.'

65

'Really?' The American could feel a headache coming on himself. And it wasn't just the rocket blast of both the mild narcotic and Svetlana's obvious stimulant properties. As it happened, several other visitors were frowning in discomfort.

A hush descended on the auditorium as the Director General settled his glasses on his nose and stood up to make the customary noises of welcome before launching into his address.

'Eighty-eight years ago, ladies and gentlemen, the European Centre for Nuclear Research was born, thanks to a handful of visionary scientists who had these positive aims: to address the ills of the Second World War by promoting reconciliation and advancement of the countries making up a continent in tatters, to atone for the ills of the atom bomb and seek only peaceful purposes in developing this powerful technology, and to counterbalance the weight of American scientific progress in the spirit of healthy competition. We chose the right place to site this endeavour, in a country lying at the heart of its many partners, in a country proud of its neutrality. We pursue our aims through what is commonly known as the Geneva spirit, and I don't mean the gin, although some of my colleagues might disagree on the type of spirit required to keep this place running.'

A ripple of laughter broke the ice of formality amongst those assembled.

'Here at CERN we have opened the gateway to another universe that lies within our own one: a universe of particles so minuscule yet so powerful that they almost seem to have a life of their own. They make us what we are. The more we discover about them, the more we discover the nature of our origins. We need vast constructs of both the imagination and civil engineering to try to grasp the infinitesimally small. This is a humbling thought, yet we are proud of the many achievements of our teams of dedicated scientists, engineers and technicians over the years. To name but some of these achievements: we have been pioneers in colliding particles at high energies, we discovered the neutral current and we established the World Wide Web and the Grid. We have learned much over the past fifteen years about the Higgs mechanism – what it is that gives particles their mass – and we have collaborated closely on many high energy projects. Our research findings have led to far-reaching technological, industrial and medical applications, and our work is made freely available in the spirit of openness and harmony that is at the core of our being.

'This is where I will hand you over to our Chief Scientific Officer and the driving force behind the Parallel Beam Collider, Professor Icarus Ashcroft.'

Icarus stood up and acknowledged the polite clapping. 'Thank you, ladies and gentlemen, and of course my colleagues here.' He pursed his lips and gazed round the amphitheatre as though still in the process of collecting his thoughts at this late stage; he clasped his hands in front of him as though in prayer and lightly drummed his fingertips together in sweet anticipation. He took a deep breath.

'You know, for all of you this is going to be the most momentous, ground-breaking day of your life. One which will make you say, I remember I was at that place on that day.' He looked triumphant. 'You won't be able to forget it even if you want to. I can't tell you how excited I am, how very honoured I am, to be the person who sets sail on a new voyage of discovery, a discovery as great I think as that of quantum mechanics and Einstein's special and general theories of relativity. You're in for a big surprise,' he added, glancing down at the Director General.

'Comparing himself with Einstein now,' a colleague mocked in a whisper to his neighbour. 'Is there no end to the Archangel Gabriel's ego?'

'Firstly,' Ashcroft continued, 'we can announce that the Parallel Beam Collider is the new child of CERN. It is no longer a baby – you all know it has been subjected to nearly a decade of building and testing. It is a strong growing adolescent with enough years behind it to prove that it has a thousand times – yes, a thousand times – the energy muscle of the ILC and is certainly capable of producing the Curry boson. Many of you already know about the research I've been doing which bears this out. Now, I know that what you and also my colleagues here are expecting me to do is give a brief resumé of what the Curry boson actually is, what type of clustering effect it has on other particles, what it decays into after the small fraction of time it remains in existence, and how it affects us and our environment. It is an awesome force to be reckoned with. You have been provided with all this on the chips handed out at reception, and I must apologise for not touching on the subject myself here and now. I know I'm stepping a bit out of line, and my colleagues

67

here will be thinking I've had too many late nights on site. However, I have something of far greater importance to tell you. It is something which will, in fact, open up the new world of the nuantum, as opposed to the quantum, particle.'

The DG looked up, startled, and was about to say something but Icarus stayed him with a hand on his shoulder.

'Imagine, ladies and gentlemen, a particle even more powerful than the Curry boson. One that is, to coin a term, a re-engineering particle or Midas particle. Now, there's a lot about this particle I don't yet know, but it's not just any old quark, it's not just some muon or gluon or graviton. It has a form of consciousness, and such creative properties that suggest it is capable of independent action. I'm telling you that it's all about us; it's been lying dormant and undetected but it can now be woken. And it will be woken in about three hours' time when the PBC kicks in.'

10. THREE PLUS ONE PLUS ONE

Same day

There was a visible stir in the auditorium, and the DG and a couple of Icarus' colleagues stood up and murmured in his ear.

A voice called out from one of the aisles in the auditorium. 'You mean you lot will finally invade and defile God's domain to abuse the building blocks of life!'

A sharp intake of breath was heard throughout the chamber. A man with a goatee beard, his eyes flashing, was on his feet and had been joined by two companions. Stein recognised them from the crowd outside the entrance, and Ashcroft also found the faces familiar. That man with the beard worked in a research lab, which one was it? SISI, the Sakharov Imperfect Symmetry Imaging experiment, one of the new detectors designed for the PBC.

The three men quickly unfurled a large banner with soft, wavy green and blue capital letters that read: DCF.

'No interruptions please!' called one of the organisers, pressing an emergency button, but the group remained standing, and the security guards stationed about the auditorium descended silently, like black cats, on the men in order to remove them.

However, the DG, already numb from his CSO's unscripted and below-the-belt speech, which had yet to deliver whatever fire it had, and better later rather than sooner, pulled himself together, waved at the guards to hold back and wait. He murmured something to Gayle Richter, who nodded, and returned his gaze in the direction of the bearded speaker who was continuing in his coldly polite tone.

69

'You know, everyone, whatever this latest revelation is by Professor Ashcroft, the darling of high energy physics, it is a resounding confirmation that this organisation wields a corrupt power on us all. It's not actually creating anything; it is tampering and destroying. CERN may have started with noble aims, but has the Director General ever told you about the spin-off developments that corrupt governments and individuals are now fighting over? He is knowingly or unknowingly lining his own pockets at the world's expense. Did you know that in the last ten years there has been more exploitative scientific intervention poisoning our world than was the case in the entire previous century? And look at the Grid. That alone has brought about change on an unparalleled scale, dwarfing the Internet and all before it. Your power has grown at the same rate as your supposed generosity, Mr Blipp. Many of you here are no less than parasites wishing to grow rich on the misfortunes of others, whether that involves taking advantage of these scientific breakthroughs or just passing on the bad news in as sensational a way as you can, you know the sort of thing: Scientist predicts End of the World.'

The security guards were responding to a bellow from an aide and again advancing on the protesters, but the DG raised his hand once more for patience and finally spoke into the microphone.

'Ladies and gentlemen, I understand that two of these unscheduled speakers were until recently in our employ. Since that is the case, and since they have chosen to ignore our policy of transparency in order to cause disruption and confusion, let them now hoist themselves by their own petard and demonstrate why it is we do not welcome such devious-minded people in our ranks. We have nothing to hide.' He sat back, folded his arms, and nodded reassuringly at his agitated aide, muttering, 'Five minutes max.'

'You know, I have not finished!' Ashcroft hissed in fury, but Henri Le Baut did not even glance at him.

'It is only by coming right inside this organisation and working here that we have reached our informed view,' continued the protestor in clipped tones. All of you here need to wake up and see what's happening. First we achieved the ability to blow up our world. We've had our hearts in our mouths ever since. Soon we may also have the potential to blow ourselves clean out of our universe. What is small is indeed most powerful.

The deeper that manipulators such as Ashcroft delve, the more they invade a domain reserved only for God. Logic dictates that at this rate they will be invading not just our physical environment but maybe also the afterlife that is hidden from our sight. Science is not the answer to everything. What about spirituality, the soul? Are our children to inherit only laboratories and test reports and cold facts, not our hopes and dreams? Ladies and gentlemen, we must stop these people. They're power hungry, they're playing God, they're people corrupted by the lure of infinite power. Subatomic particles hold the physicists in thrall, and the physicists together with their state and transnational sponsors may now be holding the entire universe to ransom.

'You know who we are. You've got our information chips. We are the Defenders of our Future Children. We are the global majority to which you belong. We represent the ordinary man on the street whose life is circumscribed in every way by living on synthetic drugs and genetically modified foods, producing a genetically engineered family, being made obsolete by computers and then being subjected to their continuous surveillance. And all the while he pays taxes that could instead fund a better, more humane quality of life but are being sunk into ultimately self-destructive research. That man on the street is losing every shred of his dignity. He has nothing to pass on to his children. Well, we are standing up for him, and we are standing up for you.

'None of us has forgotten the Bloody Green Revolution*. We haven't gone quiet these past seven years; our activities have simply been forced underground by the international alliances and multinational conglomerates with vested interests in research they want to protect. We only justify violence when it is specifically targeted at the guilty. Think of the violence they perpetrate on us with their policies: the chaotic weather patterns of global warming, the refugee camps being set up inland to receive those coming from coastal communities, the steady mass migration to the poles, the landslides, the looting in urban areas, the robbing of liberty and loss of livelihood, the resurgence of fascism, the mortuaries filling up with victims of escalating natural disasters. We speak with the voice of logic; we represent the billions who wish only to preserve what we can of our planet and environment.'

A number of delegates and members of the audience were now vacating their seats.

71

'Good God, man!' Icarus barked at the DG. 'Their five minutes are well and truly up. They've had far longer than I did!'

The DG's mouth twisted in anger. 'Enough!' He flicked his hand at his aides in a gesture more akin to an emperor delivering a verdict from his throne. 'Let it not be said we are not democratic at CERN, but now remove them.'

The guards tore down the banner and started bundling the protesters out, back up the aisle in the direction of the exit.

'There will be no hiding place for you child killers!' the lead protestor shouted. 'We are many! We will have our day before your machines destroy our children's futures!'

He glanced round, as though expecting to see something, and a shadow of sudden bewilderment crossed his face. His companions, equally bewildered, followed his gaze.

'What possible purpose has this served?' Ashcroft demanded in the DG's ear. 'This will be all over our screens and front pages in no time. You can forget all coverage of my particle and the PBC! It seems my life's work is in ruins; I've had no time to explain myself; I shall sound like a raving madman!'

'Your announcement sounded like it had little to do with CERN,' the DG snapped back. 'It seemed instead to have everything to do with your own personal ambition and resentment at not being sufficiently recognised. You're good, Icarus, very good, but being a team player seems not to be one of your strengths, and I've warned you before about being a loose cannon. How can I trust you? And as for this bunch of no hopers — well, it helps to know your enemy, and quite frankly that seemed rather more urgent than your pretty little speech. Now if you'll excuse me...'

He turned grim-faced to make eye contact with his aides and token gestures to pacify the audience. Svetlana, several rows back, ever the blonde mighty magnet even in a public arena as large as this one, fluttered a little wave at him. Henri's steely gaze glanced off her without responding.

'Tch, tch, not a happy happy Henri,' Svetlana murmured.

The struggle between the still-shouting protesters and the security guards served only to tighten the knot of frightened people clambering over both each other and the rows of seats for the exit. It choked the only path of retreat for the protesters and their captors.

The protesters, now barely visible, were lashing out when a number of shots were suddenly fired, the reports ricocheting around the Chromathene dome. There was a stricken hush, and then a communal gasp of panic. The angry knot of people unravelled as all three of the protesters fell to the ground, blood trickling through their ears and nostrils, their locked arms pulling down with them the guards who had drawn their firearms and were now staring down at their dying charges in horror.

Every face in the chamber was lined with terror. There were screams from various directions. Amid shouts to seal off all exits and even louder shouts to be allowed out, the melee moved to the outer wall of the amphitheatre, blocking the path for the security and emergency services. Marco walked steadily up the aisle towards the main exit, at the same pace as those around him.

The American postgraduate was scrabbling over the backs of seats, looking for his professor. 'Wait for me, what do I do?'

'What do you think? Get out of this place as quickly as possible!' came the irritated reply.

The graduate glanced back at Svetlana who had ripped off her earphones and appeared flushed and breathless as she teetered on her high heels. She was obviously in an agitated if not excited state; he couldn't just abandon her.

'Let me see now… you get out, sir, and I'll just go and help.' But the prof had already gone.

Jonathan Stein was standing well back from the action, jabbering into his IDO, pointing its high res digital lens at the action. The sweat was pooling in the hollow of his throat and between his shoulder blades, and his face was shining. What a story! He tried to remember what Blipp had been telling him; could Blipp have foreseen this? He could see the man right now, over on the dais with Gayle. They seemed calm and detached somehow, taking everything in the way he was doing.

Not for several seconds did anyone notice the woman, sitting slumped on her own in one of the front rows, her cloud of soft brown hair twisted at an awkward angle.

'Brooke!' came a strangled scream, and the crowd turned to see the Chief Scientific Officer taking the floor in bounds and throwing himself on his inert wife, cradling her head, calling and shaking her.

'It's Ashcroft's wife,' the whisper darted round. 'She's been shot.'

Where was CERN's medical officer at a time like this? Who'd been doing the shooting?

'Gayle!' Henri le Baut bawled. 'Stop standing about. Get a doctor. Someone get a doctor! Quickly!'

He could hear one of his aides shouting at the guards by the main exit. 'What the hell do you think you're doing, letting this lot out? What sort of security situation do we have here? For Christ's sake, what do we pay these guys for? No one's doing anything!'

A couple of minutes later a hush fell on the few journalists and stragglers left standing in shock in the auditorium. There were shufflings and mutterings of the security guards clustered round the bloodied and prostrate bodies. A medic several rows away was pumping his arms downward in the vain hope of reviving Brooke Ashcroft. He stopped, bowed and shook his head. The hush was as unnerving as the panic. It fell so thick that it was nearly tangible. The only sound that carried up and around the dome like a trapped bird was the ever more hysterical weeping of a man, covered in his wife's blood, rocking and crying, 'Brooke, what have I done?'

It was bizarre. How could it be that one minute he had the world in his hands, and the next minute he had been plunged into the blackness of losing everything?

The police sirens were already screaming up the Meyrin road that Stein had driven along just an hour or two earlier. Forensics and medical teams and a crack police unit were being sent in, donning their gloves and making routine checks on their equipment.

The rush of delegates had poured out of the building, the young American postgraduate holding the arm of Svetlana Grigoriya. Pushing the young man into an office she had decided to give him the treat of his life. It had all gone so well that the excitement was just too much and anyway Henri was, should we say, occupied. The medics, in the meantime, started to examine and see what could be done for the seriously injured and confirm that certain persons were dead, but the police also wanted these in-situ for precious evidence and for consulting with CERN security. Most incidents on site were settled internally under the terms of CERN's unique cross border status, and this was only the

74

fourth occasion during CERN's existence that the Swiss police had been summoned.

As on past occasions, the dealings had been fraught with bureaucratic difficulties. Both governments had agreed on the appointment of a neutral police specialist to deal with any incidents.

The former head of the Hong Kong anti-terrorist police, detective inspector Wai Chan was now happily settled as a Geneva resident, enjoying a high salary and unique status.

And so it fell to him to come to this atrocity and find some answers.

11. LOOKING TO SPOT THE TINIEST THING Same day

Wai Chan stood at the entrance to the amphitheatre like the embodiment of a Chinese lucky cat. The drumming of his podgy fingers was forming greasy marks on the Chromathene plastic of the dome as his bright blue eyes viewed the peaks of the Jura mountains in the distance.

It was just after midday and the sun was high. For Wai Chan, who was a fan of twentieth-century westerns and Hong Kongese kung fu movies, this high sun always reminded him of the gunfights on patches of dust outside dilapidated saloon bars. This particular gunfight was rather more hi-tech, but the ingredients were just the same. He savoured the ingredients as though they were on his lips. An act of terrorism or revenge or what? Best to keep an open mind until the data from the legs in the forensics is conclusive.

Wai Chan had a particular talent. It lay in spotting the tiniest thing overlooked by all those about him, which was perhaps why he took a shine to the like-minded people in the particle physics community he found at CERN. He was said to be fascinated by really big things too, such as the size of the Swiss bank account set up in his name on relinquishing his old post and functional apartment in Kowloon. Whatever his preferences, he now owned an Italianate villa on the lakeside and a helicopter pad in the walled and gated Montalègre district. And who else would the local police authorities turn to now a terrorist incident had occurred on his new stomping ground? Expert advice was needed, unfortunately it confirmed the necessity of his appointment and proximity.

The Director General gave Wai Chan a hearty handshake, and the necessary approval to pull the entire human and material infrastructure of the place apart if necessary, in order to get to the bottom of this outrage. The complication of indirect diplomatic involvement in this particular case meant that a conduit like the DG was needed to help keep the politicians at arm's length. Not that the detective could know about the man's private affairs; Henri le Baut was concerned about the revelations of alleged corruption by do-gooders and no hopers, and he took comfort from the fact that the deaths in the amphitheatre might provide a convenient smokescreen to negate the need for any wider investigation into the revelations contained in the terrorists' speech. He had his own political masters, and they wanted the truth, but they were complicit in all his dealings and certainly did not want it disseminated to all and sundry.

Wai Chan was in fact happy to let things run along their normal course as far as possible at CERN despite the incident. Best to keep things calm, especially given the high profile nature of this case; also best not to squander vast sums of money by shutting down operations there.

The police had cordoned off the area and gathered the mixed bag of high-ranking officials and scientists on a grassed area as though they were prize cattle. Difficult as it was, given the personalities and egos involved, they carried out Wai Chan's clear instructions to confiscate every piece of recording equipment in sight, line everyone up for a body search, and take a detailed statement. Everyone was issued with a UV sun hat and various chairs were brought out with jugs of ice cold water. The place resembled some sort of surreal unplanned picnic.

Just as thick as the hush left in the amphitheatre was the one that filled police HQ in Geneva during the toothcomb examination of the digirecords later that day. The faces gathered round the glare of the screens were frozen in consternation. Four people had died in the auditorium: the three protesters and Mrs Brooke Ashcroft.

Shortly after midnight, as he was pulling off his tie and stretching out on the gel sofa with a nightcap and yet another data file, it occurred to him that there was something else right under his nose that he wasn't seeing. News had come through that the gun used was a gun unique to CERN, and yet the security guards had only fired in self defence and they had guns set on stun dart prefix.

77

He sifted again through the wad of notes in his lap. Two or three people had observed that there had been a fourth man in the company of the terrorists as they had entered the reception area. They describe him as tall, dark, lithe and athletic in build, clean shaven with a sallow complexion, handsome, most likely somewhere in his thirties, and wearing an immaculately tailored suit. He had been seen talking, albeit briefly, with the other men and there was no photograph or statement from him after the outrage.

Wai Chan pursed his lips and pressed his fingertips together. He saw before him a particular individual whose face had flashed across the screens back at the office. He'd want a picture search undertaken and positive identification as soon as possible. It was all coming together although there was a long way to go yet.

He also thought of the headlines that would be on the digiviewers and plastered across the papers at the breakfast table. You simply could not have had a better press presence than there had been at this event. And maybe these future terrorist martyrs had made their mark more fully than they could ever have imagined.

12. GRIEF AT HASLINGDENE

When the digi-com rang out in the hall, and Elsie went to answer it, Mrs Nimmo scrambled to her feet from where she'd bent over cleaning the skirting boards, but was unable to get to the hall table fast enough. She had a sudden, awful feeling that something was wrong. She had felt a jolt only an hour or so before and had clutched her heart, yet it was beating normally. The feeling reminded her of touching an electric fence round a neighbouring field, which she had once done in her childhood.

'Wait, Elsie!' she had called out, but Elsie had already put the receiver to her ear, stiffened in shock, and dropped it.

Mrs Nimmo had snatched it, listened to what the caller had to say, murmured an automatic 'thank you', and returned the communication device to its antique cradle.

The click it made sounded so final. That was that, then. Forty-nine years wiped out in an instant and several lives wrecked. No more peals of laughter from the sitting room or humming from the kitchen garden or soothing words from the study when Icarus wanted feedback on anything and everything. No more banter with Sam or calm, practical encouragement for Lycian. No more sessions with Elsie on the sofa pouring over their research or brainstorming cryptic wordsearches, or just heart to hearts.

'No.' Elsie pushed Mrs Nimmo's arms away and remained stiff. It was the first time she didn't respond to the ever ready and warm embrace.

The police called round a few minutes later, too late to prevent the impersonal digi-message from doing its worst. The Ashcroft children were collapsed in a row in the sitting room like broken dolls. The police wanted close relatives informed, close friends too, but the children looked up dumbly, glanced at Mrs Nimmo and shrugged.

'They've got me and Mr Nimmo,' their cleaning lady said stoutly, 'and Mr Nimmo's on his way as we speak.'

Mr Nimmo did not need asking, as it happened, for he had had the same jolt as his wife. He was already only two hundred metres from the house, and was jogging at a rate which would have tested most long-distance athletes.

'The children surely need someone else for support, Mrs Nimmo,' a WPC urged.

Mrs Nimmo untied and flung her working overall aside. 'Well, appearances can be deceptive,' she retorted.

'You live at the lodge?'

'That's right. The best place to be under these circumstances, and we're not budging.'

'There will be no need for that, Mrs Nimmo. But Professor Ashcroft especially will need a lot of support, so we suggest –'

'You can send all your people in,' Mrs Nimmo replied. 'Bereavement counsellors, detectives, you name it, just as long as Mr Nimmo and I are consulted first. You will find that Professor Ashcroft will be in complete agreement on that, and in case you think he's not in a mentally fit state to do so I can provide you with a sworn affidavit that –'

'One thing at a time,' the WPC interrupted. 'We know this is a very upsetting time for you all.'

'Good grief,' she said five minutes later, as she and her colleague returned along the drive past the rhododendron borders and lodge with its conical mini tower with turrets and pretend battlements. 'Not many families have relatives with as strong a feeling as these two. I think it will really either kill or cure them.

Her colleague pressed the button to raise the barrier. 'It's not natural,' he said. 'Different people react in different ways, we can't expect normality at such a time.'

Over the Ashcroft's kitchen table, while the Nimmos sat clasping mugs of Yorkshire tea and hoping in vain that the children would fall asleep from the sedatives if not from sheer exhaustion, the Bugz Zon and Zleo inside them considered what their next move should be, outside the obvious defensive shield they had erected unknown to the humans around the vicarage.

Mrs Nimmo was waiting for an IDO message to find out which plane the Professor would be on the day after that, and Mr Nimmo would be stationed at flight arrivals to ensure a safe welcome. Zon and Zleo sat at the kitchen table late into the night with their hosts and felt their own equations moved by the grief they were lodged in. Contact with individual beings was a destabilising experience: the stronger the link the more control they had over their hosts' direction, and yet the stronger the link the more vulnerable their sensors became to unBugzish signals. Zon and Zleo felt firm in their resolve, but they felt something new too. Ziel had made a decisive move and the plan conceived those thousands of years back was in danger of failing.

82

13. THE LUCKY CAT VIEWS HIS PREY

Earlier that day Wai Chan was sitting at the desk in the hi-tech police facility which had been airlifted to the site, immobile as a statue, paw-like hands pressed together just under his double chin, staring unseeing out of his office window. The questions buzzed around in his head like a plague of flies. He was itching to swat them all, but he had patience. He wanted each fly to land one by one on the back of his hand so he could observe their every detail. He knew a fair bit about ecoterrorism, but it did not take a great leap of the imagination to suspect that, whatever form of protest the three men with their banner had planned, it was unlikely to have involved their being gunned down.

He had run the usual checks immediately of course, pulling up police, library, immigration and CERN records and then comparing notes. At the slightest flutter of his podgy fingers he had every piece of technological armament placed at his disposal: every frame of digi footage from the blue laser cameras and every pixel of information on IDO, the Grid and Super-G, plus every second of straightforward digicom contact. A black-out was imposed on all outgoing information at CERN, and all incoming information was being subjected to intense round-the-clock scrutiny.

Who the killer might be and what possible motive he or she had for the public killing of three unarmed men and the wife of a scientist was obscure. Was there more than one killer? And why hadn't it been the scientist himself instead of his wife, if as was clearly the case from his impromptu speech, he had something significantly alarming up his sleeve to unleash on the world?

83

It was not long before the protesters were identified. The Defenders of our Future Children had been prominent during the Bloody Green Revolution, and even though their operations had since become more covert, the police had no trouble keeping tabs on the ringleaders and the general groundswell of their thinking. This incident seemed, in contrast, just to have been a peaceful protest, with the high profile event they attended providing all the publicity needed.

A peaceful protest. If life were so simple.

There was the issue of the guns too. How had the killer or killers gained access to a CERN gun? It had either been authorised, apparently without the normal authorised user's knowledge, or at least unlocked and removed for use. And why had the bullet earmarked for Brooke Ashcroft been so, well, exotic? He could only think it was to make doubly sure that the shooting was fatal. Whatever the case, CERN security and its procedures would now be subjected to a complete overhaul once the police inquiry had been dealt with.

Then there were the interviews. After some delicate questioning of the dignitaries present on the scene, there had been the rounding up of the witnesses detained on their leaving the building. After that it was time to focus on particular individuals, and Wai Chan had drawn up his list without further ado.

The CERN Security Chief, James Drew, provided helpful information on the organisation's security systems. He identified the gun that had fired the bullets; it was a type used by CERN, but this particular one had not been issued by the organisation. Drew reckoned his job was on the line, and yet he didn't know where anyone, himself included, could have slipped up.

The Security Chief's job was most definitely under review, so the Director General told Wai Chan when he was called in after Drew. Henri le Baut pinched the bridge of his nose and screwed up his eyes with weariness as though to stem an oncoming headache, and then resettled his spectacles in their rightful place. Heads would roll. CERN was fortunate to have the best detective on the case, he made that clear to the entire staff, and he was expected to get to the bottom of things in no time.

This sort of terrorist outrage was all part of the territory, of course, le Baut reflected. When a global organisation such as CERN received as much funding as it did, and appeared to have the powers of a mini sovereign state, envy and resentment and hatred were sure to result. These protesters were really no better or worse than the rest. He had simply allowed them to have their say to try to understand them, to allay their fears and quash their hatred. Yes, the shootings were a mystery. Still, it was a testament to the solid security on site that these incidents were few and far between.

'Do go ahead, Inspector, please, look at the accounts. There'd be nothing out of order there. Ashcroft? Poor man. Good friend and colleague. Known each other ten years. Bit of a surprise, that speech of his, yes — but then this was the type of organisation where people were expected to stay on their toes. Working in close collaboration with – who else did you say? Miss Grigoriya? Ah, well now. She was a good physicist and a good friend.' And that of course was all the Inspector needed to know. But if anything else of interest cropped up, the Inspector would be the first to know.

The Chief Scientific Officer was not ready to receive visitors yet, not even the Detective Inspector. The professor had been sedated despite his protests. Malicious word had reached Wai Chan that the guy had suffered apoplexy from being denied his born right to hold court and present his latest magnanimous offering to the world.

Wai Chan pursed his lips, consulted his list and moved on to the two women, the model scientist and the tidy brunette. Funny how his sidekicks perked up at this point and wanted to be in on the interviews.

Svetlana Grigoriya was a Russian emigrée with a doctorate in both high energy physics and applied mathematics who was now resident in Italy. She was the owner of a canalside palazzo in the throbbing heart of Venice and a Palladian villa in the Arcadian setting of the Veneto, residences that were more suited to landed gentry or a business magnate than a scientist, if one cared to make the observation. She had, it seemed, a golden touch. Wai Chan dug up details about her non official CV. She had come from nowhere, from the flat river landscape by the Tura in Siberia. Her childhood had been spent playing in the dirt of her uncle's chicken farm on the edge of the town that was home to her reputed ancestor Rasputin. Her nomad mother took her on the odd occasion to live in a yurta in the harshest depths of winter – the sort of

85

winter long forgotten since global warming and the adolescent Svetlana had learned to cope with extremes in life. She couldn't break free from her old life fast enough, despite the long train journey across the Urals to St Petersburg and the far edge of the world. Having persuaded a semi-retired and jaded businessman in first class to part with his bang-up-to-date IDO and nanoputer, in return for some strictly non business affairs to relieve the boredom of the journey, she alighted at her destination and found lodgings with a friend in a run-down capsule apartment. Her meagre savings secured a fast-track advanced pico-puter correspondence course to obtain the scholarship she dreamed of in order to gain a degree in physics. The semi-retired businessman found a new lease of life when she soon came to keep house for him.

Svetlana opened further doors by dropping hints about her illustrious, if infamous, ancestry. She had Rasputin's charm and charisma. Everyone liked Svetlana: she worked hard, played hard, netted men of power and influence and gave them, like she gave Henri, exactly what they desired. Svetlana only ever expected the rough, and when she got the smooth it whetted her appetite all the more.

How appearances could deceive, though. Grigoriya looked at first glance like a bimbo, what with her precariously low décolletage, crotch-length hemline and teetering heels. But Wai Chan spotted what his sidekicks did not, that the sulky look in that doll's face did not necessarily mean 'come hither'. It could equally mean serious business. And that was just up Wai Chan's street.

The woman came into the newly arrived state-of-the-art incident room, crossed her long legs and arms, sat back and fixed her green-eyed gaze on him. There was nothing Wai Chan thought of asking that she could not answer. It was like ping pong. Ashcroft? Good friend and colleague. Very, very tragic. His wife? Please, Mr Inspector. Too tragic. Aware of anything unusual leading up to the big day? No. Not here all the time, anyway. It turned out that Svetlana had connections here, there and everywhere, from the highest tier of government down to the street trader. Everyone loved her. She had brains and beauty, she was (according to the CIA, Interpol and MI5) a clean living girl, and she enjoyed widespread popularity among friends and colleagues. Wai Chan stroked his chin and pondered. What a saintly image. So saintly in fact that she seemed curiously detached. She had to prove herself though, given her deprived background and all that. Wai Chan noticed the type of company she kept when he saw her out of the interview room. Were those two men in fact bodyguards? One looked like an oversized American quarterback with scaffolding by way of a skeleton, the other a Sumo wrestler who had consumed a skip full of bricks.

Gayle Richter was called in next. The stunning brunette was in some ways a carbon copy of the blonde. More chic though, she wouldn't go blowsy within another decade or two – and somewhat warmer in personality, but then that went with the job. She was adept at masterminding publicity events, coordinating speakers, drawing up guest lists, consulting on the catering, doing the introductions beforehand and seeing to acknowledgments afterwards. She was discreet but always at your elbow. She knew everything about everything, but wasn't the type to dish the dirt.

'Although you can tell me,' Wai Chan urged her, leaning forward. 'After all, you seem to know more about the comings and goings in this place than anyone else. I expect a superhostess has super observant skills.'

'Indeed, I try to do my job as efficiently as possible, those three protesters either worked here or had grade five clearance.'

'Maybe it's the system that's at fault, inspector' Gayle observed.

'Yes, true, my dear and it's well to know how to use it to one's advantage, n'est-ce pas?

'Oui, Monsieur.'

87

14. IN THE POWER ROOM
Same day

Svetlana and Gayle were in what they dubbed the 'ladies' power room', comparing notes and ruffled feathers over the Detective Inspector's interviews. A lady's man he was not. His minions had dug them out of their offices, dropped them in the interview room and then returned them to their offices as though they were counters in a board game.

Svetlana was looking in the mirror at her companion while the two of them touched up their lipstick. Svetlana's was a thick gloss of chilli pepper red, while Gayle's was merely a few dabs of matt warm grape, its excess removed by a tissue.

Svetlana gazed at the rings under her bloodshot eyes. 'God, I feel rough after yesterday,' she sighed at the mirror. 'You know how I usually manage to take things in my stride, Gayle.'

'So I have heard,' Gayle remarked. 'It's good you're off home tomorrow for a couple of nights of rest.'

'Yes, Henri can be a little distracting at times but don't worry, my mind is on the job, so to speak.'

'On that topic you know the PBC can't just be put on hold. He needs Ashcroft whatever and so do we. And of course he'll come round to the idea of Ashcroft's Midas particle, he's just miffed he wasn't in on it before and was therefore shown up in public. Injured pride, that's all.'

'And he's in a dream position what with all his lovely money,' Svetlana observed. 'He needs Ashcroft and Ashcroft will soon realise he needs us.'

'To think that Ashcroft's been sitting on a box of goodies all these years,' Gayle said. He's quite a dark horse. I've been doing some digging, and there's some family history about this chest being handed down. He wants some recognition not just for himself but also for his ancestors. They seemed to have been on the edge of things in the shadows, do you think we have underestimated these hangers on?'

'No, and I personally can't see the point in looking back,' Svetlana said, lining her lips with a razor sharp pencil. 'We go only one way and that's forward. Boxes of primitive carbon compounds never were my thing. And as for seeking glory, well, you need to stick your neck out and not hang back. That's the way of this world, and ours I'd say.'

Gayle adjusted her silk scarf. 'This is all devastating for Ashcroft.'

'It certainly is. I intend to have a little word with him. He needs bucking up, and it wouldn't surprise me if he throws himself back into his work in no time, especially if Henri proves cooperative. I will do all I can to help him. Everything's in limbo right now but it will resolve itself.'

Gayle sighed. 'There's the launch to see to all over again. It'll be more than a headache reconvening everyone, and lets make sure it's first class travel home.'

'You'll come up trumps; you always do,' Svetlana smiled. 'Anyway, it can't happen soon, given this police investigation. That fat cat policeman has really got his work cut out. And once I'm back I'll have my work cut out too, keeping Henri sweet and bringing Ashcroft back into the fold as well as seeing to my own stuff. A second launch should just be a more low-key affair, surely?

'Very low-key, if you ask me. Yes, but all the more eventful.'

89

15. DO NOT DISTURB
Same day

Jonathan Stein had a terrible night's sleep after the killings that day. If it hadn't been for the interview with Blipp the day before the CERN incident, he would have been convinced that he was experiencing some drug-induced rollercoaster inhabited by little green particles.

The ups and downs in his life had come so thick and fast that they were blurred. He'd got his first major scoop landing the assignment to attend the PBC start up. He'd then had a hell of a journey coming over, summoning up his courage to face his demons after the plane crash a year ago and almost needing to be poured off the plane from fright. He'd got his second major scoop the next day at the Blipp Corporation headquarters, where he'd been fed – forcefed, red hot information beyond his wildest dreams. The food had been good too. He'd gone to bed that night on a full stomach and a churning brain. He'd then woken up invigorated with a superman strength he'd never experienced before. He'd stayed invigorated too.

As if all this wasn't enough trauma and ecstasy at once with regard to his professional life, personal life and his mental and physical constitution, yesterday there were the shootings in the amphitheatre. He witnessed the move of the Black Queen in the most public manner leading to the annihilation of the superparticle (yet again). They needed to save

90

humankind before the PBC would be used to her own ends. On leaving the amphitheatre Stein had promptly asked his boss if he could follow up on the story and go to his old university town of Cambridge. No wonder Stein had had a dreadful night. He got the official story off to his editor the previous afternoon while the adrenalin was still pumping, and he was now going to ask the room courtesy nanoputer to draw the blinds, flick on the Do Not Disturb sign outside his door and will the world to go away.

There were continual bleeps coming from his bedside table. Blipp was feeding him with more IDO messages. Stein jabbed at the OFF button and pulled the covers over his head. Blipp could 'blipp off', he thought, but the messages carried on with or without power.

16. THE CAT ON THE TRAIL
16 June 2042

Detective Inspector Wai Chan was the cat that got the cream; he regularly forgot his manners, not least with female colleagues. With his satisfyingly ample girth he didn't give a toss about the fat police, which is why he refused on principle to visit the States even though he'd been required there in the way of work on many occasions. He invariably lulled people into a false sense of security just as a tiger might look cute, but we know a swipe from its paw could take your head off. He acknowledged the suffering of victims and he went out of his way to exact his own retribution, and not always within the confines of the legal system.

Wai Chan knew how to get things done, and it was enough in the CERN case to ensure the full imaging of Mrs Ashcroft's body in the shortest time possible to release it for burial. Three days on from the CERN shootings the woman's death had begun to resemble the collapse of a house of cards, in the form of both the DG's and the CSO's state of mind, CERN's reputation generally, and the potential cost of idle machinery to spiral. One minute Ashcroft was saying that he wanted to die along with his wife; the next he was saying he wanted to get back on track as soon as possible if he was to find any meaning to go on. Best therefore to do so as soon as possible, of course, and if he wanted a quick funeral then it should happen. He'd flown back last night with the body to his waiting and grieving family in Cambridge. Wai Chan had dispensed with polite interviews now. Hard graft was what was needed, and two leads had cropped up.

First there was the American student found in a storeroom. He was in intensive care for treatment to the 90% burns on his genitalia. Not pleasant but original Wai Chan thought. 'Wow, she blew my mind' the boy had managed to gasp to the medics, and it was true, he was acting like a seven year old.

'No points for guessing whose unhealthy libido that might be,' one of Wai Chan's English colleagues observed.

In the meantime, Miss Grigoriya needed pulling back in for questioning. But she wasn't about. Funny, that. Left yesterday for home, something about being away on official business. She would have to be handled with care. And then, of course, there was the director general and his involvement to deal with. Then there was the digi-scanner sequence. They'd got a few fuzzy images of a man's hand, wrist and watch as they slipped round the shaking shoulders of an elderly woman who was being escorted out of the amphitheatre. The watch was distinctive. It was, Wai Chan knew from personal interest, the latest Patek Philippe on the market. There were also several frames charting the course of this watch, down corridors, stairs, through fire doors, the old ALICE tunnel, and then gone – presumably worn by the same man caught on camera sprinting along the perimeter on the edge of the Meyrin road. They'd gone over the records and footage of the blue laser cameras swiping at the main entrance. There'd been several Patek Philippes on show, of course, but only one hand matched the one with the long slim fingers that they now recognised, and the chip on the back had been swiped very shortly after those of the terrorists. It belonged to Marco Andrea Bergamasco, thirty-three years of age, Italian, café owner, hired hand, hired gun, with mob connections in Treviso.

Wai Chan pursed his lips. Treviso seemed the place to be.

93

17. ZYBERIA—
another time, another place

The beam of microphotons that struck Zein in his repose signalled to him that the black phase was nearly over and the new white phase of leadership would begin.

As heir apparent, if not future joint leader of Zyberia he took particular interest in the metronomic switching of the control of the great empire that coursed its way to the edges of the known universe. The microphotons struck one billionth of a zicrosecond before Zein's mental units began their automatic countdown to the start of the white phase. His scotopic vision absorbed the brightness. He now clicked into routine motion, consuming precisely measured clumps of exotic Zo matter specially harvested for elite Bugz, both black and white.

Zein set off, tracking along coordinates that had been programmed into his mental units several millennia ago when he had been in the early energy-building stage of his existence. These coordinates, plotted the instant his equation had been completed, were permanently entered by default unless he took some trouble to click alternative mental units into place.

New white phase, new function phase. Zein was fully charged once the clumps of Zo matter had been transformed into energy in his multi-ringed ballistic-shaped body. He tracked past the familiar line of decaying statues fronting the old Library, their clusters of architect Bugz hard as the hardest zargonite, their uniform square plinths marking precisely the even intervals of space dividing them from both each other and the route.

No Bugz, indeed, had fully researched the reasons for the fall of classical Zytopia, but the potential to do so certainly existed; it simply required a Bugz with exceptional mental energy and a near infinite supply of positivity z units to kick off the process. The top-tier Bugz were in agreement that such potential existed; and the time seemed right, although routine function had to take precedence of course. There was always the future.

18. A VISION OF THE FUTURE

Zein focused on the sequence of events planned for this white phase. The Adjustment of the State of the Equilibrium was held only once every one hundred zicroyears, when the top generation which ruled from the Apex relinquished and transferred power to the succeeding one. The black and white interchanged in harmony: the dominant one to rule, the subordinate one to check. The aim was to achieve a perfect majority, namely a beautifully minuscule one, as with all the Bugz' votes cast only a very small majority was needed. During this transition period, Zyberia's harmony laws dictated that the outcome be perfectly predictable as well as satisfactory. One issue that Zein would raise in the new white phase was the recent lack of consensus on the purpose of conserving the decaying building blocks of Old Zytop, such as the statues by the Library.

The majority of Bugz eligible to vote favoured simply accepting the present status of the ancient engineering Bugz and duzz that made up the foundations of Zyber, and to maintain their utilitarian function where possible. However, the recent reading of 0.000004 expressions of opposition had provided strong evidence of a growing segment of the population polarizing between a complete bottom-up rebuild of Zyberian society and the urge, such as Zein had, to question and study these structures, to chip away at the origins of Bugz life that constituted its rich historical archive.

Investigation was therefore imperative to this new approaching white phase, and Zein intended to use his influence over more enlightened

Bugz equations and discover more about their Zytopian heritage.

As Zein made his way to the Apex, a strong and clear rush of archaic TT Bugz hit him. They had been transmitted from Zyberia's outermost margins, the so-called empty quarter, and the symbols and concepts they formed in his sensors were mystical and intriguing, yet as hard as zargonite. He believed it was the oldest message he had ever received. It appeared that they provided the answer to a question, or what he presumed was a question. They claimed that the matter for rebalancing the State of Equilibrium lay in the Empty Quarter, beyond which a route was signposted:

`Do not enter. Beware nothing. Salvation awaits.`

Each of the TT Bugz was infused with a zigzag symbol.

The impact of the message was so strong that Zein decided he would attract Zim, a close associate to review the content and make comment.

Zim was charging himself for the activities of this white phase. Half his lifespan had been devoted to the teaching of logic and function to the striplings in his sphere of contact. Their inbuilt advanced equations meant their capacity for mental and physical energy was greater than could ever be the case for those lower down the pyramidal structure such as worker and engineering Bugz, and the countless swathes of bottom-tier waste Bugz below them, but these lower tiers would probably argue that philosophical study and debate did not build the physical reality and structure that made up the Zyberian empire.

The scholars Zim taught were naturally in an excited state this phase. As was his habit, Zim would be taking them out of their confines in the Academy. Not for him was the deadening inertia in the enclosed spaces dedicated to learning, where bodies at rest might mean minds at rest too. He preferred regular exercise and stimulation in open vistas, tracking round the white columns of the old Zytopian facades and through the shaded areas where stray microphotons sparked and vanished. At the end of this black phase, however, and in the welcome company of Zein as well as his pupils, he made his way to the Open Chamber, outside the Apex, whose smooth paving stretched out and curved away under the vault of Zyber's sky.

Just before the change from black into white phase all segments of Zyberian society had started gathering here, and Zein, Zim and the

99

scholar Bugz merged with the mass. Zim's detectors swept round in an arc to note movement, density and energy. Here was an ideal opportunity for his class to see logic and function in action and not just in the abstract.

Zleo, from his position among his fellow Bugz near the Apex, detected Zim and Zein on the periphery of the crowd and straight away attracted to them, showering on them the usual polished messenger Bugz of recognition and harmony.

'There are concerns about the Equilibrium,' he told them, his rings fizzing with pent-up energy. 'The Universal Energy Monitoring Centre has reported large-scale aberrations of late from their energy readings. It is not at all clear how smooth the transfer will be. It is even less clear which of the two orders will gain the majority, for the gap is much smaller than is desirable. The black Bugz may yet retain power. The white order may not rule after all, my friends.'

Zleo's warning triggered a tingling in Zein's memory banks from the strange TT input he had just experienced. The answer lay in the Empty Quarter and beyond. The answer to what? An answer seemingly without a question; a back-to-front deformation of logic and spacetime. And it had sounded urgent. And what of salvation – whatever that meant?

'That cannot be true,' Zim replied, and quickly adjusted his logic counter. 'I mean, that is most likely not true. I sense no such suspicions among the Apex members, and I advise them regularly, as you know.'

'But you absorb spin, not necessarily fact,' Zleo replied, 'and when you are not in the Apex you inhabit the isolated and rarefied conditions of the Academy. Whereas I travel along the public pathways and visit the laboratories incalculable times, and I sense increasing levels of discord.'

'What discord?'

Zleo reeled off his list. 'Activity resembling movements of negative energy. Maybe, in fact, the re-emergence of the mutant particles we believed were long dispersed and without leadership. The UEMC has picked up unusual readings showing the existence of three- and five-ringed particles within Zyber itself, intruders cloaked under authorisation that has come from the highest level of the Apex. A power vacuum may be developing. I fear the initial phase of a widespread and long-lived disturbance, a rising of something we do not yet understand.'

'We might be receiving a vision of the future,' Zein said, more to himself. 'A future that does not exist but is being given a probability of existence using forbidden constructs.'

'Such a disturbance cannot be true. None has been predicted.' Zim once again adjusted his logic counter. 'Perhaps it is true, then. Perhaps our equations have not taken into account every variable. Have you had some form of forewarning, Zein?'

'The consequences are clear even if the origin is not,' Zein said. 'There is a worrying imbalance, just as there is between Bugz over the issue of the rebuilding of the Library and its structures. As it happens, this imbalance is precisely why I am on my way to the Library. For when our receptors do not pick up the truth, the Library is an obvious place for consulting fact. As you know, my friends, the records of the past are contained therein, and if whatever is causing this disturbance wishes to destroy the Library we should draw closer attention to its contents. Zytop's ancient past features in my equation.'

'So since what the TT said was that an answer to a forthcoming imbalance exists out beyond the empty quarter, I need to find out more of the signature this message carries and then see if what it says turns in to reality. I am thinking that there will be a black phase maintained and this marks a schism in the order of Zyberia.'

Zein cautioned, 'You can see that this is a dangerous situation. I therefore assume I have your cooperation in my seeking out the truth there, without delay. I suggest you stay and see the outcome.'

As Zein broke contact and made for the Library, Zleo returned to his fellow Bugz in the Open Chamber to focus every unit of his thought drive on intensifying the energy of his chosen party, the one by all rights predicted to win and usher in the new white Equilibrium.

The crystalline array of the architect Bugz that formed the paving of the Open Chamber had begun to shimmer with the friction of the massed ranks of Bugz: warriors and messengers, portal keepers and higher functionaries, Bugzhists and the rare Superbugz. Each Bugz sensed the crackle of the strong energy pulls of the mass, first in one direction, then in the other.

The messenger Bugz were darting around Zim's class and colliding in excited high-energy zotons. Zleo's detectors swept round the monumental vista of stark white blocks and black bars of shadow, the slip planes and odd angles. They noted the crumbling proportions of the Apex, the Academy and the Library. They tracked the plainer, multi-use structures of more recent times that were intersected by a geometric pattern of steps and channels, thoroughfares and equidistant nuclei. Eventually these newer structures would crumble too with time, just as the old pearl gateways and pathways were left abandoned when the new Zyberia was carved out of virgin space.

Zim imaged the tense concentrations of the high functionaries and top-tier Bugz inside the Apex; he imaged the Bugzhists in their retreats, the recorder Bugz in the Universal Energy Monitoring Centre, and the indistinct but vibrating form of Ziel, the Black Queen, in her closed vault. The mass in the Open Chamber coalesced now, humming ever louder as it sucked into it all the thought-drive abroad in the Zyberian universe, until the violent force of it imploded at their centre in a core of pure energy. The resulting charge spiked out white hot and shattered, creating a cloud of plasma which billowed out on an electromagnetic shockwave, up and away from the mass. A ring of debris, first contracted in the core and then flung out in the wake of the shockwave, drifted skyward through the atmosphere and dispersed in showers of sparks.

A hush fell over the Open Chamber where all energy and spin had suddenly ceased. The recorder Bugz at the UEMC buzzed in consternation at the number five majority. And a sigh of pleasure oozed out in an effervescence of bloated zotons from Ziel's chamber. The tiny majority was black. The State of Equilibrium had been broken.

Zein received the news and thought about the TT message from earlier. This was by no means the end. Possibly it was the beginning of this new unnatural future. And it was beginning right now.

19. THE ANCIENT LIBRARY KEEPER

The ancient Library was no longer the epicentre of the Zyberian universe, and the Library Keepers employed therein enjoyed neither the power nor the grand location of their forerunners in Old Zytop. In the rebuilt capital of Zyber these high-tier functionary Bugz occupied nothing other than a near redundant backwater. Zyber was much smaller in size than Zytop, and it had shifted off the original site, leaving the rebuilt Library near the rim of the capital's innermost energy ring of defense. Zein assumed that the Library had remained on its original foundations because of its imposing structure: a façade and atrium of fine architectural Bugz, though even these did not do justice to the grand repository of the sum of Bugz knowledge. The older, stable parts of the Library had been renovated as far as was possible with inferior engineering particles that rubbed ring to interlinked ring with the fading archaic splendour itself, long shrouded in duzz from the legendary Quake.

On crossing the building's threshold, Zein nearly always switched on to auto visit, scanning a part of the Library's data he had not yet encountered. The multiple trails of his multiple visits for multiple purposes were recorded in his mental units to recall the tiniest fragment of useful information in carrying out his natural function of checking formulae, comparing equations, seeking symmetry, mapping a course or solving a puzzle. As a member of the Apex he theoretically had unrestricted access to 100% of the information available.

He suspected, however, when he crossed the threshold that such access was not entirely unrestricted. There were parts of the Library even a Superbug could not reach.

103

On this occasion, and given the recent communication and disturbance, Zein was not in a passive frame of mind. He was in erratic mode, off at a tangent, zigzagging through the maze of layered messenger particles, ignoring their nudges and whispers. There was another source of information, he was sure, a hidden source where messenger particles lay cloaked in duzz untouched and undisturbed. He had come across a few brief references over the years to the Flame that had burned, that still burned, within the depths of the Library. Was it legend or reality, and what was its purpose?

The past needed conjoining with the future, and Zein knew of only one Bugz who could help in this matter. He would attract the faded energy signal of Zotl, the near-transparent Library Keeper. This ancient sage, whose brittle energy bands toppled at a sharp angle with decrepitude, was on the cusp of entering his umpteenth half life. However, his meandering equation held true, and it was as rich in fact as was the public institution it served. Library and Keeper seemed inextricably bound.

An arduous process was underway to duplicate Zotl's equation on a number of receiver Bugz for the Keeper in waiting, whose sole task right now was to internalize and assimilate this information while he waited for a good billennia to take over the post.

The existing black phase leadership had ordered the duplication process to commence, but this process was taking much longer than anticipated, either because Zotl wished to hold back data or, as was the official line, his energy bands were so weak that the signal for duplication kept cutting out, and what purpose was there for the exercise unless a 100% success rate was achieved? For now, therefore, the honoured holder of the post was indispensable.

Zein penetrated the depths of the building and detected Zotl's signature as he tracked his timeworn coordinates through the shadows and archives. The two Bugz held each other in high regard, the old versus the new. The old appreciated the shorter lifespan energy of a powerful academic particle with that old-fashioned value of integrity. The new appreciated the rich mine of information that could only be accumulated in a revered equation now worn from an elongated lifespan.

It seemed that only magnetic attraction kept the Keeper's body going. Its spin had long since slowed to a halt. Zotl had subjected himself to several energy transfers in recent zicromillennia in order to boost his mental faculties, blow out the fog of trivia and avoid total stasis. It was generally suspected in the Bugz fraternity that he had become ductile, easily influenced with age, and that therefore, while he possessed the know how, he lacked the qualities required of someone commanding a position of trust.

He was one of the last of the ancients who could recall the ravages of the Quake which had raged across the Zyberian cosmos and whose rolling mantle of duzz had suffocated the few remnants of Old Zytopia.

Even Zotl's unique and data-saturated equation did not extend to the scale of the information housed in the Library's buried vaults, let alone the detail, and he was never convinced that there was any Bugz deserving enough to be granted access down there.

Zein's messenger particles hovered and hesitated in the ether before tickling Zotl's sensors in a hush. 'I require access to the writings near the hidden Flame, good friend.'

'Yes, I know,' the Keeper floated his quavering messenger Bugz, 'you have asked before, Zein, and my answer will be as before too.'

'You mean, no.'

Zotl gave an involuntary jolt and swept his sensors round in a wide arc. 'You will find the index in the vault you were in during the last black phase.'

'I'm not after the index, good friend; I have internalised that. I require the actual writings, the data surrounding the particle known as Zareth and his time. I understand they are concealed somewhere in the layers of duzz in this hallowed place.'

'This is a name my receptors have not heard for a good many billenia. The Flame, you say?' The old Bugz compressed his sensors into a narrow slit to view his visitor. 'So what is your purpose? What exactly do you believe you will find? Choose your answer well, because I need to know that you know exactly what you wish to find. Only the person who knows his exact way and the exact nature of his equation can ever hope to find what lies within these walls.'

Zein considered the uncertainty of the knowledge he sought; he considered too the effect of the TT message that had impacted his sensors. Any feeling of curiosity had now become need. Even to the extent of approaching this garrulous old Keeper.

'Let me show you this symbol, my good friend,' he said. The three arrows pinged out into the ether, together with the curious word salvation, and the Keeper snatched them with unexpected dexterity and examined their exotic properties. 'Let me tell you,' Zein explained, 'that I have a long way to travel and need great help from what lies in this Library. I am not here to study but to take decisive action to change events. I will initiate actions, the directions and clues for which may be found in this place.'

Zotl's waving feelers spent some time probing the finer points of Zein's equation. There was no denying the Superbugz' distinguished signature track, sound principles, positive magnetic attraction and high energy rating, all of which appeared to display a sense of predetermination that the Keeper knew to be rare, if not unique.

'Of course, to access anything you might like requires Apex authorisation,' Zotl said, chanting his usual mantra, 'and to access what you really desire requires authorisation beyond that, namely from me in my capacity as Bugzhist Order elder and senior Apex councillor. Regarding the symbol and the coded word you name,' he mused, 'the word salvation was the encrypted rallying call for the white Bugz at the great Battle of the Bars. The symbol is identical to that which adorned the armament heraldry of Zareth and marked the signature of each of his followers. I gather you have received a communication?'

'Yes,' said Zein, regathering and ordering his properties. 'A TT message that directed me to you for help. It also appears to provide an answer to something that has not yet happened. A vision, you might say. It is complex and open to interpretation depending on one's spin.'

'Employing secrecy is behaviour most unfitting for Bugz,' Zotl broadcasted loudly on a grand billow of puffed-up messenger particles, then glanced round and tilted his receptors forward to envelope Zein in a conspiratorial manner. 'But my good friend: in this particular case it is behaviour that is very necessary indeed. It has been written long ago that a new leader should rise and challenge the existing order. What has not been deduced is which path that leader will take. Long ago also I was given the task of keeping these precious artifacts and data safe to aid the process of change, and I have to say the task has become ever more burdensome as possible future conflict has emerged. As the most junior assistant in the Library after the Great Quake I was witness to the most senior sage of this august establishment being obliterated. As you no doubt gather from the power lines running through keeper Bugz equations, this was not achieved without considerable difficulty. As it happens, I require no more proof of your purpose or identity. I see you for what you are, Zein. I have been waiting.'

The Library Keeper's rings suddenly lit up with a pearlescent energy as he shook the duzz off his coils and swelled his immense equation so it filled the chamber. The crackle and energy that coursed through the mighty particle dwarfed Zein's own, revealing the front the Keeper had put on for the Apex and all and sundry since the time of the Quake.

'You see, my friend,' the old Bugz announced, 'all is not always as it seems to be, and it is sometimes best to keep a low profile, so as not to attract the wrong sort of attention.'

Zein gazed at Zotl with awe as the latter's equation expanded from its compressed state to reveal many rich and ancient texts that now streamed out after so many millennia of being held in check.

'Until now, that is,' Zotl went on, his liberated equation still expanding. 'All Zyberian keepers are on full alert. Number five is too narrow a margin for stability, despite the undoubted appeal of such a wonderfully small number. This constitutes numerical weakness, not numerical harmony. The prospect of yet another prolonged black majority is not good for Zyberia. It is, however, a sign of other events predicted in the old texts, and therefore, my friend, your visit is not a surprise. For some reason, you specifically have been selected as the high-tier particle that can restore stability.'

'Then I'm your Bugz,' Zein replied with an effusive display of z units, 'and with your permission I will waste no time in –'

'You are clearly an advanced scholar and an elder Bugzhist rolled into one,' Zotl declared. 'A perfect combination. Who better to understand the contents of the revered and sealed Chamber of Zareth which houses the Flame of Zytop and to act on that information?'

'Exactly, good friend. So it would appear that caution and stealth combined with lightning speed is in order if I am to view –'

'Now then,' the old Bugz held forth, 'let me give you a more in-depth history of the secret cavity beneath the library and the text contained in it.'

'I'd be delighted,' Zein said, with the elated feeling of somebody poised on the edge of discovering some great truth.

'My analytical units insist that you know... well, no doubt you will absorb sufficient data for your specific purposes once I locate the correct set of encrypted cypher keys, so please bear with me while I excavate these drifts of duzz. This may take some time.

'And while I'm looking I will tell you something else. If my short-term memory banks serve me well, which isn't often these days,' the revitalised Keeper rifled quickly through his memory banks, 'I had a request from another visitor three hundred and seventy-one zicroseconds ago to view the writings in the Chamber shortly before the black phase majority was confirmed. The last time I had any request of this nature was... now, let me see... ah! 19,183 zyber years ago, when Zyberia experienced a brief surge, and a State of Imbalance was declared for a good few millennia until harmony prevailed. I remember it as though it were only the last white phase because it was so unusual.'

Zein was curious to know which previous visitor had made the request, but Zotl was intent on fumbling in his internal fogs even after finding the keys to the Chamber and requiring Zein to propel him down through the labyrinthine layers of time.

20. THE WRITINGS OF ZARETH

Zein was sent on a near impenetrable path chiselled out in the Zo-like mists of time by an army of curiously high-tier structural particles, which opened out on a richly appointed chamber. First he wandered through the ancient meter of Zomer and the chronicles of Zerodian. Then he scanned a furled list of unintelligible energy equations and wondered at the ancient symbols on the way. After that he found himself entangled in riddles posed by Zareth and those faithfully recorded by others.

Zareth had been a seer Bugz: he didn't just predict what could be; he predicted what would be. Zareth's spin suggested he was not a pure Bugz. He predicted what the future held, yet Bugz were neither mentally nor physically able to travel forward in time. Zareth had greyed and blurred with time and still held an appeal to the few that had some memory passed on in their equations. Zareth was a conundrum. He had posed extraordinary questions about why Bugz existed and where they had come from.

Zein's sensors then fell upon a familiar symbol: three arrows. Zein wondered at it yet again. What did it mean? It was somehow familiar, for the TT Bugz had assumed its shape, Zotl had required it be shown in order to grant access to the Chamber, and now here was Zareth's signature in the same form and emblazoned in the glory of ancient Zytopia.

Zein's sensors now fell upon a script as faded in terms of matter as the shambling coils beneath which the Library Keeper hid his light, yet as clear as white phase light in that it contained no symbols or cyphers. The pure text dashed along in rough loops and quick strokes as though the anonymous scribe – a Superbug or high functionary, very likely did not want his activity observed. Zein settled down to absorb the content. This was surely an account never relayed to the generations of thinkers and communicators in the Academy, for there was no mention of it on the curriculum.It had certainly not been mentioned in the index he had inspected on his previous visits, perhaps because it had been slipped at random between long registers of equations, only to lie undetected ever since.

At the zenith of Zytopian civilisation, the scribe recorded, a series of experiments had been carried out by a group of high functionaries in the black priest function of the Bugzhist Order, an unauthorised and unpredictable undertaking designed to explore the very creation of particles. The last of these experiments was one of those undertaken by the black priest Zess, known as the Uncorrected, when his increasingly extreme experimental values finally got the better of him. Zess's remains had been interred in some faraway trading colony, his ancient shadow having been preserved, but no zecho or a puff of memory energy remained from his passing. Even advanced zectroscopic examination subsequently failed to trace his existence apart from this shadow burned in ancient scribe particles.

A further consequence of Zess' final failed experiments was the release of a number of hybrid particles, later known as the W, X, Y mutant strains. Such was their toxicity and unbridled force that they had blasted through the three defense rings of Zytop, leaving the gates difficult to reseal.

The escape of even minute quantities of such semi-evolved and uncontrollable rogue particles represented an unprecedented and considerable threat to Zyberian society. Automatic and rapid self replication was one feature possessed by these rogue equations, and it was activated by exposure to wisps of negative energy that could be detected out in the Empty Quarter on the margins of the universe. The anonymous scribe could not have put it in the following terms of course, but the effect was akin to introducing maggots to a carcass.

In time, therefore, the scribe continued, a certain locus on Zyberia's fringes was populated with blackened rogue particles devoid of signature tracks and analytical units, particles whose sole tilt was to channel their negative charge into aggressive expansionist behaviour. Their haunts gradually depleted the fringes of any other form of force, and the outlying colony nuclei of the most important pearl gateways and Zytopian settlements were bolstered with greater defences and warrior Bugz.

On a remote bridge between three inverted cones of antimatter, the W, X, Y forces solidified in their opposing camps and assessed their respective strengths. There arose from among the y strain an exceptional antiparticle known as Yun. He had a structure composed of five interlocking rings, reputedly more powerful in terms of energy and negative charge than were possessed by the top-tier black Superbugz in the Apex.

This antiparticle grouping led by Yun had evolved, so the scribe had understood, to counter the mobilisation of the x forces under the leadership of Xawn, whose blunt analytical units had enabled his hordes to clone the negative matter within them and thereby replicate without the need for an external trigger. Their increasing levels of nomadic encroachment as a result of this population explosion had forced the Y strain to switch temporarily to a more neutral charge and seek occupancy under Zareth's protection on the fringe of Zytopia betwixt it and the empty quarter.

Little was known of the w strain, whose members kept themselves to themselves, except for the fact that Wit, their leader, was reclusive and extremely unstable, while many of his w subject particles had an unstable spin, they were likely to disappear randomly and were prone to self-annihilation. Their winking in and out of existence was put down to a lack of intelligence. It was difficult to categorize something that was literally on its own wavelength and no one else's.

The remorseless expansion of Xawn's power and the x particles' suspicion and misunderstanding of the treaty between the y strain and Zareth soon culminated in what was best described as a civil war within the rogue strains. Zareth had tried to introduce a buffer zone between the mutant strains and Zyberia, but this strategy had failed. The outcome led to a great gathering of mutant hordes who had mobilised in the Empty Quarter in order to lay waste to Zytopia.

The scribe quoted Zerodian, the only known witness to the Battle of the Bars, who described how the rogue strains rapidly decayed, coalescing as they did so in viscous clouds and appearing to submerge into a dark convergence whose horizon he dared not go near, a vanishing point noted here as the gates of Zareth.

It was said, the scribe continued, that the great wreckage of the battle site remained intact, undisturbed by anything more than trails of memory energy and anti-energy suspended in a field of bankrupt forces.

It was here that three of Zareth's followers had found the remnants of his energy and messenger Bugz, and had brought these back safely, to incarcerate them with full ceremony in the sealed chamber beneath the ruins of the Library of Zytop.

Zein knew something of the aftermath of the fall of Zytopia and the long life of the new black age with successive black queens in power. As these eventually shrivelled with age and the smog of darkness lifted several millennia later, both white and black Bugz lost in the Quake were restored together with the ancient laws of Zytopia: the laws of regularity and predictability, symmetry and harmony. The white and the black order that was now threatened

THE CHRONICLES OF ZERODIAN

Denuded of energy from slipping and sliding through the sketchy passages of script, Zein was glad to turn to the clear-cut structure and narrative of Zerodian's chronicles. According to these, a battle had taken place on the rim of a void too desolate to imagine, at the end of a route too convoluted to describe with accuracy. Those who had travelled this way had met with untold obstacles. In fact Zerodian himself had not safely returned. He had perished in the shifting deserts of duzz during his return voyage, entrusting his chronicles to the then senior Library Keeper who had been specially summoned from Zytop.

A codicil written by this Library Keeper made mention of a pearlscape plotter that gave detailed coordinates to find the site, coordinates fixed by Zerodian. This plotter had been intended for each of Zyberia's portal keepers, but Zein could find no such device hidden here. Perhaps it had faded and fragmented into waste Bugz.

The deepest recesses of the three-sided Chamber were choked with duzz particles. They constituted floating heaps, evidence of their disturbance from the presence of the earlier visitor, and before long Zein discovered a long and unnatural narrow hollow of space in one such heap. Something had been not so carefully removed.

Zein was ready to depart. It took him a while to work out how to exit the Chamber, for the Keeper, so unaccustomed to exhuming the codes for this place, had given him a slightly muddled exit code. Or was this a slightly muddled exit code? It might well be a test set by the Keeper.

Just as Zein solved this particular riddle, the aged Zotl reappeared.

'Do you know where Zerodian's pearl plotter is?' Zein asked.

'It should be where I laid it those many millennia ago. You are displacing my receptors; I had actually come this very moment to advise you to take it with you, and also a particular piece of text.'

'Were you the custodian that met Zerodian?'

'No, I was the assistant to the Library Keeper, and he felt that the information needed to be held by somebody not so important and high profile, and therefore a potentially high risk target, but by somebody junior and 100% reliable. It was a time of great disturbance.'

'Yes. So who was the visitor who called earlier?'

'They had authorisation but did not have access to the information that might alert them to the pearl plotter,' Zotl said simply.

'But look, you can see that the duzz is disturbed here.' Zein swept his sensors wide. 'Even a stripling Bugz' zectroscope would pick up the presence of the thief and reveal their identity.'

'Zzzzzz. Yes, we must look into this.' Zotl's coils bulged and deflated like bellows. 'I have my suspicions but I wish to be certain.'

'You say it was recently,' Zein pursued, 'so the perpetrator may still be in the library.'

'Indeed they may. Therefore, true to Bugz principles of logic and conduct, and true to the complex statutes I have observed to the most trivial messenger Bugz throughout my tenure here, I will follow established lines of enquiry.'

Having emerged from the Chamber, Zein made straight for the communal area where, he hoped, the other visitor might be found. For a visitor to leave the Library with data so sensitive and secret that possibly no one even knew of its existence meant that this clever act could not be regarded as a violation against Zyberian law, be it white or black.

21. THE PEARLSCAPE PLOTTER

Zein scanned the rows of Bugz absorbed in study and analysis, and his sensors pinged the familiar and attractive signature of Zag. Her body was contracting and spinning with concentration, her high performance detectors scrolling up and down the curious figures and cyphers and text in front of her.

Zag was a well-formed high-tier functionary Bugz, quiet but ambitious and rather precocious, known for the superior code-breaking skills handed down through her distinguished zen ancestry.

She alerted herself to Zein's majestic approach with a gush of zuons, as though welcoming the interruption. The two knew each other well, for they had shared study paths at the Academy before Zein had been elevated to the Apex Council. Zein was still attracted to her, remembering the many exchanges of positive messenger Bugz they had had over time.

'My friend!' Zag exclaimed, reclining and stretching. 'You find me engaged in my favourite pursuit.'

'I don't observe you here often,' Zein's messenger Bugz darted back. 'I would have assumed that you'd absorbed most of these writings long ago, yet something has brought you back here to this phase. By my reckoning (which I apologise cannot be accurate without more intensive calculation), you are here twenty-eight or twenty-nine times more often than you are in your normal area of work. Is this place such a rich mine of information that it cannot be exhausted, even by you?'

114

'There is nothing here that I have not studied,' Zag replied, 'but there is plenty of data that despite even my skills – I have yet to understand.'

'Is it not fruitless and boring, not to mention heavy, to reabsorb material which you carry within you from the first reading?'

Zag beamed. 'As it happens, Zein, I am consulting a text which has remained buried for millennia and contains wonderfully obscure symbols and codes.'

'Really?' Zein observed, casually.

'During the course of my normal research I found I required access to classified material handled only by the Library Keeper, who as you know is such an obstructive old Bugz. While in the chamber which contained it, I chanced upon a list of strange equations that I have duplicated for further study, and the list included a reference to the document I have now here before me. This is a body of ancient instructions, chunks of which have been encrypted not only to verify their integrity and authenticity but also to ensure secrecy, a most unBugzish and intriguing reason, as I'm sure you'd agree, my friend. As it happens, Zein, I'm most relieved to see you, for having extracted and duplicated this text, all for scholarly purposes, you understand, I now face a problem of a very different kind.'

'Which is?'

Zag's messenger particles were silky smooth. 'To return this to its rightful place in the vault without being noticed. I am well aware that even minor indiscretions do not go down too well with our cantankerous friend Zotl, but it was thanks to him and his stuffy ways that I felt inclined to take this information without his express permission, and on exiting I sidetracked him again in order to extract this document and view it at more leisure. I'd duplicated the list of equations down there but had no time to duplicate this text as well. Furthermore, the atmosphere in the place was so oppressive that I needed the clear positive energy of white phase light to sharpen my zen faculties.

'As a result, this text is now duplicated as well, as are the fluctuating spacetime coordinates that have wreaked havoc with my analytical units. The old Bugz will take a very hard line with me should I own up to all this subterfuge but he is bound to be more malleable if you approach him, given your superior connections. I am after all just a sub – functionary whereas you have Apex status. You see my predicament, Zein!'

'Indeed I do, Zag, but if I help you in this I need your unequivocal assurance that this data download of yours will not be transferred to others. The risk to my reputation is great of course, plus there is another motive that you need not concern yourself with.'

'I do understand, my friend. You know, my experimental values briefly got the better of me, so irregular, of course.'

'You should give your experimental values a good outing as often as you wish, Zag, but not necessarily with state secrets concealed even from the Apex. You are, for all you know, on the edge of a conspiracy and I want to keep it contained. I speak to you as an elder. We cannot risk any naïve code fumbling.'

Zag fluttered some feathery soft messenger Bugz straight at Zein's core. 'I do understand, Zein. Thank you. I'm sorry to cause you trouble.'

She handed the ancient pearl plotter to Zein. It was the most curious and confusing item, containing glowing clusters of inter-changing particles which kept separating and reforming in the shape of overlapping coordinates of constantly changing figures. Each bore a panel of text as rich and unintelligible as the equation list stored in the Chamber.

'And what is this ancient codex about?' Zein asked innocently.

'It provides the travel coordinates to a far-off location that is described in the scribe's text as 'something and nothing',' Zag replied lightly.

'Something and nothing'?'

Zag smiled. 'It may take some time, my friend, for you to internalize even the broad outline of the contents, given the difficulty that even a zen articulator and code-breaking Bugz like myself encounters in trying to grasp it. Some of the interpreting Bugz I'm resorting to are not actually official (in case you saw what I was doing on your entry), and in fact the use of these has not been sanctioned at a senior level.'

'Are you telling me,' Zein asked, 'that we are carrying out illegal historical research on files that have been stolen?'

'Zzzzzz. Yes.'

'And classified information at that, designed mainly for portal keepers?' Zag persisted, incredulous.

'That is the function of my equation. I do what I am told, Zein. I do not seek to interpret for myself the sense of the material I handle; I simply seek to communicate it.' Zag paused.

'As a member of the Apex I demand an explanation of what exactly this material is, Zag.'

'Very well, my friend, if you are, as you say you are, doing me the favour of speaking with Zotl. It is a pearlscape map for navigation purposes, a particularly complex one for it also serves as a zen spectrum for TT communication via pearl portal keepers, well, for those in the days of Zytopia.'

The two Bugz pored over the labyrinthine markings of the plotter, their sensors tingling as they examined the coordinates marking the route. These coordinates stood out bold and true despite changing their values every split second. They were encyphered, of course, to confuse all but the map's authorised users. The Bugz followed the course of the glowing line on the map. It curved through the Zytopian pearlscape and merely flickered where it crossed ill-defined contours. It scorched a bullet straight path, however, as it finally dissected the vast unmarked space that filled a third of the document. This leg of the journey appeared to contain no resistance, no obstacle.

'The Empty Quarter,' Zag explained. 'It is apparently filled only with duzz, waste Bugz and weak mutated particles, plus some shreds of memory energy left by soldier Bugz and rogue particles annihilated in a conflict reported to have taken place in the distant past. Look, here lies what might well have been a battlescape. It could be the 'something', as opposed to the 'nothing'.'

'Anyway,' Zag concluded breezily, 'this funny old plotter can't be of much relevance today except as an antique curiosity. The portal keepers from those times are probably annihilated or well into their twice life, and the routes shown are no doubt long since blocked or following different coordinates to allow for the swirls in the pearlscape. An archaic fragment of no particular interest, then.'

Zein thought of the recent UEMC energy readings in the far reaches of Zyberia and the unusual particle trails found in Zyber, the ensuing State of Disequilibrium and the coincidence of the transmission of the TT Bugz bearing a trove of new information on Old Zytopia.

'What is this?' he asked, pointing to a dark orb marked Nothing on the far side of the Empty Quarter. 'Simply an uncharted region? An unusual density of duzz?'

117

'There is no description of it,' Zag answered, 'save that it is marked by some dark convergence, blacker than the blackest pearl.' She paused to scan Zein's reaction, and added, 'This text in the panel suggests that a warning signal blocks the entrance to this zone. This is not a portal, my friend. It simply says what you see: nothing. And you know me, Zein,' she said carefully. 'When something is obscure, it is tempting to seek clarity. Don't you think?'

Zein's logic counter jammed momentarily at the thought. This was of course the obvious place to look, for his own purposes. But was this an elaborate trap? Or the question to the answer he already had? Or indeed the embodiment of the answer to the question?

Zag's frequency was raised to an expectant hum. She tilted towards Zein so that her messenger Bugz barely brushed his sensors. 'Zein, my friend, I sense that you have a strong and positive charge to seek out knowledge. Let us be frank with each other. You know that my function is always to go where some would rather I did not go. I know that you have great influence with Zotl, and that for your own purpose, whatever that is, as well as mine you wish to learn more from these old writings. So what are we waiting for?' Zein joined Zag's frequency and hummed as well. 'Maybe it's written in our equations,' he beamed.

22. THE DEPARTED RETURN

The coffin blocked out the light as it rocked gently on the shoulders of its bearers. Icarus stared straight past his sons as they stumbled under the strain of both weight and nerves. His younger son, Lycian, received assistance. His multiple sclerosis was plaguing him, but he was somehow invigorated enough to support his mother on her final journey.

Icarus put one foot forward, then the other one, then the first one again. He felt Elsie's hand tucked through his arm. The colour had drained out of the shapes and blocks of stonework and trees around him; their lines were indistinct.

He walked his familiar route through Haslingdene's graveyard, past a silent and still row of family members from previous ages. Their resting places were arranged in order of chronology as they ringed out from the church with its crumbling tower and ancient weather-cock. Icarus' eyes glided past the patches of peeling sandy coloured stucco, the brick repairs and the draped ivy. They glided past the weathered chest tombs and gravestones half sunken or bent double. He knew all the names. There was his own namesake close to the church porch: Icarus William, better known as I Will the elder, who departed this life in 1723, distinguished Fellow of Trinity College, assistant to Sir Isaac Newton, beloved husband and devoted father, who 'from the tiniest fleck on a wave fashioned the puller of tides'. His memento mori was a tiny triangle atop a zigzag. There was his son Hector William, lichen speckling the beadwork scrolled round his inscription. And Philemon James, born a century and

119

a half later, the Greek column stonework marking his spot eroded and split by rusting iron cramps. And also Hespera Mariah, Victorian matriarch, her gravestone stooping under the redbrick wall that led out to the avenue of thin limes and beyond that the open fields.

Icarus didn't see the dark figures of the others lined up round him for the committal. He waited for the box to be lowered and mechanically threw down after it a spray of Rambling Rector, creamy white clusters that had graced and scented Brooke's kitchen garden and snagged anything that came near it apart from its keeper. Time to stop all this now. Time to go home and find Brooke stepping out of the French windows with a nice pot of tea. Icarus waited to be led away, waited to be tugged by Elsie past the line of crumbling blocks again.

Svetlana attended the funeral on behalf of the Director General who was still very busy talking about the security breach and handling inordinate press attention. She stepped forward to poke the sharp toe of her black patent leather shoe into the dirt left piled on the side of the grave by the diggers. With one firm and dismissive movement she tipped a shower of earth into the space below, and departed for her flight to Venice having left a bouquet with a note from the personnel at CERN.

Next morning, when Icarus didn't find Brooke in the house, when her soft hair didn't leave an imprint on the pillow next to him, and when her smile didn't greet him at the breakfast table, he shrugged on an old coat and strode out along the water meadows, his trouser legs slapping his ankles as they became sodden with dew, and he squelched down to the river to watch a family of ducks. They pushed off from the shore in alarm, and he followed their ripples out into the dead black calm and the mist.

When you get to the end of the line, the way he had got to the end of the line, when you did not recognise the pastiche of the world you now lived in, you either died a slow death where you were, or you could try to push off to some other place, some other time, escape. The black ripples swirled round his brain and drew him in. He stepped forward. A discarded wrapper floated into his vision. It was in the black and purple colours of a popular chocolate bar, but it was printed in different wording.

`We can bring her back.`

120

He reached down to fish it out, but it was just beyond reach and bobbed after the ducks. He stood and gazed out across the water, unaware of the time and unseeing as some students and holidaymakers picked their way over the tussocks with their rolled up towels and bags of sandwiches.

Back at home, he left a note in the kitchen asking his children not on any account to bother him, and he retired to his study with the digi-com turned off, looking listlessly at his surroundings, at the things he normally loved. 'We can bring her back', said the crabbed wording on the old papers on the oak chest, said the neat print in his in-tray, said the titles on the worn book spines around him, said the nanoputer text as his hand brushed the display. He looked glumly at the strange cuneiform characters that spelt out their message.

'I must be cracking up,' he said aloud, and gazed out over the lawn.

He sat until the shadows began to lengthen. He heard sobbing in the hallway, brief scuffles, silence again. He heard something being placed on the floor just outside the study door and the shuffling step of Mrs Nimmo's puffy feet as she retreated down the passageway. He heard Lycian's knock which he did not answer. When another knock some time later was followed by the turning of the handle and the unsuccessful wrestling with the lock, he heard Elsie cry, 'Come on Dad, open the door! What are you doing?'

Two minutes later her face loomed at the window, framed with cupping hands to block out the low sun of evening. He forced a smile and waved at her to go, indicating he would come out. And as he rose from his seat the nanoputer bleeped to alert him to an incoming message. It was a file that had downloaded and opened itself. The characters looked slightly smudged, sooty. It was in code and yet it was intelligible to him, not that he could fathom how. All of this was merely a trick of the imagination due to severe stress, he knew. And yet, when he read it again, all it was was a message from the DG, saying that when Icarus felt strong enough to return to the fold he would be ably assisted by Svetlana Grigoriya, the Russian quantum physicist who was overseeing a project on cosmic wave radiation at CERN but whose work could tie in closely with his own in order to give him support on the PBC project. He had seen Svetlana at the funeral, totally over the top even when soberly dressed. She had brought flowers, tied with an extravagant black silk bow, on behalf of the DG at CERN.

He had noticed a small folded letter tucked into the DG's card. It was a brief message from Svetlana, in astonishingly inelegant crabbed handwriting, saying that she looked forward to seeing him in two days' time, back at work, if only for the invaluable pep talk she wanted to give him.

The family had close family friends here at home now to provide support with practical matters and to talk to the children. All three of them seemed reasonably calm, perhaps too calm, they were probably suffering from shock. But nobody could talk to Icarus. Brooke had been his life force, Brooke had added heart to his life of numbers. Still he knew he was doing his children no favours by shutting himself away and moping.

Like his namesake in Greek mythology, he had flown high and come crashing to Earth. Placing his hands over his head and leaning on the desk he wondered how everything could go so wrong. He would need to build bridges with Henri le Baut or he would never achieve recognition for the Ashcroft name. Unpleasant as it was, he would have to grasp the nettle and return quickly to CERN. His second love was his research, certainly now that Brooke was gone. Mrs Nimmo could look after the children, and they were young adults now anyway.

Pulling himself out of the battered leather armchair, he picked up his beloved Gladstone bag and started to pack the necessary items for his return to Switzerland. He would fly again.

23. THE BRIDGE
16 June 2042

Sam needed an adrenaline rush that evening after the funeral. He just had to expend some pent-up emotion and frustration. He grabbed Lycian – good old Lycian always came along, and they made their way to the Cam, getting there as the last of the day was draining away.

'What about Sis?' Lycian had asked as they'd slipped out of the house.

'She's with Mrs N; the two of them are trying to talk Dad out of going back to CERN. Seems like all we male family members want to just get out of the place.'

'I don't know why I'm letting you talk me into this,' Lycian grumbled, and was still grumbling the same twenty minutes later as they clambered into a punt and pushed out. 'I feel lousy, I want my bed. I'm so tired I can hardly steer.'

'Stop splashing that thing!' Sam hissed. 'Sound travels a long way at night. You seem to be going in entirely the opposite direction to where we're meant to be going, Lyce. I swear you're winding me up. Turn round! And lighten up, we're trying to get a buzz out of life for a bit, remember?'

'Oh really?'

'Get away from all the doom and gloom. Look, I think I'd better take the pole before you sink us. Hey, see Clare Bridge coming up? I've got to tell you something. I haven't told anyone else, perhaps because I'd sort of forgotten with everything else happening. And you can tell me if you think I'm mad.'

'You know the answer to that already,' Lycian sighed.

123

'Seriously. When I climbed over the other day I saw something in the water. Well, not something in it as such, but a funny reflection. The light went all funny, I mean. It stopped sparkling on the surface, as though a cloud were passing overhead, and all the sparkles condensed into a really bright letter Z. I looked overhead to see what might be creating it but there was nothing, and when I looked down again everything was back to normal.'

'You haven't been taking some banned substance, have you? Or too many Zappers maybe?' Lycian asked. 'Come on, Sam, you're just overworked, I reckon, and now, what with Mum…'

'It was weird.'

'A trick of light, perhaps. There'll be some scientific explanation.'

'You know, I want to tell Dad,' Sam said. 'He loves poring over those strange symbols in that chest of his, doesn't he? But given he's not exactly in a receptive frame of mind right now I guess I'll have to wait. Lyce, what do you think a Z means?'

'It's the end of the alphabet, it's Alpha and Omega, the end of the world.'

'Don't be daft.'

'Who knows?' Lycian said. 'Maybe you need your head examining, by one of the hall porters, they must see so many lunatic students come and go with fanciful notions filling their heads. Maybe the Z is the first sign of madness?'

Lycian steered the punt to the side of the river just below the walls of New Court, St John's College. The Bridge of Sighs loomed above them, the light stone of its cloistered construction and the barred and unglazed windows gleaming in the moonlight.

'OK, Sam, this is what you wanted to do. Get on with it and then I can make for my bed. Or, hey, I've just thought, we could go and see old Arthur at Trinity about your head. I understand he once threatened some drunken student doing African Studies that he knew the recipe for shrinking heads and it was best done while undergrads were under the influence. Not that he mentioned whether the head was still attached to the body at the time, mind you!'

Sam was already poised to leap off the punt. 'Now don't leave me in the lurch again, Lyce. I don't fancy another cold bath, thanks.'

124

'What do you mean, leave you in the lurch again? It's not my fault that you're out of shape and unable to get back in the boat at the agreed moment. You simply crawled over Clare like a snail.'

'Now, now, broth', jealousy will get you nowhere,' Sam said smoothly.

'Anyhow, I'm off. See you in ten. You know, this bridge might be a hard climb, but it's good fun. It's not tiring the way night climbing can be, it's not like chimneying up walls or putting in all the heavy arm work you need for drainpipes. And it hasn't got any of those vicious serrated bowls you occasionally have to worm your leg over to get up.' Lycian grinned at the memory of Sam's 'little accident' once.

'Ha, ha,' Sam said, leaping lightly off the punt. He moved along the wall, climbed up and along the side of the bridge to the middle, and proceeded up the grating. It was always difficult to ease yourself over the crenellations at the top, but by reaching far enough across you would find a good handhold and the rest was easy.

The descent on the other side was simply the reverse process. Sometimes, when he felt more energetic, Sam wouldn't go down straight away; he would scale the west face of Third Court on the opposite bank to New Court, following a succession of ledges up to the roof. This was a severe climb despite the obvious route up, but one was rewarded by an easy descent. However, the Bridge of Sighs was enough for tonight. He felt as drained as Lycian.

'Are you relaxing and enjoying the view up there?' Lycian hissed from below.

'Wait.' Sam was finding a purchase for his right foot and manoeuvring down the stonework past one of the windows. He froze as he saw signs of life within the college.

Looking through the window, a nanoputer, apparently discarded, was on the floor next to the inside of the far wall. The curved CPU was raised, as though its user had deliberately crouched down to work from it where it was. It was blank, but as Sam's eyes alighted on it it flickered into life to project an image that shimmered in the air above.

A blaze of pearly light zigzagged across the screen and faded as the liquid crystals reformed in what Sam took to be the wedge-shaped and arrow-tailed symbols of archaic cuneiform script. He had seen this script pictured on the clay tablets illustrated in some of the books in his

126

father's study, books handed down the generations from his nineteenth-century archaeologist ancestor. He had also seen the script in some of his father's scribblings. The curious crosshatching of the lines made him think of runes crossed with oriental characters crossed with computer code text, all unintelligible, and yet now, as his eyes took in their formation, he found he could read it.

WE ARE THE BUGZ

The message scintillated in the form of virtual characters in the air, and warmed him. The palms of his hands and the soles of his feet seemed moulded into the curves of the stonework. He almost felt at rest, as though there were no pull of gravity in his rather precarious position.

'Sam!' Lycian hissed again, resting on the pole.

'We want to cross over. But we want to do it safely, with an assistant. You need to help us. And to do so, we need to help you.'

Sam felt a rush of both elation and exhaustion. He was transfixed, and yet he couldn't stay perched where he was.

He looked down. 'Lycian, hold steady.' He dropped into the punt. 'I'm going mad, I really am. Perhaps I do need a shrink. Or at least a drink!' He turned away with his shoulders shaking.

'What is it, Sam?' Lycian asked gently.

Sam motioned for them to move further upstream, away from the buildings and echoes. He pulled out his IDO and began navigating the touchscreen, but his finger trembled too much even to turn the display on.

'Here, Lycian, key in Bugz, will you? No, I mean 'Bugz' with a 'z' at the end. The 'z' must be important. It must be the 'z' in that reflection in the water, you know. Oh God, I'm cracking up, I'm not coping with Mum gone.' He recited for his brother the text he'd read on the laptop. Perhaps it hadn't been such a good idea to come out tonight.

Lycian remained silent. He steered the punt toward the dark waters and ghostly branches on the small waterway heading up for Bin Brooke, and crouched next to Sam to peer at the screen. The air moving in from the surrounding wetland area clung to their skin; the boys shivered despite their warm clothing.

Sam keyed in 'Bugz', and the recently observed pearly zigzag floated across the screen. 'Sam. We have reason to contact you. We face a time of disharmony. There is a force that threatens both your world and ours. There are two outcomes: one black, one white. To influence the outcome, we propose mutual cooperation. We need to help you to help us. To prove to you that we can help you, we need the three assistants to meet us outside Peterhouse on Trumpington Street tomorrow at 3pm. The three of you must arrive alone.'

The glow faded and the IDO switched itself off.

'I didn't switch on the IDO, you know, Sam,' Lycian babbled. 'It just came on and directed itself!'

'What does it mean by assistants? What on earth is expected of us? And why us? Who are the three assistants, is Elsie included?'

'We obviously move in exalted circles.' Lycian sounded like he was on the verge of hysterics. 'After all, remember that Will Ashcroft the elder was some sort of assistant to Newton.'

'Yeah, yeah,' Sam answered, and buried his head in his hands. 'If you ask me, this entire word is going crazy. What with Mum gone and Dad almost off his rocker, I don't know that there's much left to faze me any more.'

'Well, I'm coming with you, Sam,' Lycian said. 'You don't think I'm missing out on this?'

'More fool you. Better bring the straightjacket, then,' Sam said.

'This could be dangerous.'

'Better let Elsie in on this first thing too. And now you'll be glad to know I'm as ready for bed as you are, Lyce. I wasn't expecting quite so much excitement tonight.'

ZYBERIA – A BLACK PERSPECTIVE

Ziel had, like Zein, received the faint and curious TT message from the far reaches of Zyberia, but unlike Zein she was not recharging her equation for the shift of power, at least not the shift in power dictated by zyberian protocol. Having already ensured the malfunction of the pendulum of change in the Assembly voting structure, it didn't take long for her to think up yet another mischievous plot that would possibly rid herself of the main opposition.

The TT message had come from some deranged particle who apparently had access to the Apex codes of old. The jumbled message of 'SALVATION' and implied harmony was no doubt intended to have universal appeal since it had been sent to both herself and her mirror Bugz, but the main effect it had on her was simply to tweak a number of cyphers in her self-preservation coding. The arrival of this message was not desired, for it caused even more confusion. The message needed immediate investigation, particularly given the social and political turmoil she had just precipitated, and whatever SALVATION meant needed to be turned to her advantage.

Zag, whom Ziel had secretly groomed for higher office in the new black phase, should be given the message too in order to conduct a pre-emptive search in the library. Unknown to her white Bugz compatriates, Zag was relaying information from the white to the black and this had been useful in a number of instances. Her most important show of loyalty to Ziel had been the corrupting of the recent transition data to favour the black continuance in power. The impossible had happened, through the annihilation of certain white Bugz and their replacement with mutant particles that to all intents and purposes looked like the originals. Where these mutants differed was in the most important area of all, that of allegiance, skewing therefore the voting in the Open Chamber.

The technology for such replication had been brought by three powerful particles known as Xit, Win and Yaba who had settled their differences to deal with Ziel on the enlargement of their areas of control at the expense of the old zytopian fringes.

129

Zag although resenting the arrival of the three allies, had helped deliver the result that Ziel required and continued to filter valuable data on the plans of the white Bugz.

Making her way to the Library and handling the perfunctory refusal from Zotl by calmly providing the code in the TT message plus all the extra necessary Apex codes he could throw up, Zag entered the concealed chamber on full spin to absorb every detail contained within. And to avoid the obstructive blocking of Zotl and a lengthy interrogation procedure, she flouted Library rules by removing an unusual plotter artifact and some copies of ancient text she knew would prove interesting to Ziel.

In another corner of Zyber, after a hastily convened meeting between Ziel and Zag to corrupt the information in the plotter and leave that on show, the Black Chamber was humming with expectation. With Zag's duplicity in her plan to dispatch her white adversary Zein to some far away Annihilation, Ziel could now silence the calls for restabilising the harmonic pendulum of power sharing. With the information copied and the bait set, all that was needed was for Zag to appear leisurely in spin and calm in energy level while waiting in the common area of the Library. If the pearl plotter did its job in the doctored state as engineered by Zag, it would guarantee that the navigator using it would blithely follow the pearl roadways expressly advised as highly 'annihilation evident' in the text. The idea had a certain Zess-ness about it, a rather crude idea for a Superbug such as she was, she had to admit, but nevertheless irresistibly effective.

Zag having handed over the corrupted pearl plotter to Zein, reported back to Ziel in true double particle fashion that the dice had been loaded and thrown; the 4D binary game* between the two mirror Bugz was now in progress. Zein had absorbed the information fed him because he was predisposed to it. The Black Queen oozed bubbly zotons of delight at a plan perfectly conceived, at the thought of the permanent disablement of the pendulum to make it a thing of the past, and at the impending annihilation of her mirror opposite Zein.

The TT had been useful because of Zein's respect for that legend of 'Zareth'. The deformity that sent this couldn't have planned it better for her purpose.

24. ZIEL'S PERFECT PLAN

Ziel flexed the voluptuous coils of her equation within the labyrinth of her vault-like fortress next to the main apex structure. All had gone reasonably to plan and the Apex council was left with no alternative but to continue the black phase of rule. Her new allies from many zyberleagues distant had conspired and provided the Zessian replication technology to tip the balance, and Zag had expertly inserted these rogue particles in the right place at the right time. This was done in the knowledge that if such illegal activity was ever discovered it would be considered the opening salvo in a major conflict – a so called schism in the equilibrium. It would mean a disruption of harmony which neither the white nor black members of the current ageing ruling generation in the Apex would sanction, but one which Ziel considered essential for progressing Bugz society.

The objective of harmony could in the long run be achieved, but the means would be just a little different. The idea of power sharing was a noble one, but its inherent flaw was the wavering back and forth from one set of values to the other. Ziel's estimation led to a neutralising of anything that could otherwise be worthwhile. Furthermore, it seemed that if anything the pendulum had been swinging more towards the white, and this would, if allowed to carry on, make her existence even more uncertain.

Furthermore the second part of this strategy was an opportunity to quell the opposition permanently. The mutated W, X, Y particles wanted

131

to be officially recognised and carve out their own part of the Zyberian universe without threat from Bugz. Well, as long as the white were silenced, the black had no objection. The rogue hordes had a dash of black thrown in their equations plus a store of illicit research, and that would be well worth delving into. When she followed Zien on his suicidal trip, what better way to guarantee that nothing of disadvantage could happen in her absence than by justifying Win's, Xit's and Yaba's presence as an honour, to see the final demise of the white.

It would be a welcome adventure during which she could keep her scanners trained on them and at the same time witness and confirm the annihilation of Zein. Simply mention the word Zareth, and they were foaming negative energy in their rush to desecrate his final resting place or to finish the job started at the great battle all those millennia ago.

Yes, she was thankful for the TT, but something was burrowed deep within the self-preservation programme that said 'beware messengers bearing gifts'.

25. THE QUEST
(ZYBERIA)

Zein's preparations for the journey along the coordinates given by the pearl plotter needed to be started immediately, straight to the Empty Quarter and the mysterious dark convergence, and the means of getting there needed to be as fast as a TT Bugz, faster than the speed of light and true.

Research conducted at the Academy under the direction of Zim and Zag had revealed further secrets contained in the coded text from the Library, including a reference to the annihilation of Zareth and the cause of the Quake. No one, however, not even Zag with her zen* powers, could crack all the secrets to be found therein without devoting several millennia to the task, for it became clear that they would have to sift through not just layers of data but also the stultifying barrier of duzz. Zag's duplicated files showed a duzz layer that sandwiched both the anonymous scribe's account and Zerodian's chronicles, a layer that protected information within it suggesting the existence of several hidden chambers under the Library apart from the Chamber of Zareth.

Zein's immediate task was to muster a crew. He targeted those who were resistant to the forces of plotting and spin and who remained stable under stress yet highly charged to channel their energies to the good. These would in turn select a group of accomplices to aid them on the quest, a quest to follow in the tracks of Zareth, find the possible reason for the Disequilibrium and put measures in place to restore harmony.

133

He chose four adherents. There was Zim, his fellow academician, whose recording skills made him the ideal Bugz to log the journey. There was Zon, the warrior Bugz, who would arm the vessel. There was Zleo, Zein's fellow Bugzhist, whose thought drive would maintain morale. Lastly, there was Zag, whose code-cracking skills would navigate the vessel along the pearl coordinates and decypher the Library texts.

Zein chose in addition a handful of junior Superbugz and functionaries, and then commissioned under the utmost secrecy the finest Zireme ever to be built. It was crafted with the most precious buginos, jewels of the early Zyberian universe, and powered by clear energy through enhanced zyclear technology. It was a vessel equipped with high-intensity scanners and a zectroscope to guide them with arrow precision through the twists and turns of the Zyberian pearlscape and bring them out in the void beyond.

The vessel was named the Zargo.

The departure from Zyber was done with great secrecy afforded by the status of Zein and the great particles gathered for the hazardous journey. The journey of the Zargo would itself be enough for another full book* but suffice to say it negotiated the gates of zyber and headed towards the Empty Quarter, as it passed from portal to portal and navigated the unknown hazards of the outer pearlscape towards the nothingness beyond, an unseen shadow the colour of jet and the shape of an earthly arachnid followed in its slipstream.

26. LIFE ABOARD THE ZARANTULA

Like Zein, Ziel had also secretly constructed her own craft to follow the Zargo. This is in part why the Apex remained oblivious to Zein's activities, Ziel wanted to witness the final demise of the great white strand of Bugz and it was essential she covertly help the process. Zag was also proving invaluable; she had passed on many engineering secrets including zyclear modifications known only to the great Zim.

All had not gone entirely to plan on the journey, now energy levels were wearing thin, and Ziel wondered at the indomitable nature of the Zargonauts as they simply sailed through all the annihilation evident hazards the original pearlplotter had said to avoid. Zein's overcoming them all represented according to Ziel's reckoning the most zicroscopic probability ever to be realised in the history of Zyberia. In contrast, by the time she came zipping by with the expectation of finding particulate debris she was finding the areas visited aware of intruders and prepared to give a very hot reception. The backwash of Bugz disharmony reigning on board was making the travel experience on this adventure trail more dangerous than Ziel or her ally mutants had counted on. No wonder they were on the verge of mutiny.

By way of compensation, however, as well as having the correct pearlscape map, the Zarantula enjoyed yet another advantage, Zag's researches had unearthed a block of archaic Zarethian text which contained an interactive preservation equation. This artefact had proved its worth by issuing its own messenger Bugz whenever it sensed a threat.The artefact had been calibrated many aeons past and was therefore alive to the dangers lurking on the old pearl road. Certainly right now it was giving out increasingly agitated danger signals, as the Zarantula entered the Empty Quarter and the site of the battlescape.

Sitting as she was in the slipstream of waste Bugz left by the Zargo, Ziel considered her next move as the region of dense antimatter that had been looming up for many zyberleagues ahead hove closer into view.

Ziel's ultra-smooth sensors curled up and around the Zarantula's scanner to take in the image looming large on its display. She marshalled the messenger Bugz in front of her. 'Zoom to close proximity. How far is it to the dark convergence?'

The scanner coughed up its spiky data Bugz.

```
First contact:    battle scape
                  16.84 zectars at current zyclear power
                  Caution - latent life indeterminate
                  Annihilation rating: 6.2
Second contact:   dark convergence
                  39.47 zectars at current zyclear power
                  Extreme caution advised
                  Annihilation rating: infinite probability
Mass:             indeterminate
Energy:           infinitely negative
Age:              indeterminate
```

'Zzzzzzzzzzz. A most handy and dangerous disposal unit.' Ziel turned to address her second in command. 'Regarding our destination, Xit, the conclusion I draw is that anyone entering this Bugz-forsaken place has a 0.0001 by 10(-26) probability of coming out again. We will have to see if our mirror friends are ill advised enough to enter or if we will have to persuade them.'

Ziel's mental units were invigorated by the negative import of this information for all of two glorious zicroseconds before they jammed and refused momentarily to accept the information her sensors were now picking up. Ahead lay an enormous black convergence that emitted no light and never sank below the horizon. It hovered in a state of semi-collapse, corroding all around it and drawing tatters of cloud into its dark rim. It resembled a vast maw, placed in the outer stretches of skin of the Zyberian universe, sucking in through swirling lips the flesh of its own being.

In the foreground, the first point of contact before this consuming vision of Armageddon, was an area identified by the zectroscope as once being filled with opposing charges. An ancient battleground, lined in chequerboard fashion, choked with duzz and littered with ancient pennant cyphers.

The Zarantula's scanner noted that the Zargo was racing far ahead across this unforgiving landscape, straight for the blackness. A splurge of negative energy zotons rose up from the Black Queen's bloated core and exuded a hum of deep pleasure. If Zyberia had or at least needed a dedicated waste site, this surely was it. And if there was a good place to have Zyberia's problem disappear once and for all, then again, this was surely it.

Ziel needed to keep morale up. The Zarantula carried on board nothing other than a motley crew of legitimised annihilators drawn from every non-descript and forgotten crevice of the universe. Their warped mutant charges meant that the only way they could be kept focused on the job in hand was to wreak destruction for its own sake. The unlucky recipients of this black largesse were the portal keepers stationed along the pearl road they had followed and the odd vagrant particle.

It was, as it happened, the brand of good old-fashioned destruction that the legendary master annihilator Dez* would himself have been proud of – not that there was any chance of dredging him up from the sludge of his twice life. Dez was a dark legendary profligate Bugz who would as readily pump you full of antimatter as he would bestow upon you a velvety messenger Bugz of condolence on the misfortune of having crossed his path. Such had been his crimes that his energy rings had been unceremoniously dismantled one by one by the dread regenerated Zess* of Zytopian black priest particle notoriety, and they had been posted high on each of Zyber's thirteen gates by way of warning to anyone who might consider pursuing the same career. Zess himself had later in his life also fallen from favour and not exactly suffered the same fate but certainly had been neutralised and banished to some hole on the edge of the old Zytopia. Ziel considered her crew as zlow life of similar calibre, on the lowest rung of existence, who, if left unchecked were guaranteed to take the Zyberian universe back to the nth root of Z all.

Some form of amusement for the troops was to be had if the Zarantula's progress was to prove less painful, and preferably together with the odd dash of discovery and occasional gobbet of annihilation. Roll as much negativity into the experience as one could, Ziel felt: it was all part of being a great and magnanimous leader. In addition to that, teach the crew her particular creed when fighting the foe: once seen, always forgotten. Meaning, in effect, that it was not helpful for anyone to announce or record the arrival of the Zarantula. Those the vessel passed should go their own merry way, if they had any sense, and she would then go hers. Those who thought of picking up and passing on just one inconsequential stray messenger Bugz would have a rich tale to tell, therefore making pre-emptive action on Ziel's part the only answer.

Ziel had rehearsed the story that only she knew. The Zargo, she would say, had journeyed to its own destruction, driven on by some unBugz-like quest. All aboard would be remembered only as annihilated zeros, sweet zeros, one and all, to be commemorated in the great halls of the Apex that were stuffed with the heraldry and clean-cut pomp of hard structural Bugz carved out in that shape. 'O hail the zeros!' Ziel mocked inwardly. Zeros were the perfect number and shape; they represented a closed circle and no escape. What could be more perfect than a zero? To make sure that this tale, the passing of the Zargo, would be told, Ziel left a trail of messenger Bugz to trumpet their contents at the most mute of pursuers.

Yet she had to keep focused on the task at hand. The local reception at each pearl entrance varied in scale and calibre, and her rogue allies received on occasion much more than they gave. The Zyberian universe still had lurking within it its fair share of undiscovered dangers that could serve up their own unpalatable justice, levelling all ranks to a duzzbin of Bugz waste in a forgotten and uncharted empty quarter of nothingness.

Oh, well. Ziel considered on the other hand the delicious joy of the hazards of this journey. You might fade away into your twice life from sheer boredom; you might just as easily meet an untimely end as a result of some unforeseen adversary nibbling at your mass or discharging antimatter all over you. Unpredictable outcomes equated with unadulterated excitement.

However, all this being so, there was a particular downside to this quest. Unloved by her bickering crew, it was really beginning to rankle with her logic counter to see how the Zargo was continuing to survive after all this time. The probability ratings were a nonsense. The unnerving feeling that in fact the quest was meant to be, one ordained by the Bugzhists, one that sanctioned Zein's actions, gnawed at her very core. After all, wasn't she just a dissatisfied black Bugz who secretly admired her mirror particle? She had to admit that the resilience of the Zargonauts in overcoming every obstacle put in their way was impressive. If she and Zein were ever to have a direct exchange of messenger Bugz, a most unlikely event, of course, she would send him several exotic zo particles of admiration.

It had seemed at the outset to all aboard her ship that there was one clear winner in this quest, and their aim had been to share in her glory. That glory, however, was now seriously tarnished. That was one of the very few things they could agree on. Also, if this trip was in some way ordained in terms only understood by Bugzhists, what could she do to stop events already recorded in the great pendulum of their universe?

Ziel was fatigued by the defective and zlobb-like behaviour of her attendants on board. She also resented the fact that she was expected, like every other lower-tier zole, to kowtow to the portal keepers en route, Bugz of mere second-tier status with petty pearl-parochial concerns whose properties lacked all metropolitan finesse. It could not be denied, however, that the pearl knowledge these functionaries possessed was staggering and extremely useful to her, as were their unsurpassed authority and their TT hotline to all regulatory units of the Zyberian universe.

Ziel therefore polished her interBugz skills by filing the jagged edge of her equation, and attracting to each portal keeper with smooth and most humble messenger Bugz, for her purpose was clear. It was to tail the Zargo and give it just a final quantum nudge beyond its intended destination, ensuring it had zero chance of returning to upset the harmony laws of Zyber, now revised in her favour. The great clock was ticking and the sooner it signalled the return back to Zyber the better.

27. THE ANCIENT BATTLESCAPE
Empty Quarter Zyberia

The Empty Quarter was just as the scraps of legend had said: a zone of unquantifiable and lethal nastiness. It lay scorched and soured into a state of bankruptcy where after the expiry of all life even the process of decay had ground to a halt. Zein's mental units were contorted. All was motionless yet not at true rest.

The region was the black diadem at the end of the great thread of portals that led from Zyber. It had presumably been important in the past, for the whole route was lined with ancient structures now covered in the duzz of ages past.

The fabled battlescape mentioned in the zerodian text spread before the Bugz, and beyond that loomed the dark convergence. The Bugz were awestruck by the pall of the grey miasma that was unadulterated negative energy hanging off the site.

The Zargo edged forward across the site. It was not the desolate, featureless landscape the Bugz had first understood it to be. It was a multi-dimensional chequerboard stretching out in all directions as far as a Bugz sensor could reach, with a crisscross of towering cones of ash and duzz studding its squares. The cones appeared to be ancient and shrouded structures standing sentinel, needing only the faintest spark to reignite hostilities of long ago, and the lines intersecting them were shallow trenches. The maze of white and black was disorientating for the Bugz as they travelled up one column and down the next; they could not tell which way was up, tilted or sideways.

The Zargonauts now switched on their zectroscope to full power to inspect more fully what lay in front of them, and instantly an eerie atmosphere of a violent past filled its display in the form of the irregular swarming of armoured Bugz and the felling of heraldic equations. Was this what put an end to the white pearl of Zytopia? Would this provide an answer to the fate of Zareth?

The Zargo's zectroscope, jumping from the charge of such ancient and intriguing data, set itself on maximum time rewind, a function never fully tested. It began cranking back in time, fading out the vivid surroundings of the present and entering the fuzzy images of ancient history. The Bugz were rivetted as it laboured backwards.

They strained to track the action and identify the key players. The zectroscope had an infuriating habit of coping well enough with recording the periods of relative inertia but then cutting out at any sign of action. It also cut out whenever Zein required it to zoom in on the unique signa ture energy banding of a leader particle or an unfurled heraldic equa- tion. Despite the Bugz' wrestling at the controls to keep the sensors focused on events on the ground, it was actually happiest swinging upwards and recording instead the dreamless starscape up above them. This malfunctioning seriously displaced every one of the Zargonauts, even the ultra-placid Zleo.

Several zyberleagues behind, the Zarantula's zectroscope was picking up the same histories. Ziel was busy tweaking the ON/OFF functions of this much more basic model and having even less success than the Zargonauts with viewing the more interesting pieces of action.

Only jumbled readings of the histories of the place were picked up at first; they merely confirmed that there had once been a clash of forces and smashed equations on an unprecedented scale. However, as the zec- troscope zigzagged back in time through the cones and columns of battle, the Bugz saw how the duzz retreated, revealing the warriors that once did battle here, their armed components snapping back in place with military precision, their harmonic messenger Bugz ringing out ancient battle zymns.

These were not simply hordes of uniform warriors acting on blind loyalty, however, though these too existed and were arrayed in terms of their Zessian stamp. These constituted the greatest gathering of the most powerful top-tier equations ever seen in Zytopia, equations that dwarfed the sum of the equations of the Apex members themselves.

141

With a rush of cosmic duzz and a flash of light the warriors and their engines advanced at breakneck speed, each side headed by pennants and cyphers, the air filling with the whine of rogue Bugz and explosions and blinding tracery at the point of impact.

Ranged in front of the zectroscope and paralysed with shock, the Zargonauts found they were not just witnessing from a distance but had inadvertently wandered on the stage of a virtual theatre of violence. Just as the warriors were within a zicrosecond of seemingly bursting in on them, the display's surround imaging kicked in, flashing and blocking off all external stimuli from real time, and accelerating the Bugz forward through virtual history.

One moment the Bugz were traversing along the bottoms of the shallow trenches and over collapsed energy fields, and the next they found themselves buffeted by walls of force sliding in on them. In this virtua world they tore through carnage, through the wrecked zyclear wreckage of craft they had seen only at the Academy, through an army of rogue Bugz that loomed up and swarmed round them, and through air filled with exploding matter and annihilation on a grand scale. The Zargo's zectroscope was hit by an unseen virtual energy source lobbed at its centre, which threw several frames out of sync and nearly disabled the device permanently. The Bugz' sensors were fogged. They felt the rush of wind and flash of light on all sides, pummelling them in their squashed space of fear, and yet they passed through the violence at a remove. There was no heat in the fire, and after the initial battle roar of the advancing ancient warriors the Zargonauts picked up only muted sounds of disharmony: the harmonic zymns of Bugz competing with the discordant whine of mutant particles.

In and out of the wings of this theatre there slid closely packed streams of abnormal particles, headed by the pennants and cyphers of unrecognizable mutant X, Y strains and the secondary W strain that evolved as a result.

The arrayed particles of many impure strains gained momentum as they approached the white warriors now seen in compact phalanxes facing forward on the dark horizon. Zon recognised among the white

144

vanguard the distinguished emblems and equations of several of his warrior ancestors, while Zein and Zleo were attracted to the positive and silvery pearlescence with which the white Bugz suffused the black field they inhabited.

Where were the black Bugz? Ziel wondered. Surely where there was white there were also black. So far she had only seen rogue Bugz ranged against white. She swung her zectroscope off at an angle to the right and there they were, ranged in a defensive arc topped with two winged horns, in the charateristic black Bugz stratagem of Zhan that Ziel knew well, apparently holding their energy in reserve, perhaps until the rogue hordes had completed their mission. Quite what they were waiting for was perplexing.

As the eye of the Zarantula's zectroscope refocused on the centre of the battlescape, and as the eye of the Zargo's did the same, the Bugz were now stunned by the spectacle of not only a yawning black hole but also the colossal annihilation vortex hanging off the site, a vortex rising out of the layers of smoking annihilation and curling high into the starscape, inhaling every shred of energy and exhaling only the shrivelled carcasses of waste Bugz and the odd puff of memory energy. It resembled a corkscrew and chess board all in one shimmering entity with shoals of spent Bugz and mutant equations that glided upward to its pinnacle. From the pinnacle the Bugz could just make out the faint arc of a bridge, its far end lost from sight. Zein and Zag recognised it as one according to legend formed at the time of the mass extinction here. How this vortex had transplanted itself to this place was a mystery, because it was normally anchored at Zo.

The zectroscopes of both vessels now distinguished a silver light, glowing at the heart of the white company arrayed before the rogue masses. It scintillated in an irridescent manner repeating the message 'SALVATION to me', and it pulled towards it pure and rogue particles alike, in the same way that the black hole behind it pulled in all manner of Zytopian matter.

As the grey and striped forces advanced across the plain, their orderly lines began breaking up and skidding about, and as they did so, the watching Bugz saw a singular particle, a curious lumpen mass with tendrils extending from a barrel-like body. The creature would crawl along, pause, and then move forward or sideways with astonishing rapidity,

145

sweeping aside and obliterating all mutant strains in its path. The higher the number of swathes of rogue mutant particles that disappeared, the more the convergence seemed to expand. And the more the convergence expanded, the fainter the scintillating light at its heart became until it too was extinguished along with its company of white warriors.

The zectroscope of neither the Zargo nor the Zarantula could zero in on the nature of this extinction. Instead, both their displays were bombarded with a series of crabby messenger Bugz to report a malfunction of their scopes. While the Zargo's zectroscope clunked and whirred, Zein consulted his Zargonauts for their interpretation of events.

'It is surely the battle that drew to an end the age of Zytopia,' he said.

'Everything here tallies with the descriptions in the texts,' Zag said, 'down to the pearlescent particle at the heart of the white, plus the chevrons of rogue hordes that pinioned the white Bugz on each side.'

'The black convergence seemed to swallow the whole group, white and rogue,' Zleo observed.

'So whatever we seek has already been annihilated, and we are here purely to understand that fact? For what purpose?' Zon asked.

'You have heard of time rifts or time slips,' Zein said, 'Maybe it is a physical phenomena which means nothing in fact, or maybe we need to look at the reason for the message more closely and examine the battle.'

'I noticed the heraldic equation of Zerodian,' Zim said. 'And I also spotted the creature of irregular mass and exotic properties with an incredible perfection rating.'

'I see no course of action except to move forward and examine this dark convergence,' Zag said. 'Salvation, remember, Zein. That is the positive message amidst all this negativity.'

'I sense the black ooze ahead has a grip which cannot be broken,' Zein pointed out, 'So we have to be clear that this will be extremely hazardous. Spread all of your observation particles and view the state of our quest. We may end up as no more than memory energy. Think of the many great particles now lost on this journey: Zipio, Zander, Zeiner, Zercl – all annihilated with their engineering and warrior Bugz.

'Those that wish to take the pearl road back,' Zein continued, 'can take a segment of the Zargo and depart in stasis, but I as the leader will have to continue even to annihilation.'

146

No one volunteered. There was a unity of purpose on the Zargo which extended beyond the natural tight bonds that kept particles in check, and it was with renewed vigour they decided to venture nearer the dark convergence.

Zein consulted the craft for its zyclear power reading. 24.6 zegas. Nothing like enough to return to Zyber. It was a case of act or be annihilated.

'Let's at least leave behind a zecode capsule with TT transmission that records our journey to date. It may eventually reach Zyber to inform any who follow us and wish to keep a record. Our quest may shed light for others, even if it reaches only this far.'

With only the scanner to direct them now, the Zargonauts moved cautiously forward into the dark convergence.

Ziel's zectroscope had overdosed on data just like the Zargo's, though not so much through exhaustion as through the frustrated actions at the controls of X particle leader Xit. The crew had been staring for some time now at a persistent small circle of light in the centre of the blank display. It glared like a baleful eye, and this together with the slow response mechanism of the machine generally, had maddened them. The Zarantula's zectroscope had only ever been intended for the simple purpose of answering to ON/OFF and YES/NO and getting the crew from Alpha to Beta, not for indulging in flashbacks to the past, however exhilarating they might be.

However, the zectroscope, while it was still functioning, and for all its inadequacies, was just in the process of displaying a perfect and lingering multi-colour, full-screen and close-up image of the radiating equation of Zareth, complete with subtexts and references and all a Bugz would ever want to know about the meaning of Zyberian existence, when the raging and unseeing Xit brought his full might down on the controls and blasted the device to smithereens. A deathly silence reigned on board.

The splurge of excited zotons that had been bubbling forth from Ziel dried up instantly. She struggled valiantly to keep her coils in check. She tried to console herself that salvation, which surely meant the full and perfect equation, the Zo constant of every Bugz, would soon be theirs anyway. With the destruction of Zein, the possibility of finding a clue to Zareth remained an illusive enigma. It had to be sculling about here

147

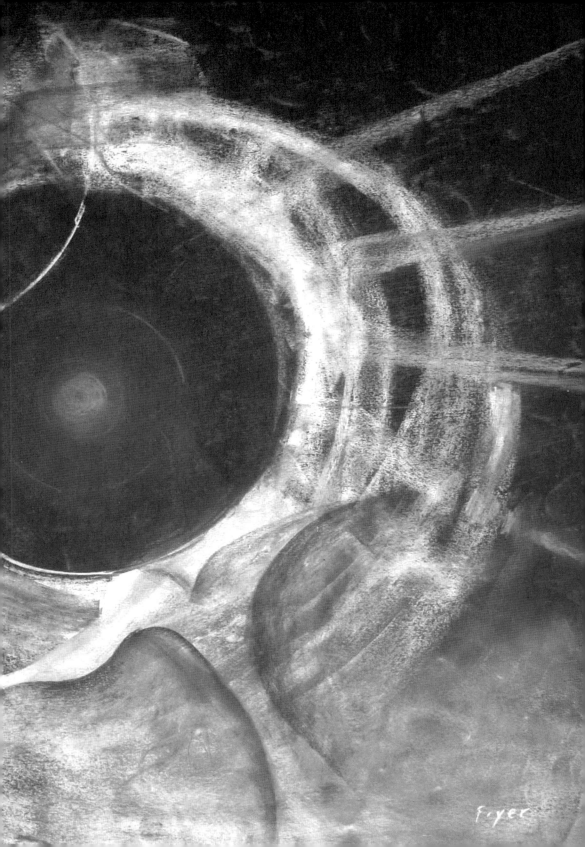

somewhere. All she would focus on until it was found, therefore, was the reliability of the scanner's directions and her mastery of the zlow life on board. Somehow, though, this line of reasoning proved to be of little comfort.

THE DANGER (NOT) SIGN

The Zargo's outer shield had been damaged from the ravages of the voyage so far. Its zyclear engines were faltering. The waste Bugz required for consumption were adulterated with the shrivelled and toxic kernels of the tainted X, Y, W strains strewn across the battle site; they would soon clog and choke the zyclear core. Refuelling and repairs were becoming urgent. All the Zargo had left was a small, albeit very powerful, emergency reserve of pure positive clear energy.

After the uneventful time spent roaming the battle site the Zargonauts came to the conclusion that the signal they had picked up in the throng of the battle was connected to but not coincident with the TT message received at Zyber.

They then found themselves jolted out of their rather listless state by a pinging of buoyant messenger Bugz from the main scanner. It had registered in the far distance a beacon, bobbing and clicking out a programmed series of messenger Bugz.

This beacon indicated the next obvious place to look, and yet again it had properties it shared with the original message and its powerful link was the extant Zareth particle and its ancient pedigree. The beacon clicked out:

Danger. Nothing ahead.

Its appearance was blasted and indented. It resembled an object for target practice, yet it had clearly survived several billennia, the hallmark, maybe, of a great maker.

'Something or nothing', Zein and Zag thought. The bobbing beacon had now come into close view, and beyond it Zag had located a curtain of throbbing messenger particles.

Danger. Nothing ahead, the beacon reminded them.

150

'Nothing to fear then,' Zein remarked to his crew, with swelling experimental values. He commanded the Zargo to start using its emergency reserve of clear energy to set a course for a large opaque eye-like swirl that seemed somehow to defy the numbing pressures exerted in the dark nothingness surrounding it.

This next stage was crucial: it was a case of fine manoeuvring if the Bugz were to avoid the thing's grip. A sense of uncertainty, something so alien to him, now welled up in Zein like heavy anti-matter, reaching unprecedented levels. He was able to quell the unease, for a soothing fountain of Z units began spiralling up from depths of the ancient Zarethian text in the Zargo's hold. They secretly refreshed and reinvigorated each one of the Zargonauts and willed them on their suicidal course, reinforcing the need to seek out 'salvation'. The ship itself was warning of the text's influence on all the Bugz' sensors and its probability of annihilation reading 100% if they took the action previously advised. The mission was reaching a deathly conclusion.

Zag viewed the wavering zectroscope, and pinged a discreet and encrypted messenger Bugz to the scanner of the black ship that followed several zyberleagues behind. 'We're going in,' she reported. 'Get ready to catch me.'

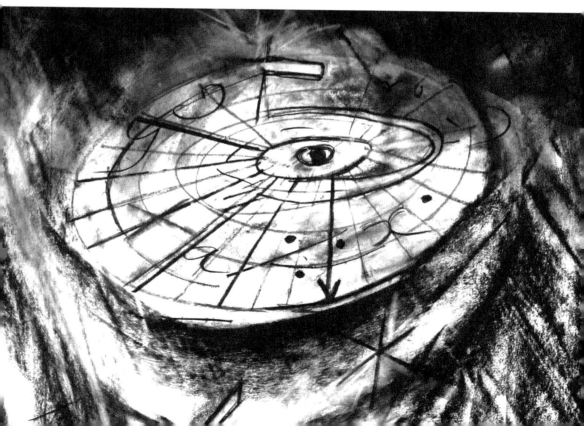

28. INTO THE DARK

Zleo supervised the fixing of the Zargo on two great anchors that were implanted in twin supernovae in the quadrant nearest to the Empty Quarter, as an additional force to counteract the dark convergence. The vessel hung like a dainty, shining buckle on the huge belt that was the vast rim of swirling black maelstrom.

A course was set past the battered beacon into a zone of neutral charge that swirled in the form of a giant eye in the all-embracing blackness ahead. The Bugz were braced, yet all there was, it seemed, was nothingness. The antimatter storm raged outside the calm as energy and matter were sucked in, crushed and converted in the enormous convergence. Somehow by miracle this calm spot existed 'twixt matter and antimatter' as though it formed a neutral area of truce.

As the discovery particles pinged back and forth, the tell-tale sign of the signature of the original message received at Zyber emerged. An exact match, came the crystal-clear communication from the Zargo.

Zein studied it. 'It appears,' he said, 'that something exists in these impossible conditions that has the energy to transmit this message halfway across Zyberia to us, using ancient Zarethian code.'

Interspersed in the message of SALVATION were the messenger Bugz:

```
No----thing  no ----thing .fear ..annihilation ..energy spike pure energy..
No -thing  no ---thing ..fear ..annihilation  energy spike  pure energy
```

As Zag prepared to jettison and all sensors on board were trained on the bottomless void opening up beneath them, a cluster of pure white energy bolts suddenly slammed into the rear of the Zargo like a spiked ball and chain, whiplashing round the stern and burying itself in the vessel's flank, fracturing both anchors attached to the supernovae, and impelling the craft forward at an alarming rate.

There was not even a zicrosecond's reaction time. The Zargo plunged into the grip of inky black pressure, a vortex of semi-collapsed matter, scattering half its vector Bugz and all its precious buginos. The Zargonauts' analytical units began descending fast into senselessness. Every thought, every sensor; everything slowed to an elongated muffled growl, every origin, every purpose, every goal. There was no meaning any more, not to the quest, not to Zyberia, not to a single equation of the Zargonauts, there was no meaning for anyone except for Zag, who remained composed. With her last pulse of energy she fashioned a single messenger particle, hardened and in her multi-striped encryption went darting up and out and away.

The anti-energy shield buckled. Chains of armament Bugz stripped off the Zargo as it descended through belts of increasing pressure and unfathomable density. The Bugz were sucked deeper into the stygian darkness through a storm of radiation bolts and density fluctuations.

The Bugz' Z units shrivelled to nothing. Their vessel was being crushed and turned inside out; their own individual histories were bending round on themselves in never-ending loops. Whatever reserves of positive clear energy had remained on board now radiated away in a series of gravity waves. Whatever their destination, it could bear no relation to the dimensions of time or space that determined Zyberian logic and function. And without these, the wave function of the Zargo would finally be extinguished with every particle on it.

This was surely THE END.

At this point Zein issued his last instruction to the Zargo, to blow up the precious last reserves of clear energy particles in the zyclear engines and to reinforce the movement forward to add momentum rather than reverse as logic might suggest. What other particle would have taken this course when all had failed? Yet this is what Zein did.

The thermonucleur zyclear detonation cut through every law of phyzics, propelling the Zargo into a fifth and unstable dimension where even time had no sway and where nothingness itself was flotsam.

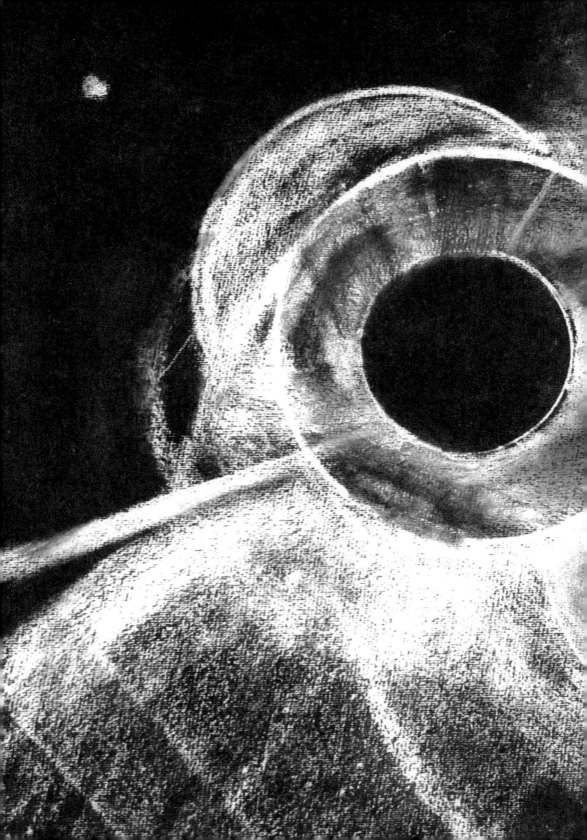

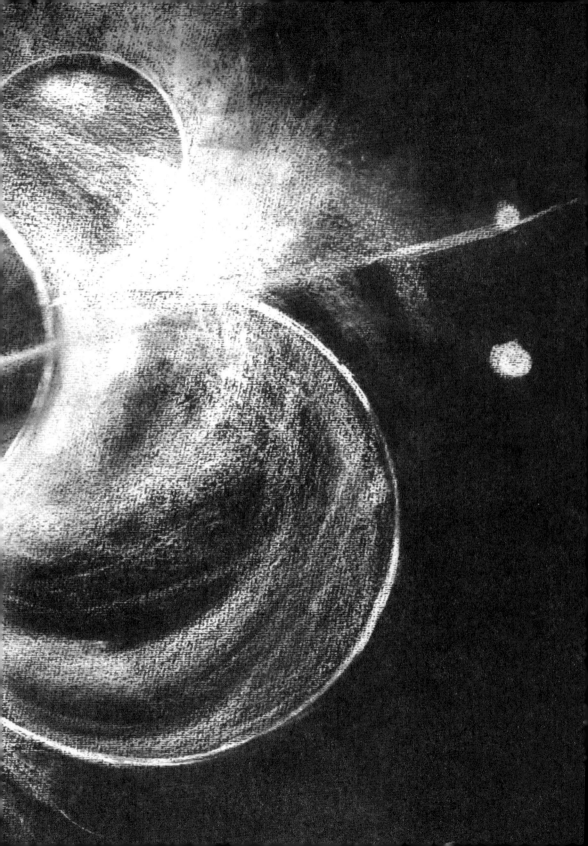

A MISSION FULFILLED

Ziel's mental units, which for millennia had sluggishly matured in a sour froth in the unlit pores of her vault before embarking on this thrilling hell-ride, were more concise than most. The information they received and absorbed might be the most complex known to Superbugz, but it was habitually reduced to two simple chunks for the purposes of interpretation and output: YES and NO.

The spectacle of the Zargo coursing into the great black eye and up-ending itself had made the trip worthwhile. It had all happened so quickly in the final analysis. She had had a perfect view to witness the obliteration of her mirror craft. Yet it still all seemed underwhelming. The new State of Equilibrium was assured, but it just didn't seem possible.

The failure of her servant Zag to jump ship in time and rejoin her comrades for the trip home was not such good news either. The second-tier Bugz code-breaking skills were unsurpassed. Ziel had viewed the zectroscope for some time, impatiently willing the Zargo to pop back into existence amongst the tatters of matter on the event horizon. She continued to scan the giant black eye, wondering what had finally precipitated her mirror ship's self-annihilation given it had shown such resilience during the quest. As for Zag, well, no Bugz was indispensable.

Xit wasn't, for instance. He might be a direct descendant of the commander of the X strain who had had a lead role in the zectroscope replay of the Battle of the Bars witnessed, but then there were plenty of other direct descendants to vie with him for black stature. He might be fierce in terms of both force and loyalty, but then so were all the others. Then there was Zedex. True, there were not many binary particles with a fickle black/white nature like his, but Ziel was never quite sure whether the advantages of binary particles outweighed their disadvantages. A hybrid of pure white Bugz stock and the rogue X strain, particles like Zedex were deliciously useful as double agents and decoys, but only as long as they were smart enough not to cross her. And then there was Win, a W particle produced from a watered down X, Y hybrid strain, a specimen both extraordinarily strong and extraordinarily dense. All matter and no mental units.

156

That was fine, though. All Ziel required was to get the Zarantula from alpha to omega with a crew prepared to martyr themselves. Yet Zag, well, Zag had been rather more useful than that. Ziel decided she wanted something even better than the conclusive readings of her own scanners. She wished to feast her sensors close-up on the fate of the Zargo.

Something urged her to order the Zarantula forward; it was maybe that message which had drawn them here, or maybe the ancient artefact in the hold giving off soothing Z units. A quick zicroprobe report of the area wouldn't hurt. She ordered the Zarantula's prow to turn into the neutral miasma. There was nothing for it: the craft would have to slip right through into the no-go zone. It glided gracefully into the area of neutrality, and its crew was soon rewarded with the violent spurts of distorted and distended messenger Bugz jettisoned from the doomed Zargo, plus the broken fragments of an encrypted messenger Bugz from Zag.

Good. Done and duzzed. Time to get off home to Zyber.

Ziel was poised to flick off her receptors, order the ship about and make the fastest possible pearl route to Zyber. However, as the Zarantula swung round it was assailed by the twin fireballs of the supernovae which in the end failed to hold fast the anchors of the Zargo. The anchors had not fractured as assumed but had dragged the enormous balls of energy that constituted their moorings into the path of the Zarantula, juxtaposing the immense positive energy contained in the two bodies with the great gaping mouth so eager to chew up the pieces. The Zarantula was no more than a sitting duck, albeit a powerful one.

The Black Queen coated her navigators in a thick film of recriminations as the supernovae hit them broadside on, and they all now felt themselves sliding backwards, being sucked round and in in ever-decreasing circles. The feeling was actually quite pleasant. For once Ziel's YES/ NO mental units wavered between their two settings. This must be the state a binary particle experienced the entire time. Not that Ziel had time to reflect on this interesting sensation, for the Zarantula was then hit with a further wad of intense energy which made it inevitable that it would follow the Zargo into the void.

'Oh, ZESS,' Xit sighed recalling the creator of all mutant particles in some expletive as the entire world turned inside out and swallowed up black with white. He was beyond fear and anger, so corroded with black were his sensors. 'Isn't this the annihilation limit? After all we've gone through.'

'I need to survive,' Win babbled.

'Wait till I get...' Ziel raged, but with only five zicroseconds of time left till meltdown life on board the Zarantula entered its blackest phase ever, for the toxins of nothingness drugged every unit of thought or function remaining to the crew. They could only sink into a stupor deeper than any that could be induced by duzz. The black and the rogue Bugz, so keen to nudge the Zargo over the rim, had received their own last quantum nudge with a vengeance.

It was not quite curtains yet. Dragged back up at one point and shaken in the zicrosieve properties of the shallows in the dark convergence, the Zarantula in its odd sifted form was then propelled even faster into the convergence. So near, yet so far...we...continue...shadow...Zargo.

BUGZILLA

On the rim of the dark convergence the many-tendrilled Bugzilla surveyed and scanned about on its age-old mission of hoovering up debris, extracting every jot of data, discarding the empty shells and waiting for its master to return. A routine toil since the Battle of the Bars when the white Bugz had almost been destroyed and his master Zareth had drawn the rogue forces to their oblivion. He had waited as commanded until his time sensors had finally reached the predetermined point to send the message. A message coded at the time of the battle, one that would be recognised by friends, who would come to rescue his master from the great black thing that was eating up the universe.

As anticipated, a craft had arrived and surveyed the sign – the sign intended at least to warn those who came near that they would meet their oblivion at the instigation of Bugzilla, who had been programmed to protect the site. There could be no recriminations, because all had been told.

All had gone to plan, and the Bugzilla had propelled the craft into the blackness while at the same time extracting the information it required. What its complex onboard programming hadn't expected was a second craft of almost identical design and equal status to appear. A hint of concern drove a hard reality surge through the creature-vessel's logic that maybe the first craft wasn't the expected rescuer.

158

Best make doubly sure.

He did get a glimpse, however, of the glowing Zarethian artifacts contained in this craft as had been in the first, and by the same probability he recognised that they should both be propelled into the abyss to make absolutely certain, his master's rescue.

In the meantime he would review the data he had on the two craft, and wait as he had done during the billenia for his master to reappear, perhaps in an uneasy truce with the boiling mass of blackness below.

29. INTO THE UNKNOWN

In the beginning there was nothing.

And just after the beginning there were the Bugz.

The pinpoint energy released by the zyclear engines ripped through the membrane of pulverising pressure that had rearranged space and time. The unnatural birth out of the nothingness took the form, initially, of a rent that opened in the underbelly of the dark convergence, and then as a back blast that blew its half-consumed and bilious matter back out past the rim into the Zyberian universe.

A cosmic fireball in the rent exploded in three distinct phases at zicrosecond intervals as the partly digested contents spurted out and expanded in a virgin vacuum. The back blast spewed ancient mutant particles in an upward effluence, slicing the edge of the rim and defying every rule of particle phyzics. The triple blast and smaller back blast alike gave exultant freedom to matter and energy that had somehow, almost impossibly, survived in the dark convergence.

The event lasted only a fraction of real time, yet the pressures and densities to which the smallest of particles was subjected meant that a whole universe of matter was disgorged before the membrane staunched its wound with a sickly rumbling and the frothy remeshing of whirling forces.

The Bugz and waste particles spilled out in their zillions, architectural and engineering Bugz, warrior Bugz and waste Bugz, and any other particle unlucky enough to have been consumed in the countless

160

millennia that constituted the timeless span of nothingness. In the midst of the waste were the Zargo and its shadow craft firing their engines almost in unison. There was a third and larger blast as well, some other part-detonated entity, perhaps, or maybe the spasm of the whipping in and closing of the rent.

There was no adequate record of what exactly happened, because the zectroscopes and compatible monitoring equipment on each craft had started malfunctioning before the lurch into the black hole, and they did not revive to record further data until the crafts were launched on the other side in an expanding plasma of charged electrons, nuclei and other particles of varying sizes.

The mariners were swept up and borne aloft in different directions on a massive, curling crest of energy that sped for hundreds of millennia through a sparkling sea strung with necklaces of nuclear clusters – hydrogen, helium and a blinding array of other elements combining and forming and of course all manner of Bugz. These necklaces of stardust solidified in the subatomic foam, they were washed out into deep space, and the friction of their forming and stringing together forced the preservation programmes of the two vessels to come coughing back to life. The original zyclear engines were gone, but the slow and gentle process of self-healing and self-restoration was able to take its course while the two crews with their cargo remained oblivious to their onboard preservation programming looking over them.

The lone ships of fortune, oblivious to each other's existence, still surfed the giant wave of energy through the afterbirth of the universe, and as the wave finally dissipated they gobbled up the last bubbles of Zyberian energy that had propelled them along this course, leaving in their wakes a glowing froth of intercosmic virtual particles and waste Bugz.

The Zargo and the Zarantula, dulled and decrepit from the ageing that the nothingness had imposed on them, limped on while regaining strength slowly. The original particles that constituted the Zargo's crew replicated themselves endless times over as their energy burned and they were annihilated.

The cargoes somehow remained entirely intact and, if anything, regained their gloss. Maybe it was the equations contained therein, or maybe the stamp of their Superbugz heraldry, but in this new spacetime they had not only survived but also flourished.

THE SIGNAL

The Bugz on board were in stasis. They had slept through the most fantastic proto-universe party of their lives, had they but known it. Then the Zargo's chambers received a jolt, activated by a clear external signal to wake its passengers. The Zargo was infused with a light emanating from the chunk of Library text. It pulsed with the reassuring rhythm of symmetry and harmony, with the same message that had prompted Zein to embark on the quest – only this time it was more detailed, for it carried the archaic royal encryption that demanded an immediate and instantaneous response. The source of the message seemed to be beamed from far off.

Zein was slowly re-energised. His access code no longer seemed valid, but the energy freeze-packed within his coils required only the lightest brush to unleash its spring-release reaction. The pulse from the message jolted up in quick succession through each of the energy rings of the Zargonauts, and at the same time flicked the scanners into life. The displays were sluggish at first: they showed only the black-and-white scene of myriads of constellations and recorded only the hiss of cosmic microwave background radiation. Zein reviewed their present position once the main scanner spelt out its updated data. Great swathes of armament, structural and engineering Bugz had been lost from the Zargo.

Its main scanner reported that the archaic Library texts had been activated presumably by contact with some marker left by Zareth. It seemed the presence of the Library texts had prevented them from being annihilated in the dark convergence. The scanner noted that the vessel's main structure was in its fifty-sixth reincarnation, with each of its subordinate particles likewise replicated and containing identical programming.

THE QUEST RESUMED

The Zargo was more than the sum of its parts. Now that Zein and the other Zargonauts were wakened, the craft pulsed ever more strongly with the glow of its cargo. The zectroscope sighed deeply and stirred. It too was picking up the signal; it too discerned the signature of Zareth.

This unmistakable Z signal bleeped above the hiss of radiation, a signal shaping the messenger Bugz into a reassuringly familiar zigzag. It repeated the word, this time even more succinctly:

Salvation.

Was salvation here? Had Zein's plan worked?

Time was no longer folded in on itself; for all they knew it had straightened out again. They had punched a hole through to a far side after all. They had passed through a tear in spacetime unlike any other gateway, they had ripped open a hole where none should have existed, defying all laws of Zyberian phyzics. They had emerged in an altered state and yet were still together. Did Zyberia still exist? Was it still in some other place, or had it been sucked into the void with them? Was this neither Zyberia nor a new universe but the twice life after annihilation?

Zag and Zim remained neutral. Their experimental values were more prosaic: Zag thought only in terms of codes and Zim thought only in terms of mathematics. As long as there existed a wave function, they would plot the route to its destination. Whether this was their twice life, or whether this was another universe where they had no sense of time and possibly no world to return to, the Bugz could not for the time being see any purpose in the quest. The single link with Zyberia remained the signal which begged them to explore further this strange place. It was strange that the signal still remained intact through all that had happened.

Also, more than anything else, the Bugz wondered at the pulse of the Z signal which seemed to plug ever deeper into them. The more they wondered about it, the warmer and brighter its dynamo became. Its glow came from a familiarity of something from their home.

'It's actually a distress signal,' Zein said suddenly.

'If it's a distress signal, it's not salvation,' Zon argued. 'In which case I know where I'd rather not be heading.'

'We have no option,' Zein said.

They continued to gaze at it. It was the only signal they had to connect them somehow to home; it was also the only signal to guide them anywhere.

163

Zein ordered the rebuilt zyclear engines to be fired up. The Zargo leapt forward. The reactivated zectroscope was picking up a string of anomalies and had recalibrated itself on what was only a poor approximation of the Zyberian scale, in order to gauge the alien topography of the surroundings. The Bugz could not believe the readings. They realised they were experiencing something both alien and yet familiar. For here, on the other side of the blackness of nothing, was a mirror image of sorts of what they had left behind.

FRIEND OR FOE

Zein was soon alerted to an object of clear familiarity in this universe. To use a simple analogy, he sighted in his telescope another island castaway sailing on the horizon.

The Zarantula had escaped the dark convergence in the slipstream of the Zargo, and with its comatose crew, splayed antennae, defunct zectroscope and hiccoughing scanner, was grimly determined to hang on to its mirror vessel with every pincer-like feature it possessed, especially now it too was receiving the glowing signal.

The signal appeared to come from a dusty white clump of carbon, a long and desolate shore of a hundred billion stars. Beyond they glimpsed a halo of hazy sunlit blue. The strong sonic breeze coming off the milky shore was the radio noise of hydrogen; it swelled above the hiss of microwave radiation, and beckoned both vessels with a signal from a near forgotten legend, for which the Bugz needed to use archaic text as a receiver.

All felt calm and serene. The incandescent messenger Bugz had pulsed a welcome, as did this friendly wave of hydrogen. They were not alone. Zein knew they certainly were not alone when a discovery Bugz of purely Zyberian appearance hove into view and scanned the Zargo. At the same time a streak of thick sooty messenger Bugz stained the Zargo's scanner and clogged every pore in the display. They fizzed, 'May Zareth's charm be forever with you, my mirror Bugz.'

30. MIRROR CONTACT

Ziel was far from content. She had awoken, not in the luxurious comfort of her Black Chamber but in a cramped corner of the bilge of a near wreck. She and her rogue crew had been conserving energy in their frozen time capsules onboard. Her YES/NO analytical units still remained confused, for the surge of well-being she felt on recalling the Zargo's annihilation collided head on with the all too vivid action replay of her own demise. Her memory banks sloshed with hangover images of the pell-mell rush towards a zero-sized destination of infinite density. There was no one at their post when the Black Queen buzzed and threw negative energy zotons around her coiled eminence as she crackled into life.

A quick appraisal of the new-look stretch ship, Zarantula, had revealed several substandard structural particles. However, the advanced preservation programme on board had been preserved. All the original particles on the ship apart from the elite Bugz had been drained of their energy and the ringed husks discarded.

Despite the Zarantula's limp state, it was now, like the Zargo, glowing in response to a flickering beam ahead, which was infusing the nugget of Library data on board and was pulsing the word Salvation. The beam came from what looked like an exotic paradise: a milky white shore with a bluish haze beyond it. Ziel oozed several zotons. There were still some pleasurable things in life for the taking.

The Zarantula's scanner was picking up another signal now. It was a faint blip, like a ghost emerging from the mist. It came from that maddeningly indestructible mirror ship, the Zargo, and it was marked with Zag's encrypted signature.

Ziel was still woozy. Her units simply could not straighten out the YES/NO function. The Zargo was still at large: NO. Oh, NO. The Zargo was familiar, trustworthy, hard-working and therefore most useful company when on an unknown course to an unknown destination: YES. Plus Zag was still alive: YES!

The Queen sighed. 'Oh well, if you can't annihilate them, combine with them.'

Her sensors therefore dolloped out a generous helping of positive messenger Bugz, anchored their Z formation with the crabbed signature of Ziel, and sent them shimmying on their way to her Apex rival and future co-ruler over Zyberia, her one and only mirror Bugz, Zein.

When the Z of black messenger Bugz stained the Zargo's scanner, it took less than a zicrosecond for Zein to recognise the signature.

Zein considered. For Ziel to be here, she must have either come ahead or pursued them through the black hole. Her craft looked familiar and as emaciated as his did. He was both appalled and comforted to find her here.

'What are you doing here, Ziel?' he addressed the scanner.

The crabbed messenger Bugz danced. 'I might ask the same of you, Zein.'

'I presume you're after me then? I can't believe you were just casually cruising by.'

'I didn't want you to be on your own, my mirror. Dangerous journey, and all that.'

'You've clearly been prepared to follow me through thick and thin. Very thin in fact. So touching. You know my mission, then?'

'Indeed I do, Zein. I know perfectly well that you took covert action not befitting of the white principles of a Superbugz; that you made off with the most precious of data from the innermost sanctum of ancient Bugz knowledge without Apex approval. Well! I could not stand by and see the laws of Zyberia being violated, and I could not stand by and see you travel the black road toward likely self-destruction without understanding your purpose.'

'Which is?' Zein challenged.

'A noble purpose, apparently, my mirror, despite the less noble measures taken to follow it. You seek to understand the past in order to understand the future. I can complement your skills, you know. You tend to stick to rigid rules, while I prefer to be more pragmatic and tweak things a little. Since we're here together, we Bugz must now attract together to pursue this quest and discover what is meant by this tantalising and ancient message.'

'How surprising and reassuring that you too ponder the mystery and meaning of life and that you tried to save us, Ziel. I thought your interests lay in the opposite direction.'

'I thought you might say that, my mirror. I like to surprise. So I trust we can now collaborate?' The silky black messenger particles zipped around the display in a flirting fashion. 'And I have something to show you. Something you might like very much.'

'Which is?'

'I have a very interesting Zarethian artefact just like you have, and maybe our putting the two together may furnish some clues as to why and how we come to be here. I have been picking up a signal as presumably you have too.'

At which point the Zarantula purred into view on the scanner, drew alongside the Zargo and emptied an unexpected barrage of discovery particles and warrior Bugz straight into its flanks. The shutters of Zon's analytical units slammed down instantly and triggered a rapid reaction on the part of his own forces. The two ships then locked into a fierce but contained sparring match. Ziel sweated zotons of excitement, which coagulated and swept round her in a mantle of negative energy. The Zargo's warrior Bugz bounced off it, stunned.

'I knew it,' Zein sighed. 'Put Ziel and Zon together and you will expect a jousting match, and it's a case of function first, logic later.'

'If you ask me,' said Zim, 'time would be better spent information-gathering. It would be easy enough for us to send a discovery Bugz on board the Zarantula while all units are focused on this unnecessary formality of combat. What did make that harridan follow us, if not to gain access to the Library material we have and use it for her own purposes? Anyway, given where we are, we may well need her as much as she needs us.'

167

'Very true,' Zein replied, and dispatched a tiny white discovery particle on a wide arc round the crossfire and swashing folds of Ziel's negative energy fog. It wormed its way through the interleaved linkages of armament Bugz and lodged itself in the Zarantula's abdomen, a toxic cavity stuffed with gobs of data intended only for Ziel's private consumption.

DANGEROUS SPARRING

The streams of particles firing from both ships and colliding midway lasted until Ziel was glutted with the excitement. The little spat stopped as instantly as it had started, and it was time for business.

'I would not be what I am without some confrontation and I wanted to test you are still worthy of my alliance my mirror' Ziel's messenger Bugz observed.

Zein's reply was equally obvious. 'Of course we would have expected nothing less, and best to get such disagreements done with now.'

'Yes, logic prevails,' said Zein.

Ziel flexed her analytical units and cautiously arranged her black messenger Bugz on Zein's scanner like pieces in the binary game. 'My friend, I suggest we combine on this quest. We are, you surely agree, mutually dependent on each other. I for one do not intend to hang around in the middle of nowhere, and all we have to go on is a version of the same signal which maybe has drawn us both here. Let's get to the source and find out how to get home. Could you therefore accept my negative energy if we meet, say, at the equidistant point between us, do you see it? – next to that waste heap of broken atoms?'

The two Superbugz attracted for an intimate little ring-à-ring, and Ziel revealed to Zein the data she also had from the Library. Despite the fact that Ziel's was detailed, accurate and exquisite while Zein's was abridged, corrupted and just cobbled together, the two Bugz' Z units sent up peace signals in no time, for here was a chance to compare discovery Bugz and shine information which might help them find the source of the signal and then get home. As Ziel put it to her mirror, Zein, 'We Bugz need to draw forces together. Close together.'

It was a case of survival. Unlocking the gateway back to their universe was imperative. And finding the question to the answer.

Ziel hymned a note sagely. Clarifying the Library texts was not quite as imperative as a return pearl portal home, but she agreed it was desirable if securing the passage required a tedious long wait. They would after all need something to occupy their time. The Zyberian protocol of consensus would naturally rule – at least until they made contact with anything non-Zyberian which stood between her and the trip back.

As the two Bugz were about to disconnect, Ziel's memory banks spat out in front of her consciousness the image of the sticky limbed creation scouring the waste on the outer edge of the black hole. A disgusting and completely singular creature. Her parting shot to Zein was that her messenger particles could not compose a summary character annihilation worthy of it. Zein could not help but agree that the encounter had been less than pleasant.

As the two Bugz split, and the Zarantula buzzed up and away, the discovery particle that was lodged in the ship's abdomen stirred from a toxic stupor and tumbled out into crystal clear space. Gorged with data but low on energy, it limped back to the last known coordinates of the Zargo, only to find the craft no longer at the same position. It found only the start of a trail of energy ripples and Z units, a trail that disappeared off the limit of the particle's range. Setting a course and shutting down all but its survival settings, it followed the dwindling trail, intent on completing its mission.

31. THEOREMS IN ZYBERIA
The Creature by the Dark Convergence

On the rim of the dark convergence the creature known as Bugzilla had carried out the latest part of it's mission successfully and was as ever waiting for its master to return. Programmed to analyse and sweep debris and keep safe the area of its master's demise, it was computing that it had helped send two helpers rather than the one expected. Also unexpectedly, as its memory recorded soon after the craft had been dumped in the darkness, a blackened fire-ridden bolt had exploded from the black eye and the contents had proved too hot to detain and examine in depth, and they had damaged one of the creature's trailing scanner tendrils.

The data gathered was of an imperfect nature, but it analysed the back blast materials as being familiar and dangerous former adversaries of the creature. Programmed to guard the dark convergence, it could not track these mutated enemies until given new instruction by its master. The data gathered flowed into its immense storage banks.

Three mutates last seen at the Battle. - Wit, Xawn, Yun

annihilation - 8: very dangerous.

Substance - heavy ionic matter, mutated.

Age - recreated time - Zessian epoch, late Zytopia.

Other information — time delay with danger increasing.
Link to primary objective.

Annihilate at first opportunity.

Track and annihilate soonest.

The Council of the Apex

Shortly after the start of the quest, the Apex Council of high-tier Bugz had convened on two important matters.

The first was the fact that Zein had left Zyber and travelled through an old portal gateway last used in the age of old Zytopia, and that he had been followed by Ziel. Two newly commissioned and powerful zyclear-powered Ziremes were missing with enough armament, engineering and Bugzhist monks to sustain a very long voyage. Nothing had been heard from the craft, and they had left without due clearance, regulation portal passes and without pearl plotter coordinates. The Apex Council, once they had traced the path of the Zargo and Zarantula, agreed to despatch Apex-authorised discovery particles and assemble a heavily armed fleet of Zireme Scouts to search, make contact with and bring back the errant successors.

The second matter to resolve was the continuation of the phase of the black Bugz, there being enough disturbance and disharmony already in Zyberia without the apparent jarring of the pendulum of leadership of black to white. This would last until the next natural pendulum phase when white would naturally resume power.

A real concern for both the white and black Apex Bugz was how and why the pendulum of harmonious power-sharing had changed. It pointed to some infiltration or contamination within the voting process, one intended to create a disturbance. If it be known, an even bigger threat was identified in the news of this 'disturbance accomplished', and that threat lay in the underclass of errant zoles messenger Bugz class of mercenary particles which habitually made its existence out of information and data retrieval. A complete data embargo was placed on the Council deliberations, and more security was placed on the thirteen gates which bisected the three rings round Zyber.

As the new measures for security were put in place, a mercenary messenger particle laden with highly secret Apex communications infiltrated the third ring at the eleventh gate. Packed with additional energy for a long voyage, this disturbed binary particle departed on a course that would lead to the empty quarter of the Zyberian universe. The Apex carried on its duties oblivious to the reason for the disequilibrium and the data stolen from secret Apex council meetings.

THE SECOND RISING BEGINS (ZYBERIA)

As the Zargo and Zarantula passed through the domain of nothingness they had unwittingly released from their billennia-long suspension in a black prison the most toxic and destructive form of mutant particles ever to have existed and the only imperatives these particles remembered were the planned overthrow of Zytopia, the treachery of the black Bugz at the Battle of the Bars, and the subsequent trap laid by Zareth which had led to their long incarceration in the dark convergence.

The mutant strains under their three ancient leaders Wit, Xawn and Yun having scorched out of the nothingness acted swiftly; they channelled the aimless blast out of the hole so that it set them on a course to the location so familiar to all three. Absorbing or obliterating everything in their path, they made set to return to their ancient zone of conquest on the outer fringes of the old Zytopia. It did not take them long to re establish their leadership because of the vacuum left at the departure of Xit, Yaba and Win with Ziel. They settled quickly into a period of rebuilding and observation of the new zyberian universe on whose fringes they had eked out an existence.

One of the major things they desired was to regenerate and re-energise their creator Zess or at least investigate the cache of secrets which still must exist, an act that would need to be accomplished with some secrecy lest it be construed an act of open aggression. However, the rogue Bugz felt, having been to the giddying edge of annihilation and back, what danger could be worse than the threat of nothingness they had experienced? Having probed the social structures of the new Zyberia, it soon became apparent that what was left of Zess, a few scorched data files and some smoking memory energy, had been forgotten by the new Zyberians and could easily be removed by sending out a covert mission of low impact. Reawakening their creator, the notorious Zess particle, would require first a quick keyhole incision of energy into the Bugz empire to recover the remnants and then possibly a dash of self-alchemy and grafting to see if any of Zess' properties could be regenerated. The time frame for the re-emergence of the returned mutant particles was not a clear-cut one, but slowly the tendrils of their influence began snaking out into the grey area that formed the outer buffer of Zyberia with the Empty Quarter.

It was on one of these foraging expeditions that a mercenary messenger particle was found and detained, and brought before the newly evolved Zess. Zess was not the original particle of all those billennia back, but rather a recreated entity of some immutable alchemy that the three leaders had rediscovered. He was now a figurehead for the tripartite leadership, and was himself created by those he had created. Any scraps of original purity the Zess of old had possessed were now corrupted and further removed from the Bugz' concept of harmony. The mutants had made a point of honing Zess' already formidable data extraction capabilities, a useful quality when it came to the slow decapitation of other particles.

The markings on the high functionary mercenary particle recently brought before Zess showed it had ventured far abroad, possibly with some purpose deeper than the norm. Although bathed in Zo energy and carrying the Bugz signature on its surface energy bands, it soon became apparent that it was not of Bugz origin. Not that this mattered, for Zess had never yet encountered a particle that would not finally give up its store of data if put under enough pressure. The information it contained was indeed most interesting as it bore the cypher of the ruling elite of Zyberia. Almost historical in nature, it told of the disharmony and possible weakness created on the loss of two Superbugz from the Apex and the ensuing vacuum which would lead to instability.

Wit, Xawn and Yun considered the circumstances of their own release and the three amplifying waves, recorded by them, that had washed through the belly of darkness. Clear signature particles of zyclear energy had alighted on the dollops of rogue mush all about. They bore an encrypted message telling of some particle called Zag being trapped.

It seemed possible that the events outlined in the mercenary particle's store of information might be connected to their own escape from the black hole. In fact, the demise of the future ruling elite of this new Zyberia was somehow inextricably linked to their own escape from the nothing. They had an opportunity to live a second life, this time in a changed universe scarred from the Quake in the aftermath of the battle they had fought in. They were busy sending out their own brand of discovery particles to ascertain the exact status of this new Zyberian foe.

It appeared that there now existed an opportunity greater even than that when Zess was in his first incarnation, to finish the job not finished all those years back, which was to overthrow the Bugz empire. This time the treachery of the black Bugz would not stop the overwhelming outcome, to strike at the core of Zyber when the Apex elite and rulers-to-be were travelling over the horizon on the vortex to their twice life.

Zess was therefore left to play with the particle. As plans for the encroachment and attack upon Zyber were made, he prized open the striped, kernel-like shell of the unusual particle. It was like nothing he had ever seen, but he sensed something familiar from somewhere far back in the haze of his warped memory banks, a recollection perhaps of this curious zero signature.

As the particle distorted and screamed it seemed to enjoy being slowly annihilated. The more discomfort inflicted on it, the more zuons it exuded. It took all the joy out of destruction when particles actually willed themselves up the rungs of the ladder to their second life. Either this particle had lived in such torment that it welcomed release, or it actually enjoyed being pulled apart ring by ring for the sake of it. Both theories were disturbing, even for the most disturbed particle that had ever existed.

32. A BLUE SALVATION

Back in the universe so unfamiliar to the Bugz, their new alliance of white and black saw the beckoning signal of Salvation looming large on the zectroscopes, and they streamed towards it across great distances, plunging up and down through the portals that reared ahead and leaving in their wake a froth of cosmic rays and debris. The pearlscape plotters were on a high melodic hum as they charted the best course through the welter of data, every sensor flared and alert. The unfamiliarity demanded even more care navigating than the tricky contours of Zyberia, but despite its rough surfaces it teemed with welcome particles and clear top-up energy for the zyclear engines and also replacement armament and engineering Bugz.

As the two craft wove in and out Zim demanded they slow down for him to record every anomaly, of which there were many, but Zein and Ziel had their sights set firmly on the only link to their past: the beckoning message and its location. The signal, they discovered, emanated from a small hydrogen burning system with eight major satellites and attendant comets. It was in itself totally unremarkable, worthy of no more than a zicrosecond's bored blip on the scanners, but it was dwarfed in size and spectacle by a colossal vortex of unfamiliar colour and hue that floated like an umbilical cord off the silvery moon of the third satellite out, a watery blue planet which bathed in the glow. The vortex resembled a bouquet of overpowering blooms. It was a wonder the solar system from which it hung was not dragged out of orbit.

177

Its richness and splendour inundated the zectroscopes and sent the Bugz' sensors reeling, for in terms of nature and shape it was reminiscent of the vortex of annihilation in the misty outer reaches of Zyberia at Zo. But whereas the chequerboard of the pearl vortex was gated with satisfyingly complex cyphers to channel the passing equations to higher thought and fulfilment, this colour cornucopia contained mighty pendulums that swung back and forth, barring the path of any particle lacking the requisite coding.

As the craft descended the Bugz were not at all prepared for the next assault on their sensors. The place shimmered and hummed with the burgeoning atom linkages of primordial life. Tucked in the blue folds of high-energy gases was a mini cosmic garden, teeming with organic carbon compounds and amino acids.

In this goldfish bowl of exotica the perfection rating simply went off the scale. Whatever had defined the classical age of Zytopia, whatever lay beyond the Bridge of Annihilation, this was surely paradise.

The Zarantula went into overdrive as Ziel cruised about in an ecstasy of zotons. She was already winkling out the treasures of mini-spirals of blackness that erupted from the bursts and collisions of particles around her. She might not know what greed, lust and violence meant beyond their Bugz definitions of accretion, excessive positive charge and turbulence, but she knew she was attracted to them.

While Zein was engaged in his own fact-finding expedition, Ziel fixed her detectors on Xit, the leader of the the X strain whose depleted hordes back in Zyberia no doubt still relished the thought of swarming on Zyber in the aftermath of the Disequilibrium. Xit was her new and dirty alliance. Rough and ready, not the slightest refined, but that suited her fine. Great mass, rogue energy and loyal support were what counted for a captain who alone called the shots. She kept him in line along with the other two mutant strain leaders Win and Yaba, and also the deliciously ambivalent binary particle Zedex who provided a frisson of excitement even to routine function proceedings.

She considered the Zargonauts. Repellent in terms of charge, of course, but all of considerable use given their noble equations which would soon be focused once more on the nitty-gritty of getting home. Let those with a penchant for hard work get on with it, on her behalf too. She had ports of call that beckoned just as much as did the signal.

178

Zein for his part oozed Z units.

The scanners of both vessels were moving across the ever-changing surface, noting the multiple layers of information embedded within it. Zim was already combing these riches, clicking over and over in his analytical units the searchword Salvation and picking up only a weak signal. If this was from Zareth, he was clearly in a near zero-energy state.

Weak as the signal was, however, it still pulled the Bugz on. It brought them to a pyramid formation of compounds erected by a water channel on a desert plain, a place where hydrocarbon creatures containing the intriguing but as yet dormant Bugz-like equations scurried back and forth. There were multiple layers of information in this primitive construction, all potential clues, crumpled like the leaves of plundered text and code in the Library of Zyber and needing decyphering.

A positive charge surged through the Bugz. They had made a connection. Both pyramid and equation fragments matched the nuggets of Zarethian text on board the vessels. Zim was already combing these leaves of text, noting the content which indicated that the sentinel signal marked the resting place of Zareth, who was in a serious low-energy state and near to annihilation. His message of Salvation, presumably for himself and others, seemed a paradoxical riddle.

Some of the particles were recognisably Zyberian, those that had catapulted out of the black hole with the Zargo and the Zarantula. Most however were the colour of this planet. Their equations were only partially numeric, they were neither engineered nor mutated, and the energy they contained was neither light nor dark yet radiated the familiar pure glow found in Zyberia. It was clear to the Bugz that these Earth particles existed in primitives who did not understand the equations within them. The Bugz noticed too that when the DNA host was annihilated, the resident particle made its journey up through the ticking pendulums of the colour vortex hanging off the moon in the same way that the Bugz made its journey up the pearl vortex from Zo. Zleo wondered what sort of twice life these equations had.

Zein asked Zim to see if he could return the signal by transmitting a crystal-clear Apex code of greeting. Ziel had, however, already broken the agreement to consult her mirror Bugz in advance by peppering the signal's curious antique receptors with her own impatient messenger Bugz. The result was that the signal simply vanished after floating in front of the Bugz' sensors with a highly polished aplomb. It read:

SALVATION comes from UNITY.

There was nothing for it but to wait and study the equations around them if the Bugz were to find any meaning in the riddle. Ziel had forced the lock and, it would seem, broken it. She hastily sprinkled a few apologetic messenger Bugz over Zein; yes, the fact-finding was important and should be done carefully and methodically, even if she did have her own impatient agenda.

As the two sets of Bugz waited and observed the Bugz equations themselves all began to be slowly affected as the time passed and the hydrocarbon life forms evolved. Direct contact was restricted initially to observing these primitive equations close up until the idea was raised that some form of linking with them for the purposes of experiment might be good. The disagreements between the humans, extreme and illogical forms of white and black, provided a rich source of record-keeping.

It wasn't long before the Bugz' sensors were drawn to the sight and sound of clashing forces on a narrow pass through the mountainous terrain of an area we know as central Greece. There they saw that day became night under the hail of flying missiles as thick as the spat between the Zargo and the Zarantula, and the superior might of Xerxes' Persian army was blocked for three days by the fierce defence of Sparta's elite troops. The Battle of Thermopylae was a reminder of the channel of blackness the Bugz had passed through; it brought to Ziel's mind the success of penetrating a bottleneck of resistance to have her own way, and it brought to Zein's the brave actions of Zareth's forces replayed on the zetroscope and the subsequent Quake that had swept over Zytopia.

The drama of activity here was however as nothing next to the vortex towering above them wherever they went, hanging off the barren moon, trailing off in an ever-widening spiral into outer space, a cornucopia of colour splashes shot through with striking pendulums.

It was clear to the Bugz that weaving their way in and out of human activity would be simple in comparison with traversing this deadly vortex.

Yet the extreme forms of white and black activity and the impenetrable fastness of the colour vortex above did not deter the wanderers. As they explored the burgeoning civilisation of mankind their calculations found astonishing levels of connectivity between their own equations and those on the surface of the planet.

The attraction was incomprehensible and irresistible. Unknown to either Zein or Ziel, this new environment was starting to impact heavily on their equations, making them draw odd conclusions, but like all things which are imperceptible these changes in their make-up occurred very slowly, and of course, even if subject to scrutiny they would appear ever so minute and inconclusive.

33. THE NEW ZYBER
Earth 270BC

It was among the olive groves and turquoise coves of Ancient Greece that the Bugz decided to make the first real contact with their primitive counterparts. Curiosity as well as frustration at receiving no further signal meant they could no longer hold back. The new sights, smells, sounds and feeling were with time impacting on their sensors. Not that Zein or Ziel or their crew would ever acknowledge such entirely unBugzish reactions even if they were fully aware of them.

They were just focused on the calm and order around them. What could be more satisfying for a Bugz than moving through a cool light world, strolling up and down the stone steps and marble paving of concourses among lofty pillars, ornate gates and public assemblies? What could be more satisfying than to go about one's business like a good patrician? The layout and complexes of the Greek citadel were an echo of the elegance and sophistication of Old Zytop.

The democratic state of equilibrium gave order and symmetry, the regulated activities of the Olympics and theatre gave harmony and intercourse. And what could be more pleasing to the newly awakened Bugzish sense of the aesthetic than the geometric design of adornment and the concept of the mosaic myriads of small pieces making up one large whole? Then there were the colours: the silver-grey of rocky outcrops, the gold of the beaches, the emerald of the pine forests and jewelled boughs of the orchards. A treasure-house of nature far removed from the thick layers of duzz that blighted their own world.

Ziel was off-guard and feeling increasingly intoxicated. She and her crew had abandoned ship to take in the sights of the monumental architecture, the phalanxes of warriors, and the heady collections of bucolic and exotic literature. Her mind map could not resist sculpting her own bust. The inevitable lack of any physical features of interest on it would be of course be compensated for by the highest quality of the hardest black marble or preferably zargonite.

Zim had gravitated to the academies, which were humming with positive energy and sophisticated messenger Bugz in the form of rhetoric and debate. They spoke of the world about, the universe beyond, and more interestingly the world and the universe within. Man was stripping back the layers to the smallest of the small and zeroing in on the atom. Bugz-like ideas were being seeded in every centre of learning. Euclid drew up rules of geometry. Others drew up epic accounts of past pearls. Plato envisaged Zytopia on this Earth and a new code of laws. And Epicurus heard a silky soft, dark buzz in his ears that advocated the pursuit of pleasure.

Moving among this mass of increasingly refined equations was one with a stronger glow, a pupil of Plato's with lisping but highly evolved messenger Bugz and analytical units uncannily Bugzish. The lure of this equation turned the Zargo's nose straight in its direction, while the crew of the Zarantula indulged in hedonistic self-abandonment.

Aristotle with his glowing equation was unquestionably top-tier for a human. An academician, he walked in shaded open spaces with his scholars. He observed and recorded the habits of living specimens, he explored their universal habitat, and most importantly, he argued that the building of Zytopia required the systematic collection of universal knowledge. This knowledge included awareness of the inert Bugz of potential energy within each human being, of what he called the soul. The Bugz wondered at this. The S units of the soul might equate with the Z units of their well-being.

Aristotle's teachings spread wonderment among his fellow humans as well as the Bugz – wonderment, and ultimately rejection by those of more rigid equations. Aristotle went into self-imposed isolation and his collection of data went to the great Library of Alexandria.

Zein and Ziel sighed in unison. The humans were making some progress, but at this rate the Bugz' energy levels would run out long before their way home could be found. New Zyber was great, but it would be even greater if one could accelerate its development. The Bugz were on a roll through the long white pearl of Ancient Greece. They surfed its culture and politics and dabbled in the froth of adolescent equations.

So far the policy of no contact had prevailed. You might think that Ziel would have been the first to test the waters, the first to jump out of her depth. You might think that a Zargonaut of sound analytical units would be the last to succumb to temptation and an uncertain outcome. But then the Bugz were not quite the Bugz they had been, now that they were sampling the delights of a soft blue planet promising 'salvation'. The black Bugz had been contaminated by them. The Zargonauts had been touched.

PATHS OF DISSENT

Zein considered that the equations found in the humans could be equal to Bugz, if they could develop. This respect for the danger implicit in contact was diametrically opposed by Ziel, who considered that at best humans may be a means to an end. There views were summed up in the following statements:

Zein: 'Treat their equations as future friends and let us gently impart knowledge.'

Ziel: 'This place exists for now and the Zareth particle has laid his stamp on it. Let us leave nothing when we go.'

34. THE CONTACT DECISION

After Aristotle they detected the man called Archimedes. His equation possessed latent qualities well in advance of the majority of others. It was thickly stamped with black and white logic while interlaced with delicate strands of rainbow. It appeared to complement and bridge the two worlds the Bugz knew.

It was agreed that Zim would connect with this equation, examine its properties, especially the S units, and report back on the outcome. The result of this action was the Bugz' first indirect contact with man and the setting in place of a train of events of great importance to all. Archimedes was chosen by Zein to be the catalyst for human scientific development in relation to communication in the future.

Archimedes was hit by the full power of Bugz equation linkage while bathing in his tub. After stripping away his human coat of grime he proceeded to strip down all the complex layers of geometry, hydrostatics and mechanics to the pure and simple. His function might be to design and construct tools and machines for carrying out the work of others, but his heart lay only in the Bugz spirit of pure mathematics of form and function and the beauty of science. His equation drank from the pool of knowledge at the Library of Alexandria, and constructed three spheres for the study of other worlds. The first was a celestial globe, the second a planetarium to imitate the motions of the sun, moon and five planets, and the third a curious bronze orb containing visible inner workings that no one could identify. The first steps were taken in devising a system capable of counting every grain of sand in the universe.

185

Zein was busy on another fact-finding mission and Ziel was off on little pleasure trips, but Xit was poised at the helm of the Zarantula with every sensor on lookout. The strength and glow of Zim's presence on a human equation, even one as advanced as Archimedes', were not lost on him. The X Bugz harboured designs of his own regardless of the no-contact policy agreed by Zein and Ziel.

Given the conflict between Greeks and Romans at this time, it seemed a perfect opportunity to see how well Zim could influence Archimedes. What if he could thwart the overwhelming power of the Romans, who were at this very moment, in 212BC, attacking the settlement of Syracuse on the island of Sicily? It seemed it could be done. The machines of war devised by Archimedes were holding back the Roman general Marcellus now laying siege by sea. All well and good, except that an act of treachery led to the sacking of the city.

Xit, annoyed at being denied the privilege of making first direct contact himself, had decided to act on his own and enter the equation of a Roman centurion. Zein, Ziel and Marcellus could whistle. Xit's human host then sought out Archimedes with a view to carrying out his own little experiment: annihilation. Get rid of an upstart human equation. The forced entry, the first ever recorded, of a mutate particle in a human equation created a violent ripple of negative energy, which dictated a new strategy for Zein at the expense of Ziel.

The unsanctioned killing of Archimedes was captured on the zectroscope, and so was the astounding after-effect, a zecho that rang out when Zim exited his host's equation. But Zim had achieved what he had wished. He had planted in his host a seed of thought that would grow independently of its origin. Archimedes' discussions were annotated by another hand and his writings and automatons were smuggled away and later placed for safety in a wooden chest. The great man's train of thought was kept alive. It wasn't just the Bugz flitting among equations in search of the nectar of human life and transmitting it from one to another. It was man himself who passed his knowledge on to others for safekeeping.

I looked down from the balustrade in the courtyard as my master, on his knees and engrossed as was his wont in his calculations, bade the Roman centurion standing over him to wait with his demands until his calculations were done. The soldier, amazed and impatient with his own business, struck forward with his gladius, thus piercing my master's back where he knelt.

My master, rolling on to his side, uttered with his last breath words barely audible but which to my mind sounded like, 'Time will run for all men'.

I closed the heavy door slowly and swung the wooden bar across it. Grabbing the papers and the bronze orb most treasured by my master, I pushed them into a jute sack and made my way out of a hatch on to the tiled roof. The wind was blowing smoke from the harbour and it burnt my lungs as I loped along the rooftops. I could hear the hammering on the door, the screams and angry noises from the street below. I was using a familiar escape route, a handy one over the years for visiting various men friends, especially when my master did not wish me to leave the house.

I could see the turmoil on the Eurialo as I hopped down on a low roof, grabbed the rungs of a rusting ladder and accessed the city wall that ringed the northern part of the Epipolae. This area was totally free of soldiers, for all the troops had either fled or were fighting for their lives near the main square in front of the temple of Apollo on the island of Ortygia.

I made my way down to the bottom of one of the bastions and squeezed with difficulty through one of the slots in the wall to the moated area outside.

It was a long drop, and having twisted my ankle it was all I could do to limp off past the old quarry area of Plemirio and then the olive groves after that. I had left Syracuse not a moment too soon. As I looked back at the city I loved, I saw only smoke billowing high in an azure sky.

I thought of finding refuge with relatives a good number of leagues away high on the slopes of Etna. To get there I felt it best to follow the coast before sweeping back to the east, thus avoiding the roads. However, I knew I would be facing a long slog, what with Romans marauding the countryside on the lookout for any bit of booty or easy sexual pleasure.

I made other plans. With the sack of precious contents over my shoulder I found rude shelter near Catania until I was able to catch a merchant boat. It would take me to Patara on the coast of Lycia.

Extract of account by Hedra, Archimedes' assistant.

Zim exited Archimedes as he rolled over in the courtyard, and Xit followed in short order when his own host was executed at Marcellus' command. Even Archimedes' enemies grieved at the killing of a man so exceptional and admirable. Zim was as profoundly affected by his host's untimely death as he was by the energy-shattering zecho. In fact, he found himself nearly dragged off the Earth and up into the pendulum vortex. It was clear that his equation had in some way been altered in the process of linking.

Zein observed Zim's equation with interest. 'Zim, we are all disappointed in our mirror particle. She seems to have abandoned her post and let her crew run amok. I need to speak with her. But for now tell me about the linking; what have you learned from it?'

190

Zim had dusted himself off but his spin was slow. 'Firstly, I can say that, although it seemed at first inconceivable, the match between my equation and the other was near perfect. Secondly, I am no longer what I was before. The stain is indelible. Lastly, given the match, we have to consider that we may in the past have existed alongside each other. I have a feeling, Zein, that such matching needs to be fine-tuned, for if the linking is not good enough the host equation could tear it with its crude spikes, whereas if it is too perfect it may flip our own equations with its smoothness, perhaps irretrievably so.'

'Are you saying, then, that linking could lead to the human equation taking over our own? What do you call it – flipping?'

'Indeed so. But I trust you will keep this to yourself Zein; a little bit of knowledge is a dangerous thing.'

'Zzzzz. Yes. But the zecho on exiting could not go unnoticed. Look at our fellow Bugz. They're stunned. A fine human equation has made his travel on the vortex.'

The remains of Archimedes received an appropriate burial. They were deposited in a grave together with an epigram that referred to the column-shaped headstone placed above it. This column was surmounted by a cylinder and a sphere, the symbols that formed the basis of Archimedes' unique equation.

Over time this spot became concealed and entangled with neglect, then detected over a century later by the Roman statesman and orator Cicero, and after that returned to the same concealed and entangled state as before. Archimedes may have been forgotten by his fellow humans but not so by Zim, who on Zein's instructions ensured that the female servant with her jute sack and twisted ankle was granted safe passage and assistance for the benefit of generations to come. Her sack contained the records of the armillary inner spheres which next saw the light of day at the hands of the great astronomer Ptolemy of Alexandria, who studied them in AD150 but did not know their real importance. Hedra proved to be the first in a line of assistants, the first to carry the baton. It simply had to reach the end of the line, whenever and wherever that may be, for it contained data of primary importance to human contact with Bugz.

It was as well that the Bugz acted when they did, for the abstraction of the Greeks was quickly replaced by the practicality of the Romans.

35. EARTH EMPIRES (PHASES)

The long white phase of Ancient Greece had been a most satisfying study. Zein reflected on the priceless contribution that the most meagre scrap of information about these Earth particles would make for the vaults of the Great Library. Ziel for her part reflected on the priceless contribution that the power and influence provided by these particles would make in Zyberia. It was clear that the equations around then were evolving all the time, and the more complex and powerful they became, the greater the chance for their being harnessed appeared – although a gap was now yawning between the caution of Zein and the hedonism of Ziel.

Zim and Xit were able to provide an exclusive 'insider view' on their hosts, although Xit's equation had had the misfortune to be contaminated as a result of forcing the fit with the host. He sparked and discharged erratic bursts of energy, causing Ziel considerable annoyance, until, that is, she became captivated by the delights of the newly emerging Roman empire and its militaristic advance.

36. CONTACT WITH ZARETH
Earth date AD27

While Zein mused on the logic of humans and Ziel remained more focused on their function, the scanner on the Zargo suddenly filled with the familiar message that had haunted them. It was the same signal that had been interrupted by Ziel's heavy hand at the pyramid.

Salvation and Unity ----- Salvation and Unity.

It emanated from a tightly coiled equation long dormant but now stirring within a human host. The equation suggested duality, the ability to flip to white or black. It combined matter and antimatter, energy and anti-energy. It was spotless, its signature was richer than that of the two Superbugz combined, its message was unequivocal. It was surely Zareth, although neither Zein nor Ziel in their state of awe wished yet to mention this.

The host for this equation was found not in the centres of Greece or Rome but wandering on the exposed margins of the Roman Empire in a region known as Palestine, radiating light and gathering adherents to hear his radical message.

This superparticle called upon them to abandon old habits, control instincts and usher in a new and eternal white phase. His appeal was based on the power of morality, from which conduct, function and logic all flowed, and to Ziel's incomprehension and disgust it flooded straight into the Bugzhist cores of Zein and Zleo and the human-tainted cores of Zim and Xit alike.

193

The messenger Bugz transmitted were few and charmed, they were soft and gentle, yet they prized open holes in the hard and brutal structure of empire. It appeared that no contact could be made with the superparticle, but he was affecting his host in such a way as that it engendered both fear and attraction in others. The host was causing a stir, for the force within it was radiating tremendous energy and challenging the egoism and self-indulgence of his local power-brokers and the Roman overseers. The host also seemed to be employing engineering Bugz to change matter on the planet. Miracle-working, as it was called. And he was spreading messenger Bugz telling of a vision, a future leader of a future kingdom.

Relations between Zein and Ziel had been smooth enough while drawing comparisons with Zyber in Greece and Rome, but this third superparticle surely meant a change, if not an abrupt end, to that. Three was destabilising, especially as Ziel quite enjoyed the success of Rome.

Ziel understood the feeling of changed probabilities; she saw only too clearly the intensity of the soft blue S units emanating from the particle's golden glow to wait for the benefit of the doubt as to which side it would take, hers or Zein's. There now existed an unstable balance of power. She would not tolerate it. Salvation, if it meant anything, now seemed to imply the destruction of the black and her casting out of the Apex, for the warm tints of blue and gold seemed to equate with a perfect white pearl. Thoughts of salvation were replaced at zyclear speed by survival.

Ziel mobilised her annihilation squad and placed at its head the Y mutant Yaba, and on reflection, the now human-contaminated Xit. She decided that the binary particle Zedex with his disturbed black/white tilt was too unreliable to send, and the other attendants were simply inferior. Her plan was to support the Romans and help remove the threat and send the particle zooming straight up through the pendulums of annihilation.

Xit fulfilled his function, although he felt a drag on his core by the human element now staining his equation. It was relatively easy to reinforce the fear of the ruling elite of a new leader with powers beyond the norm, yet he was well aware how special that life was. It was, after all, what had triggered the great battle that destroyed the possibility of the rogue particles expanding out of the waste area they inhabited. Xit thought of his place in history. He would be honoured as the great leader that had finished the job started by his powerful ancestors, the annihilator of Zareth.

Ziel, meanwhile, provided Zein with her rationale for the action. The superparticle should be neutralised for observation, but the human could be brought back to life, be given a new identity and then slide off into obscurity. He had drawn far too much attention to himself and if it was Zareth wouldn't he be more careful ? She deployed her silky black messenger Bugz encouragingly at Zein and complained terribly about the unstable actions of Zareth. Didn't Zein himself counter against affecting the balance on earth, what was this super particle doing?

Zein viewed the effect this intervention had and looked with interest at the assistants of the special human who spread his teachings like some ripple from an energy source in Zyberia. The effect was interesting because the wave form grew in height as more ripples were created even though the rulers tried to annihilate the effect.

Apart from one other occasion to come about a couple of thousand years later, this was the only instance of Ziel agreeing to use time-shift alchemy to split time in two possibilities.

Zein considered the unsuccessful communication attempted with the superparticle. He knew that Ziel would be a future threat to its recovery were it allowed to flourish unchecked. From what Zim was telling him as they consulted each other on the Zargo, the better the fit with the humans, the more effective, therefore the more dangerous, it was.

'Are you saying that Ziel will always try to disrupt your moves?' Zim was asking.

'If we end up colliding over Zareth the entire planet could be destroyed,' Zein answered. 'You saw her negative reaction to your entering the Archimedes equation. Xit's intervention was just a front; I have no doubt it was her doing.'

'So how do you propose to keep her happy while still exploring the possibility that this planet offers some clue to our own future and reason for coming here?'

'We will have to sate her appetite to some extent while following our own course. It involves risks that according to the Zargo's calculations means a 42% chance of a favourable outcome. So we're throwing Bugz logic to the universal winds here, but we may have useful human allies in the form of the assistants.'

'We're using humans as bait to achieve our own ends?' Zim asked.

Zein struggled with the conflicting Bugzhist values at his core. 'Well, yes, to put it bluntly and logically. But we are also thinking of increasing their worth on this universal game and maybe giving them a say, faced with the queen's undoubted enmity'

'And what of Zareth and the salvation signal?'

'If Zareth is as tenacious as the Library texts suggest,' Zein sighed, 'it's logical to assume that either he cannot contact us or he seeks to do so via human hosts, therefore there is every possibility he will do so again. I can't say when though. All we can do is employ our best calculations and observe the shifting data around us. As I say, there is no Bugz logic here; we are faced with constant uncertainty. Careful observation, pragmatism and measured contact with our hosts are all we can rely on if we are to avoid annihilation and the complete failure of the quest. Given that our mirror Ziel throws in extra uncertainty for good measure, I believe, some of the equations around us may need to be sacrificed for the greater good.'

'You mean the Bugz' greater good?' Zim asked.

Zein nodded. 'Precisely, but you know that human equations are contaminating, influencing all of us. Only the core of the Zargo with its anti-energy shield remains 100% unaffected.'

'I am developing a consciousness for these creatures,' said Zim, 'I would not disagree with your logical appraisal.'

37. FURTHER CONTACT

The Zargo and the Zarantula flitted among the strings of pearls that wove the Earth's history together. Despite their policy of limited and controlled contact, and despite the protection of their anti-energy coating flaking with wear but still effective, the vessels now felt the trickle of strange sensations leaking in, the same mingling of S units with Z units and zotons that had already entered Zim and Xit's equations. The trickle was perhaps welcome; the two craft had to adapt in order to survive.

Zein and Ziel had their own agendas to follow, and they both looked around uneasily for signs of the re-emergence of the superparticle, a potential ally in Zein's eyes, a threat to an uneasy truce in Ziel's.

Ziel had no time for musing and analysis. She gallivanted through life and the odd host human at the same time. She left the sinking ship of Rome in order to pitch camp first with the Goths and then with the Huns. She rode with Attila at the head of his hairy and stunted but mighty equation, as his hordes laid siege to countless populations. Some of those that fled would lay the foundations of Venetian civilisation, a seat of elegance fit for a queen, a Black Queen on a malaria-ridden swamp. Having enjoyed such little diversions as joining Columbus on his chequered voyage of courage and brutality and then bathing in the strange eternal fire on the rocks of Chimaera on the Lycian Coast, Ziel returned to pleasures of the haven that was Venice. And these pleasures were irresistible. The protection and isolation the city-state enjoyed within its energy ring of the lagoon afforded it the status of power-broker and empire-builder, and from this handy vantage point Ziel could don a mask and train her sensors on her mirror Bugz binaryboard moves.

197

Then there was the culture. Ziel could not resist dabbling, especially in the design of the aptly named Bridge of Sighs, which connected the prison cells to the interrogation chambers. A simple structure of white limestone that reminded her of the light-coloured facades of Zyberia whose visitors passed along without knowing where they were heading. It mirrored the legendary bridge in Zyberian legend, supposedly at the end of the vortex of annihilation. Ziel's connection with the Doge had remained unbroken from the Byzantium Empire and she, in a sense, had made it her independent home on Earth.

Meanwhile, Zein was pursuing his own more methodical strategy and was encroaching on Ziel's home turf of northern Italy. Zleo's equation was found to be a near perfect fit for a scientist with Bugzhist leanings as strong as those of Archimedes had been.

'The universe cannot be read until we have learnt the language and become familiar with the characters in which it is written. It is written in mathematical language, and the letters are triangles, circles and other geometrical figures, without which means it is humanly impossible to comprehend a single word.' (Galileo, Opere Il Saggiatore)

'Beautiful,' said Zein.

To which Zleo replied, 'What does this mean?'

'I am not sure for certain, but it seems this place is affecting my equation.'

'Is it not so, Zargo.'

'Indeed it is', confirmed the Zargo's data drive.

Galileo Galilei's early years had consisted of a monastery education, and he retained a sense of loyalty to the Catholic Church. He combined reflection with the rigour of scientific analysis, and he also, in a move away from the teachings of Ptolemy, which put Earth at the centre of the solar system, embraced the view of Copernicus, which put the sun at the centre instead.

Galileo ascended the leaning tower of Pisa to observe falling bodies, he climbed hills with his assistant to flash a lantern on and off and observe the speed of light, and he developed various devices to view the big in the small, the detail in the distance, such as a telescope trained on the solar system. Galileo noted that smooth-looking surfaces like the moon were in fact irregular and that the Milky Way was not 'nebulous' but filled with a multitude of stars.

Zleo gave his host a quantum nudge to have the courage to speak out, to redirect man's energy away from blind faith to scientific research and the publication of its results. With the Bugz equation tagged on to his own to steer him in Zein's direction while lighting up a trail for man, Galileo did not disappoint. There was his 'Starry Messenger' in 1610. There was his acclaimed dialogue on the great world systems in 1632, a work banned by closed human minds for the following two hundred years.

Ziel contented herself with a campaign of containment to serve as a warning to Zein's designs. She saw the burning of heretics, such as a neighbour of hers in Venice, a certain Giordano Bruno. She watched with satisfaction as Galileo headed for a confrontation with the Pope Urban VIII, and she then dispatched Xit to the equation of the Commissar General of the Inquisition. Putting her own machinations above the cause of science was most unBugzish, but this was the politics of survival: the Italian scientist was a threat to the equilibrium, and she would play Zein at his own game, starting with the issuing by the Vatican of Codex 1181 against Galileo. When Zein openly defied her with the publication of Galileo's dialogue in 1632 she ensured the man's public humiliation and imprisonment in his own home at Arcetri. Thus enfeebled, Galileo welcomed, in October 1638, the perfect live in companion Vincenzio Viviani*, a Florentine youth of sixteen years with a great aptitiude for mathematics.

Ziel made it clear, however, that she could be magnanimous. She had had the rack and other instruments of torture lined up and ready for those unfortunates who fell on the wrong side of her 'for and against' divide. Those opposed faced slow annihilation of course. But, after three years of living under the threat of torture and death at the hands of the Inquisition, Galileo secretly finished his work on the 'invisible forces' during his final years under house arrest.

His sight was dim but his memory and purpose were clear. He remembered the spectacle-maker from Flanders who had aided him in his first scientific and commercial success (his marine telescope among the merchants at the Campanalia in Venice). His head moved impatiently on his pillow, and Vincenzio leaned over his master's bed to hear the murmured words, 'Be good and pass me the wine, my friend, and then tell the guards you will need to make a trip for me to get ointment for my eyes.'

'Yes, master. As ever, I will simply explain to them that I am pandering to your ravings.'

Galileo's lips worked and his breath rattled. 'All these years they have sought to denounce my ideas but they cannot suppress them. Gather my papers and instruments and flee this place. You must travel to Leiden in Holland. There lives a lens-maker who is acquainted with a publisher of scientific works. Here, Vincenzio, take my seal in order to secure your dealings. I feel you will be safe.'

'I will miss you, master,' Vincenzio whispered.

'And I you.' Galileo touched his servant's shoulder to pull him closer. 'Vincenzio, you and I know what is in that chest. Our work is added to that of others who have gone before us, and it must be passed on. It is like the layers of an onion skin, being gradually removed one by one.'

'I will guard it with my life.'

'Now, lower the works out of the back window and retrieve it once you have spoken to the guards. Make sure you get well clear tonight. God speed, my son.'

During the course of his journey, Galileo's assistant found he had been entrusted with a number of unusual spheres, a lunar telescope and a document containing heretical material: a theory on inner matter.

Zein watched the servant slip away in the dead of night through the olive groves, and willed the man to go faster, to pass on the information about the inner sphere of creation. He felt displaced, for since the appearance of Zareth hundreds of years before, the Earth seemed awash with the strange values and colours of religion, the opposite of Bugzhism. It was imperative to get back on a more scientific footing. He sighed. He was only too well aware that Ziel had countered his move with Galileo's arrest. It suited her purposes to use religion in its blackest form.

Zein thought about the one missing piece needed to complete the body of learning on all laws of nature at the Bugzhist Centre of phyzics. It was known as the Zo constant, for Zo was where it had first been identified.

Some said that the black priest particle Zess in the age of Zytopia had reduced the constant to zero and used the secret knowledge he had gained from this to create the rogue particle cultures that streamed from his laboratories and to explore other dimensions, especially the fifth dimension. His studies had surely indirectly led to the mutant rising and constant threat to Zyberia's pendulum government. Perhaps the answer to the missing Zo constant and to all physics lay here, in this alien place with its message of salvation.

Whatever the case, and whether for good or ill, after the equation-jumping of Zim at Syracuse, Ziel in Ancient Rome and on the Russian Steppes, and now Zleo in the learning centres of northern Italy, Bugz contact was assured in the quest to seek answers.

On Galileo's death on 8th January, 1642 Zleo exited the genius equation with a numbing zecho. It displaced every property within the Superbug. After so many years of living within a human equation, the effect on him was even more profound than had been the case with Zim.

And on the passing of Galileo's equation, a new and similar one came into the world hundreds of miles away in a Lincolnshire village in England. The Zargo took note on its zectroscope and decamped to the centre of learning nearby, the backs and water meadows of Cambridge, where Zon was able to zero in on the bright intellect and simple tastes of a young student at Trinity College.

38. ZEIN'S STRATEGY CONTINUES

It was 1665, the plague was ravaging England, and the young Isaac Newton had woken up one night in a sweat from a dream of swirling symbols, fluxions and garish prisms. It was no wonder his brain was filled with the fantastical, for Zon had entered it the previous week while studying prisms in great detail and was now having an argument with the stubborn human equation he had found here, an argument in which there could only ever be one winner. As it happened, once the tenacious Bugz got the better of him Newton realised he was quite content to hide himself away and engross himself in Bugzish things. Zein viewed the scientist with mixed feelings. Being locked away in study was wonderful for making progress in scientific thought, but Newton's argumentative nature and innate suspicion of others stealing his ideas did not help spread the word. As it was, it took years for him to take into his confidence the one assistant he hired to carry out his experiments. Will Ashcroft was young and quick to learn, and the older scientist grudgingly came to lean on him.

Newton did well. In many ways he took up where Galileo had left off, what with his interest and ability in the areas of motion, mechanics and gravitation, optics and light, and rigorous experimentation. Zon found himself lounging in a hotbed of ideas, what with his host's work on the binomial theorem, calculus, the laws of gravitation and the refraction of light. Newton identified that a luminous body emitted light in the form of a multitude of minute particles travelling at a hundred and ninety thousand miles per second in empty space. He then demonstrated that every particle attracts every other with a force inversely proportional to the square of the distance between them. Zon observed and occasionally took over the experiments with the fascinating pattern formed by the dispersion and separation of colour. And Newton didn't stop there. His deep interest in alchemy led him to study the nature and structure of all matter formed from what he termed 'solid, massy, hard, impenetrable, movable particles'. His deep religious sense attracted Zleo. The reams of manuscripts he produced on many topics attracted Zein. The Bugz hardly saw an end to the man's talents.

However, it was while Newton and Ashcroft were discussing telescopes and the concept of time at the newly constructed Greenwich Royal Observatory that the Bugz really pricked up their sensors. humans were now establishing time coordinates for sailors at sea. The next logical step, and an essential one, was to establish time coordinates for the Bugz, not dissimilar to the pearl coordinates that guided the Bugz through the fourth dimension in their own universe.

'Will,' Newton was saying, 'We have shared so much. Where I have gone in both scholarly pursuits and in flights of fancy you have gone also; you are still at my side even when discussions turn to seemingly foolish notions of time. You know what I know, no less.'

'I follow in your footsteps.'

'You do more than that, as well you know. For all that your name is not well known, I will commit to paper while on my deathbed that you are to be credited as much as I for the discoveries we have made.'

'I hardly think so, sir.'

'Well … you have aided me in every little thing while tolerating without complaint a most cantankerous person. We both understand my nature, Will. I won't marry, you know. I have strife enough to contend with in my profession.'

'And given that you won't marry,' Ashcroft ventured, 'and also given that neither you nor I wish to have our treasures purloined by your rivals and objectionable sycophants in London, I wonder if you would be agreeable to submitting to my own safekeeping our unpublished, and as yet unpublishable works?'

Newton beamed. 'Indeed I am, dear fellow. Where I am going, where you will go too one day of course, I have no need of manuscripts. They must be kept aside for the more inquiring minds of tomorrow, not those of today that bandy about outrageous and narrow-minded accusations of witchcraft.'

Several years later, when Sir Isaac was laid to rest and Zon made an exit from the bad-tempered old equation he had warmed to, an oak chest of items was delivered to Will Ashcroft's house at Haslingdene. It contained a note, secured to the curious and ancient copper orb that Newton had often examined.

```
Will,
Your worth is known by those that count. The secret
of nature lies in the palm of your hand. Keep it
safe for those who await it.
Isaac
```

'Of course,' Ashcroft whispered, as he cupped the metal sphere and saw it glint in the light.

A SHINING EQUATION
Switzerland 1895

A young man working at the Swiss Patent Office in Bern, hundreds of miles away and two centuries later, was one who awaited it, even if it he didn't know it till near the end of his life. Every minute property of his shining equation was already being scrutinised by the Zargo's zectroscope.

'Incredible,' Zein remarked.

'If it's real, then it's credible,' Zim reminded him with common Bugz sense.

'Look at him. Here's a man who's already on his way to understanding the relationship of time to the speed of light. He can see that while the laws of physics are maintained each individual sees the values of time, mass and distance differently. Look at the equation within his equation: $E=mc^2$. The man's on the brink of working out the laws of pearl portal travel, my friends.'

'And more than that,' Zleo added, 'his analytical units are suffused with S units, the essence of humanity and a humble awareness of a superior presence.'

The Zargonauts regarded Einstein's equation with awe. It combined almost Bugz-like complexity with clear and calm simplicity. His view of nature was one that included an almost god-like presence. He would do well amongst the Bugzhist monks at Zo, busy in their search for the elusive Zo constant. Even Ziel sidled over to admire an equation that had developed with none of the fundamentals of teaching from the Academy of Zyber. What both Ziel and her mirror particle Zein were agreed on was that this equation was so bright it could burn them both. Best not to pass through the flame but to stand back and feel its warmth.

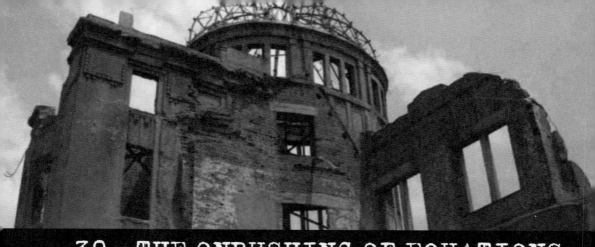

39. THE ONRUSHING OF EQUATIONS

WORLD WAR 2

Gayle adjusted her crisp white blouse and grey pencil skirt and lifted her leg in a pose so reminiscent of Hollywood's starlets as she posed in the full-length mirror. She painted sharp lines of crimson on her lips and smiled at herself. The car was already waiting for her to step out in the dust and oppressive heat and drive her to Zero Hill. The eve of an act of planned massive destruction was hardly cause for joy, yet Gayle felt a sense of elation. As the PA to Robert Oppenheimer, the man spearheading the effort, she knew what high principles and hard work had driven him and his entire team this far.

As the world had sunk deeper into war the Bugz had gathered at a deserted spot in New Mexico, a plateau surrounded by deep tree-filled canyons, to see the elite of the scientific community set up a cyclotron, van de Graaff generators and other apparatus. They had built a nuclear device that was the indirect product of the work done by physicists such as Einstein and Niels Bohr. 'A practical military weapon' was the term given it.

At 5.29.45 am on the morning of the 16th July, in the 'Jornada del Muerto' personnel from the Manhattan project had tested 'trinity', the first nuclear bomb.

Robert Oppenheimer recalled: 'We waited until the blast had passed, walked out of the shelter and then it was entirely solemn. We knew the world would never be the same. A few people laughed, a few people cried, most people were silent. I remembered the line from Bhagavada Gita, the Hindu scripture:

'Now I am become death, the destroyer of the world.'

206

Zein and Ziel were training their zectroscope lenses on events from different perspectives; Ziel was not concerned which side finished this war as long as the technology was developed and Zein of course, like the other Bugz, remained in particulate form not connected to a human.

Ziel was oozing zotons at the turn of events. She had no intention of being on the losing side in anything; certainly not in a mini binary game on the surface of the planet she visited ever more frequently. She had been in her element among equations examining such ideas as that of purity and a master race. It was even more enjoyable than in the days of Nero when she bathed in narcotically induced destruction.

Zein, meanwhile, saw the bomb as an undesirable necessity. Zon saw it as a fighting force for good. Zim saw the collaboration of so many sharp minds as a mental force for good. Zleo was staying low on the Zargo and wishing it would all blow over.

After the test, plans were advanced for the annihilation of many equations in the enemy nation of Japan.

They were there on 6 August 1945, at the start of the mission itself, when the B29 Superfortress bomber that was to fly to Hiroshima stood ready on the runway. Zag felt a rush of zuons at the sight of the name of Enola Gay emblazoned on its side in stark black messenger Bugz.

'Enola Gay,' Gayle said slowly, speaking to herself. It meant something to her alone. 'You know, I do like that name.'

Out loud she said to the technician next to her, 'I simply must take a photo in honour of the occasion. Don't you go reporting on me to security; I'm indispensable to Mr Oppenheimer. By the way, I gather the bomb being dropped today is called Little Boy and the next one lined up is Fat Man?'

'Yes, ma'am.'

'Are they named to match the crew on board?' Gayle asked with wide-eyed innocence.

'Whatever do you mean, ma'am?' the technician answered, flushing and moving away.

Gayle stood near the American air force officials as together they watched the plane arc with triumph above them, and zuons and zotons scattered like black confetti in its slipstream. Ziel thrilled to the rush of air under the wings of the plane and the shockwave as the bomb hit home.

It took only one extra neutron to be jiggled into a uranium nucleus already stuffed with neutrons for the glue of the strong nuclear force to become unstuck, and for the multiplying releases of further neutrons and split nuclei to take place. These exploded in the form of disappearing mass travelling at a substantial fraction of the speed of light; its flash tore open the sky with no sound, emptied itself, pushed out the air and bounced off the moon.

The world reeled, but for the Bugz this display of force was no more than that of a stone thrown in a pond.

'In the perspective of the galaxy, it was the most insignificant flicker. Our sun, alone, explodes the equivalent of many million such bombs every second All the scrambling commandos and anxious scientists and cold-eyed bureaucrats: all that is but a drop, the slightest added whisper, in the enormous powerful onrushing of the equation.' (David Bodanis, E=mc^2).

40. THOUGHTS OF HOME

Increasingly, Bugz scanners considered the location of Zareth. Where was that glowing gold and blue signature that winked in and out of the most special of human equations, only to face speedy annihilation?

The superparticle had been all but forgotten. The same deep glow still emanated from the Zarethian files in the holds of the Bugz' two vessels, although it resembled more a dimming electric bulb. The quest was idling along its various ports of call, and the word Salvation did not quite have the lustre of old.

Zim, Zleo and Zon, each one now touched by their linking to a human equation, were discussing the path ahead.

'Zim, do you think we will ever return to Zyberia?' Zleo asked.

'I would have said yes before,' Zim sighed, 'but now I am no longer convinced Zyberia should be our goal. It's all so confusing and imprecise. You know, these days I find whenever I have the odd game of binary chess with the functionary engineers that I lose. And I used to be Academy champion!'

'So you think Zein's decision to follow the message from Zareth was mistaken?' Zon asked.

Zim slowed his spin in thought. 'Not exactly, but I think that artful old Bugzhist Zotl in the Library has a lot to answer for. It may be that we all, Ziel included, were manoeuvred into this by subtle scheming of his. Perhaps he was bored, perhaps he wished to unearth secrets himself and use others to do so. Either way, it seems he played on the ambition of both white and black Bugz to control the pendulum.'

209

'Do you not think the equations we find here on Earth are critical to our return home? Might that not be suggested in the texts?'

'Indeed it appears so, but you surely notice like I do, my friends, that fresh interpretations can be drawn from this text the longer we view it.'

'Just what is meant by Salvation?' Zleo wondered aloud. 'And if this Zareth is so important, what drives Ziel to annihilate the human hosts he selects? Why does Zein simply stand back and prevent us from drawing a defence ring around Zareth? If we don't offer him protection how can we hope to understand his message?' His sensors bristled. 'I know Zein fears all out war and large-scale human suffering, a mighty black pearl here on Earth, but how much worse can it get having just experienced two world wars?'

Zim sighed. 'Zon, what do you make of this?'

'Zein is a true white Bugz: calm and methodical, keeping all options open as long as possible. He is confident that Zareth will reappear, given the texts. You see he has his assistants in place, our human allies, you might say, who pass the baton of progress down the generations, and this has not been challenged by Ziel, at least not yet, for she is solely preoccupied with the here and now and the dramatic. Of course Xit, Yaba, Win and Zedex are supremely confident of their thick mass and rogue energy. Quite frankly, they would not notice such subtle moves, they wouldn't even see the logic of it all until it burned clean through every coil round their rotten cores.'

The Bugz smiled most unBugzishly, but such a reaction came naturally nevertheless these days.

'You could say, then, that the master strategist is pulling in a frayed net slowly and carefully so as not to lose the catch,' Zim said.

'Exactly. What an excellent Earth analogy, my Academy theorist,' Zleo remarked. 'Feign a weak charge and be seen to retreat in one's own field, but at the same time draw into the field with you the charge of the opposition. When you have it in place, contain, neutralise and, if need be, annihilate them. Remember the Zytopian strategist Zama's teachings: `CONTAIN, NEUTRALISE, ANNIHILATE.'`

'Zzzzzzzzz. Sounds zeazy,' said the Bugz.

The conversation turned to the human phases they found themselves in. They wondered at the extremes of human equations, the way they could swing from dropping atomic bombs to advocating peace. A Bugz

210

was either white or black, and he never fluctuated from one side to the other, unless he was a binary particle like Zedex, of course.

It was still hard for the Zargonauts to understand how Zein could be complicit in the annihilation of so many human equations for all the talk of his strategy of caution.

'Perhaps a white Bugz isn't always true white?' Zleo asked. 'And a black one isn't always black.'

The Bugz sighed and coiled up. They were finding themselves rather confused here on Earth, contaminated even, after linking with host human equations the way they had done.

'The main thing,' Zim said by way of comfort, 'is that the focus is now on peace, and we know our good friend Zein is behind that in his usual subtle way. That is a prerequisite to finding the meaning of the quest. Now, my friends, as we know, the calculations from the Zargo's zectroscope and scanner suggest that we need to recreate the exact conditions that occurred when we entered this universe. The time coordinates can shift but the pearlscape dimensions must be approximately the same, not easy in a world like this where everything is so frustratingly inexact. I have consulted with Zein on this many times, and we are agreed that we need a machine of man's devising to aid us. We believe it is written in the texts, and anyway, while we like to think that we can move heaven and earth, that is not strictly true without assistance, even assistance from those we have perhaps viewed as our inferiors.'

'A man-made device to help us return to Zyberia?' Zleo asked.

'It's either that or annihilation, even if it's only slow decay from lack of energy.' Zim consulted the scanner to locate Zein, who was only just leaving from Los Alamos after comparing the detailed analysis of the blast with Zag and a highly satisfied Black Queen.

'The next step has to be to convince the inhabitants of the planet that there are better uses of the technology then annihilating each other' Zim confirmed.

'This will mean more direct influence then ever before,' advised Zein, 'and more risks.'

In other circumstances Ziel might well have been captivated by the drama of the alpine scenery. However, at this moment, while the Zarantula was speeding back to its pleasure capital she was more focused on a vast construction site by the Meyrin road leading out of Geneva. So here was another hive of industry: she had come from the atom city in the US to the accelerator city in Switzerland.

She was witness to the epic transportation from Belgium of two sixty-tonne magnet coils for assembling a synchrocyclotron. This machine was not the first of its kind, nor was it the biggest, the best, the most powerful or the most destructive in the world. It was simply a good machine. It was a force for peace, built by the fledgling European Centre for Nuclear Research in a neutral sovereign state. It was a particle accelerator for learning, for keeping Europe's enquiring young minds busy until the next, more powerful accelerator would be built to unlock more secrets of the universe.

41. CHARTING AN UNBUGZISH COURSE

As Zein returned to the Zargo it became clear that a new uncertain probability lay ahead.

'Let me outline the next important steps,' Zein said to his assembled crew. 'We know that the truce with Ziel has to be maintained or she will destroy this special place with her excesses. This truce is, however, preventing the re-emergence of Zareth given that he faces the threat of annihilation at her hands. It seems we are cornered. We counterbalance the Zarantula in terms of mass, energy and power; we find ourselves in a position of uneasy equilibrium.'

'Does that mean we need to change the rules of the game or dare I say it, cheat?' Zleo asked.

'Well we have more binary counters to play with on this human chequerboard, only they just don't understand their worth, at least not yet. My plan is to make a contact with them'.

'Surely we've already done this?'

'Yes, we have influenced and linked on to their equations, but it was bound to be the case that we would in fact have to open their eyes, make them aware of us.'

'You mean, enter into dialogue with them and get their help?' Zim interjected. 'Help with our research, or simply help for getting us back to Zyberia?'

'Human equations are the only things of note we have found here, apart from pretty scenery,' Zein said. 'We have to believe there was a purpose for the sending of the signal and the presence of Zareth if we are to make sense of anything. What else is there, then, but these equations?'

213

'And do you think they are the equal of ours, Zein?' Zon asked.

'My friends, you have all felt for yourselves how beautiful but flawed they are. I am not jumping to conclusions, you know me, but it is certain that our contact with them has accelerated their development for both good and ill. We have so many unanswered questions about them, that the Zargo's data banks are simply crammed with so far unintelligible theorems and constructs on their origin, purpose and so on.

'We have just seen how fragile human survival can be and the equations are linked to the fragile DNA, even with my mirror Bugz Ziel mostly just watching from the sidelines. Consider this: if something were to rouse her anger, she could scrub this planet down to its shiny metal core in seconds and blow the quest sky high.

'We have been trying to keep this uneasy truce with Ziel, while linking with the humans to aid their understanding of the inner world. It now appears that the efforts will be rewarded soon, because they are now making attempts to physically understand the inner world. Who knows, they may even finally understand their own equations.'

At Zein's nod in his direction, Zim then clicked into action: 'We find ourselves having to adapt our ways to this place, therefore our only hope may lie in charting an unBugzish course, one which relies on hope, chance and having the humility to depend on others to aid us. It is the so-called 'fate theorem', which I have managed to glean from one of the Library texts. I know it all sounds very 'Bugzhist teachings at Zo', but we cannot find anything in the functional Bugz thinking which matches with the equations we find here. As it happens, it applies very well to the man-made device strategy we were discussing earlier. Speed and timing will be the final differentiators in the confluence of our actions after the past two thousand years. The quest for truth and salvation is a tributary running into this confluence but the main stream has been and must be our return to Zyberia. We will let Ziel play her game and hope she thinks she is winning. In the meantime, we will try to elevate the pieces as planned on earth in this dangerous game so they can help us and themselves. It is a strategy we started all those years ago and it may tip the probability in our favour.

'The physical aid to us returning to Zyberia is a human machine in the making as we speak. It is at the European Centre of Nuclear

214

Research on the outskirts of Geneva, and the scanner tells me that the Zarantula has just a few zicroseconds ago been on a reconnaissance trip there. The end of the quest could well be in sight. Ziel wishes to return as much as we do, despite her mischief making, she will surely cooperate if not join forces with us, once we are good and ready to approach her.'

'Remember, Zein, she did not follow us here on purpose and we don't know what her mission was, it may have been to seek our demise,' countered Zon.

'As ever,' Zein put in, 'caution is the best policy. This plan must remain known only to four of us. I do not wish data to leak to Ziel's flapping sensors. I'm therefore instructing the Zargo to delete the record of this meeting.'

'But what of Zareth?' Zleo asked.

'I do not know,' Zein said, and sighed. 'You know, it's enough right now just to think about that mirror adversary of mine.'

42. OPPOSITES MEET AGAIN
July 1989

A second parley of the two Superbugz was needed, and this time Zein demanded that it would not be in a particulate fog beside a duzz heap. Ziel wanted it near either the warm aroma of a chocolatier's, or the cool gleam of a watchmaker's, or the tempting strings of a puppet maker's. Zein ignored all that ('This is business, Ziel') and chose instead the squeaky clean and functional environment of the Large Electron Positron collider, constructed at CERN in a 2.8 kilometre long tunnel and ready for bringing online in July 1989.

'Look,' he said, inviting his partner to admire the clinical appearance and high perfection rating of a non-evaporable getter strip, a component dreamed up by man for producing ultra high vacuum. 'And look at these,' he added, indicating to her the series of accelerating cavities, superconducting coils, tanks and transformers, detectors and magnets. 'And now ...' Zein threw the switch at the moment the team of scientists in the control room did the same, and two counter circulating beams of light instantly began streaking round them.

For the next six hours the Superbugz stood mesmerised in a crowd of a million million repeatedly colliding particles. These were carried by beams circuiting the 2.8-kilometre-long ring more than 240 million times and covering a distance of 6.5 billion kilometres. Humans were definitely opening doors for them. The Superbugz saw how millions of Z particles, the carriers of the weak force, were produced in the collisions. Six years later they saw the LEP upgraded to become a W particle factory.

Five years after that, they saw the machine shut down to make room for its successor, one that would achieve a collision energy seventy times higher.

Zein oozed messages at Ziel. 'Things are looking up, my friend. This place speaks for itself. Acceleration technology is enjoying an accelerating speed of progress. If its Z and W particles today, and the Higg's boson tomorrow, what's to say that there won't be W, X, Y particles and Bugz after that?'

'So true,' Ziel confirmed.

'And aren't you also impressed with the spirit of harmony, cooperation and mutual understanding that prevails here at CERN?'

'Well, yes, of course, since you mention it. Which Bugz would not be? But Zein, may I share with you my innermost thoughts?'

'I'd be delighted, Ziel. There's no one else around except for these carbon bipeds.'

'Well, my mirror,' Ziel said with a petulant swish of messenger Bugz, 'now we're here at the gateway with the key in the lock and the gate about to swing open, I hope you're not going to hold us all up with the niceties of scientific research and strict safety procedures and noble ideals about saving mankind. Remember it's our return we seek. In the spirit of harmony I would of course, like you, prefer to avoid mass annihilation, but let's just consider that a bonus. By the way, now we've established our escape route from here, have you had any glimmer of the problem particle?'

'I take it you mean Zareth?'

'Well, he does have a bearing on all this. You know my views, my friend: two's company and three's, well, destabilising. We must avoid tipping the perfect energy balance between us, wouldn't you say? In the spirit of our mutual cooperation I've sent my annihilation squad all over hell's half acre these past centuries looking for him.'

'And thank goodness you have.'

'You say?' Ziel's sensors blinked. 'I am very surprised you are in agreement on that, since you weren't before.'

Zein stroked his sensors calmly. 'Well, let's say that I'm as pragmatic as you are, Ziel. Perhaps his power and energy is such that it would be a threat to our counterbalancing each other; perhaps it is not possible to make contact with him anyway, or perhaps he simply expects us to learn what we need to know just from being beckoned to this blue planet and from studying the Library texts we have with us.'

'By the power of Zo! Maybe this planet has some good negative effects after all, my mirror, even for you! Anyway, enough of the talking; let's decontaminate ourselves and get out of here now.'

'Well, we can't go just yet,' Zein said.

'No, true. The humans are making good progress, but this machine does seem a bit on the small side.'

'And when we do, we'll go together.'

'That is my desire, my shining white mirror.'

'And with this planet left intact.'

'Yes, of course, if possible.'

'And with the answer to the quest as well.'

'Now, that's what I would term excessive optimism, and it's an optional extra likely to harm our relationship,' Ziel cautioned.

'Oh, all right then,' Zein answered lightly. 'Zareth should be left in the past. Let's not get hung up on that, as long as you accept the need to seek salvation for all, for man as well as for ourselves.'

And as the two supreme entities returned to their respective craft, they agreed that harmony was restored. They each had their own twist to their interpretation of the conclusion of the quest, of course, but this need not hamper short term cooperation and Bugz solidarity.

EQUATIONS FROM DIFFERENT PERSPECTIVES

Think of Zein as a Leonardo da Vinci figure and Ziel as an Hieronymous Bosch. These were contemporaries who viewed the world in different ways. Both were concerned to bring about universal harmony and both had met up in Venice. In the same way that the two artists made shrewd observations of the rich social tapestry of merchants, politicians, soldiers and visionaries, who made up the Renaissance world, so too did the two members of the Apex elite in the early twenty-first century. Both pairs, human and Bugz, were out of the ordinary and both pairs understood the equations needed to make up the key pieces in their armoury.

218

In a rapidly changing world of mass communications and technological breakthroughs where all progressed at an accelerating rate, the Bugz found they had a bewildering choice of human equations. The two mirror adversaries felt obliged to choose which was the best course of action. The better the fit, the more control, but equally the more chance of permanent damage to both host and Bugz.

First there was Stein. A fresh-faced physics exchange student, with a hungry look and an eye for detail, who arrived on campus under the auspices of the Cambridge-MIT Initiative and who enjoyed taking in the quaint sights of the spires and quadrangles. He liked the beer, he liked the music. At times he seemed in fact more than a little distracted by these pastimes, when what he was really meant to be doing was getting his head down to some work. His tutor at the Cambridge-MIT Initiative despaired at times. The boy was bright but he wasn't focused enough. He seemed more interested in talking about what others did than actually doing things himself. He'd have to pull himself up by his academic boot strap once he got back to the States.

The Cambridge-MIT Initiative was a novel institution which had been a runaway success once it had got truly off-the-ground in the 2010s. Its focus was on funding research into quantum technologies and to foster commercial interest in the form of spin-off companies in emerging industries such as magnetoelectronics and bioinformatics.

The many pairs of feet that over the decades had crossed the marble floor of the reception area had borne leading academics, politicians with international clout, captains of industry and business magnates. They couldn't fail to notice, as they passed through the grand portal, the zigzag emblem carved in the silver white arch above. It was a curious and slightly crooked design with a slight gap in the centre, rather reminiscent of Adam's index finger receiving the spark of life from that of God in Michelangelo's painting in the Sistine Chapel.

Then there was Svetlana, hand picked by Ziel. A platinum Cleopatra crossed with Machiavelli, a simply dynamite equation and a perfect arrangement of well-developed human sensors. The same lineage as Rasputin, and thanks to yours truly, whom simply everyone wanted to know, more connections than she could ever hope to cram into an address book the size of an archaic telephone directory.

219

Ziel observed Zein's carefully chosen player and Zein observed Ziel's fit for purpose pawn. The spotty youth with the keen enquiring mind versus the catwalk model with a nuclear physicist's brain. Ziel shrugged. 'Svetlana will eat him for breakfast,' was her private TT to herself as she locked on to the Russian female's equation and gave her host an incredible adrenaline rush.

Then there were Mr and Mrs Nimmo. A former boxing world champion from Wales and an Irish landlady from Cork. Robust and combative equations for Zon and Zleo. The handyman and housekeeper would be in close attendance on the Ashcroft family. The courtship and marriage of the Nimmos caused some consternation on the Zargo. Here were two Bugz bonded in human form, whereas in Zyberia the most intimate pairing that could ever happen in interparticle relations was a mutual transfer of data or energy. Were the Bugz missing something besides the Zo constant?

Zein's interests were even better served by Icarus Ashcroft marrying Brooke Cassidy, an Ivy League American with an impeccable equation. The line of assistants seemed to be ensured.

Then there was Bertholdt Lipp, chairman of the Blipp Corporation. The German telecommunications magnate's global domain with its IDO technology and Super-G network provided an ideal low frequency communications channel for Zein. The Blipp headquarters were but a stone's throw from CERN, and if it be known, which it wasn't despite persistent rumours, pots of funding went via Blipp's extended empire into the pockets of governments, who in turn fed it back into CERN and gave the Blipp Corporation ever more favourable contracts.

Not a single blip disrupted the Blipp empire.

SVETLANA'S RUSSIAN HERITAGE

Ziel considered her position in the light of Zein's seeming good fortune so far. She retired to her end of the metaphysical binary board and marshalled her crude but effective pieces in front of her palazzo in Venice. Svetlana had, thanks to the courtesies paid her by a coach load of Italian businessmen on a fact-finding mission to St Petersburg,

220

acquired an elegant abode overlooking the Bridge of Sighs. Ziel could see how the white pieces at the opposite end of the board had entrenched themselves in Cambridge. The Zargonauts were back in their old habits, refining their analytical units. No surprise there. But why they would choose to link to the equations of a charwoman and a former boxing champion turned school caretaker was beyond her comprehension. On the other hand, linking Zim to a German and helping him build a media communications empire with a simple logo and a global presence was rather smart.Zag had manoeuvred herself into place at CERN with both mirror adversaries insisting she did so for different reasons. Zag after all was strange in either universe.

Ziel looked around at her crew. They were not that enterprising, it had to be said. But then it suited her simply to have them at her disposal. Just give them menial jobs which fooled them into thinking they had the power they wanted. Sharp suits and gold wristwatches, e. laser automatic weapons and underground connections did wonders. Simple earthly things staved off boredom. Enrico and Vittorio were two of Papa's henchmen who looked looked like Sicilian tomatoes, sun-bronzed, sweet but a little common, but once the Bugz equations of Xit and Yaba had locked on to their own ones they found they possessed an inner strength that was unmatched even by the lion strength of their former boss 'Papa'.

Not that earthly things staved off Ziel's boredom. Things had, at first, looked promising when construction of the Parallel Beam Collider at CERN had started up in 2035. Ziel was poised to barge in with a host of engineering particles and get the job done in zicroseconds, but she reluctantly agreed with Zein's logic that the impact of such miracle working on Earth would probably kill off all the human scientists with a string of heart attacks, and that wouldn't do. The humans could, after all, construct the machinery as well as she could, even if it did take them longer with their bolts and screws and wiring. They might, with their combined knowledge, be able to make the damned thing work which was more than she could do. Even a black Superbugz stamped all over with Apex credentials and consumed with ambition had her limitations.

In the summer of 2033, when Icarus Ashcroft left Cambridge to take up his post as Chief Scientific Officer at CERN and put the formidable

Mrs Nimmo in charge of life at Haslingdene vicarage, rumours abounded that the CERN administration was benefiting from more than just the increased contributions from its member states. Not that these rumours could be substantiated. It was true that the organisation, with its consistently high profile, commanded greater sums to put at its disposal, but these could all be sourced to public bodies and private benefactors using legitimate means. Still, it was strange. Just where did so much money come from?

The speed of funding and progress was still not fast enough for Ziel, and she voiced her boredom and impatience to Zein.

'So what more can I do?' Zein asked. 'Do you expect me to make the Earth move for you, Ziel? This instant?'

'I certainly do, my mirror. After all, you're well in with our human hosts, and I like someone with connections.'

43. THE BLOODY GREEN REVOLUTION New Years Day 2035

It had started out as a popular movement against increased industrialisation. The burgeoning of financial metropoles in China and India had snatched the balance of power away from the old Western economies to the new Asian ones. Increase in the average surface temperature of the earth by two degrees as a result of global warming since the start of the century, plus the population movements and recurring natural disasters, had seen increased pressure on scarce food supplies. These had been now augmented by the large scale production of GM foods, distributed with bureaucratic precision of course, with due deference to creaming for the operators.

The movement known as the Defence of our Future Children had started peacefully enough in London in the early 2020s, but, as is often the case with any problem allowed to simmer, it was something simply waiting to boil over. It did so over something fairly innocuous, across the Atlantic in that bastion of individual freedom, the USA. It concerned the increasingly restrictive regulation of food supply and consumption and the increasing intolerance of obesity in the West. This, mixed with the increasing social and racial disharmony as a result of displaced centres of population, brought about the groundswell of discontent soon known as the Bloody Green Revolution.

The ecoterrorist movement could trace its origins as a global force to be reckoned with to a fairly innocuous event at a house in a particularly rundown area of Harlem, New York on New Year's Day, 2035.

It was during the period shortly after the implementation of controversial legislation for monitoring the consumption habits of particular

223

individuals on the basis that obesity was in fact a social crime. This apparently run-of-the-mill spot check by the so-called Fat Police* rapidly escalated into a showdown which resulted in two deaths. This in turn heralded the start of a crackdown on individual freedom imposed by an overly zealous city mayor whose grandfather had died in the 9/11 atrocity. Anything anti-establishment was not to be tolerated. He deduced that a show of force was needed to calm the protesters.

He deduced wrongly. The severity of force used on this one event triggered a backlash against all governmental controls, acknowledged by many of the world's governments to be an unprecedented but necessary infringement of civil liberties. The violence spread throughout the Eastern Seaboard with many lives lost, and soon spread like a raging fire right round the world. Tens of thousands of civilians were killed in places as far apart as Greenland, Buenos Aires and Shanghai, and the reverberations of the movement remained a canker for the world's leading nations, barely coping as they were with drastic climate change measures and the financing and coordinating of aid agencies. The movement appeared unstoppable. For all the violence, the many popular movements that sprang up under the umbrella of 'the League of Green' advocating the protection of the planet and the children of the future had become revolutionary causes with which even the most conservative-minded found sympathy.

While the world's economies were in turmoil, the likes of organisations such as CERN were fortunate to have a political lid kept on the amount of resource going into them. It was a fact that certain high ranking government officials were receiving sweeteners in the form of patents and commercial rights for their constituents and powerful connections for themselves. The privileged were getting fatter and the poor thinner.

The ecoterrorists were winning the day. They had begun mobilising a global underground army. They advocated simple values, simple lives regulated by a simple government. The fact that they advocated the use of force to achieve it was not quite so palatable, but in a world of extremes, there seemed to be no alternative. The rising, soon known as the Bloody Green Revolution, had come about as the result of a neighbourhood police officer in New York being snubbed by a girl and meting out his own form of retribution on the girl's overweight brother.

Brother, policeman and sister were now dead, and the brother hailed a martyr in the fight against scientific globalisation. So it is, that the biggest of world events can come about from the smallest and most inconspicuous of origins.

44. A LIGHT AT CAMBRIDGE
Early Summer 2041

Now, six years later, it was 2041. The Parallel Beam Collider was about to come online and the test firing was set a year hence, with thousands of technicians and support staff from over fifty countries swelling the already formidable array of physicists and mathematicians at hand.

Zein had carefully built up and deployed his crew to influence key personnel in line with the Zargonauts' adopted fate theorem. His centre of activity was Cambridge and his chosen host equation, a nonentity in terms of human status and one so scorned by Ziel, but probably the equal of Einstein – a rather hazardous linking, therefore, given its untapped potential, but necessary for the final push. Zon and Zleo were at Haslingdene vicarage, to all intents and purposes helping Mr and Mrs Nimmo with humdrum domestic duties. Zim was lording it in Blipp's Geneva office and surveying the vast telecommunications empire that covered the Bugz' binaryboard. Zag was in Geneva too, keeping tabs on any person of note passing through CERN's door.

Ziel was busy constructing, in spider-like fashion, her web of contacts and intrigue in the underworld of organised crime in northern Italy. She was well and truly embedded in her host equation, and had ensured that Svetlana's bulging portfolio had gained her both a high-profile job on the PBC team and also the ear of the Director General. Not that Svetlana had to be at CERN in person too often; Ziel was loathe to part with the pleasures of Venice, taking in the carnival and a night at the opera were just the ticket for one smart, well-connected lady.

All was going to plan. Yet something was different. There appeared a faint but familiar pinprick of gold blue light in a quiet, leafy corner of Cambridge, which radiated out from the redbrick walls of an orchard garden. It was the same light that had shone in a corner of the Roman Empire, before that, it had gleamed beside an Egyptian pyramid and before that, out in space in the form of a beacon which had drawn the Bugz here.

Svetlana Grigoriya was sipping a large gin and tonic as she cruised down the Brenta Canal at sundown at a celebrity-studded corporate event. The messenger Bugz that suddenly gave her linked equation a cold drenching was a rude shock. Her lurching and tipping the gin and tonic down a neighbouring female's cleavage as a result, did not create a very good impression, nor did they improve her networking skills. As Svetlana's body sank at her fellow guests' feet and her eyes began rolling like one possessed, Ziel exited her host mid sentence, and Svetlana never did finish her casual conversation on matters relating to obscure high energy physics.

Half a zicrosecond later, back at the helm of the Zarantula, Ziel trained the zectroscope straight at Haslingdene vicarage. Things had been going to plan, but there was no doubt about it, Zareth had reappeared and was very close in proximity and relation to the family her mirror guarded well, the Ashcrofts.

How could Zein have possibly known about the superparticle's appearance? In truth, he didn't, but it made no difference to the fact that Ziel thought she was losing control and like any dangerous creature being backed into a corner, the only answer was to react and regain the initiative.

Why the Zareth particle had chosen Brooke Ashcroft was clear, the match of equation was near perfect. The coincidence of the strands of the assistants and the reappearance of Zareth geographically on earth was debated endlessly by Zleo and Zim.

It was the odd thing about this place that uncertainty and the improbable occurring was a possibility. It made it exciting and dangerous but it threw Zein's plans and probabilities, set those years back, into disarray. The 'fate theorem' seemed to be working in overdrive as if this was some testimony to its effect.

45. THE CRASH
6 August 2041

Flight number Bii29 took off right on time at 1035 hours on 6 August 2041 from Newark airport, bound for London, exactly ninety-six years after the B 29 Superfortress had taken off from Los Alamos. The giant Airbus C980 accommodated 834 people from all walks of life all of whom expected to travel in perfect safety, as its Rolls Royce Bio fuel engines had a flawless safety record. That record was about to be blemished.

Mrs Joan Nimmo, who had arrived at the airport in good time after an enjoyable week visiting friends upstate, had shuffled up the aisle clutching her boarding ticket and extraordinary heavy bag. She was looking forward to getting back to her husband and charges at Haslingdene vicarage. She always missed the children when away from them, and she knew they felt her absence keenly too; their parents were so often either at Cambridge functions or allowing their lives to revolve round CERN. She found her seat a few rows from the back, and sent Brooke a Super-G mail. The air hostess reminded her to switch the IDO off shortly.

Jonathan Stein was eighteen rows forward on the same lower deck, devouring the audio-visual material his editor had given him. It consisted of several brief biopics on the growth of the League of Green and its interface with the scientific issues concerning food production in a world coping with climate change – all heavy stuff but interesting. Stein found himself drifting off and remembering that big juicy steak smothered in onions and barbecue sauce that he had consumed in Chicago all those years back. He was rudely nudged back into reality by the beaming stewardess who had been down to apologise for the delay in handing him the two cartons he had ordered, one containing 'spring water' and the other the hot Nutria-meal of the day. He read the writing on the carton as he tipped the slurry into his mouth. 'Steak and Fries with Greens. Only BERNI Tongue Teasers give you, in one direct hit, the essential vitamins packed into a wow factor great taste... ENJOY.' The 'ENJOY' was a command, not an expression of good wishes.

Closing his eyes to force down the disturbing mush, Stein considered his forthcoming visit to the Astrolab, a department of the Cambridge-MIT Initiative, situated among vineyards just outside Cambridge. Funny, the name made him think of 'astrolabe'. Maybe it was intentional. And once at the Astrolab he'd be making his way to the rather shadowy, so called Innerlab where they were conducting some revolutionary research into the production of negative energy density matter. He'd got a foot in the door, thanks to some old Cambridge contacts there, and his boss had decided, after some sucking of teeth over budgeting, to let him go economy class.

On the upper deck and enjoying much better fare was Gayle Richter, who was at this moment flicking through the digi-airline mag and pausing to study a picture of the Superfortress and its crew which ninety-six years earlier had carried the atomic bomb over Hiroshima. She had been on a business trip from CERN to give a presentation to several top US defence officials regarding the latest new spin-off developments they could buy into. They had listened politely to the details about the Parallel Beam Collider, and had dutifully smiled and nodded. Their focus lay elsewhere though. In the closed inner sanctum of the New Pentagon they were rather more interested in the cutting edge peripheral developments in superconducting metals for use in military hardware that could rechannel energy; they were also more interested in the virtuagog glasses, which could be used to brief agents via a synoptic download, of sensitive military sites and could run simulation programmes showing battlefield plans before troops were deployed.

Enrico Raviele might not be wearing a sharp suit and shades on this particular day but, even in a soft cord jacket and a beachcomber shirt, he still oozed Italian charm. He had been mulling over which smooth chat-up line to employ with the tidy little cherub two seats away, but she seemed engrossed in some frustrating game on the airline digi-mag. He looked at the giant red Ferrari chronograph on his tanned, hairy wrist, and contrasted it with the delicate black and gold time piece on the porcelain-skinned wrist feverishly working away at some game. The two of them were truly worlds apart, even though they occupied first premier seats just a few metres away from each other. Enrico had been sent by Papa from Venice to see some of the family in New York, not so much for a happy reunion and the usual back slapping, but to deal specifically with a thorny inheritance issue in which Papa was the sole beneficiary, even if the New York cousins didn't think so. Sadly, Enrico had failed to put them right on this, despite every friendly persuasion tactic he'd dreamed up. Papa would not be pleased, he had fewer relations stateside, but there was no doubt who the beneficiary was now.

The plane had a bumpy takeoff, and it never reached its destination. It had been delayed by a couple of hours due to some electrical fault now allegedly put right, and had roared along the runway and lifted into the steely blue darkening sky. That was when it was hit by a Thor-like thunderbolt. The aircraft exploded with the noise of a thousand over-loaded electrical nano connections. An eerie light from nowhere suddenly came dancing down the aisle of the plane, cloaking the four humans unknowingly pre-programmed to remain intact. Seconds later, the plane fell apart in three pieces at the end of the runway, scattering cargo and blazing fuel in the form of a giant exclamation mark on the ground, as the main piece of fuselage ploughed to a halt on its upturned nose.

The firefighters and ambulance crew had come battling through the roar of fire and smoke, and it had taken two days to recover and identify the bodies. There were miraculously four survivors.

Once Enrico Raviele had come to consciousness a couple of weeks later and read the names of his fellow survivors, he felt rather sick. He did not know, could not know, why these names meant anything to him. Since Xit had extricated himself from his host equation at the point of impact of the plane on the ground, Raviele was experiencing memory loss. He stared at the names, closed his eyes and slept. He'd better pull himself together or the meagre pay cheque due him would be even more meagre.

The media scrutiny that ensued over the following weeks was not quite what Ziel had in mind, not when she'd thought the four surviving human equations along with their hundreds of counterparts on flight Bii29 would face annihilation. Also she hadn't really relished the prospect of Xit's demise, but paying that price had been considered worth it.

As Stein felt himself borne away in the aftermath of the crash, he felt a curious rush of strength course through him. It was hope born of nothing, it seemed. He had so much to find out, so little time to lose. It wasn't just the obvious, it wasn't just the euphoria of surviving against the odds and seeing life in a new light. It was something else. He simply couldn't explain it, any more than he could explain why as a born and raised American, he felt more at home in Switzerland.

The vastly expensive enquiry into the causes of the crash, which was still continuing months later, came to the conclusion that the metal components and electrical nano connections on flight Bii29 had been physically changed. Alchemically changed, rather like the turning of lead into gold. NASA made the astonishing claim that the impossible had happened. An on-going investigation still ensued about the causes of the crash, never mind the highly unusual changes in atomic structure of components of the aircraft.

Zein had not anticipated Ziel's move. As the plane flipped over he saw that her strategy was to attack key host equations now. For over two thousand years he had put up with her apparent need to blood let, to retain the balance ingrained in their Zyberian make-up. There was near symmetry but not harmony. He had put up with the Zargonauts' grievances over this fact. The nascent Zareth-style superparticle had appeared behind the walls of a Cambridge vicarage. What if Zein and his fellow Bugz, bereft of their human hosts, were now to find that this being their best possible ally in harmony as well as freedom, would be annihilated once more?

With Superbugz effort he had cast a mantle of positive energy over all four special passengers on the plane. He had to save the unique human equations, just as Ziel felt it necessary to annihilate them. Clearly Ziel had no real concern for the eight hundred or so human equations sent on their journey to the Bridge of Annihilation as a result of a tremor of dissatisfaction that shook the Zarantula, at yet another plan thwarted. Whatever contact Zein had with Ziel from now on was not going to involve a cosy ring-à-ring.

46. THE ZECHO IN THE AMPHITHEATRE 13 June 2042

The American student had been looking forward to the launch and the firing up of the Parallel Beam Collider. He hadn't been quite prepared for the rocket blast that assailed him where he sat in the firing line of Svetlana's peppermint breath and predatory sights.

However, his surprise was as nothing compared with the rocket blast of the superparticle zecho that sent Ziel and her fellow Bugz in the amphitheatre reeling. Even the crew of the Zarantula paused in their cruising and pendulum gazing and wondered if there had been an earth tremor. And not long afterwards, they received a sharp hiss of messenger Bugz from Ziel summoning them to her side. She would like the time shift just enacted to be cleared up as best as possible, to remove any traces visible to Zein and Zim.

Bugz never used to feel sick, but the millennia of exposure to humans had gradually contaminated their once rock-hard cores, and this experience almost turned their cores inside out. Gayle Richter and Berthold Lipp could do no more than join the throng at the exit and shuffle out in a dazed fashion, their ears ringing and the Bugz equations within them momentarily stunned. Stein managed to retain a cool head; he'd kicked into work mode and was standing well back from the action jabbering into his IDO. Zein was not so composed, however. This zecho had been much worse than the one created as a result of the superparticle decoupling from the carpenter, all those centuries ago, and it had been much worse than enduring the plane crash a year back.

232

He was mourning the annihilation, yet again, of the main reason they were on this planet and the only solid link to Zyberia. Zein secretly hoped that contact with Zareth might give some clue to their return outside of his plans at CERN. Ziel's actions were senseless and blind. The light had beckoned, and surely did so for a reason, even though it was not yet communicating. Would it rekindle yet again, or had this zecho been final? Zein's Superbugz properties seemed to shrivel for a zicrosecond into the farthest recesses of Stein's equation, as though wishing to creep into the ignorant bliss of the human condition.

Even the equation-jumping Ziel, nearly immune to zecho blasts, received a nasty jolt on this occasion. The crackling of Bugz tension in Svetlana's virtual earphones from the moment the Ashcrofts had entered the amphitheatre had been unbearable, and as a result Ziel felt the wretched woman sink in a momentary swoon. At the moment the American student had hesitated in flight and turned round, Ziel had got Svetlana propped up on her high heels and was already breathing cool, clear energy into her. With her blonde hair askew, her chest heaving and her pencil skirt riding up on one hip, Svetlana looked like a Barbie doll dragged through a hedge backwards, and the bedroom look had the desired effect. Despite his feelings of panic, the student leapt over the backs of the seats to the rescue. He had the pleasure of whisking Svetlana off her feet, carrying her out of the mayhem, and then running with her down an empty corridor and barging through an open door into a small storeroom. The student could not have dreamed of such an intimate moment. What he could not have dreamed of either was seeing the long, painted nails rise up round him like flames, and feeling them claw his neck and pull him down among the boxes and strips of foam. This time Svetlana was not having another swoon.

233

47. A PLEASURABLE ENDING
Same day

The old ALICE tunnel where Marco made his escape went under the Meyrin road, and at the far end he sprang up a short flight of steps. The steps emerged in a field hut with a door already unlocked and the alarm disabled. He heard sirens and saw a crowd gathering over the road. Traffic was fast grinding to a standstill. He sprinted along a perimeter fence and headed for the gap indicated in his instructions. From there it was a short walk down a gravel track to the road. He merged with a stream of passengers wandering about the pavement and battling to board an eco-tram to the city centre. Tempers were frayed, voices were raised and bodies were pushed, and Marco squeezed quietly among them. He stood as squashed and as invisible as could be, and gazed out of the window while he munched on an energy bar.

He saw in his mind's eye the scene five months earlier sitting at the oversized ebony desk in Papa's office overlooking the Brenta Canal in Venice. He could never understand why the chairs in there were so high that you sat like a little boy with dangling legs; your feet not quite touching the floor. Yet Papa over at his end sat with ease and leaned forward with purpose on his elbows. Was it his overpowering presence, or was it the effect of some skilled architectural engineering designed to flatter?

Papa had the expression and the dress of success of a man who liked to remain jovial, and who usually was good-humoured, but who knew sadly that business was not so good now the East Europeans and the Chinese were muscling in on his territory. He had sighed and looked

234

deep into Marco's eyes. One or two of his many sons had let him down recently, and it was hard to know whom to trust any more.

'But you won't let me down, will you, my boy?' Papa appealed to him.

'I have never done that, Papa, and I never will.'

Papa smiled as though instantly reassured, raised his glass and felt the grappa slide down his throat. Marco Bergamasco didn't need telling twice. And he wanted Marco to know that he knew that. Marco could do anything from taking an old granny round the fruit and veg market to whipping up the fervour of an international environmental campaign. As long as the money hit his account straight afterwards, Marco was your man in whatever guise you wanted.

Marco stepped off the tram near an underground car park. The bonus would be winging his way since the mission had gone perfectly. His fee had instantly gone up from five hundred thousand to a million euros; not bad for a couple of months' research and preparation.

He thought the better of retrieving his Alfa Romeo. Better to use public transport.

Back in his army days as part of a crack unit he had taken ten times the risk for a pittance. The true appreciation of his worth now, however, meant that he could afford the good things in life. His bank was just down the road, actually, and as he sank into the back seat of the automatic bus he loosened his collar and rolled his neck a couple of times to relax the muscles while he scanned the healthy balance in his account on his IDO. The money was already in there, bang on cue.

The screen flickered a little, and the sculpted cheekbones and dark green eyes of Svetlana hove into view. Her recorded message fell from her lips like the chink of lucky charms on a bracelet being dropped tantalisingly before him.

Mmmm, she was set to meet at four o'clock that afternoon, exactly as planned, and the Beau Rivage Palace hotel on the lake front in Lausanne was the location. Much more inviting than the carefully chosen non-descript backwater lodgings he had arranged for himself overnight before heading back to Venice. Maybe they could head back together.

When Svetlana opened the door to the hotel's Imperial Suite she looked rather different to the vision he had seen in the amphitheatre just a few hours earlier. Her hair was loose and swept in an ash blonde waterfall round one shoulder, and the folds of ivory satin that traced her body curves left little to the imagination.

'Come in, Marco, I have some vodka on ice. Time to relax a bit, don't you think?'

The satin folds followed her movements with slight caresses, and his outstretched hands followed instinctively as he stepped into the cool elegance of the room's gold and white salon furnishings. He reached round her waist as she turned towards him with slightly parted lips and also with his glass.

'Cin, cin!' she smiled, clinking her own glass on his and backing out on to the balcony with the backdrop of the lake and mountains beyond. She draped herself over the railing like a classical statue. She seemed impossibly beautiful.

Marco barely put his lips to the glass, and he paid scant attention to where he discarded it. He didn't need the alcohol to feel the heat and excitement rising up within him. The prospect of devouring this angelic vision in front of him seemed almost more attractive than his bank balance. Mind you, it was about time he received this particular reward. The woman had spurned his recent advances, although that perhaps indicated how alike they actually were. As cool as arctic foxes. Well, he could play the game.

The side slit of her extraordinary negligée creation defied gravity and slid up over her hip as she placed one leg at a provocative angle to reveal a suspender belt. She allowed him to tuck his finger under it and lean forward to kiss her throat. She gently transferred his grip, guiding his hand up from the belt and under the hem, up to the gossamer light silk stretched across her thigh, while all the time breathing heavily.

Marco was now intoxicated, and she knew it. She could see, as his lips travelled down from her throat and he began groaning, that it was more than just the heat of the moment that was forming droplets of sweat on the nape of his neck. She took a long slug of her vodka, gazed patiently over the waterfront below as the latest in her line of lovers continued doing his thing, and sighed with pleasure.

She loved men who made the moves and considered themselves powerful, and what she loved even more was their realisation, their belated but very stark realisation, that something entirely different was about to happen to them.

She raised his chin with two teasing fingers and drew his lips up to hers.

'Oh God!' he murmured as she locked on to his jaw with an aphrodisiac kiss. She let her glass smash at their feet as she now began half biting him, clawing at his back and kinking her right leg up round his hip, allowing him to force her further over the balcony railing.

Marco could not believe how churned up he felt inside; he was feeling sensations he'd never felt before. He could not know about the re-engineering Bugz that had slipped under his skin just moments earlier. It was not long, though, before they made their presence felt. They began playing merry hell with all the warmest and most tender parts of his body, stinging and annihilating the subatomic structure that made up bone, flesh and blood.

'Oh God!' he repeated, more in surprise now.

It rippled through every vein and every muscle, for it was directed to consume every particle of this tanned hunk from the inside out. After a few deep probings here and there, which made its host gasp from both pleasure and pain, it went about its work quickly.

Marco's last vision of this world, a split second before he shrivelled like burst bubblegum, was of the gold halo of Svetlana's hair, her doll-like and expressionless eyes, and the shimmer of the lake and cloudless sky beyond. Moments later the unconsumed remains of his outer skin hung from dead lips that in turn dangled from the side of Svetlana's mouth. It was as though his whole inner body and all the organs it contained had been excavated from the inside out.

Svetlana plucked the shrivelled head of hair between finger and thumb and removed the offending article from her mouth. The punctured bag of skin still twitched in intense pain. It was a beautifully intact trophy although, inevitably, it had made a real mess of the negligee. Time to freshen up in the bathroom. Svetlana held the human carapace at arm's length and hung it on the back of the door in the manner one might a bathrobe. She used to have a sizeable collection of such trophies, but now she only kept the really important ones back in Venice to muse over like the ardent collector she was.

Svetlana smiled. She had had her few kilos of flesh, and Marco now took up less room and was less annoying. Almost as good as having a healthy bank balance. And now it was time to travel back to Venice.

Papa might not be thrilled at Marco's non-appearance, but the job was done and it had gone perfectly.

She made a point of not looking at her face in the mirror as she splashed water on herself and dabbed on the exquisite designer perfume. She lived life to the full, but she didn't always like living with herself. To have real fun you often needed a mask to steel yourself. And that's why she didn't care to look at the naked face in front of her. That's why the City of Carnival was the place to be, even if it was slowly sinking under the rising sea levels on the surface of this blue paradise.

48. FLIPPING SVETLANA
14th June

Ziel stood on the Bridge of Sighs, a welcome and peaceful distance away from the Zarantula, and surveyed the scene, not just the view of the shimmering Venetian lagoon outside but also at the pawn she was placing on the binary board in front of her. She would rack up human emotion no end to achieve the ultimate scientific achievement. Lifespans had a beginning and an end; particles popped into existence and popped out again. It was clear, though, that while human lifespans popped out of existence, they still lived on for a while in the form of memory energy, which triggered an outpouring of grief. Blend this human grief with a bit of unique time shift alchemy Zessian-style, and you could create a powerful illusion. Powerful enough to bend the most advanced human will to your doing, and right under the braced energy rings of the enemy.

Ziel liked flexing her new power. It was useful having Svetlana to get men to do what she wanted without having to coerce too much. Plain creation and annihilation of particles was too clean and boring. In contrast, coupling the way that she and her W, X, Y attendants did with the murkier end of human equations provided the adrenalin of danger and unpredictability. This decidedly unBugzish trait was not one to be exalted, of course. And who could know if serial zecho-transiting was harmful in the long run? Her equation would need thoroughly flushing through once she returned home to rid it of the dirty elements accreting to it. She knew that only the immense negative energy locked in her multi-ringed structure was preventing outright corruption. The many years of locking

239

on to human equations and manipulating these carbon creatures had meant she was as supremely effective at manipulating as they were supremely ignorant of the manipulation.

Svetlana was also peering at the murky blue water through the grilled window of the Bridge, and as she did so she twisted her pert rear end round to one side to allow the flow of tourist traffic to squeeze past. She felt a tugging on her skirt, and looked down to see a girl with pale blue eyes and a freckled complexion looking back up at her.

'Excuse me, miss. Have you seen my mummy?'

Svetlana bent down and drew the little girl to her. 'What is your name?'

'Amelia, miss.'

'Your mummy should have told you not to talk to strangers.'

'Yes, miss, but you look kind.'

'Well, we had better find your mummy then.'

The girl's eyes filled with tears, and she rested her head on the cradle of Svetlana's perfumed neck. Svetlana was flooded with a strange sensation that passed through her normally impenetrable exterior – tender warmth as opposed to fierce heat, and she patted the girl comfortingly, like it was her own child. A child, a progeny, an odd and yet appealing concept.

A moment later Svetlana heard a cry of anguish. 'Amelia, oh Amelia!' She stopped short when she saw Svetlana. 'I'm so sorry! I hope she hasn't caused you any problems. What have I told you, you young madam! Running ahead and disappearing round corners!'

'She's been no problem,' Svetlana assured her, at which point the girl released her grip and gave her a kiss on the cheek. Svetlana smiled at the unusual tingling sensation. The girl grasped her mother's hand and skipped along to the end of the bridge, threading through the tourists and slipping out of sight with not so much as a glance back.

A brief flicker of remorse and loneliness, involuntarily passed through the normally impervious facade of Svetlana's face. It ignited a spark within her. She liked it, the girl and it was like a craving that was difficult to understand.

The heavy tolling of the Duomo's bell snapped her back to reality. She thought of the history of this place, the shuffle of prisoners once led along this narrow passage of grey gloom between their cells and the

240

interrogation chambers. They had glanced through the cracks of daylight here and wished they were somewhere else. They had dreamed of the ultimate release to come, one which no walls or bars could hinder. Svetlana felt trapped at times, for all her power. She remembered the pain and remorse of those she had tortured and killed in a past time. Ziel roughly jerked the strings of Svetlana's equation and brought it back in line.

Svetlana's thoughts switched accordingly to the cracks of light flashed up by particle collisions in human accelerators, and of the wider cracks of light to open up at CERN once the Parallel Beam Collider came online.

The Bugz were thinking of their release too. Ziel would prize these cracks open even wider, with or without the help of the PBC team, now she understood better the lie of the land.

Unbeknown to her an insignificant connector node in Ziel's equation had flipped from negative to positive, a bit like red to green lights on old traffic lights. Powerful human emotions of procreation, motherhood and survival imprinted at some dawn of time began to trickle feed into the deep recesses of Ziel's immense coils.

49. ZARETH AND THE ZESSIAN TIME SHIFT

Zareth's time on earth up to CERN

Zareth's massive equation had been healing slowly during the billennia. His energy rings had been damaged and he required a graft of a new perfect equation to complete his rebirth.

Before entering that convergence, he had left a set of command protocols on his battle-scarred craft the Bugzilla, and afterwards drawn the rogue particles into the darkness. The Bugzilla was to guard the rim of the convergence and extract data from anything coming close, and was also to annihilate any mutant Bugz skirting by or tumbling into the convergence. If and when certain explicit conditions prevailed, the craft was to send a coded message requesting help from Zyber.

Zareth had then vanished, and had existed in a bubble of pure energy, unable to break free of the black void. The word salvation had been the rallying call of the white Bugz at the great Battle and Zareth felt sure that any survivors among these would recognise his signature provided on this communication. The deep ancient royal encryption would mean that only a select important few would understand its import and the identity of the sender.

Time had stopped in that convergence, as had all reference points for judging one's existence. Nothingness, a zero state, was all there had been; it had been no more and no less than the end point of being, the summation of all that had run its course, run together and run out.

242

Then, an incalculable age later, he had sensed the presence of his Bugz rescuers, only to feel the great wave of their zyclear energy surging past the bubble he had survived in.

This was closely followed by a similar second wave, whose power he chose to reinforce by managing at last to channel the energy he had left into a third great wave of his own making, one which burst through the back of the dark convergence with the others. Thus the three great waves of pure energy blasted out into a virgin vacuum.

Thrown into a new existence and new universe, the superparticle soon came to rest on the satellite of a small solar system, a satellite in the form of a blue planet. The whys and hows he had been unable to deduce, but this place had something very special about it. From the primordial ooze on its surface there emerged a host containing Bugz-like equations. Zareth was able to influence these primitives to construct a token pyramid not dissimilar to the Apex in Zytop. From within this structure he erected the communicator to continue sending the salvation signal in the hope that help from Zyberia would arrive.

As Zareth slowly healed, it was clear that within the equations found on this blue satellite there was something missing. It seemed that, in common with Bugz' desire to search for missing parts of a jigsaw within their equations, so human beings seemed to be seeking an answer to their existence. As a particle might spin one way, it might equally have a mirror that span the other way. Perhaps a particle could have a multiple spin, each spin balancing the other to form a complete whole. This was exactly the particle Zareth considered himself to be until he reached this new place. How could he heal such an equation as his in this new universe? Imagine if an equation such as his already existed amongst the equations found here. The union with such an equation could accelerate his healing, and perhaps alert his awareness to greater things? It was the thought of such a union that Zareth had been exploring in his consciousness at the time of the arrival of the Bugz he took to be his rescuers.

It was this thought that had stayed with him while he had rested within Brooke Ashcroft's equation these past few years. As he healed he felt the presence of other Bugz round about, although he could not and in a sense did not wish to communicate with them. The danger of removing the human host shielding his equation was that while his rescuers might detect his presence, so too would the particles who had destroyed other human hosts.

Brooke's had been the strongest host equation so far and now it had been prematurely snapped and tossed away. It seemed recent host equations Zareth chose to convalesce in were quickly annihilated. The linking to Brooke these past few years had confirmed to Zareth that near total reconstruction was possible. The fit was almost perfect, and this meant that the damage inflicted on him in the dark convergence could be fully repaired.

Zareth's idea of attracting his rescuers had certainly failed if the Bugz drawn here were determined to destroy his various human hosts at every opportunity. During the last five thousand Earth years, Zareth's healing ability had not extended to putting up a defence to prevent a host annihilation. However, the sensation on exiting Brooke's equation was predetermined and he had a plan of sorts that might deceive the killers. Zareth might still be weak but he was now fully alert. This was not as previous annihilations. Time was being manipulated and prevented from running its natural course. He could see twin paths of action suddenly opening up ahead of his host, one signifying death and the other life. He was at the same time aware of the brief delaying of time by an unseen hand and the deliberate selecting of one path over the other.

Zareth had not witnessed the like of this since the time of the trial of the black priest Zess and his deconstruction at the behest of the outraged Apex. That was when Zess had flouted the laws of symmetry, tampering with other dimensions and thereby ushering in such abnormalities as the rise of the mutant strains. Illegal experimentation with time shift, the weighing up of probabilities while suspending time and splitting it into alternative strands before allowing it to re-entwine and continue, had been a fact.

The object that ripped into Brooke's body and killed her had been one probability, while the dart that simply stunned her, a projectile coming from a gun which could be set on kill or stun at the mere flick of a finger, was another. The selection of one or other outcome, kill or stun, could be and had been suspended for a fixed period. Once one outcome were selected and realised, it would follow its clear and irrevocable path as though no time shift had happened in the first place. Time would cover over the rift, leaving little trace of the interference. Thus was the idea of 'outlawed time surgery' born.

During the split second that the attack on Brooke took place, it was clear to Zareth from within Brooke's equation that the consultant advising on this botch job was not a master of such arts. Her shooting was catapulting her into a state of neither death nor stun; it was leaving her suspended. And the only possible practitioner of such a Zessian experiment was, he believed, somebody with or familiar with rogue properties rather than a pure Bugzhist positive or negative charge.

Zareth had been aware of the presence of other Bugz here on Earth since the annihilation of his third human host, but he had not counted on mutated X, Y or even W particles. He could not accurately determine what his course of action would be, now he had powerful enemies tampering with his future. It surely meant that the distress signal he issued on his own arrival here had been intercepted by his enemies. But who were these particles and were they a mix of ally and foe? These answers were as yet unknown, and would remain so as long as Zareth stayed within the confines of a human host equation. He would need to exit regardless of his host's circumstances in order to find out these answers, and now, he knew, was as good a time as any.

If the assailant or assailants were fully anticipating his exiting of the equation, they must assume that exiting was inevitable even if the host were not annihilated but left only in a suspended state. They would not therefore know what Zareth knew, that he did not need to exit, but he still would. He would turn to his advantage their novice experience in the practice of time shift. As the projectile impacted, splitting time into two strands of probability, his lightning reaction was to decouple voluntarily, giving the impression that he had done so automatically. He braced himself and passed through a false zecho of his own engineering. The experience inevitably proved bruising, but it was nowhere near the scale of discomfort of what would have been the real thing.

In this way Zareth passed out of Brooke's radiance and away from the crumpled frame of Icarus Ashcroft leaning over her body in the amphitheatre, his head in his hands, unresponsive to the comforting arms round his shoulders and the kind words in his ears. Zareth entered outlying shadows whose veil enabled him to restabilise and take stock of the situation, and he picked up straight away the powerful signatures of other Bugz. It was the first time since his strength had seeped back through his rings that he could view the configuration of his would-be rescuers/annihilators.

Their equations were apparently post-Zytopian: less advanced, dulled and ambivalent, still relatively rigid and blinkered despite long-term exposure to the soft and challenging vistas of their surroundings. Two of the Bugz, however, seemed more responsive than the others. One of them was linked to a journalist in the press stand, while the other was linked to a business mogul in the field of mass communications. A third Bugz had an equation equally powerful but exceptionally narrow, tainted as it clearly was by over-dependence on human contact, a certain type of human contact, and therefore irreversibly corrupt. There was a fourth presence too, so Zareth noticed. This was not strictly a Bugz, however, nor was it even a mutant Bugz. It had another quality, one whose clean rawness and striped coils stirred his depths for it seemed faintly familiar, yet this rawness appeared almost as dark as the abyss from which Zareth had emerged so long ago.

Zareth chose not to attempt opening a channel. He simply absorbed the details of their familiar and near-identical properties, and juxtaposed those with the unfolding of events around him. He needed to act whether he could communicate or not. The splitting of time like a burning fuse to serve some particular purpose was ominous. Such a dark art could mean only disharmony and destruction. Despite his fuzzy understanding of his circumstances and a certain sense of alienation, Zareth was increasingly aware that he felt part of this world, and that it felt part of him. There was surely a purpose to his awakening and to this connectivity, and the purpose was surely not the snapping shut of his own equation in the wake of Brooke's. He was, in any event, on his own search for salvation, which seemed intrinsically entwined with the life forms he had found in this new world. There was a familiarity, almost a necessity to seek a linking of equations and each time he chose a new host, his healing increased and the fit got better.

The elusive Zo constant, which existed in all Bugz equations was almost reduced to near zero.

50. STEIN FOLLOWS HIS INSTINCT

16 June

After the events at CERN and a hastily convened meeting with Blipp, it was clear to the superparticle now lodged in Stein that events were coming to a conclusion. The various strands set those years back were being cut or woven in a new pattern and were changing the probabilities of success for the white Bugz strategy.

Ziel had targeted the Ashcrofts, and it seemed logical to move back to Cambridge, which had become, in effect, the earthly base for the white Bugz.

Zein had never experienced anything like this linkage and even though Zim often spoke of the connectivity with Archimedes Zein could now see how difficult it must be to leave the human host equation.

Blipp had asked Stein what they should do regarding the situation that had occurred at CERN. The roles, it appeared, were now reversed. Blipp was actually asking advice of Stein and taking direction regarding the need to meet back at CERN once the assistants had been gathered. How did they think the security had been breached and how had Svetlana been able to launch the pre-emptive attack at CERN? What had happened to the presumed Zareth particle and had Zein noticed there was some 'time slip' at the event?

Stein had digi-com'd his editor, who was clamouring for the story of what had happened at CERN. It hadn't taken much persuasion to get a few days off to see if there was another interesting angle to be pursued at Cambridge in England.

Boarding the flight at Geneva airport on the 16th June, Stein was aware of the intricate workings of the aeroplane and how inefficient it was, burning a mix of bio fuel and the heat it wasted. The more that Zein integrated with his equation, the more the world around him came more into focus. He could see the latticework structure of the chemical assemblages and the forces that held them together. The domain he controlled could command a hierarchy of particles as intricate as any human society.

On arriving in Cambridge, Jonathon Stein had IDO'd Mr and Mrs Nimmo. Having briefly met the couple it was clear that Ashcroft senior was distraught. The other assistants who had great potential were also showing erratic and illogical behaviour.

In either case, Ziel had visited the funeral and played the masquerade in the guise of Svetlana while being viewed at a distance by the Nimmos. It took a great deal of restraint on the part of Patrick Nimmo to stop Mrs Nimmo from tearing into the Russian scientist. At the meeting with the Nimmos, an amended plan was quickly convened which required talking with the Ashcrofts and enlisting their assistance.

'Now is the time Patrick, we will need to convince the younger Ashcrofts quickly that we are trying to help them, but I could equally see they may think we are the cause of their woes. How did the Z go down the other day with Sam Ashcroft?' remarked Stein.

'I think he knows something happened and it has sown a seed in his mind that something unusual happened', Patrick replied.

'And what of Brooke's funeral?'

'A sad occasion I have to say, and one that makes us even more confused about our identity. You will find it equally difficult, Jonathon, I am sure.'

'Yes, I know because I was at the shootings in CERN and saw the effects first hand, it was let me say disturbing and confusing to see it from two perspectives. So, as far as you know the professor will return to CERN and what of the other assistants?'

'Two are on the Cam burying their sorrows and Elsie is at home talking with some of the relatives who attended the funeral,' volunteered Joan Nimmo.

'You both know that Brooke is probably not dead because we have not picked up the signature zecho of her annihilation, all we have is interference in a 2 minute 23 second time slot after the shots were being fired. We need to gain the confidence of the Ashcrofts and maybe illustrate how this dead and 'not dead' might work,' said Stein.

'It would be wonderful news if Brooke is not annihilated.'

'Are we sure, Stein?'

'I am told by the Zargo that her signature equation lives on but she is held captive not far from CERN, this is why we need to convince the younger Ashcroft's to join with us.'

Patrick reinforced his view. 'Well let us start now, because Elsie is very sceptical and the only way to get her along is to convince Sam and Lycian.'

'For sure and in the meantime I will put another part of the plan together for when we get them to meet in Cambridge. It will have to involve somebody that Elsie likes or she will think it is a hoax. I will somehow get this Christian to meet us in central Cambridge. He can be the sacrifice and us the saviour, and until we meet more formally it is good to see that you are joined on the earth's surface, Patrick and Joan.'

At which point the Nimmos headed towards the river Cam in the hope of making contact with the Ashcroft brothers and left Stein to make sure that the time slip demonstration could be put in place.

Stein had lots of probabilities to look at for it was a certainty that Svetlana was moving on her own path. The Bugz may view this as some form of binary game but the human part of Stein's equation still tugged on Zein and he could see that Earth could not be destroyed simply at the whim of his mirror.

51. MORNING COFFEE AT SVETLANA'S 17 June 2042

Svetlana had a second ghastly night, as bad as her first night back home in her Palladian villa since returning from Geneva. She couldn't understand what was happening to her. She woke in a sweat as though someone had shoved a thousand volts through her body, and had difficulty stemming the nosebleed that erupted as a result. She'd been getting these nosebleeds quite frequently, along with increased headaches from using electronic equipment and endless buzzing noises. And the nightmares of late, all to do with being swallowed up by some vast black hole, were making her doubt her sanity. She might just need a medical check up when she had more time.

She got herself a strong coffee and a Zapper, and heard her IDO bleeping. It showed a cryptic message, something about the lion calling by at eight to close in on the kill. The symbol in the bottom right corner was instantly recognisable: the glowering lion's head betwixt three legs.

Svetlana growled her response at the IDO. The display showed 07:50 am, barely enough time to stagger in and out of the shower, scrape back her long blonde hair and climb into a silk trousered kimono affair she'd discarded over the back of a chair.

The bell jangled, and the virtual image on the room's viewer of the gateway and front entrance to her Treviso villa flashed up Papa's antique convertible, driven by a tanned and attractive deck chair attendant lookalike. Papa's tanned, whiskered face and slick white locks hove into view.

'Ciao, Papa, come in,' Svetlana called.

The gates slid open.

Svetlana lurched down her marble staircase, tying her silk belt and pinching her cheeks to get some colour in them. She stumbled to her knees halfway down as she felt an unexpected and warm surge of elation. It tingled every erotic zone on her body and made her momentarily faint. God, she could feel so awful and she could feel so good at the same time. She arched her feline body, rose unsteadily to her feet, took a deep breath and drilled in military fashion on her ten-centimetre Cuban stilettos down the stairs. Ziel was back and she meant business.

'Sveti!' Papa called from the entrance hall as the maid opened the door with a curtsy and he pushed past with outspread arms. If the sight from his own stunted height of the long lithe figure of Svetlana, towering on high heels and still several steps above him, was unnerving, he was too much the master of smoothness and self control to let it show.

'I had such a quiet evening last night, you know. I was lonely, just me and the cat. And I'd been so looking forward to some company.'

'I left you a message,' Svetlana said. 'I needed an early night. You'd rather have me bright-eyed and prepared for our important business, no?'

Papa could see that the woman looked fantastic. She glowed with energy. The young man could see it too. Papa prodded him forward while keeping his eyes on Svetlana.

'Fabricio, this is Svetlana. Svetlana, this is my great nephew Fabricio. My latest trainee, you could say. He wants to know everything about everything because, I assure you, right now he knows absolutely nothing.'

'And I want to know everything,' Fabricio breathed with glazed eyes.

Svetlana smiled, showed the two men into what she called her salon where she held court, and tinkled the bell for refreshments. 'Where are your son and grandson?' she asked. 'You look almost naked and vulnerable without them, Papa.'

Papa flushed. 'Out on recruiting business. They were free last night, you understand, when you were expected, but they had other appointments to keep this morning. May I ask where our good friend Marco is?'

Svetlana snorted. 'He did the job, that is the main thing. But I must tell you that it, ah, drained the life out of him, poor guy. So he had a very early night, wherever he went, and he will keep his mouth shut, that I promise.'

Papa pulled out his diary. 'As long as there are no loose ends, when will you be coming round, Sveti? We'll just deal with the preliminaries for now, but we need to fine tune time, place and logistics with all present.'

'Tonight then. Here we are Papa, grappa, pastries. Let's cut to the chase and discuss funding first and foremost. As you know, I don't need to consult anyone else on such matters. I write my own cheques.'

'This funding,' Papa sighed, and scratched his stomach slowly. 'I suppose I shouldn't look a gift horse in the mouth. However, a man like myself who puts a price on every little thing gets rather nervous not knowing where all this money is coming from. It does not grow on trees. Yet somehow I'm almost tempted to believe you have a bottomless purse. Ha! So crazy, I know. Now, my dear, I know you don't want to disclose confidences, but if you could just give me some clue as to…'

Svetlana smiled demurely as she knocked back the grappa. 'As I said, let's discuss the funding, not how the funding is sourced. You disappoint me, Papa. And after totting up all the figures I wouldn't mind a bit of rest and relaxation. Care to join me, Fabricio? Or are you off on a spot more training with Great Uncle Giuseppe today?'

'Fabricio does have a lot to learn from you, my dear,' Papa answered without glancing at his great nephew, whose sudden coughing fit showered pastry flakes on his lap.

'He certainly has, Papa,' she said. 'You know it can't be all work and no play.'

What sort of an address was Villa Nero Zero? Wai Chan grunted in surprise at the fact file on his IDO, and stepped into the back of a police speed boat which drove him along the Brenta Canal in that direction. Ten kilometres away, Svetlana walked down the front steps of the Villa Nero Zero with her two bodyguards and sped off in her Riva Super Aquarama, also along the Brenta Canal but towards Venice, past other great Palladian villas and neat gardens towards the urban squalor of Venice. She had her g-tunes system on full blast and the wind in her hair, and she felt good. It was a perfect summer's evening. She slowed at the approach to the palatial gates that fronted the Casa Trinacria del Leone di Venezia and looked up at its gaudy red and gold symbol above the archway. The three-legged lion of Venice. Many had heard of Papa but few had the privilege of direct acquaintance with him – that is to say, had knowingly seen him.

She placed her lips near the electronic panel by the gate and murmured her arrival. Its voice-recognition software picked up the unique properties of her voice and flashed the details to some flunky.

'Code?' he asked.

'Fab,' she breathed. The gates opened. And Sveti reminisced, the boy had been fab, just as Papa had thought. Shame there couldn't be a repeat experience with him.

Papa Giuseppe Flammia Cassaro grew up in the dusty streets of Catania in the 1980s. Now in his seventies, he was the patriarch of a

Sicilian family empire that had expanded to encompass the Veneto in the past thirty years. He did his fair share of dirty work since the age of eight, and he knew how to keep his head down while doing it. He grew up at a time when the Italian government was cracking down on the old ways and competition in the world of drug-peddling and racketeering was fiercer than ever. He was at the forefront of calls to see in a new society. A gloss of straight companies and society connections in the media and local government ensured that Papa was perceived more like Father Christmas than the run-of-the mill businessman he modestly described himself as when evading the spotlight.

Papa was proud of his chosen coat of arms. He'd once had long hair and the fortitude of a lion and he had a prodigious member reputed to be as sizeable as a third limb. Three legs made up for height. He blamed his parents for his 1.55 metres, who else could he blame? But he still venerated their grave back home, a mere two-minute stroll from the runway for his jet when he could drop by. His parents were not able to play God when they gave him life and form, but he could. What his parents could not bring about in the way of grandeur he provided instead, hence the optical illusion built into the design of his office, hence the specially designed furniture and raised cushioned seats in his Bugatti, hence the carefully orchestrated photographs in which he appeared larger than life.

Sveti was this very minute walking into his office and noticed the odd perspective, it somehow annoyed her Bugz vision of existence. She could walk all over him, but she wouldn't. He would keep his men as close to her as they would like to be, to make sure his retirement package saw the light of day. And his retirement package had just got a fair bit fatter. Word had reached him that the Swiss police were offering an unprecedented ten million euros reward for information leading to the capture of the perpetrators of the CERN shootings. He needed to match that sum to keep some people's mouths shut, as he had said to Svetlana that very morning. She said she would effect an immediate transfer, and the money came into his account just after lunch.

A small fortune would be needed for the takeover this woman was planning. It seemed a harebrained scheme, what little he knew of it. She called it 'creative' and 'liberating', and it involved a giant machine, the

255

brainchild of a mad professor. Papa knew nothing about subatomic particles. Nor could he understand the whys and wherefores of targeting the professor's wife in the full glare of publicity, and then, in the wake of heightened security there, staging an even more ambitious event. It wasn't even as if they'd be able to just blast their way into the place; apparently it had to be a covert operation of some sort lasting at least three or four hours. Papa could think of no rational explanation for Svetlana's thinking, neither political, economic, social nor religious. Whatever it was, it most probably involved Russian agents seeking to cause trouble and using ecoterrorists as the fall guys.

Still, money talked. The advent of competition from the Russians, East Europeans and Chinese meant that the family business was in need of a serious cash injection. Svetlana Grigoriya played Fairy Godmother herself when she walked into his life last January with a pay cheque for thirty million euros, and that was just for the ecoterrorist incident. A further hundred million would be winging its way to him with the takeover of the PBC machine. There was only a low risk of things going awry; the woman was clearly bedded in with the Director General, so she was in every sense on top of things.

Life was good. Papa's son and grandson would be taking over the business the minute the deal was done, and he could spend his days pressing olives and sitting on a bench in the sun with the other old boys or, if boredom set in, making the odd little weekend trip to the Alps or his latest investment in Greenland.

'No sign of Marco, Svetlana?'

'Staying low, Papa.'

Where was Fabricio?

'Oh, gave him the day off,' Svetlana smiled. 'You don't miss him that much, surely? I would not want him sitting in on this anyway, how could I trust such a young puppy? By the way, can I introduce you to Enrico and Vittorio, I have found the need to have some of my own security in these troubled times.'

'I know, Svetlana, and I am glad you took my advice. I know the families and they are good boys'.

'I hope so Papa'.

Svetlana's IDO bleeped. She answered and smiled. 'My maid, Lucia,'

256

she mouthed at Papa, listened for a few moments before switching the IDO off so as not to be disturbed. 'Just as well I have my bag packed and in the back of the boat,' she said. 'I had a feeling a certain visitor might be calling by. Be prepared to be the next in his little digi-address book, dear Papa.'

Papa didn't bat an eyelid. Roving detectives and missing hit men could wait. He wanted the deal thrashed out without delay and with a hefty advance paid up.

It was agreed. The date of the takeover was to be 21 June 2042, just eight days after the initial outrage, an auspicious day in the calendar for the entire world. Midsummer, when the power drain on the grids of France and Germany were at a minimum and enough electricity would therefore be available for sucking into one massive surge. And if every terawatt of that were not enough, Svetlana would flick on her IDO and squeeze some extra capacity from her friends in Russia, no problem. This would be the mother of all switch ons.

It would have to be at night time too, of course, with as few people around as possible. The venue was the enormous void housing the Ashcroft detector on the Parallel Beam Collider site at CERN, and there'd be no problem with access. The Director General would make sure they had the requisite passes, well, he wouldn't know the full story, but he'd know that some important experiment on a rather more modest scale was needed and as some compensation to Ashcroft the family could be present in memory of Brooke.

Papa was anxious to know about his boys' exit. Would there be some sort of explosion, for instance? Which was the safest way out? Svetlana assured him no one would know a thing, no one. Papa didn't like vague reassurances. He glowered and thought about how much the bitch would have to lose if things didn't go to plan. The woman was an easy target. Even if she scrunched her hair in a hairnet and dressed in a bin liner and old flip flops she would stick out a mile in some busy street. No problem for training the barrel of a gun on that cold heart of hers. Svetlana was getting a reputation for people disappearing round her. While Svetlana was discussing the mountain retreat in the Alps where the final planning would be made, Papa was reviewing the latest court case involving one of his associates. It seemed fairly mundane now that this Russian she-wolf was on the scene.

257

53. THE PERFECT MATCH
17 June 2042

As Zareth detached from the equation of Brooke in the amphitheatre at CERN his survival mechanisms had clicked in and recalculated its locking code in the search for a matching human equation. Until now it had taken hundreds of years of scanning the ever-changing equations on the surface before locking on to one successfully, but Zareth was on this occasion powerfully charged and not damaged from an untimely death of his human host. He needed not only refuge to complete his healing; he realised from the moment of his awakening that he would need the perfect fit to regenerate fully. Zareth hoped the charge he had dropped would replicate a zecho from the annihilation of a superparticle and maybe confuse his host's attackers.

The locking code identified itself unexpectedly quickly, only a few days after the exiting of Brooke. The download of vast quantities of data offered a deep draught of energy that his mental units would need to distil later.

Surging at near light speed, the powerful Zareth particle homed in on his new host where he sat a little dejected at his workstation in his room at Haslingdene vicarage.

Lycian sat hunched and exhausted in a household made even more gloomy by his father's early morning departure for CERN. His human equation was dimmed with grief, and yet it appeared to be not only as unblemished as that of his mother but also aglow with pearlescence. Zareth knew the location extremely well and was surprised to find that the relation of Brooke had such a strong reciprocal signal. Why this had not been apparent before was a mystery.

The fusion of Zareth with Lycian was extraordinary in that there was no sparking of discord, the fit was perfect as a whole object being created without refraction. Lycian was like his mother only even more special, a fragile vessel containing a perfect, diamond-hard, scintillating equation that astounded him. It was like nothing else he had seen in Zyberia or this place, it was a perfect match for his own equation as if it had been created in the same mould. The linking resembled a godly transfusion of healing energy for both, and Zareth felt more alert than ever before. The details of his past were becoming clearer as the mist started to clear.

Lycian was not immediately conscious of the presence within him, nor the surge of energy it brought with it. He experienced only the murk of blindness ahead and complete incomprehension at the passing of the lifelong protector and nurse that had been his mother. Her death had been a senseless act by a group he had some sympathy for.

Zareth was stirred to his very depths. He found he could understand the boy's process of mourning, this most human and most unBugzish of emotions. The attack on Brooke did indeed seem an illogical act. An illogical act to the human mind, that is, but one that was certainly logical in the analytical units of the perpetrator. Zareth knew also that Brooke was not dead and he wanted to infuse his host with some optimism. Analysing the data from CERN he was picking up the white and black signatures as well as another equally powerful presence. He sensed much more now and saw that the Nimmos were also powerful particles and there was also the craft from his home.

Turning his thoughts back to his new host, he could also sympathise with Lycian's battle against a constantly malfunctioning system, the result of damage to internal pathways for sending signals. Even this ailment seemed to replicate Zareth's own damage he had sustained as he drew the rogue leaders into the dark convergence. There was some strange parallel in this young human he had not detected before and maybe his equation had only become active recently. Could it be the outpouring of grief that had triggered the change or could it be the link to his mother which they both felt ?

Lycian had been diagnosed at a relatively early age with multiple sclerosis. He had already had two years of relapse and remission, with the bouts of remission becoming ever shorter and the relapses ever worse. He had received all the latest treatment: scans, implants, testing and a range of drugs. Brooke was always there, at his bedside, in the consultant's room, cheering him on during his periods of remission and not dwelling on the doom and gloom of it all. And she had had a curious little habit. The medicines in Lycian's bathroom cupboard were stored in old-fashioned brown glass bottles. She wrote on the labels 'Drink Me' or 'Eat Me', as though willing these to contain magic potions. His eyes fell on one of these bottles on his desk as he wondered. He felt he could look inside the very structure of the tablets and knew they were primitive and would not help him greatly. Almost involuntarily he dropped it from his hand on the floor. This was not magic.

He replayed in his mind the appalling events at CERN. Yes, he did understand the grievances of the environmental lobby, even those held by the more extreme elements within it, and who didn't know the world was turning into a hostile place? The UN and its individual member governments had met force with force during the Bloody Green Revolution, and that force had not been like for like; it had been the horrifying spectre of global autocracy against individual liberty wherever lawlessness had not already taken hold. However, the murder of innocent bystanders in the cause of helping the future environment didn't add up. For some reason he didn't feel sad any more, there was some hope for the future, his and his mother's, he couldn't shake this new found optimism.

When a short time later Mrs Nimmo was stooping and quietly sweeping up the fragments of brown glass with a dustpan and brush, she paused to raise a hand and place it on the boy's shoulder.

'We are all more sorry than you would ever imagine.'

'Sorry about the glass Mrs N.'

'It's nothing.'

Later that same day Lycian stood in his bathroom fingering one of the other brown bottles in wonder. He was beginning to feel quite strange, very different, and stronger. He didn't need the tablets anymore and the grief passed like some storm.

In the same way that Lycian was becoming aware of the change within him, Zareth was becoming aware of Bugz within close proximity to him, within the energy ring of Cambridge, within the garden wall of the vicarage itself. They seemed to be standing sentinel, defending what? Keeping something within? Their presence provided strength. He wondered about the Bugz further afield at CERN. Once they became aware he had a new host they would surely come after him again. If they did come, he hoped his healing, which was progressing now at an accelerated rate, would help him defend Lycian. An anger seemed to swell in the particle sending out a strong unique signal of defiance.

261

54. DOUBLE JEOPARDY
Same day

Stein watched the Ashcroft children travel into central Cambridge. It was nearing the time for their three o'clock assignation outside Peterhouse college. He saw Sam's loping figure, striding ahead with ease, head slightly down, dark hair flopping over his eyes. There was Elsie, walking abreast with Lycian, more hesitant, looking at him as though wishing to say something.

'Come on, Elsie,' Lycian said, aware of her gaze. 'Isn't this – whatever it is – just the most incredible thing that's going to happen in your life? Apart from – you know, Dad's discovery.'

'Look, Mum's just died, and now this. I don't want to be some 'assistant' in something I don't understand. And I swear to God if this is some prank I'm going to–' Elsie broke off, and quickened her pace. 'Lyce, I swear you're walking quicker! Normally I can easily keep up with you!'

'Must be the adrenaline.' But Lycian knew otherwise, although he simply couldn't explain it.

Zein was ensconced in the journalist but had every sensor trained on Lycian. The boy was living proof that the shining equation of the nascent superparticle had feigned his annihilation and returned, alert yet silent. It had escaped the trick of time shift at CERN and had rapidly and unerringly moved to a new host, although still making no direct contact. Of all the billions of human beings on this planet it had almost miraculously chosen Lycian, the descendant of the family of assistants conceived thousands of years before by him. The Zareth particle was operating entirely out of his control, yet in the mathematical thinking of Bugz it was inconceivable that these paths had not meant to cross. Zein felt as though he were coming under the spell of what man called 'fate'. Either that or he was, as the Bugz' hosts might put it, losing it. And either way the situation was unBugzish, and was tying his logic in knots.

The pavement outside Peterhouse was heaving with afternoon shoppers, a hubbub of tourists, students and locals.

'Wherever, whatever, they are, they're late,' said Sam. 'It's bang on three… now.'

One of a string of cyclists was threading its way past them along the gutter, squeezed between the kerb and a passing bio delivery van. The cyclist's front wheel wobbled as the scanner mirror on the side of the vehicle glanced off his right arm, causing him to swerve into the path of the following vehicle and tumble over its front with a sickening crunch before landing on the road. In the next second the cyclist lay deathly still like a life-sized rag doll, blood oozing from his head.

Before the three Ashcrofts or any other person could even gasp in response, there was a slight flickering of air, a low rushing of sound, and then pitch black followed by broad afternoon daylight.

'Wherever, whatever, they are, they're late,' said Sam. 'It's bang on three now.'

'Did I – did you – just say that?'

One of a string of cyclists was threading its way past them along the gutter, and Sam recognised him. 'Hi, Christian!'

Drawing to a halt near the kerb, Sam's friend looked round and was caught a glancing blow by a passing white biovan.

'Bloody lunatic!' Christian shouted. 'Anyway, what brings you here? By the way, what can I say guys, it's more than shocking.'

'It's a difficult time for all of us,' Sam said hastily. 'We're here because we're supposed to be meeting someone, well, maybe more than one, we don't actually know.'

'OK, well, I hope you find them in these crowds, hope to see you soon Elsie', Christian said, remounting his bike. 'Anyway, your Dad's asked for some of us to join him urgently in Geneva and I'm going to pack. Under the circumstances we haven't any choice but I wish it was in happier times… and I'm just so sorry. See you later, guys.'

Elsie and Lycian touched Sam's arm in agitation. 'What happened there? Did you just see that cyclist getting hit by the Bio and then lying dead in the road? What happened?'

'It was Christian. But he wasn't –'

And what's this about the boffs going to help dad?'

'I'm going to have to g-text Christian and find out what's happening'

Sam's IDO chimed out its melodious tone and the display glowed.

'What has just been demonstrated is what we call "time shift". Imagine if the first outcome had been allowed. Imagine if it had been someone close to you. Imagine being offered both that outcome and the second one at once. Imagine if this has already happened once before?'

Svetlana's lilac polka-dot shoe barely touched the brake as she swept through the gate with a fluttery wave and a hot kiss blown at the guard. Always a fail-safe ploy to distract him from checking the scanner under his nose. The magnetic strip on her windscreen sticker was valid, of course, but it amused her to have proof she could gain entry without it. Her Lamborghini sped up the narrow road and yanked over at a sharp angle in the no parking zone.

No matter how workaday her surroundings, her entrance always put a gloss on things, something the DG could not deny although he winced at her excesses.

The car door slid open and Svetlana uncoiled her endlessly long legs, pulled out her Dolce & Gabbana bag after her, jammed her skin-tight mauve body tube down over her buttocks and tossed a light jacket over her shoulder. She removed her shades as she stalked through the doors, dropping her keys into the hand of a conveniently placed functionary deep in conversation with the receptionist.

Always so disappointing, the utter plainness of the place, especially after the flamboyance of Venice. Svetlana had mentioned this during her long pillow talks with Henri on those occasions when his wife scuttled home for the latest grandchild's christening or dutiful visits to her mother's nursing home.

Her senior post on the PBC project was a direct result of him taking on her hefty CV as his bedside reading for a couple of nights. He liked what he saw. She was not the Russian bimbo many others took her for

265

with her jaunty gait. He knew she could push energy frontiers with the best of them, and not just in the pleasurable sense.

She wasn't planning on being here long, not with the pug-faced inspector on the warpath. But making contact with Ashcroft was paramount, and she knew just where to find him. He'd made a beeline back here as soon as the funeral was over and would be in the most receptive frame of mind.

Svetlana paused outside his door and rested her thigh against it to compose herself as she knocked gently. The offer she was about to make simply had to work. She had to use whatever means were at her disposal to get the man's cooperation, and a strange flush came over her, not unlike the one she had experienced walking down the staircase in her villa.

Ziel, despite her two and a half millennia of skinny dipping in human equations and abandoning herself to the exhilaration it brought, suddenly felt a strong urge to uncoil her energy rings and exercise her own immense power. This was one occasion when it was in fact frustrating having to confine herself within the parameters of Svetlana's body, impressive in an earth sense though it may be.

Yet Ziel knew, as did Zein and the other Bugz at last, that this linkage was essential were they to have any chance of returning to their own universe. The time the Bugz had spent equation dipping or at least observing this species at close hand had proved that, no matter how much raw energy abounded in this universe and no matter how much of it was expended, there was still scarcely a glimmer of hope of return.

There was only one way out of here, and it was by driving their human hosts. The time was now, on this clump of carbon and hydrogen called Earth, at a location known as CERN, with the calendar coordinates 21 June AD2042.

Ziel clicked around the inside of the synoptic paths that made up Svetlana's brains. It was almost impossible to route these paths in exactly the direction you wanted. In fact it seemed best to let well alone and just pinpoint in the manner of keyhole surgery the areas where influence was most needed. A sensitive approach was most needed now because the killing of Ashcroft's wife had rested on a single premise: to have him turn to them in grief to serve Ziel's interests, even at the expense of his life's work if need be, in order to recover his precious mate.

The door opened quietly, and Svetlana stared into a long thin face lined with grief and exhaustion. Ashcroft looked ten years older.

'Nice to see you, Sveti. To what do I owe the pleasure? I'm trying to get back in the swing of things but you understand I just need a little time.'

'The PBC is the last thing on my mind right now, Icarus. I'm simply concerned for you, and I am here as a colleague and as a friend.'

'Thanks, I'm OK, I mean, I'm OK because everything's pretty unreal.' Ashcroft sighed. 'I just put one foot forward and then the next. That's when I actually remember to put one forward and then the next. My brain cuts out at times.'

'Actually, so does mine,' Svetlana said. 'I sometimes wonder if I'm allergic to electronic equipment, I get such headaches. Not a big problem, of course, I don't want you thinking I'm not up to the job.'

'That could never be said of you, Sveti! Here, sit down, excuse the mess. You know, being without Brooke is like losing half my body. I don't know how I'm going to function in the future.' Ashcroft ran his fingers through his thinning hair. 'Anyway, how is Henri? Professionally, I mean. Sorry, that was uncalled for; I don't mean to pry into your own affairs.'

Svetlana laughed easily, crossed her legs and smoothed the body tube as low over them as she could. 'You don't need to apologise. Everybody knows even if nobody says out loud. I like frankness far better than nudges and winks. Anyway, you know Henri; he questions whether he shouldn't have stopped the protesters from the outset. But you know he is reasonable and always tries to see other people's points of view. He wanted a chance to refute them in public too.'

'Instead of scheduling an impromptu speech from uninvited speakers, I just wish he'd heard my speech and my point of view,' Ashcroft said bitterly.

'Your impromptu speech, you mean,' Svetlana said, but with a smile of sympathy. 'We all know you had something important to say, but it wasn't what we expected you to say, and Henri's quite a sensitive soul and he's a little bit hurt you didn't confide in him.

'I know, I know. He didn't mention it in the card he sent with his condolences, not the time and place of course, but I know he got quite a surprise, and he also feels he's partly responsible. He wishes he could turn back the clock.'

'Don't we all? But don't worry about dear Henri; he will get through this. We all benefit from his undoubted wisdom in such matters because, as you well know, he gets all the funding he wants, and he let's us get on with the job without endless bureaucracy and interference.'

'Has he sent you to keep an eye on me, Sveti?' Ashcroft asked suddenly.

'Not at all; he sends his best wishes and sympathy.'

'More like a loud silence of disapproval, I would think. I am a loose cannon, as you know. And now my mind's off the job anyway.'

'I know you are still grieving, Icarus. It's only natural, given what happened.'

Ashcroft changed the subject. 'Anyway, I have some news on the terrorists. It seems a man escaped down the old disused ALICE tunnel and the police are trying to tie up the images with those from the amphitheatre. The digi-viewers were for the most part disabled but somewhere along the line they picked up an image of a Patek Philippe watch on a wrist. They're trying to get a reading from the mass of finger-prints and check it with the international DNA pool.

'The joys of modern technology,' Svetlana said. 'Just think, if you can get a fingerprint match off a smudgy image, how much more amazing would it be if you could reconstruct a finger?'

'I'm sorry?'

'I'm talking reconstruction of bits of time to change events here, Icarus. That's what I wanted to see you about, actually. You may think you have an exciting piece of research up your sleeve but I tell you I believe I can go one better.

Now sit comfortably, because what I am going to tell you is going to be a pleasant surprise. It's going to shock you very much but it's a wonderful surprise too, like heaven must be.' Svetlana brushed some imaginary fluff off her lap in a business-like fashion, looked straight into the bleak grey eyes opposite her, and continued. 'You know you said about turning back the clock of time? What if I said I had way of accomplishing this and bringing back your beloved Brooke?'

Ashcroft sat frozen, still not comprehending. 'I'm not up to mind games, Svetlana, and I would say that this is black humour at its worst and hardly appropriate. In fact it's perhaps best you go, because I have had enough to cope with these past few days. Thanks for the sympathy and support. Let's leave it at that.'

'Look at me, Professor, don't glare, look into my eyes and hold my hand. It is warm and my perfume is sweet, is it not? And now, imagine I am Brooke. You miss her so very much.'

'This is truly offensive.' Ashcroft lunged past her to open the door.

'Well then,' Svetlana persevered, 'imagine instead that I run your project exactly as you like, no ifs or buts, that I guarantee all funding you need, and that I have a pleasant little chat with Henri about you and your future. And, more importantly, imagine you have Brooke back.'

'What are you, some bloody lunatic?' Ashcroft exploded. 'What the hell are you saying? That Brooke can be brought back in some Frankenstein-like experiment?'

'It's not quite the fiction drama you imagine, Professor,' Svetlana flashed back. 'What's more, I can guarantee it will happen quickly. Brooke will be returned, shall we say, perfect, unblemished.'

Ziel buzzed in the darkest chambers of Svetlana's body and observed with interest Ashcroft's reaction. He spread out his hands in mock appeal.

'And how is this achieved?'

'I have my connections. I don't divulge confidential information. You understand that.'

'No, I don't. If you're saying this is scientific fact as opposed to ludicrous fantasy I expect some sort of explanation.' Ashcroft gave an hysterical laugh.

Svetlana flushed in momentary confusion and made a pretence of examining her painted fingernails. She did wonder herself how it was done. The information fed to her had come out of the blue; it had been fascinating, fantastical, and yet it made sense. She had at no stage really questioned its validity. It was as though her understanding and acceptance of it had been implanted, not logically grasped. She could not properly account for it.

She composed herself and briefly outlined the technical points she recalled, while Ashcroft returned to his seat again as he tried to absorb her words.

Thank God he knew next to nothing about the biosciences, she thought. She could dazzle him with the terminology but was no more qualified than he to give a lecture on the subject. She must, however, get

269

this right. Ashcroft had his dreams of grandeur and barrier breaking in the field of particle physics, but so had she. And CERN was a honeypot of sweet, sweet funding. A little pillow talk worked wonders, and Henri was being especially communicative these days. Furthermore, now that Ashcroft was out of favour, Henri was even more receptive to any suggestions she might make.

Ziel felt her old confident self. Who would ever have guessed that the accidental results of a Zessian time experiment conducted in a sunless refuge in Old Zytopia, results then stored like black magic seeds in the mental units of a few mutant particles would germinate and prove a successful and earth-shattering ploy in another universe?

'So what do you want from me?' Ashcroft asked with a shaking voice.

'One little thing,' she smiled.

'Which is?'

'That we carry out some little experiments which push the PBC to the limit.' She handed him a black nano file with a golden zigzag border. 'I have an outline of them here. All you have to do is supply certain modifications.'

Ashcroft pulled out a wad of A4 paper printed in a curious, mock-cuneiform font. 'Modifications for what purpose?' he asked.

'To drive home as soon as possible some very, very small but essential points. You see, like you, I am doing some research of my own. This machine is important to us both. I think we both know it represents life itself. It is cutting edge material,' Svetlana added as Ashcroft reluctantly opened the file. 'You and I will work side by side, and your reputation will be salvaged, you will have your wife back, and everything will be right, Icarus.'

'You won't see me again, I guarantee,' reassured Sveti.

Ashcroft's eyes were glazed. 'I can't give an answer to all this just like that.'

'Brooke…'

'What do you mean? Where? Has her grave been desecrated?' Ashcroft cried. 'I don't believe any of this. Just go, get out!'

'Calm down: her grave looks no different. Ivy will be climbing on the headstone as we speak. Even so, we are talking about bringing your beloved wife back. Now do we have an agreement?'

Ashcroft made for the door, ready to bundle her out. 'What's to stop

270

me right now ringing the guy in charge of the police investigation? I'm sitting here talking to my wife's murderer, for God's sake! And being subjected to harassment, subversion, blackmail; his ears must be burning already!'

Svetlana pursed her lips, uncrossed her legs, and tapped a polka-dotted toe with steely impatience. 'Feel free to do what is best, Professor, but I am offering you the chance to get Brooke back perfect and just as before. I can even arrange for a new identity for you both and your family. Make the Earth move for me, and you'll get everything you ever wanted, and when this is over you need never work again.'

Ashcroft fished out his IDO, punched in Wai Chan's number, sighed and clicked on CANCEL. He glared at Svetlana sitting nonchalantly in the chair. 'You complete and utter bitch. You know I have no choice but to go along, even if it means only one day extra with Brooke. OK, let's not waste time then. Just how do we work together, and how do I know if I can trust what you say? Who's in on this with you?'

'That's better, Icarus. I'm relieved you're not going to shoot the messenger. Sorry, I didn't mean to say that. A little indelicate. Sorry. And Icarus–' she tapped the side of her nose. 'I have my sources, that's all you need to know.'

Svetlana stroked the briefcase on her lap like a pet kitten, and extracted an IDO chip in a black velvet pouch. The chip contained instructions for Ashcroft to absorb at leisure. She also produced a cheque made out to the sum of five million euros. 'An advance for you, go and entertain your colleagues. They need cheering up too. And here's a blank requisition signed by the Director General. You know how close I am to Henri.'

'Good God! Is he in on this as well?'

'Not exactly, but let's just say that he and I have an understanding, and it helps smooth so many negotiations. Like I told you, he wishes he could turn back time.'

'So all the stuff that protester was going on about is true?' Ashcroft demanded. 'Henri's just a criminal after all and I had respect for him. All these years we've worked together... I need to see Brooke and speak with her before I do whatever dirty work you have in mind.'

'Of course, of course, say tomorrow, I'll set up a short conference call on the IDO. You can speak to her. You will know you won't be talking to a voice recording, I promise. And Icarus, let's not introduce any complications. It will be a happy ending for all of us. Remember, if you think about contacting the government authorities you will never see Brooke again, and what will that serve? You will end up with your career in tatters. Or you might be joining Brooke under that headstone. We will simply get someone else to do the work. Remember also that if you try to explain the truth, and you know only a fraction of truth, the police will take it you've gone totally insane with the shock of your wife's death. Now, we may not have the friendship we once had, my dear Professor, but let's not have that affect our new and excellent working relationship,' Svetlana continued. She smiled broadly, reached over and patted his arm playfully.

He twisted his mouth to resemble a smile of agreement. 'No, let's not, Sveti.'

FROM THE WHITE PERSPECTIVE

The time-shift experiment with the cyclist had worked, not that Zein took much pleasure from it. The rule of limited contact with humans was now over and he just had to face the new reality… Somehow his strategy was soiled and it was getting dragged further off course like the wreckers' light welcoming the captain and crew to their own destruction.

Ziel's actions were sickeningly obvious. Brooke was no doubt alive and held somewhere, and now Icarus was back at CERN he would be vulnerable to persuasion. He would be in the pocket of Ziel and this was the only thing Ziel could do to get the principled scientist to do her bidding.

Zim was feeding Zag with the Super-G messages coming from Svetlana, but there was trouble getting them decoded. The others were concentrating on the defence of the Ashcrofts and their residence. Zein wanted the three children back there.

These were all fire-fighting measures, not precious time spent to return to Zyberia. Zein thought about Zareth and the linking with Lycian; he had not anticipated this all those years back in his calculations. It returned his thoughts to the reason he had journeyed this far with such risks.

They still remained.

Human beings, surely, were still the means of getting back to Zyberia. If Zareth had the power himself, surely he would have used it, for both himself and for them? Stein, Blipp, Gayle and the Nimmos, and Ashcroft himself with his years of research, were giving of themselves to help them. And Lycian glowed alarmingly with superparticle strength.

Ziel had ensured that Ashcroft would now help her with her own brand of salvation involving some nuclear meltdown at CERN. Ashcroft was to ensure the draining down on an unprecedented scale of the resources of at least two national power grids. His PBC machine needed to whip up strong enough particle collisions to smash space and time into zicroscopic fragments on whatever scale was necessary with no heed for the consequences. The collisions must rent a hole in the fabric of this universe, so that Ziel could fire her way back to Zyberia.

It was time the Ashcroft children knew the truth, and fast. They had to act to save their parents and possibly the whole planet. Perhaps they needed the truth brought home to them more clearly. They were heading home in a daze right now, and they needed to spring into action.

As Stein viewed his charges' journey back to the vicarage, he knew that the time for direct communication with the Ashcrofts, face to face was quickly approaching.

FROM THE BLACK PERSPECTIVE

The coercing of Icarus Ashcroft had metaphorically moved Svetlana towards the middle of the binaryboard and she was viewing the events right under her nose. She had moved to the alps after the sojourn in Venice, to put finishing touches to the machine that would propel her home. She had two hefty earth body guards with her with her mutant allies ensconced within them, and she was pulling every string in Svetlana's equation. She'd pulled off her own time-shift experiment, and Ashcroft's wife was now being held as the essential bargaining piece. The power of Ashcroft's grief was working wonders in terms of her own modifications to the PBC.

Ziel was no longer bothered about decontaminating her equation back on board the Zarantula. All her equation-jumping had made that process too tedious. She had therefore relinquished effective command of her ship, trusting it to her fiercely loyal rogue particle attendants, Win and Zedex.

As for these, life on board was becoming monotonous. There was only so much pendulum-vortex-gazing, that you could do before your senses glazed over and slid into stasis.

Even the ship's zectroscope had given itself over to hallucinatory images in sickly colours. They looked rather washed out in one corner, as though sunlight were falling directly on the display. But it wasn't ordinary sunlight. Zedex' jolt passed through the coils of his fellow Bugz. There was no mistaking the radiance of the Zargo over Cambridge. There was also no mistaking the strange pearlescence that had emanated from there before and had now come back. It broke like a summer sun through the zecho fog created by the exiting of Zareth from Brooke's equation. At first it was ignored as some aberration of the scopes, maybe a shadowy memory of Brooke and the particle that had lived within her at Cambridge pre-CERN?
Zedex fumbled and tweaked the zectroscope a little to the east, to CERN, where several black smudges erupted and ran into the sickly colours. They saw Ziel positioned with her sensors drinking in the professor and his lovely machine.

The attendants buzzed. Best not to bother Ziel now; there was no time for that, and, anyway, she'd be proud after they'd dealt with this little problem to know that her crew had shown initiative. Rogue particles weren't really meant to show initiative, just blind loyalty, but hadn't she always moaned and wished that just for once they would?
Win would head the annihilation squad, and Zedex signed up too.

There was no doubt in Win's analysis that something had gone very wrong with the time shift, if the Zareth particle was being detected in Cambridge. It was not the issue of failure but the reaction of Ziel that concerned the crew. Certainly, the strike had been deemed a success, but the probability of having a superparticle of the immense power of Zareth active would tip the balance greatly.

56. STORM OVER CAMBRIDGE

18 June 2042

Stein had walked from his hotel and looked out over the garden of the vicarage at Haslingdene. If he had had a watch he would have tapped it with impatience. This would be afternoon rush hour at its worst, and not just because of the time of day. He could feel in his core the onward rush of almost imperceptible vibrations, of a tightening band of charged particles disturbing the Bugz' protective belt round the city. The trees and buildings round about looked a shade darker than a moment before, and the sky had assumed a glassy look. It was not the eerie light of a thunderstorm, however. The silent onward rush was unmistakable. A plume of magnetised gas was being discharged from a great height, it issued forth in the form of a giant arachnid with bolts of destruction on its limbs, and it came quietly as if on filaments of ethereal energy ionising particles as it descended menacingly to anaesthetise its prey.

The navigation systems of several aircraft on various flight paths to Stansted and Heathrow started to malfunction. Beyond them and outside the atmosphere five satellites were pulled down out of orbit, and three astronauts carrying out routine maintenance on space station equipment were subjected to lethal doses of unknown toxic radiation.

The Nimmos and Ashcrofts were charging around the vicarage, chucking things in rucksacks, the Nimmos barking out orders with no explanation and the Ashcrofts looking bewildered. OK, it was fine to go off on a whim like this to their Norfolk cottage, but why the sudden rush? They'd know soon enough. It was as well that Patrick Nimmo had a wrestler's muscles and Joan was equally strong for Zon and Zleo within

275

them decided to force the family out of the front door and pile them into the MK9 1961 imperial maroon Jaguar. As they shut the car doors on them, a pulse passed through the city. It was the precursor of an attack and Zon knew this all too well. You could hear the next door's dog barking and more animals, as if they knew something that humans hadn't detected yet.

Stein was preparing his own response to the challenge on the way, for certainly he intended to protect Cambridge himself with all the power at his disposal.

The entire city of Cambridge was grinding to a standstill. It was being slowly stifled in the cage of an electromagnetic fog, which descended in a perfect web to seal it off from the outside world. Automatic speed regulator transmitters went blank. The robotic tram system was disabled and people were getting off and walking to their destinations. Digital signals were jammed, IDOs crackled and cut out, electrical substations started to steam and power cables glowed.

All communications systems within a ten-mile radius of the city buckled under the overload as the heavy particle fire from above disrupted the charge on every nanochip in every electrical component.

'For heaven's sake get a move on, Patrick!' Mrs Nimmo bawled at her husband as they bolted down the old A10 into the centre.

Horns were blaring illegally and police sirens wailing. The world was going stir crazy.

They passed the debris of several chimneys and electrical antennae and dishes which had been toppled on the road. Several people had abandoned their cars and were running along the road, waving their hands. Someone was screaming; a man nearby was kneeling and pulling a travel blanket over a lifeless body by a smashed motorcycle. The acrid stench of an electrical fire enveloped them as they rounded a corner.

'Good grief, look at Trinity College!' Elsie gasped. A pall of smoke hung above what looked like no more than a building site.

Zein had fought Zedex in the grounds near Trinity and although successful in annihilating his adversary, an energy mace had scythed through part of the college injuring a number of students.

Mr Nimmo turned pale and gripped the steering wheel even tighter, as he felt the ramrod force of Zon's positive charge kick through the core of his being and stream out of every pore. This volley of z-saturated energy zeroed in on the patch of dark fog that was hovering and drifting eastward after the Jaguar, and a zicrosecond later a thunderclap rang out which shattered window glass in all directions. Mrs Nimmo involuntarily clutched at her husband, and he blinked hard as though trying to steady himself. Lycian was groaning for a good minute and then became transfixed as a glow emanated round his body.

'Stop the car, something is happening to Lycian.'

'We can't darling, whatever has happened to him, he is okay, he has survived maybe the biggest test.'

Sam pulled at Lycian and felt the small discharge of static. 'Did he get hit with lightning?'

Mr Nimmo advised, 'Well yes of a sort, that was a special sort of electrical storm which is more dangerous than you could ever imagine.'

'Patrick...'

Mrs Nimmo distracted Elsie by the view outside the window. 'Look, a daytime Aurora Borealis, almost unheard of,' Mrs Nimmo explained to the three in the back as the particles took the form of a great winged beast that assailed the web to punch holes in it.

Unknown to the others, the rogue particle Win tried to destroy the super particle in Lycian. Shocked literally to its negative core, it received a blast of positive energy that except for being distracted by his human host would have meant the end of Xit. Thankfully the energy ceased flowing and he was able to limp off leaving other particles to form a fighting retreat.

The lights hissed and crackled in the form of a pyrotechnic display until a small but dense black column of fog descended before them, obliterating the view. The Jaguar's saloon's 3.8-litre engine began to splutter.

'They're shutting us in,' Mr Nimmo muttered, as he slammed the accelerator to the floor with undue force. The converted bio fuel engine responded urgently as the modifications put in place by Zon delivered hundreds more horsepower. Patrick had never liked the engine conversion on this classic car and for sure it now had F1 performance as they sped through an old industrial area and out of the city perimeter and down the emergency services lane of the crowded motorway as though fired from a great cannon.

The family trusted in his driving skills and shut their eyes again, until Mr Nimmo braked a a minute later to a more comfortable speed until he finally stopped on the hard shoulder. They were back in sunlight with birds flying from the direction of Cambridge, one of them fell on the bonnet of the car burning, its wings scorched as if it had been in a fire. You would have thought it was a normal June afternoon, but it wasn't. They craned their necks round to look at the blackened horizon behind them. A slowly rotating maelstrom of electrostatic fog, impenetrable as night, had enveloped the city. But for its unnatural size it was like a web that now lay in tatters with great rents and tears and bits of fimbral electrostatic charge blowing in great gusts.

'Good driving Mr N, you sure can get some performance out of this old cat. What was that? I know we have had some weird weather, but that was something else'.

Sam looked at Elsie and Lycian in some disbelief.

'Indeed it was and thanks to Pat here we are out of it', voiced Joan.

'Just as well we left when we did, do you think home will be okay, Mrs N?'

'I just g-mailed a friend and they say our part of town isn't affected greatly; she said, telling a white lie.

'I wish I had my digi-corder,' Sam sighed.

'We got out by a hare's whisker, Joan,' Mr Nimmo mumbled, and switched on the digi channel to hear whatever early news bulletins were filtering in before he received a barrage of questions from the back requiring difficult answers. Quite a few people had stopped because the road was dotted with newly descended birds all burnt and in the last flapping throes of death.

'Yes, what happened to our feathered friends here could have happened to us Lycian, can you move that bird off the bonnet?'

'Everyone get in and let's make our way to Cromer. We can talk a little in the car about today.'

Reports were already flooding in about the strange weather phenomena over the university town. It had been violent, out of the blue, and strictly localised. A mini electromagnetic storm evidently. All broadcasts had been blacked out, nano and picoputing systems were down, and the emergency services were out in full force employing military-style measures to deal with the crisis. There had been an unconfirmed number of fatalities and four large-scale fires. One of Trinity College's buildings had been seriously damaged.

'Why are we going to Cromer, Mr N?' Elsie casually asked.

'Zzzz..It's a bit of a surprise, can you wait?'

'After the last few days, just make sure it's a pleasant one, can you?' Sam said jokingly.

57. GLOOM ON THE ZARANTULA
Same day

Life on board the Zarantula had not been and still was not a happy one.

First it had been dominated by Ziel's recent schizophrenic tendencies, then it had descended into an anarchic state of discord, because everyone feared Ziel's reaction to the ill-fated unauthorised attack on the ancient superparticle.

The problem was they did not expect to be opposed by such force. Zedex had been annihilated as had three high black functionaries and Win was so energy-depleted, he barely made it back to the Zarantula.

All defences were up as Win recounted how he had Zareth's host in his sights and then a glowing energy bolt had thundered from the entity, absorbing and neutralising the negative energy he was deploying. He had been lucky to survive annihilation because the superparticle host had been startled and cut short its withering counterattack.

The disturbance in Cambridge did not go unnoticed in Switzerland as Svetlana looked at Enrico and Vittorio in disbelief. 'What were those cretins up to?'

282

58. RETREAT TO CROMER

Stein followed the Nimmos' classic Jaguar, which had been parked and now sped down the motorway and then threaded along the winding roads of Norfolk in the early evening light. It wasn't easy for either Stein or the Bugz inside of him because they still drove on the left in this crazy country and the Norfolk roads were small in width.

Zein was coming to terms with his human host and the limitations, thankfully he knew the location because all those years back he had been to this place when Einstein had visited. His memory banks fizzed with data as he viewed the past with some affection and the church they had visited, but now the coast was changed, the sea having risen.

He had never felt so destabilised as now, and yet the word Salvation was etched on his equation. It glowed with the same light as that shining from the superparticle now sitting squashed with three Ashcrofts on the back seat of Mr Nimmo's Jaguar.

As the Jaguar cruised along the roads Zon and Zleo knew that each of the three young Ashcrofts had a robust and complex equation. Sam showed the directness and ambition of his father, Elsie showed the courage and intellect of both her parents, and Lycian had the compassion and quiet wisdom of his mother. They could, it seemed, take on board any manner of information and deal with it. The Bugz could only hope that that would include such minor details as accepting aliens from inner space, it certainly had become much more complex with the situation of the two Ashcroft parents. Bugz were able to feel human emotions

283

like guilt or hope and humour, so maybe the Ashcrofts could feel a Bugzish sense of calm clear logic and function.

As the family debunked into the cottage at Cromer and made themselves at home an hour or so passed and the family gathered in the living room with its low ceiling and seventeenth century beams. There was a pregnant pause.

'You first, dear,' Mr Nimmo nodded to his wife, helping himself to a badly needed Jamesons.

'No, you first,' Mrs Nimmo returned, out-staring her husband and stuffing the last wedge of fruitcake in her mouth to force the issue.

'This is a once upon a time with a difference, then,' Mr Nimmo said to the three Ashcrofts, 'and the happy ever after depends on you.'

Sam, Lycian and Elsie got a potted history first about the lead up to their present circumstances. They did not need reminding about their father's status as a globally recognised physicist, nor about his labour of love on the PBC project, it had often seemed closer to his heart than they themselves did, if the truth be known.

They needed little reminding about their family history, the vicarage was after all steeped in it, or about the little oak chest that took on new meaning since the talk from their Dad and the contents so lovingly, almost jealously, handled by their father. They understood that he was seeking some recognition for the contributions down the ages of their ancestor I Will the elder and a line of so-called assistants they were very vague about.

'You'll want some reminding and explanation about the Midas particle, though,' Mr Nimmo went on.

'That's science fiction,' Elsie said. 'Even the Prof's mensa boffs looked lost.'

'Dad never let on anything beforehand,' Sam added. 'I don't understand why.'

The children glanced at each other. They couldn't help wondering, in fact, about Dad's state of mind, and that wasn't just to do with Mum's death, Mum's not being here any more. There were no two ways about it: Dad was playing God. He was not the father they recognised. At worst he had delusions of grandeur, and at best he had turned on its head every value he himself had fostered in them and encouraged them to be all their lives, generous and polite, values that represented a loving family, which was more the exception than the rule these days. Mr Nimmo took another clunk of whisky and thought he'd better offer some to his audience.

This was it. Time for a deep breath and an explanation, then, about engineering particles and other sorts of particles – conscious particles. In fact, about particles in both this universe and another universe, and a desire to go back to that other universe. About the black Bugz and the Zargonauts. At this point the three Ashcrofts looked as though they might fall like skittles, but they kept their nerve.

'The Z,' Sam said to Lycian, who nodded.

The children then learned about Ziel's manipulation and blackmail of their father, about the fact that five of his students had gladly accompanied him at short notice back to CERN, ('Christian mentioned it,' they responded), and about his consent to speed up the Bugz' return home regardless of the cost to Earth.

'No!' Elsie burst out when Brooke's name was mentioned.

'I don't want to build up hope but we think that Brooke may still be alive'.

'We just buried mum in the family grave, Joan, we were all there, don't you remember?'

'Look at me guys, I swear that this is some trickery from some other place and we did not bury your mother. It was an assemblage of atoms that may have resembled her, but her soul still lives and I know her body must do also'

As the story was recounted it was unlikely that their mother would survive if Icarus did not do as he was told. They should not feel so bad about their father because it was the way of getting him to break his own ethics, probably the only way. Ziel's grand design was contrasted with that of the Zargonauts, who wished to return home leaving Earth intact.

No contest as to which to choose. The three Ashcrofts just had to grow up very quickly and take the lead. They looked at each other with a mix of deep shock, elation and resolve.

'Life's never going to be same again anyway,' Lycian almost whispered. He could not yet bring himself to mention the extraordinary strength that had been welling up in him all day. What had changed his feelings and given him powers which meant he felt he could look inside structures to the very atoms they were made of? Mr and Mrs N had said nothing that might have a bearing on it. Was he like them, he wondered? Did he have a Bugz in his so-called equation? But if he did, they weren't acknowledging it and it didn't seem to communicate anyway.

They would have to go to CERN. No one else could stay their father's hand and thereby block Ziel's move. Mr Nimmo would organise travel arrangements in the morning, they would have the following day lying low and resting up in Cromer, and the day after that they would head for London and the train without making a detour to Cambridge.

'We'll have with us on the train the journalist we told you about from the plane crash, Jonathan Stein,' Mrs Nimmo said. 'He will join us for the trip to Geneva and will explain a little more about his overall involvement in the plan.. Stein and Blipp will be our eyes and ears. And Gayle Richter will manage publicity; she knows your Dad well. You couldn't be in better hands, and at top level too.'

'The players were moving into the position as planned all those years back,' thought Mr Nimmo.

Half an hour later when all had collapsed in bed, Sam switched on the 3D TV to catch the news again, and Elsie joined them. It mostly repeated what they'd heard in the car.

The power in Cambridge had been switched off, and after the world's most amazing pyrotechnics display a lot of the electrical infrastructure of Cambridge had been damaged. It would take the authorities days if not weeks to work out the problem. The casualties and damage incurred in that short period had been appalling. And then there were the increased numbers of patients at the city's clinics and hospitals, all reporting a general feeling of anxiety and nausea, and in some cases buzzing noises in their ears.

Lycian clicked the OFF button. Sam lay back with his hands behind his head, gazing at the moon through the parted curtains in the boys' bedroom. Lycian followed his gaze, and saw a soft-coloured vortex rising off it and disappearing into space, but he decided to say nothing.

'You know how when you think worrying or crazy thoughts at night when not sleeping,' he mused, 'but everything seems to fall into place in the light of day? And how when you make sense of crazy thoughts at night, when you're dreaming, you then discover it's actually all crazy when you wake up?'

'This is certainly crazy,' Lycian said. 'But it's still true. I know it.'

'Think about it, Lyce. Here's the situation as I understand it. We're holed up here with two raving loonies who have been hypnotising and brainwashing us. There's nothing else to prove what on earth's going on here.'

'But the attack on Cambridge!'

'Fireworks and a black out. Some weird electric storm.'

'And what about mum being alive, it's just incredible, like something impossible to even wish!'

'I'd say you're in a state of denial, Sam. Best get some sleep so you can think straight. God knows we need it. 'Night.'

'I don't think I can sleep, given what is going on, our whole lives are on the line.'

Sam stared at the ceiling, his hands still behind his head. His lips moved as though of themselves. 'Who is God, Lyce?'

The Nimmos had had their cocoa, brushed their teeth and climbed into bed. Mr Nimmo had turned on a little light music and Mrs Nimmo was glancing at her IDO, receiving a message from Stein.

'I chickened out,' Mr Nimmo remarked. 'Mentioning the superparticle, that is. I just couldn't dump it all on the poor lad in one go.'

'We'll tell him on the train,' Mrs Nimmo said. 'He'll be stronger by then. Patrick?'

'Yes, dear?'

'He will need to be, that is for sure.'

59. THE RISING OUT OF THE SEA 19 June 2042

The next morning, after Mr Nimmo had booked a carriage on the super maglev from London to Geneva and Mrs Nimmo had been to market, the three Ashcrofts were coaxed from their beds and everyone climbed back into the Jaguar for what they termed their annual pilgrimage. It was always at Icarus' instigation, at the start of every cottage holiday, and everyone moaned about being expected to tag along, but this time there was no question about it. If Icarus wasn't there to nag them, they'd have to goad themselves.

Elsie in particular was still asking lots of questions because if their mother was alive surely they should ring the police ? Patrick agreed that they would go to CERN and check out the certainty of the situation and then involve the police?

A few miles inland from Cromer, Mr Nimmo turned off the main road and headed up towards Roughton Heath. It was the tradition to park the car on an old dirt track and walk the rest of the way to a strip of farmland containing a singularly uninteresting wooden hut, adorned with a blue heritage plaque and a neatly tended flower border. He liked the idea that an object so small and unprepossessing in itself could hold such significance. The hut had been temporary lodgings for Einstein in 1933 when he had fled Nazi Germany for the States and come to Cromer as a stopping off point.

The Bugz admired the hut too. Small was indeed big. It was so satisfying. It interested them for other reasons too. It represented the transition from an old life to a new one. It incorporated not only the Bugzish combination of big and small but also the human combination of the functional with the cultural. Einstein had shared his cramped quarters with a grand piano and a violin, and the sculptor Jacob Epstein had come to visit and carved a bust of him there too.

It was a bright breezy day, perfect for a walk on the seafront once they returned to the cottage. The Ashcrofts were acting calmly as though nothing had happened. It did not escape anyone's notice, in fact, that Sam seemed to be either distancing himself from the Nimmos or humouring them the way one humours a child or a simpleton.

'That wasn't just some electromagnetic storm yesterday, you know,' Mr Nimmo commented. 'Just like the cyclist you saw wasn't some trick of your imagination. Nor was the display on that laptop you mentioned.'

Sam shrugged on a jacket. 'I've simply put my brain in neutral. I'd say that's the best thing when suffering severe stress. Still, no doubt worse things happen at sea.'

Mr Nimmo had his eyes elsewhere though. He had pulled out his binoculars and trained them on the horizon just past the pier. There were the gulls, the clouds, a couple of tankers on the horizon. His gaze rested on an expanse of water a few hundred yards off the northeast end of the pier.

'Are you looking for something?' Elsie asked, and Mr Nimmo pointed out to sea for them all to see.

No sooner did Mr Nimmo spot the slight disturbance on the water than he handed the binoculars to Elsie while keeping his eyes on the disturbance. There was a slight swell, which gained momentum as though a school of dolphins were rounding up fish just under the surface. Choppy wavelets began darting in all directions and ribbons of froth skittered crisscross above them, and the swirling movement cut a rapidly broadening ring that bruised into a storm colour. The gulls above shrieked and circled and dived. Elsie stared and passed the glasses to Sam and Lycian.

'Is it an earth quake?'

The Bugz flexed their coils in concentration. It was as though some eruption were bubbling up from the depths. A muffled and distorted booming resonated in the morning air, the rhythmic pendulum sound of striking metal. It carried on the breeze and drifted shorewards past the pier where several figures could be seen standing frozen. A brief moment of calm followed. It seemed the waves fell silent, even the gulls hovered motionless.

Then in a shiver of sunlight and an eerie rush of sound the heaving body of water suddenly tilted bolt upright and streamed back on itself in bright silver cascades. The onlookers gasped. The silver column revealed a long slim cone that rose majestically from the depths, a subterranean rocket that spewed bursts of water, not fire. It rose higher and higher in a smooth steady movement, its body silhouetted and its tip glinting in the sun.

'St Peter's! It's the drowned church!' Elsie exclaimed.

'The lost village of Shipden,' the boys breathed in unison, as from the muddy boiling depths around the base of the church and the clouds of screaming gulls there bounced up the ramshackle frames of tiny cottages and jetties and the rubble of stone construction. It seemed the sea had raised an ancient offering to the gods on a bed of rich silt, soft black ribbons which now pooled and gushed out of every crack and window and channel, which mingled with the silver steamers from the steeple above, and which revealed the empty eye sockets and gaping jaws of long buried medieval dwellings.

The children's IDOs bleeped simultaneously.

Help us, said the messenger Bugz which filled their screens before streaking back to nothingness. Help us, and we will help you.

'A trick of the imagination, would you say, Sam?' Mr Nimmo asked and turned on his heel, as an approaching siren filled the air behind them on the promenade, shouts of near panic carried from the pier, and the air around them rang out with the blows of displaced waves.

60. ON THE TRAIN
20 June 2042

The SuperCeleritas maglev link at St Pancras in central London left on the dot of 10:10. The service hurtled its human passengers along an electromagnetic cushion at speeds of over 750 kilometres an hour through a blur of countryside towards the newly opened second Channel Tunnel. In contrast, its Bugz passengers felt they were trundling along at a leisurely pace rather in the manner of a nineteenth-century stagecoach delivering its occupants to the steam packet due to sail from Dover.

The Ashcroft party, ringed as they were by their unearthly and invisible shield, had been joined just as the train doors shut by the journalist who had survived the Newark plane crash.

Mrs Nimmo gave Mr Nimmo a knowing smile. The American's honest face, clear grey eyes and laid-back manner belied the power within. She also saw the telltale fading burns on his neck and on his wrists, and on greeting him she drew back her own sleeve and nodded. It had been a shared experience of the most horrific kind.

Stein had been orchestrating the resurrection of the church out at sea to convince finally the doubting Ashcrofts that they meant business and undoubtedly those they faced were very dangerous and powerful indeed as they were literally able to move earth and time.

'I didn't know about these travel arrangements till last minute,' Stein nodded at the Nimmos. 'These days I don't know whether I'm coming or going.

'I am glad I am able to join you on this important journey', Stein announced to the group. 'My editor said I could come to England to follow up the CERN story, and now here I am with you guys. I guess I'm getting back into the thick of it, hey Joan?'

'So true, and we're all in the same boat now, at least we soon will be.'

'Glad you're with us, Jonathan,' Mr Nimmo said. 'You'll find you'll feel a whole lot better after some morning coffee and a little chat with us.'

He stuck his nose back in the 3D audio-visual screen built in the arm of the seat. There was, not surprisingly, a full commentary on the electrical storm over Cambridge.

Lycian viewed and listened to the reporter, and then looked at Mrs Nimmo sitting opposite him. Not for the first time he rubbed his eyes in disbelief. It tested the limits of his sanity to believe that the homely, bustling woman who had been like second mother to them was part 'Bugz' alien.

OK then, she really was a bustling middle-aged woman and not some illusion, but she did happen to have one of these Bugz linked to her soul… Lycian couldn't really get his head round it. He knew about the soul in the Christian sense, how when the deceased was buried in a churchyard his or her soul passed heavenward, but the truth about souls and equations was amazing, the fact that they really existed in a scientific sense and yet remained hidden to man. The revelation made him think of the old story about human evolution; he no longer had a use for a tail, although he retained the bump. Maybe he retained it in case he needed it again? And as regard the soul, maybe he retained his awareness of it in case he would one day understand it more fully.

Lycian could not understand the fact that he was feeling better in himself. When shaving that morning he had examined his face, to discover it was looking more manly, more rugged, more determined.

'What's it like being Mrs N and Zleo at the same time?' he asked Mrs Nimmo, as she noticed him looking at her.

Mrs Nimmo smiled calmly. 'Perfectly normal, I suppose,' she said. 'I have known about it from the start, and you needn't think I'm schizophrenic or that Mr N has conversations with himself. Zleo has been a part of me ever since I was approached all those years back and told it would not harm me. In fact I understand that Bugz can only choose a select few hosts where the link is almost perfect. I felt privileged to be asked, in a sense, and have wanted for nothing. I'd say the match between me and my Bugz self is so good that we share the same interests, which includes wanting to care for you lot.'

'The interesting thing is that Mr N must be very special, because when we met he explained the situation, his situation. Our friendship grew of course and, well, romance followed despite the Bugz. I don't know whether they engineered our meeting, like some extraterrestrial dating agency, but I couldn't ask for a more loving partner. As our human selves we have feelings that have changed our view on this world and of course our working here has helped that too'

Joan Nimmo sighed. 'But I'm really sorry. We intended to enlist Icarus and tell you about the situation, but as you know sadly we have had our plans changed by others who would seek to return home with no care for this place. Also we haven't discussed the reason why we were led here or if the particle we knew as Zareth is still alive.'

'Also that powerful Zareth equation is the one sure link we have back to our home.'

'Equation? Which equation?'

'Did you want your magazine disc, Joan?' Mr Nimmo interrupted. 'You know, the one with the knitting patterns you were after?'

'Oh, thanks for reminding me, I was getting carried away. You know, Lycian, I was thinking of a light wool jumper for Sam, for his climbing, seeing as how he wears through the elbows in no time. And in the meantime Mr N is, I know, very keen to explain something to you which hasn't already been explained.'

'Thank you very much indeed, dear,' Patrick said. 'I had thought I could get through my viewing the newscast of the storm first.'

'No time like the present,' Mrs Nimmo said. 'Perhaps no time at all, in fact, after a few hours are up.'

The train trip seemed to vanish in the blink of an eye. During the conversation that followed, it was all Lycian could do to absorb the fact that he was now like Mr and Mrs N. It was all he and his siblings could do to absorb the fact that what was lodged within him was indeed a superparticle that defied adequate description even by the Bugz.

'Why me? What have I done?' Lycian asked, folding his arms as if to protect himself. 'Why not Sam or Elsie?'

'It should have been the be all and end all of why we are here, but

294

recent events have not been entirely predicted and even we are on a wave that we need to balance and look at the future probabilities of events carefully.'

They returned his gaze, equally confused. Lycian was different, and they wondered if they knew him.

'On to practical matters,' Mr Nimmo coughed. 'And shall we explain about what's happening when we get to Geneva?'

He said that for once they would not be heading for a conventional house once they got there; it was too risky and could prove a repeat of Cambridge. They needed peace and quiet and they had an expert ground agent to get them to their accommodation. Stein and Mrs Nimmo knew Gayle; she was of course one of the four that had survived that terrible plane crash. A nice intelligent girl. The three Ashcrofts would like her. Their dad certainly did.

'Blipp will be there too,' Stein added. 'He's taken a special interest in this whole business, and he's been a real asset in looking at various IDO communications surrounding the attack in the amphitheatre.'

Lycian sat back, and shut out the stares of his siblings by gazing at the blur of scenery and tunnels and then closing his eyes. He was tired, he suffered from the MS yet he had a new unfamiliar clarity and surge in his body that could only be the particle. It had to be the same when he felt the electrical surge in the car, he had been attacked and not even known about it. Yet according to Patrick he had fought off a particle as powerful as they come with hardly blinking an eye. Even Zon the great warrior particle in Mr Nimmo was duly impressed.

His mind raced. All around life continued in a normal vein, and yet they were facing what was probably the most momentous event in human history. Their own father was going to help serve up enough destructive force to take out half of Europe. At worst, or at best, if the Zargonauts were able to prevail, the unprecedented power as yet unleashed within CERN could be harnessed to create conditions thirteen-and-a-half billion years earlier at the time of the big bang. They would be witness to the warping of time itself and the opening of a singularity so vast that it could digest many earths in one gulp, a black pearl in spacetime for passing into another universe. They would be witness to it because they had the potential to tame it and use it. The thought was not just mind-stretching, it was mind-reconstructing.

Zareth could not communicate from within his host. The self-preservation determinant of his equation was jolted by the recent attack of the rogue Bugz at Cambridge. The attack was in part thwarted by one of the three particles now in close attendance to the humans on the train. The third particle, which just joined them, was of greater power and controlled the defence; he was locked on to the man who had boarded the train and was now spreading his protective energy rings round the group. He had positioned himself above and between his two companions so that they formed a pyramid. Zareth's mental units clicked into the same shape. The familiarity of this classic protective mantle so revered in old Zytop filled Zareth with some thought that these were the particles that he hoped would answer his distress signal. Maybe his own 'salvation' was at hand.

The electromagnetic current below the train carriage brushed his outer coils. He seemed to be on some purposeful journey or why else would they congregate and construct the protective zone.

The Cornavin terminal at Geneva was heaving with tourists, but before they found themselves forced to plunge into the crowds, the Ashcroft party was met at the barrier by Gayle Richter wearing a snappy suit and an outstretched hand of welcome.

'I'm Gayle. It's as well I got here in good time. The train staff have just been telling me that this train was fifteen minutes faster then any other train on this line before. It could have played havoc with other trains on the line but somehow, miraculously, didn't. Something to do with you lot?' She was now addressing Stein and the Nimmos, who automatically turned to Lycian.

'Don't ask me,' Lycian protested. 'I'm not sure I can take responsibility for my actions any more, I didn't purposefully make the train go faster! It just happened because I wanted to get there quicker.'

Lycian saw only the toothpaste-ad smile and the brisk demeanour of the woman in front of him, but Zareth saw straight through those outer appearances to the equation within. It had the look of being cut and polished by an expert craftsman, with ultra-smooth facets that suggested Superbug quality, yet not of a pure kind, for embedded within them could be seen unfamiliar striping. Interesting.

Gayle whisked the party out of a side exit to the waiting eco land wagons, where another Bugz, pure Bugz this time, sat inside. Bertholdt

296

Lipp deactivated the smoked Chromothene and Zim greeted his fellow Bugz. Blipp gave them a warm welcome but dispensed with preliminaries.

'I'm taking you all to my old steamer; we'll take the launch out to it from Lausanne. She's a delightful old lady, and you just might recognise her, Jonathan. One of your relatives owned it for a while after he became famous.'

Stein smiled. 'So many coincidences, and yet we know from our chat that they're not coincidences, are they? Anyway, I'm back and fighting fit, as you see.'

'Glad to see you're all well after the problems in Cambidge. I think we all need to be aware that the stakes have been raised, as has the risk.'

'Yes,' agreed Stein.

297

61. ON THE STEAMER
Same day

The Siracusa was stationed far out at the northern end of Lake Leman. She was indeed a delightful old lady, a lake steamer still trim and elegant at the grand age of a hundred and thirty years. She bobbed gently, her white streamlined shape studded with lanterns, her wooden and brass fittings redolent of a bygone age.

Her interior had a studious feel, comfy old leather, pot plants, shaded lamps and built-in bookcases. Portraits lined the walls and narrow corridors, the faces of scientists both renowned and obscure. Sam thought of Dad. These people, the ones obscured with time, were the ones for whom he sought recognition. Sam's eyes then rested on a group of men and women posing and smiling in a photo taken at the prow of the steamer.

'Here, guys, look at this. It's Mum and Dad and Blipp and some others.'

Elsie reached over, picked up the brass photo frame with tears in her eyes and gave her brothers a steely look of resolve.

Mrs Nimmo looked at her husband, and Blipp and Stein behind him. 'Poor children. The grief's enough for them, let alone everything else. They need time to adjust, and they just don't have it.'

'And I don't want it!' Elsie burst out. 'We've got a job to do, to save Dad from himself and find out where mum is'.

'We've got to save the lot of us,' Lycian said, as he pulled Elsie towards him.

His emotion filtered round and round inside the multi-coiled equation of Zareth, which swelled with the near uncontrollable force and sent out from the very core an energy shockwave of withering power. As it torpedoed outwards through the water in all directions and bounced off the lake bottom the advanced sonar on board the steamer fizzled into a wisp of smoke. The ripples that followed bobbed the boats in the marinas and slammed into the limestone folds of the Jura, where it dissipated.

The violence of its passing was picked up on the monitors at CERN and at the subterranean laboratories across the French and Italian borders. It was also picked up in the mountain retreat above Montreux, where Svetlana looked up abruptly from her little light reading on final focus quads and high acceleration gradients. Her eyes froze over, her flesh crawled and her lips parted like elastic as she spewed out a blood-curdling scream followed by a garbled and robot-like exclamation that was incomprehensible to her own ears.

'By the powers of Zo! What is this that awakens from its long sleep? What's brought this to this insignificant backwater? And how the hell has it survived?'

Svetlana lunged at her study door to turn the lock and bar entry to anyone coming by, and threw herself into a claret-coloured leather chair, kicking off her high heels, clawing the arms and arching backwards in a torment, until the possession ripped itself from her to leave her slumped and senseless. The crew on board the Siracusa reported the seismic wave to the captain, who in turn reported a small earth tremor to Bertholdt Lipp.

'I felt it all right, Captain,' Blipp said, 'and it's best to prepare for stormy conditions tonight. And I don't mean the weather'.

'But there was nothing forecast, Sir.'

'And I'm telling you to be prepared regardless.'

Night was now falling, and it muffled the lake. The glaring red fingers of sunset slipped round and down the surrounding mountain peaks, as though caressing and pulling them into blackness, as though cupping the lake in the palm of an unseen hand. Apart from the comforting company of the clusters of light coming from the shoreline, the Siracusa floated in a vast expanse, alone and, some might say, vulnerable.

Gayle sat apart from the others on the pretext of not wishing to intrude on the Ashcrofts' undoubted concern for their parents. She

299

sipped on an orange juice and considered the strong pulse that had rocked the ship. She recognised it for what it was. It was as told in the Zarethian texts. A part of the texts she had decoded after much effort but not imparted to either Zein or Ziel. Ziel would now know of course, about the connection with Lycian, the fact the superparticle appeared so much stronger and was recovering rapidly. As with all tremors, she wondered if it was the warning of a much bigger shock.

Morning brought with it a sky of the palest blue and a crispness in the air that you could cut with a knife.

Stein was alert, drinking in the fresh colour and looking south in the direction of CERN. The feeling of invigoration that had returned to him was not only fantastic but also absolutely essential: he would otherwise have buckled under the strain of the twin imperatives of helping return Zein and his fellow Bugz to Zyberia and preventing the unthinkable calamity that could befall Earth.

After a late breakfast the day was spent going over the plan for CERN. Blipp confirmed what he had feared: that preparations were going ahead for the test firing of the Parallel Beam Collider at two o'clock the very next morning, midsummer's day. Icarus Ashcroft was wasting no time, and certainly not with Svetlana Grigoriya at his elbow and she in turn had the DG in her pocket. The IDO traffic that Blipp had intercepted regarding the power drain from two national grids for the switch on was threatening a system overload. The vast bulk of CERN's employees was completely ignorant of the deadly work in progress under their noses and the modifications put in place by Ashcroft under Svetlana's instructions.

Despite being braced for bad news, the fact that imminent danger awaited all humankind was still astounding. There was no time to waste; they had to get hold of Svetlana. Gayle insisted she would track her down herself, and the three children were desperate to get to their

301

father. They had tried to contact him but had been told politely that he would ring back. Sam had received an IDO message that simply read: 'Back soon, love to you all, need to sort business out here. Dad.'

His IDO had no signal when they tried it again. It was impossible to get him. Colleagues reported the same thing, that Ashcroft was at the test facility, ensconced with his strong Yorkshire tea and a couple of sandwiches among his cables and instruments, and he had given strict orders he would speak to no one, until tomorrow.

There was nothing for it but to turn up at CERN and trust that the influence Blipp and Gayle had would gain them entrance. Reinforced blast-proof doors, alarm systems, security locks and protective coding were no barrier whatsoever to the Bugz; disabling and breaking them down, however, was a last resort. The less public awareness of anything unusual afoot the better. Surprise was usually the best weapon, and swift, clear action. And anyway, as the Bugz within their hosts knew well, they were themselves the hidden architects; the establishment and development of the entire organisation could be said to be a project of their own devising.

After a restless day Lycian and Elsie boarded the launch that evening with Blipp, Stein and Mr Nimmo. Gayle had insisted that the Ashcrofts drew lots as to who should go to CERN, as their being pent up together might prove a security risk if things went wrong. She used an expression Zein was fond of, that 'it was not a good idea to keep all their eggs in one basket'. She felt it best that Lycian should stay and be protected, and Zag within her felt it best that the superparticle should be kept away from the action. Zein disagreed. He fixed the lots so that Lycian came along. If Svetlana were to be negated he may need the diamond-hard quality of the superparticle's equation at hand. The seismic energy wave it had engendered the night before was surely the prelude to its awakening, and it might supply answers to why they were here in this universe.

'Any chance I can go ashore and stretch my legs, Mrs N?' Sam asked, to which he received the following firm answer: 'Didn't you listen to what we were saying, dear? Heading off into the wide blue yonder might get you more than you bargained for.'

Gayle stood by the deck railings and stared at the launch as it headed south down the lake, then turned her gaze on the clump of mist starting

302

to gather on the slopes above Montreux. As the evening became unnaturally colder it was slowly descending towards the town.

'I'm going to catch a movelet or do some interactive climbing, then,' Sam said, and Mrs Nimmo at a nod from Gayle followed him.

Zag, from Gayle's position by the deck railings, reviewed the defence ring system placed round the old steamer, a ring ever so slightly chinked. The chink, her own exquisite modification to Zim's impenetrable battle ring, would mean a decisive defeat for those aboard the Siracusa. It resembled the postern gate in an obscure corner of a mighty fortress being left open.

She had been keeping Ziel fully informed of events, just as she had been for the past two and a half Earth millennia, ever since her visit to the Great Library an even longer time before then, but she was becoming disenchanted with the increasingly rigid and narrow equation choking that oh so alien faculty. Zein's equation might have occupied the other undesirable extreme these days, flexible and unBugzishly fuzzy, but at least his receptiveness and connectivity with humans kept him focused on the quest, plus he had Lycian under his wing.

Zag's memory units jarred and they stirred Gayle's recollections too for a nanosecond. It was not easy to forget that Ziel had been prepared to sacrifice Gayle on the flight from the States and even to sacrifice Zag herself. They had both nearly been annihilated. Ziel claimed that she prized loyalty highly, yet she had little regard for it in practice. Anyway, she would never comprehend Zag's feelings for Gayle, for those featured in neither Bugz nor human thinking. In fact Ziel would never comprehend Zag's make up, period.

Zag did not appreciate being lumped together with guileless mutant particles of a solely negative orientation. All Ziel wanted was to cancel the other side out, whereas Zein was focused on salvation for all, including that of his enemy. Zag felt displaced between positive and negative. The negative might be dominant, but she had a growing unease that she had chosen the wrong side. Not of course that either side was right. Not that either side would ultimately matter.

MORE BLACK PONDERINGS

Sweetness and light were not top of Ziel's list of likes, but on the odd occasion they could offer gratification, and this was one such. It had been a trying night what with her little turn after feeling that seismic wave, and she could only hope that the short visit she was about to pay on the steamer would go as planned. No more nasty jolts like the seismic one, at least.

Her mind was at present on another vessel. She sighed. It seemed she couldn't leave the Zarantula for more than a couple of Earth days before discipline on board descended into insubordination. Win's little outing with Zedex and their high functionaries to Cambridge had not gone unnoticed. She had been a little distracted from that, what with so many other players on her binaryboard to keep a watch on. But was she losing her grip? Certainly not! Nothing that a little summary annihilation would not fix.

Her crew should be grateful, very grateful indeed, that they represented a minuscule irritation in comparison with the zornets' nest they had stirred up in Cambridge. The pulses emanating from the Zargo's stronghold there had struck at her equation like some ear-splitting tuning fork, twanging her equation with discord. When those pulses had rippled across the surface of Lake Leman, just a few miles away they had given Svetlana a splitting headache. They had that same old familiar signature of the superparticle. In that case, what was the zecho she'd felt at the time of Brooke's killing? Was there some aspect of time shift not fully understood? Had the fooler become the fooled in this deception?

Svetlana's IDO bleeped and showed three unopened messages from the Chinese detective. A sharp fingernail coated in deep purple gloss hovered over the display in indecision. It was tempting to string the poor man along, play cat and mouse, only this mouse had its own killer instinct. But no, silence was golden, and the best option was always, including now,

DELETE.

304

63. THE ATTACK ON THE STEAMER

Twenty-seven minutes thirty-eight seconds later Svetlana, Enrico and Vittorio were making their way down the steep mountain roads from Svetlana's mountain retreat, the darkened windows on the limo being the only concession to being inconspicuous. Vittorio cut lazy Z's down the hairpin bends as Sveti viewed herself in the large pull-out mirror, always best to be presentable when visiting. A demonic anti-energy mist preceded the vehicle down to the waiting launch at the lakeside, rolling and thickening like a gathering avalanche in a remorseless series of time-lapse frames. Its stiff icy fingers spread out like outriders, withering tree trunks and bringing permafrost to roots. The unseasonal sight on what was a perfect summer's evening would have surprised most onlookers. But then nature, black Bugz nature, gave way to no human.

Joan Nimmo sat bolt upright from her slumber on the sofa as Zleo jolted alert and detected the descending heavy mist. It was like an old horror movie film set come to Montreux, but not a man-made one.

As she issued a stream of ZZD* distress Bugz, Mrs Nimmo hurried down the corridor and knocked on Sam's door. 'Best keep inside, Sam. I'm detecting something not right.'

It was unusual she had received no warning signal from Zag on deck. The second tier Bugz was still up there by the railings and the particle Zleo within her could sense that she was also alert.

It was clear to Svetlana, setting her sights on the steamer from behind the wheel of her launch, that her plan to whip a young Ashcroft from under everyone's noses and tighten the screw on the professor was

305

not going to be a complete surprise. It was clear to Ziel as well, Zag was not alone on board with Sam in the way she had hoped. The crew on board were irrelevant to her calculations. But the matronly Mrs Nimmo had a Superbugz, locked equation and was at this very moment making her way up on deck. Zag had not alerted Zleo, which was as it should be, but neither had she attempted to block the ZZD Bugz. Why not? Was the wretched Zag in stasis or was it a trap? Either that or she was in one of her fickle moods, which were becoming annoyingly frequent of late.

Ziel took immediate action. She intercepted the distress messengers as they came spinning out of the energy ring and winged their way across the darkening water. She contorted her equation, so easy these days, in order to deploy an umbrella formation of collector Bugz. If time shift could be seen to work in this universe, then why not another Zessian art? Anything outlawed and deemed unethical and heretical, at least in Zyberia, usually implied it was highly effective and desirable. She needed every string she could add to her bow, now that Zein not only was making for her most precious prize, Ashcroft, but also had the superparticle equation in tow.

The collectors deployed caught with ease the travelling ZZD Bugz with a signature that mimicked the equation of Zleo and then admitted them into a zone whose centrifugal forces trapped their energy and scrambled their distress signal.

Ziel exhaled zotons of satisfaction as the launch she had boarded moved forward over the waves and gathered momentum, its roll displacing the volume of water and freezing the lake, creating a channel which formed a floating causeway behind the craft to the shore, capsizing those yachts out for a late sail, rocking the boats in the marinas, and sending lashes of foam across the neat walkways and flowerbeds of lakeside promenades and gardens. The peaks and high mountain slopes round about were bathed in the balmy twilight of late evening, but the lake valley itself had developed its own extreme microclimate. Yet the steamer itself remained calm in the eye of this approaching storm. The mist was closing in on it now as Svetlana sought the treachery of a chink that would allow boarding of the aged steamer. Her feline-like stride on the boarding steps could be sensed, as Mrs Nimmo padded up the stairs from below, the way a bear is alerted to defend its cub.

As Sam also now emerged from below decks, pulling on his T-shirt, his hair tousled and his eyes wide, his feet stumbling after Mrs Nimmo, there materialised from the murk at the other end of the boat three spectral figures, each partly concealed by the shreds of mist adhering to them. Gayle's body lay on the deck face down unmoving and Sam had to presume she was badly injured or dead. Another member of the crew hung off a balustrade like a broken toy.

Zleo, in his state of high vibration, wasted no time in casting about both the young man and his guardian a barrier of zicroscopic blue particles, powerful agents of pure positive energy, particles which painted out with bold strokes the stains of darkness before them. The three figures advanced slowly in a triangular formation, the most large and dense of the three at the apex. There was a whining sound; they appeared to be sucking out their own mass in order to direct a thin red line of light through the apex and straight ahead. The warrior particles initially bounced off the blue counter barrier and whipped back round the coils from which it had emanated, but it righted itself and slowly began eating through the blue, sending an acrid smoke of annihilated detritus jetting off to a great height and filling the air with the high-pitched singing of countless invisible blades.

An intense but unequal battle was now played out, each thrust and counter thrust in time with powerful and strangely melodic singing, music not unlike some great clash of keys and tones sent up by choirs holding forth in opposing cathedrals. It was the sound of merciless power and majesty.

Sam felt as though the deck had slipped from his feet, his bearings had vanished, and he was suspended in the sheet lightning of a silent violent storm filled with cutting arcs and fiery bolts that severed all sense of reality. He saw Mrs N plunge ahead of him into this curious red brightness and take on an unearthly glow. Her form was melting and deconstructing into fragments that intermingled with the blue shards of the breached barrier and the black shrapnel of anti energy. Some of these fragments were tossed overboard like confetti and vanished in the mist.

'Mrs N!' he screamed, but his voice whimpered like that of an uninvited and unprepared chorister.

The spectral pyramid now bore down on the remnants before Sam, intensifying its choral onslaught and stripping the mass from each

fragment until all that was left was a scorched outline on the oak boarding of the deck. The crescendo of feverish singing and stripping was then cut dead by a complete, heart-stopping silence.

Before Sam could draw breath there was a zecho this time, an unprecedented one. It numbed every property of every particle. Ziel and her X, Y attendants felt it. So did those on the Zargo and Zarantula. The zecho was more forceful than that of any simple exiting of an equation. It marked the end of the Superbugz Zleo and human host known as Mrs Nimmo in one. It was the second time a great Bugz had been annihilated on Earth and in Ziel's world, evened the score for Zedex at Cambridge. Bug instinct brought each surviving Bugz to a standstill as much in curiosity as in numbness and, in some cases, even sorrow. In the case of Zein, Zon and Zim, it brought acute alarm and an immediate call to return to the steamer.

Sam stared with utter lack of comprehension at the burn mark at his feet. His brain refused to function properly. Mrs N had disappeared into thin air, and he saw no sign of Gayle now. There was no time to collect himself, for in the next moment he heard and saw a soft footfall in front of him, and four strapping arms locked him in their band of muscle as though in a straight-jacket. They were sunburnt hairy arms, and in the split second as he looked up to face his nearest captor he saw on his assailant's hand a ring with a three-legged lion.

The shock of capture was as nothing compared to seeing the faces to whom the arms and gold ring belonged. Sam's jaw dropped. It was as though the once normal bronzed, rugged features of the men in their thirties with tousles of black hair had been gouged from forehead to chin into furrows of puckered flesh, puffing up the outer edges and mottling the skin in livid burns. It was though they had survived having their face slammed down into a hot griddle and then having clawed fingers dragged down the grooves. Eyes and lips had as a result been pushed into parts of their bone structure where they should not belong, and the growl from between the teeth was more feral than human.

A third face now stepped into view, and this one wreaked havoc with Sam's senses. Sultry doll's eyes with long lashes, pert nose, high cheekbones and bee-stung lips emphasised by a pout. Long blond hair skewwhiff yet still photo-shoot style as though carefully arranged that way.

Not pretty boys,' Svetlana remarked to him as she gestured to the men to lower him into the launch.

The ravages on the hosts' faces mirrored the unprecedented strain on her two rogue particles. Xit and Yaba were emptied of almost all their reserve energy as well as their normal amount. The hammering they had received from the red-blue collisions at the heart of the battle on deck had left their logic and function faculties severely fractured. In turn, two of Papa's finest had been so shaken by their unearthly ordeal that they had sunk their heads in their hands, only to find their heads difficult to raise again for their handprints had burned straight into the flesh. Svetlana should have warned them about the destabilising effects on matter of high energy bursts in Bugz warfare.

Xit and Yaba had no time to swap their hosts for a couple of fresh ones, not with so little time to go, even though they were in considerable pain.

'We'll just have to pretend your hosts are from the Venice carnival,' Ziel quipped, and she gave Svetlana a sharp jolt through her synaptic nerve.

'Stop moaning, Enrico and Vittorio,' Svetlana was prompted to snap. 'They can do wonders with surgery these days.' She then looked Sam up and down coolly. 'But you're a lovely boy, it will be a pleasure having your company.'

Sam looked round for maybe some saviour but none was forthcoming. Somehow the entire episode had lasted only a few short minutes, apparently contained in both time and space. There were movements below deck that suggested that calm had reigned supreme there, and the mist was already lifting and dispersing in fluffy baby drifts to reveal the pale blue sky and snowy peaks once more. Sam could even hear one of the crew whistling down below, as though nothing had happened. It was absurd but true.

He opened his mouth to yell again, only to have a hairy hand clapped over it, and he was bundled overboard in what seemed to be only a split second, with his face forced down to the floor of another boat, a launch. He heard the scramble of several pairs of feet about him, the panting of breath and the drilling of high heels into the floorboards just inches from his head, and it seemed the whole world roared into life as he was whipped away, who knew where, who knew at what breakneck speed. He

311

was suddenly blinded by the glare of a blast wave that erupted from the direction where they plus the Siracusa, had stood seconds before and where exploding fragments of wood, glass, metal and cloth were now raining down.

He struggled to free himself once more, and this time the grip was loosened and he looked round and straight up at the doll-like apparition that stood over him, braced against the buffeting of the waves. Svetlana's legs were long and endless, and her bosom rose as she inhaled and exhaled with deep satisfaction.

Her voice came down from a great height. 'Sam, this is a good day for you and me, and even better is to come. Thanks to our new friendship, I will ensure we both see our dreams come true. Here, have a Zapper, darling, sour cactus fruit and ginger, my favourite. I will pop it straight in your mouth as it could burn your fingers, there! I reckon we could both do with one. Sadly, because of our friend Joan Nimmo I can only offer Enrico and Vittorio this Vodka, I don't think they will be on solids for a while. Boys get some of this down you and put some on your faces, I don't like your odour.'

64. THE STIRRING OF ZARETH
Same day

Blipp, Stein and the Haslingdene household might have had the benefit of very sharp human minds plus the guidance of three Superbugz and one convalescing superparticle between the five of them, but that didn't mean they were easily able to gain access to CERN. Their half an hour or so on site should have been ample time for the Bugz to get their analytical units whirring and clicking to a conclusion, but it wasn't. The party wouldn't even have made it past reception had they tried. The days of low key red and white barriers and electronic passes seemed to have vanished. The place was now ringed with a cordon of reinforced blocks and armed guards were posted at all entrances. The personnel within might have thought that the tightened security was merely the best of human thinking and technology in following police procedures, but it was clear to all that each lock, seal and alarm system here was bristling with layers of intense anti-energy fields warped by some curious Zessian trickery. It could only mean the hand of the black queen Ziel. She checked their move.

The acute alarm felt by every member of Blipp's party at the zecho of Joan's death and Zleo's annihilation had already sent them racing back to the steamer. But when an incandescent ball of orange lit up the northern end of the lake and obliterated the twilight, Elsie looked at Lycian and Mr Nimmo sank his head in his hands and moaned. Only the very worst could have happened. The Bugz knew already Ziel had somehow annihilated Zleo. It was the signature zecho of a great equation being rent apart.

313

As they sped across the water Elsie and Lycian felt only a light flutter in their hair from the strong wind, they heard no rise in tone of the launch's engine and they saw no stormy wake left behind it, yet it was clear they would be back at the Siracusa much faster then the earthly motor might be expected to do the job.

They arrived to find remnants of the steamer floating on the surface. There was no sign of life as they scanned the wreckage in the half light. There would be no wailing sirens on shore just yet, all had happened so quickly. The cloying mist had evaporated as quickly as it had appeared. Elsie gripped Lycian so that he gave a cry.

'Where are they? Sam, Mrs N, all the crew? What have they done to deserve this?'

Lycian began to double up in agony as his stomach cramped and he looked at his sister. 'I know. I feel helpless, Elsie!'

The light from Blipp's launch scanned the iridescent surface that reflected a low moon. The temperature was freezing, and the moonlight picked up the ghostly bobbing of small bergs around them. Guiding their launch through this shifting maze of ice the party found the stiff body of a woman hanging on to some wreckage. The blue apparition was Gayle. Mr Nimmo pulled her swiftly up into the launch and bundled her in into a tartan blanket from the hold and tipped some Irish whisky through her lips.

Gayle gasped and twitched. 'It was Svetlana!' she choked. 'Sh – she killed everyone. Except Sam. She thought I was dead.'

Elsie gave a cry. 'Sam! Oh, thank God! Oh no, I mean, Mrs Nimmo...'

'So Joan is gone,' Mr Nimmo said quietly.

'Yes. Sorry. She was heroic, tried to stop them taking Sam. Paid the price for it.'

'Nimmo, I'm really sorry,' Stein said, touching the man's shaking shoulders.

'Poor Mrs N! And she was so lovely!' Elsie buried her head in Lycian's chest.

'You're saying they took Sam?' Lycian asked Gayle. 'And the crew?'

'The crew are all dead, I think.'

Zein glanced at Zim as their hosts stood back.

'More game pieces for bargaining, wouldn't you say?' Zim observed.

314

'So it appears.' Zein's messenger Bugz were faint. He was creased with the counter-currents of energy suddenly flooding his pathways, stabbing at unexpected points in his equation, twisting his analytical units inside out and yet frothing with Z units and a pure charge. He'd never experienced anything quite like this before.

'My friend, I'm picking up some message. It's downloading at a rapid rate. But I can't tell... can't tell...'

'Can't tell what?' Zim prompted him.

'It's in code, or some different transmission index anyway, I can't image it.' Zein's rings were oscillating and relaxing repeatedly. Black and white, black and white, neither black nor white, he couldn't tell, it was all blurring. He felt he was about to explode.

'It's the superparticle Zareth,' he gasped. 'He is asking who we are and if we answered the distress signal.'

Zon looked round from within Mr Nimmo's shaking frame. 'He's asking who we are? I'd like to know who he is! And if Zyberia still exists! And how we get home!'

'We haven't got time for any of this,' Zim said. 'You need to block out whatever the message is for now and focus, Zein. We have to move quickly if we're to stop Ziel.'

'I feel it's my fault Zein, how did she get through the defence so quickly and overpower Zon and Zag? It's worrying.'

'But this is it, this is the message, the light, that has drawn us on here!' Zein said, still creased.

'Listen to me.'

Zim snapped with impatience, set Blipp back in front of the boat's controls as though he were a rag doll, and turned the engine up full throttle, zyclear throttle. They had to get back to shore. Gayle needed treating for hypothermia and above all else the switch on the PBC must not be thrown. Only then could the Ashcrofts set about looking for Sam and the Bugz get cracking supercodes.

Stein leaned over the railings to retch, and Zein within him realised that the new contact with the superparticle was critical, it needed to be acknowledged right now. He couldn't understand all the complex equations and probabilities being thrown across the divide. Even his Superbugz faculties were not up to the task. They appeared primitive in

315

comparison to the data now flowing in him. He knew only one thing, and that was to find the answer to what was meant by 'salvation'.

Zareth, his analytical units told him, Zareth, his values told him, Zareth, his sensors told him.

'I am Zareth,' the superparticle told him. 'You know me.'

'I know of you. You are a legendary construct, a superparticle, you are the same, yet you are not the same,' Zein breathed. 'Your equation is far beyond mine; I cannot link.'

'I am not the same,' Zareth said, 'yet we are linked already. We are linked also to our hosts here.'

'There is no time—' Zein thrashed about in panic as Blipp's launch reached its moorings and the party climbed into the two waiting eco-UV LandWagens to speed along the autoroute. Blipp only ever expected the best for every occasion: the body panels on the vehicles pulled their power from the sun's rays by day and the Earth's energy by night and provided a bottomless supply of silent fuel.

Zareth plucked Zein out of time and space and cradled him in the palm of his outspread insignia, the emblems and cyphers of a mysterious void, the stripes and imprints of a multi-charged being. No, they were not the same, yet their equations linked perfectly.

Zareth's gaze came from every angle; he carefully turned over every facet of Zein's equation in the manner of a master craftsman. He then spoke, and clothed Zein in burnished messenger Bugz that brought to him an invigorating glow and the clarity of understanding.

'These carbon creatures contain different versions of our own equations,' Zareth said. 'They were in the distant past part of the same species of particle as ourselves and they have devolved as a result of a cataclysmic event. Our hosts' equations are familiar, but feel the rough edges of yours and the even rougher edges of theirs; they are a broad canvas of emotions. Now feel the rich complexity of my equation as it threads through yours; it is the silk missing currently in the human weave and the silk that frayed in that of the Bugz from the dawn of Zytopia. I am an extant echo of the past when the particles of people and Bugz were one, of a time given to great construction when the pendulums of time were fashioned to give rhythm and symmetry and harmony. I am the last of the great Bugz that had knowledge of this place.'

'What of salvation?' Zein asked. 'How can Bugz hope to progress without change and without an understanding of this other dimension? We are stumbling, as are our hosts.'

'It is the linking of equations,' Zareth answered. 'I have guided you here for reasons of my own survival, but you need to understand above all else that these human equations around us were as much a part of us as the black Bugz are the mirror opposite of white Bugz. They are integral to the progress needed for building a harmonious future. We may be powerful and they weak, but we should not underestimate their potential. As regards making contact with these equations, be they friend or foe, you are best advised to study the Library codex in more detail and not to play about with what could be a dangerous coalition.'

'Why are you here? Why are we here? Do you, like me, feel the sensations of colour, do you feel what our hosts call 'sadness'? Do you yourself seek a linking?'

'I was unable to link with anything but a mirror particle in this universe,' Zareth said, 'or there would have been massive dissonance. It just so happens that this very special planet is mentioned in the codex in connection with the escape from the dark convergence, and as it does contain a particle I can link with I cannot now withstand the pull of the zides beyond the bridge back to Zyberia. The pull is great and time is therefore short. Earth is the pool of salvation from which a greater Zytopia can be built even stronger then before. This link is permanent, Zein.'

'What of the Library texts?' Zein asked, feeling that his analytical units were being sapped by the entity, which needed colossal energy to reinvigorate itself.

'It is unclear how the entrapment in and escape from the dark convergence could be related to the connection to this planet,' Zareth answered, 'but the codex records both its existence and that of the great particles as yet living undetected within the primeval DNA.'

The emblems and cyphers now fragmented, the burnished light dimmed, and Zein felt the tug of the super-equations communication disconnect from his core like a wind blowing through a dandelion head.

He had looked on a window of a past that spanned two universes and a time when the equations of the humans and Bugz had been linked, an extraordinary revelation, which would change forever Zein's perception of his existence and the worlds around him.

317

65. ARRIVAL AT CERN
Same day

The short time needed for Blipp's launch to make for the wreckage of the steamer was the same as that taken for Svetlana and her two accomplices to whisk Sam to shore and pile into her limousine.

Enrico had helped pour Svetlana into the passenger's seat and was now helping her knock back a quick vodka from the drinks dispenser with a handful of Zappers for a chaser. The poor woman needed it. Her equation had been so abused by its uninvited lodger that it was fraying at the edges and most of its values were fast becoming defunct. Ziel had to kick some life into her Venetian puppets. Xit's and Yaba's hosts resembled deformed, masked misanthropes and Svetlana now resembled a lopsided mannequin.

Svetlana's IDO was bleeping. It was Papa. Best not elaborate on the messy operation at the steamer. Best not mention Gayle's possible treachery. Best not mention she herself was feeling very 'second hand'.

'Hi, Papa,' she beamed.

Papa's whiskered face and coal-black eyes loomed out of the IDO display. A look of surprise crossed them briefly. Svetlana appeared a little more worn these days, more like a high-class hooker than the classy act he'd first seen back in January. He nodded as he listened to her update. All was going to plan? Great, great. There in the next couple of minutes? Va bene. No, that was not all he was after. He'd like a few more details, actually, before Operation Cobra started in earnest. No, she wouldn't be boring him with trifles; this was his retirement package and he wanted

318

a full brief. One of the Professor's boys kidnapped, you say? Mannaggia! Papa clicked his tongue. The unnecessary publicity...

'It's blackmail, remember, Papa,' Svetlana reassured him. 'Ashcroft and his family won't talk. We've only a few short hours to go now.'

Papa confirmed that his son and grandson were on their way. They would be at the east gate of the CERN site as planned any time now. Still no word from Marco, by the way. Extraordinary. And where the hell was Fabricio?

It was Svetlana's turn to be vexed. 'Look, he was just a young puppy, wet behind the ears, raw material, and now he's gone, pouf! Forget him. Would you say he was indispensable, Papa?'

'Well, no,' said Papa.

'And did he have information he might leak?'

'No, it's true he didn't. Ah, well.' Papa stroked his rat's tails. 'Perhaps a generous donation to his family church in Marostica would appease my brother, what do you think?'

'Such a kind gesture,' Svetlana said. 'Put that on your expenses claim, and let's think no more about it.'

'Now, a quick word with Enrico and Vittorio, if you please.'

'They're sitting in the back of my limo and being slowly squeezed to death with cramp the longer we hang about. Is it really necessary? They send you their love.'

Papa laughed dryly. 'I want to make sure they haven't disappeared.'

Svetlana sighed, and quickly flashed her IDO over the back of her seat into the night gloom of the car's interior. 'Say hi, boys. See, Papa?'

'What the hell–?'

'They're worn out from working hard today. I'll be in touch, ciao.'

'Who's that guy? Where are we going?' Sam demanded.

'Tch, tch, such a fuss,' Svetlana said over her shoulder as she sped along the autoroute to CERN. 'I told you our dreams would come true. You're going to see your father. And your mother. Now isn't that nice?'

If only; it was true Sam considered that this woman held nothing sacred, everything was dispensable whether it be human's lives or their ideals.

The sleek bullet-nosed limo glided past security at the main entry on the north side of the Meyrin site. Svetlana flashed her digital sticker and a smile at one of papa's newly installed security guards and pulled over in the No Parking area. She saw the lights on in the massive temporary incident room that Mr Chan had had airlifted into the grounds. She wondered if this hound was still sniffing round even late in the evening?

Svetlana locked her hand in Sam's, whistled to the other two to follow, and trotted him across a shadowy expanse of lawn to the magneto shuttle train that then took them the few kilometres to the surface site of the PBC. The site consisted of a large hangar-like edifice with some service buildings and vast loading bays, and around it lay open fields now bathed in moonlight. It occupied the spot where the old ATLAS detector had once stood on the ring of the now defunct Large Hadron Collider, and where part of the old circular tunnel now formed one end of the new linear one. The party entered through a side door, and Ziel methodically disabled and reset every blue viewer they passed by. Svetlana paused by another door to a sealed room, which lay outside the radiation-proof sliding doors into the main area. She unlocked it and poked her head in.

Svetlana escorted Sam to a safe room just outside the radiation-proof doors to the main experiment area, for use in emergencies with an independent supply of power and running water and with a store of food, drink and clothing.

'I will leave you to link with your spawn,' Svetlana announced to the woman with a pale drawn face and soft brown hair sitting in a far corner, her head resting on a pillow. 'Enjoy it while you can.'

She pushed Sam into the room, and as mother and son recognised each other in astonishment and crushed together Svetlana remarked to Vittorio, 'I do like these moments of human emotion, especially when we know they will be short-lived; it reminds me so well that this species has not improved, even after all this time, and that it even revels in its own destruction.'

'You see what a miraculous recovery your mother has made, Sam,' she added brightly. 'Stop gawping, boy, this woman's not a ghost. Let's go and find dear Henri.'

'Ten minutes, darling,' she told the DG a few moments later, as his office door clicked shut behind her. 'I can't keep Ashcroft and the boys waiting, and you are going to join us on the PBC site in time for the switch on. I'm going on a long trip, you see, so here's something to remember me by.'

Svetlana slipped off her dress, and Henri whined in delight.

320

A WELCOMING PARTY

Papa's son and grandson and a number of hired ex-military had arrived at the north gate, moving into position at 9pm as planned at various gateways. The main group were to wait in the shadows near the lifts by the access shaft to the experiment area until they heard the click of Svetlana's heel. No response on her IDO when they tried to report their arrival. Wretched woman. Papa's son had never danced to anyone's tune before; this was his first time, and he had sworn this was also his last.

A NOT SO WELCOMING PARTY

James Drew paced the same few yards in his office that he had paced for the past two hours. He needed space to think. He had spent yet another afternoon at police HQ in Geneva looking at digifootage from the PBC launch and trying to field questions about his security staff. The ecoterrorists had been identified, as had the wearer of the Patek Philippe watch.

He could understand why Henri was beefing up security now that Ashcroft was back in action, but why the need to replace so many of his own personnel with some hired Italian security company? There were even more of them this evening, all ready in the black CERN uniforms, rolling up in specially armed vehicles.

There was another mystery. It appeared that the timings on the pico surveillance equipment had been tampered with. There was a discrepancy of two and a half minutes recorded at the time of the shooting. The clock on the surveillance bluecams had given 11.33.08. The atomic clock shown on the wall by one of the cams had given 11.35.36.

Wai Chan was meanwhile talking to his officers in the ultra-bright, ultra-clean incident area and expecting answers from Drew. Now was as good a time as any given the need for overtime on the case tonight and the frustration while waiting for the switch on.

He was voicing to his colleagues his reservations about Svetlana Grigoriya. It seemed she was at the centre of all this, and he had this curious feeling that she was standing aloof and quietly cheering on the sidelines in the manner of a Roman courtesan at the games. Wai Chan was a more perceptive man than he knew.

He wanted her pulled in. Look at her ice-cool, almost robot-like reaction in the recordings, look at the student from CalTech with the awful burns, look at the connections with that Mafia-type organisation, look at her disappearance since the event, and no doubt there was more. He wanted her badly. Even more badly than most other men did.

He looked out at the armoured vehicles outside disgorging a number of outsourced security guards, and sighed. How could he solve the killings while he only had bits of information and the Director General made sure this place leaked security like a sieve?

One reassurance was that the checks on the five students from Cambridge, the 'Prof's boffs' selected by Ashcroft to assist him, had proved clear. Anyhow, the DG had sanctioned Ashcroft's request; let Ashcroft have what he wanted if he was going ahead with firing up the PBC. The black sheep was now returning to the fold, and CERN needed positive publicity.

Wai Chan called Drew on his IDO to get an update. Drew seemed distracted. Something else was different now. There were erratic blackouts registering along the pico surveillance cameras at the head of the access shaft above the PBC experiment cavern. And there was some activity at the north gate. Blipp and Gayle Richter were there, with a party of people of different ages who were, Drew assumed, the VIPs Henri had mentioned. It looked like some bizarre late night picnic. They were now heading off on the magneto shuttle to the PBC site. Drew cut off Wai Chan's call and jabbed the number to the gate in his IDO. What the hell was going on? He had a feeling Wai Chan was about to storm in and ask the same question.

66. THE HALL OF THE MOUNTAIN QUEEN Same day

As Blipp's party were boarding the magneto shuttle, Svetlana had Sam and Brooke and her two disfigured Venetian henchmen in tow as she whisked them down a lift in the PBC access shaft, marched them past rows of safety hats and boots ('No need for that stuff') and punched in the access code by the vast double rad-proof doors. Here was the entrance to the main PBC cavern. She briefly passed her wrist across a screen next to the code panel for it to read and confirm the biometric information permitting only authorised staff safe entry into the beam areas of the site.

'Welcome to my kingdom,' she said with an exultant gesture, as the doors slid shut again behind them.

Five minutes later Blipp and his party stood at the same entrance. They were prepared for problems gaining entry into the cavern, but saw straight away that the code panel had been disabled. It seemed they were expected, and the doors slowly swished aside

Even Blipp was impressed. What lay beyond made each of them lose all sense of proportion and reality. They stood with their backs to a great cylindrical void which they entered one third of the way up. They found themselves gazing up from the bottom of a vast metallic cave of gleaming frontier technology at a forty-storey high construction, set in a drilled core of rock fifty percent wider than the Roman Colosseum. It sat god-like above a pit, which was itself a further twenty storeys deep into the ground.

323

It was Ashcroft's beloved detector. It was a gigantic catherine wheel consisting of gleaming red, silver and blue radial segments, each one packed with decapole magnets, pumps, cryomodules and power amplifiers. The detector was threaded on two vast steel cylinders, the twin beam lines, and the pit the entire construction straddled was a trench of liquid argon. This cut into the thick concrete base and metal bed plates below, and ran as far as the eye could see down a tunnel from the CERN complex, pointing straight as an arrow at the heart of the Jura mountains. From the detector itself there trailed countless numbers of cables leading to the banks of detector electronics in a smaller cavern nearby, ready to feed the gargantuan appetite of the Grid clusters round the globe.

Before this dizzying spectacle stretched a shining arena, an experiment pit snaked with coils of vanadium composite wire and thick power lines and surrounded by rows of giant superconducting magnets with the eerie look of frozen-faced sentry spectators. Behind these rose a forest of gantries and girders, their tops nearly reaching the cathedral-like Chromothene dome above.

The control room to one side was Ashcroft's retreat, his ringside Riccarro seats to the race that beat all other races, before the starting pistol had even been fired and a track that had an end somewhere beyond infinity. The low growl of pent up energy suggested all was now assembled and in place: the prototype hybrid design systems for normal conducting and superconducting radio frequency waves, that would provide a high accelerating gradient never before reached; the endless safety tests, cold tests and multiple systems tests; the nanoputer simulations, the final checks and the all clear from the commissioning team.

Blipp and the other unbelieving onlookers now heard Svetlana give a deep sigh of satisfaction and saw her stride out into the arena with hands jammed on her hips to survey her domain. It seemed that they had entered the hall of the mountain queen.

'Elsie! Lycian!' Sam yelled.

'Mum!' Elsie screamed as she recognised the figure next to Sam.

'Oh, I do like engineering family reunions,' Svetlana exclaimed in delight, popping a limited edition extra-strength nuclear-force Zapper on her tongue, and feeling its fizzling acid send a strange rush of zotons to her head. 'And we're all here right on time,' she declared, as Ashcroft and Christian with the rest of the PBC team emerged from the control room, looking dazed. 'So now it's just a case of saying our goodbyes before we have to fly off.'

Svetlana thanked Stein and Blipp for coming, gave Gayle a knowing 'tut-tut' look and expressed surprise at her surviving such a long cold ducking, and patted Mr Nimmo on the shoulder. 'Sorry about Mrs Nimmo, by the way. We wanted to save her, but I'm afraid she just wouldn't cooperate. I know you had grown close.'

'And I now hope to get closer to you, Miss Grigoriya, so we can discuss my views on the matter in a little more depth and reach a very satisfactory conclusion,' Mr Nimmo fumed.

Stein held back his shaking friend to calm him and address Svetlana himself. 'We have come for the Ashcrofts, to save Icarus from himself and any suicidal undertaking, and to understand what you're planning here.'

'Ah, my mirror,' Ziel from within Svetlana grinned as she came face to face with Zein. 'I don't mean anything bad for our human hosts. I simply want to get back to Zyberia; that's all I've ever wanted to do, and Professor Ashcroft here has kindly agreed to help out. It is my duty as leader to do so, if the elected black phase is to continue.'

'But we need the help of these humans,' Zein argued. 'We now understand something of the special qualities locked in their equations.'

'How touching,' Ziel answered. 'You've been having a little ring-á-ring with Zareth, I imagine? He hasn't seen fit to make my acquaintance yet, but I can reassure him that the little bit of mess he helps create here will help save the Zyberia that's so close to his newly acquired heart.'

'Let me get this right,' Zein said, his equation locking horns with Ziel's. 'Your idea is that Zareth and I deliver ourselves up for you to do with as you will, stand back and allow potential mass destruction on this planet, so that Brooke, Elsie and Sam can live? And what assurances do we have that they will live?'

'Exactly none, my mirror. All you need to know is that if you do not comply we will start with Brooke right now and finish a job we did not see fit to complete before.'

Svetlana glanced at her watch. 'Eighteen minutes to switch on. Icarus, time for you to prepare the very special injection batch of particles we have here.'

Ziel within her looked at Lycian. She couldn't understand why the superparticle had latched on to such a sickly human frame. He was standing transfixed, as though the voices of Svetlana and the others around him were coming from across a great divide. He felt himself being plucked out of time and space, he felt diamond seeds exploding in his thoughts. He felt Zareth's coils flexing within him. We are linked.

Ashcroft was walking across the arena to understand what was going on. He was also staring incredulously at his wife and beginning to tremble. He looked exhausted. 'I'm sorry you felt you had to come and see this. It's nearly all over now, isn't it, Sveti?'

'Indeed it is, and a good job too.'

'Don't worry, Brooke!' he called to his wife.

'Mum! It's a miracle to see you!' their children cried.

'More like a living nightmare,' she said faintly.

The deeper understanding of the danger that Svetlana was invoking from the behemoth had entered both Lycian's and Stein's heads simultaneously. Lycian's equation was a perfect fit. Stein's was nearly so. Svetlana's on the other hand was crude and reaching meltdown.

Zareth sent the clear communication Bugz of ancient lineage. 'When we get near the time you should let me join and protect you from the damaging beam.'

It was at this point that Zein and Stein felt the endless complexity and power in Zareth's equation. It was stored and banked and shielded from anything not allowed access. It was a dam equivalent to a universe of matter and energy.

'How entirely logical,' Ziel commented, 'to have our superparticle friends tell these two humans to come with us and save me the bother of having to annihilate their relatives'.

'What is this?' Ashcroft asked, looking bewildered as he became aware of the interchange between human and Bugz.

'It can't be all sweetness and light today, I'm afraid, Prof,' Ziel spoke through Svetlana. 'You can still get on with tracking your precious Midas particle, but we need your precious son and our good friend Stein to give the main PBC beam just that extra punch we need.' Svetlana strode around the arena, spreading out her arms as though addressing the multitudes across her empire. 'You know, I hadn't counted on having a superparticle as well as my mirror Bugz to get back home. What is the quaint term you use? Killing two birds with one stone. They will be going over the Bridge of Annihilation together.'

'NO!' Ashcroft roared. 'What are you saying? This was not part of our deal! What nonsense is this? What Bridge? I'm the one in control of this machine! I'm not sacrificing anyone, that's a fact!'

'Any more hysterics, Icarus, and we might have to make further sacrifices. My ugly boys are here at my bidding, and I'll have you know that the entire sum of your distinguished human equation is no more than a speck of muck under my heel.'

'This is not just about the Midas particle, Dad,' Lycian called out. 'This is not just about our planet. This is far greater; it's about two universes. Don't worry about me! I know what I'm doing.'

Ashcroft stood uncertain, white-faced and twisted with pain.

Lycian drew his sobbing sister to him. 'I must go,' he said gently. 'Be strong now, Elsie. What was a future with MS going to hold for me anyway? I'm feeling better than I have ever done, amazingly well. Do you know, I can feel everything about me, not just all the machinery in here but the individual particles that make up and fill this cavern. I am changed. Try to understand that.'

Elsie nodded without comprehending, still clinging to him.

Stein stood by them, quivering. 'I must come too,' he said. 'Somehow I know it's the right thing to do. In fact maybe my whole life was geared towards this moment. I have no relatives, nothing to tie me down, and I was empowered to make a choice, wasn't I, Blipp?'

'Indeed you were, Jonathan, but even without the agony of leaving family behind the choice you made was a brave one, laying down your life to save others.'

As Bugz and humans stood facing each other, frozen for a moment, a zicroscopic light streaked in from nowhere, hovered in exhaustion above the arena and sank with relief at having finally reached Zein, spilling its considerable weight of data into his very cell. It was the plucky discovery particle dispatched by the Zargo at the time of the first parley by the cosmic rubbish heap, backfired from the bowels of the Zarantula and finally coming to deliver its message.

Everyone viewed Lycian, with tears silently streaming down his cheeks, as he straightened his shoulders and walked steadily with Stein across the arena, both touching Ashcroft's hand briefly in farewell. They calmly climbed the platform steps and entered by way of an open-ended cap the central chamber of the detector. It was enclosed in curved plexiglass reminiscent of a helicopter and afforded those outside clear view of the two men, their arms and legs outstretched, being strapped upright by titanium bracelets into their target positions lined up with the main beam. From a distance they looked to be no more than a pair of animal skins hung out to dry from some erstwhile safari. Svetlana felt a buzz of pleasure and checked her watch again, fifteen minutes to go.

A LOT FROM A LITTLE

The particle buried in the Zarantula had extracted confidential files exposing Ziel's plan to give part of the territory of old Zytopia to the mutant particles gathering on the fringe of the empty quarter. The leaders it appeared were ranged in front of Zein in various guises.

Zein understood perfectly now who the perpetrator of the disequilibrium was but maybe not the architect. How Zag had remained undetected in the negative sense but also how the simple discovery particle survived was incredible.

More pressing probabilities including annihilation coursed through Zein's equation but the mysteries outlined needed much greater investigation.

GETTING BRACED

Wai Chan was looking at the row of blue cams in front of him, seeing the passengers on board the internal shuttle. They were all heading for the test firing of the PBC, accompanied by CERN personnel. One member of staff looked uncomfortably familiar, to Chan's liking.

'Can we run that segment of digi again and focus in on that face?' Wai Chan asked. 'Can you run a match?'

'It will take five minutes,' the man next to him said.

'OK.' Wai Chan was a man of patience, even when he felt time was running out.

Henri had called his wife after plunging his head in ice cold water to recover from an action-packed ten-minute interlude with Sveti during which his glasses had been crushed. He would be late home because of the PBC start up, he had said, and even though it was no longer the big media event he had hoped for he still needed to be there to show support for Ashcroft and his team. Anyhow, he thought to himself, if there was a Midas particle, who better to be king bountiful than him? And how much would the US pay to be part of his kingdom, given their position on the international sidelines these days? He could easily write his own credit limit and then double it.

Leaving his office, he made his way to the magneto shuttle, dreaming about the bottomless treasure chest of patents and applications to be had from a substance finer than gold dust that was able build atoms bottom up.

Leonardo Cassaro, Papa's son was also dreaming happy dreams about controlling the empire that would be his once Papa got his retirement package. He couldn't figure out why this deranged Russian she-wolf might want to pay a hundred million US dollars for this one brief night of fun, but the deposit was down and the rest was on the way. Everything was going to plan. Only fifteen minutes to go, and there may not be more unpleasantries than were strictly necessary. All that was needed was for the Professor to throw the switch. The two human targets spread-eagled inside the detector didn't look good news; there was some weird stuff going on here. However, they'd gone in quietly, and just as long as he wasn't involved…

Ashcroft had retired to the control room, ready to throw the switch. The Bugz with their human hosts were now gathered round the detector with bated breath and taut receptors. Millions of billions of electronvolts, fired from the central injector complex through a beam only a fraction of a nanometer wide, would blast the human and Bugz equations to annihilation while affording Ziel a first-class ride back to her universe. As she had said, sacrifices had to be made in this universe and the next.

329

Timing was everything, as was the inclination of the Earth and its relationship to this exact spot in this universe. The trajectory needed to be accurate to a zicroscopic degree, in order to aim the beam at that exact dark spot from where the Bugz had come.

It was necessary to go faster than the speed of light and beyond pearl-portal time travel into a little explored fifth dimension, which would throw up a ladder through the the underside of the black hole. It would be a tricky and messy experience, but Zein's and Ziel's memory banks combined to recall the precise coordinates given on their zectroscopes.

Thirteen minutes to switch on.

Henri boarded the magneto shuttle which took him to the lifts at the access shaft, to find himself joined by a bristling Wai Chan.

'You're up late, inspector.'

'Yes, I'm trying to brush up on my quantum physics. Mind if I tag along?'

Wai Chan's IDO gave a bleep, and the voice at the other end said, 'Sir. Confirmed match. Leonardo Cassaro, age thirty-nine. Mafia connections, drug dealings, wanted in two countries for questioning.'

'Monsieur le Baut, I suggest you delay the start up,' Wai Chan barked, as they stepped off the shuttle and headed towards the vertical lift to the PBC cavern.

'Certainly not. I insist it goes ahead, and it's doing so in ten minutes' time.'

Wai Chan scowled, scrolled down his IDO menu, and with a stab of his podgy finger launched the coded distress signal for special forces to descend upon CERN. 'Dragon's lair'.

The men left the lift at the bottom and passed through the vast rad-proof doors into the experiment cavern and the glare of countless sheets of vanadium-hardened steel. Into the innards of some great beast. Wai Chan gaped and dropped his IDO at his feet, as he saw one preposterous conspiracy theory after another explode before his eyes. He must be hallucinating.

'Henri!' Svetlana cried in delight, her voice echoing round the cavern above the accelerator's hum. 'How lovely to see you, darling! And Mr Chan! Mmm, my intuition told me you would not want to miss out on my little show. Indeed, you have the honour of putting all my game pieces in place at last. Now, darlings, my boys will show you up there on that gantry for the best view, oh, and put on these safety goggles if you don't wish to be blinded.'

The DG was staring at a nearby monitor. He was contorting his lips to form words but no sound came out at first. Even without glasses he knew what he was seeing on it. 'What...? Sveti, what in God's name are those men doing in that contraption?'

'She intends to kill them, monsieur,' Wai Chan said. 'Just liked she killed Ashcroft's wife and those terrorists.'

'Henri, you can stay down here with me and Ashcroft and get the best view. I will try to blow you a kiss. I'm afraid it's second-class viewing for the rest of you'.

Turning on Wai Chan, 'Don't go accusing me of murders I haven't committed, Mr Detective Inspector. See for yourself, Brooke Ashcroft's right here in the flesh. And as for those other bits of human flotsam, well, I did you a favour. We now have fewer undesirables on this planet. Boys, show all the members of our audience up to the circle, I mean, the gantry, over there. Standing room only, I'm afraid, but you'll all have your opera glasses. Oh, and it's a Z energy containment area too, best not to touch the edges or they'll spark. Gayle, you can show your true black pennants now and come over to me. I will choose to overlook that little aberration of yours on the steamer.'

Mr Nimmo and Blipp gasped as Zon and Zim within them clicked their sensors on Zag.

'A double particle,' Mr Nimmo muttered.

'How come you slipped out of my net?' Blipp demanded of Gayle. 'All my leads on you, and there were many in place, led to absolutely nothing!'

'Zag and I have been what you might call old family friends,' Ziel smiled. 'Ever since she trotted along to the Library for me at the time of the Disequilibrium in fact, when I received the same TT message as you, Zein.'

Zon remembered the uneasy feeling he had while poised at the rear of the Zargo on its quest to the dark convergence.

'In a way I'm sorry I will have to leave you, but I also have my own mission so to speak, I feel sure we will meet again', countered Gayle as she joined Svetlana near the collector entrance.

'You have my greatest regard, my mirror adversaries,' Ziel fizzed, 'that you managed to get to the battle site in the Empty Quarter, never mind get through the nothingness beyond that. Anyway, less of the niceties. There's an appointment to keep. Zyberia has to be missing its leader and I would be remiss to delay any longer our departure, in fact Zein knows we can't delay it. It is now or sometime never maybe.'

Ashcroft and his boffs watched from the control room as the group including the Ashcrofts, Chan, Blipp and Mr Nimmo were shepherded on to a platform that sent them up the highest gantry in the cavern and filled them with the sensation that they were soaring through a shining, echoing, rumbling void. Far below they saw those they had just left scurrying across the bottom of this colosseum, making final checks and preparing the sacrificial targets. Ashcroft spoke to Christian very quickly.

'When the count is on two you must try to lead the others up the emergency stairs to the safe room. I have set the emergency dump device to try and negate the worst effects of the overload. I now know it was desperately wrong to get you into this but I did not know the power of this creature.'

'We were all very scared Prof, especially when the armed guards said we shouldn't move. It looks like curtains.'

'Do as I say and tell the others, and you will have a chance.'

Nimmo and Blipp stood rigid with impotent rage on the gantry, as the Bugz within them cursed at Zag's treachery and their inability to help their leader.

Nimmo could, however, think of one channel for his frustration. 'Time for some unfinished business, I think,' he spat, turning to Enrico at his elbow as Zon at the same time rounded on Xit with his energy coils pulsing. 'This is for the loss of a beloved wife and a true and faithful friend.'

The sound of laser-guided thuds of gunfire promptly rang out in thundering echoes round the cavern, and one of the impostor security guards pitched and thudded bloody face up on the steel mesh flooring. Mr Nimmo's bear-like frame simultaneously bore down on Enrico, knocking his gun spinning over the edge of the gantry. The two instantly writhed in a tight knot, wrestling their way to the same edge, the one crushing bulk pressed against the lithe frame of the other in an even match. The two mightiest white and mutant warrior Bugz of Zyberia crouched within their equations threw all Bugz protocol and logic aside. They engaged like two gladiators who must fight to the last, to the accompaniment of high-pitched battle zymns, raised banners of anti-particle mist that lashed around them, and hurled all the weaponry of old Zyberia that they could muster: spiked energy maces, bolts that cut arcs through the air, barbs tipped with the sting of poisoned waste Bugz, until one such bolt whipped clean through Mr Nimmo, slicing him from scalp to sole with not a single ragged tear to the flesh, and flinging Xit back senseless in the zecho blast of Zon's furious annihilation. Enrico was also mortally wounded by the mace, which hung from his chest pulsating like a warning beacon. It was but seconds before his body simply disintegrated leaving a great hole through the middle and the zecho blast of Xit's annihilation.

Blipp, normally a fairly calming influence, turned on the raging Vittorio with a blue fire that one could only describe as some high energy particle laser. For such a big man Sam thought he moved more like a trained Samurai as Vittorio's head was sliced clean from his shoulders. There then proceeded a blast when the Italian heavy collapsed like a fallen tree with a withering groan. Yaba was also annihilated and the zecho blast added to the already deafening reverberation of the PBC.

'Boys! Keep the noise down,' Svetlana rapped out as the onlookers on the gantry shrank back in horror. 'The pearl will open in ten seconds. Ten.'

Zein and Ziel could feel the prickle and buckling force of building energy, as Zareth's tightly coiled and long-dormant equation twitched in anticipation of the violent surge of energy to come. The codes were locking into place. The Bugz saw how the cavern was now suffused in a curious white-black light.

In the goldfish bowl chamber of Ashcroft's detector Stein whispered to Lycian, 'I don't really know what's come over me, even though I made this choice. What gave you the strength to do this?'

'Somehow I knew the time would come when I would have a choice,'

Lycian said calmly, 'and that the choice would not be for me but for others. What real choice did I have anyway? What would life have been like as an invalid, being a burden to my loved ones, compared to a life more complete than any human could ever imagine, whereby I help countless others? I have no words to explain it, but it's as though an untold number of loose ends within me have locked together, a sort of clicking, a snug fit, a completeness.'

'Yes, to be truthful I have been lonely in my life, searching for missing clues about my real parents and I guess Switzerland is my spiritual home but I never thought it would end like this.'

'I don't think it is the end Stein, I think it may be a new beginning for both of us. Let us at least think of the greater good we are doing, but I will miss my family and I pray for their safety.'

Lycian and Ashcroft caught each other's tear-filled eyes through the plexi-glass of the detector and the window of the control room. For a second father and son stood motionless, unhearing, unfeeling, as though kept in suspended animation. Ashcroft was grimacing and battling with an invisible grip as his finger hovered and trembled over the switch.

'I will do what I can,' Ashcroft's lips moved silently. 'I love you Lycian.' Nine, eight, seven...

'You know you can't resist my touch, Professor,' Svetlana murmured. Six, five, four...

'Goodness, what a racket those Ashcroft women are making,' she added, holding her ears and wincing at their screams.

Three, two, one...

'Dad!' Ashcroft heard his entire family cry out, as he twitched robot-like and threw the switch, while at the same time triggering the rapid reaction safety mechanisms to contain the runaway beam and deflect it to the graphite dump of Ashcroft's personal design even before the massive components of the accelerator could even begin to tear apart.

Zero.

'Goodbye,' Lycian whispered, and just before the 5 TeV bullet of Bugz and subquarks slammed into his chest, his last thoughts raced through the course of his life: tree climbing with Sam, his tedious hospital trips, the musty smell in his father's study, the sweetness of his mother's bedtime caress.

335

At that split second the Bugz rose up as one out of their hosts' equations and swarmed in pyramidal formation towards the detector.

'Get down off this thing! Run!' Blipp shouted, as he and his fellow hosts felt the tearing of mental tissue and the gushing out of the charge that had bolstered them for so long. The chorus of zechoes echoed like pistol shots, and the accelerator escalated to a roar as it began delivering up unprecedented energies.

The select few gathered to slip into the main beam that would hurl them at the speed of light in the direction of oncoming particles from the opposite end and meet them at the point of collision where Lycian and Stein and their host Bugz were positioned in the detector.

All the Bugz, that is, except for Ziel. She had been wallowing in her host equation for as long as possible, and was now having incredible problems disconnecting from Svetlana, that wretched YES/NO dilemma again! In the process she had snagged her equation on blackened shards of Svetlana's own, jerked back and had her timing for entering the main beam thrown out of kilter. What in the name of Zess ? It appeared that Svetlana had no desire to run after her fellow humans. The crazed woman was gazing enthralled at the cataclysmic storm whipping up about her and engulfing the structures now trembling about her; she seemed as frozen with the clinical detachment of Bugz observation as Ziel was consumed with the ink-black urgings of a human soul that had gained the upper hand.

Ziel now heard herself, not her host this time, swearing out loud like a Sicilian fishwife. Stupid Russian bitch. She didn't know when to get off; instead she was now throwing a tantrum, shrieking that she wouldn't let Ziel go. And to her horror, Ziel found that for all her Superbugz energy she couldn't just break herself free.

At this rate she, the Black Queen, would be bringing up the rear at blast off. The loss of status was unthinkable. With an incredibly sapping crunch that caused Svetlana to double up and retch, Ziel finally untangled herself and tumbled out, threw herself into the accelerator and blasted past Zag and Win. Never let it be said that she trailed behind a second-tier Bugz or rogue particle, even if she could not get level with Zareth. That zicrosecond's delay at the mercy of Svetlana's mannequin equation had been sufficient to hand the advantage to Zareth even without the billennia of stored energy he possessed.

338

The Bugz pulsed through a series of electric fields oscillating at 50 GHz, fields created by the transfer in quick bursts of high-intensity drive beams to the main beam.

'Come, my beauties,' Ziel murmured as she saw the beam slam into the two human targets and cut into them with its zicrosurgical incision.

The direct hit fused an extraordinary mass of black, white, striped black-white and human equation that kick-started the chain reaction to end all. It catapulted the Bugz and the two human equations Zyberia-ward at many times the speed of light, straight out towards the pearl gateway that opened up a fifth dimension.

The two immense equations still locked with their human ones pulled in their slipstream the unwieldy clots of Ziel, Zag and Win.

Behind the departing Bugz the gleam of the PBC cavern and the scatter of human equations within it dwindled into a pinprick and vanished. And as the Bugz were snuffed out the PBC screens and read outs recorded the usual: multi-coloured spirals showing the trails of secondary particles that danced through their brief existence to their decay.

The flash in and out of Bugz existence would have been the most stupendous data ever to have hit the Grid had it been safely gathered in on the compressed magnetoelectronics of the waiting nanoputers. But scarcely a byte could be saved, for even as the onlookers turned on heel to flee from the gantry and the cavern, the PBC began struggling in its death throes with animal ferocity, its supports buckling and joints snapping, its ventilation systems puffing and its high voltage arteries blowing. The body of the beast had been felled by the tiniest clot passing along its spine. The zicroscopic wobble would have stunned the beam loss sensors one by one and overridden their attempts to deflect it into the beam dump, had Ashcroft not quietly taken emergency measures to contain the apocalyptic destruction he had so well foreseen.

Ashcroft had sprung out into the arena now, and was drowning in a torrent of emotion and a stream of melting copper fast pouring out of the colossal machinery behind the target chamber. His lungs were filled to bursting as he shouted at all about him, as though gesturing in triumph over Svetlana, but his voice was lost. He was beside himself, both ecstatic at the spectacle of unprecedented particle collisions on the screens before him and racked with unimaginable grief. Both he and the two

339

strapped men in front of him stood with their figures contorted by the extreme heat and eerie light of shattering explosions, until the golden rain of metal obliterated them from sight.

Henri was fused to the rail he had been handcuffed to on Svetlana's instructions as the glow reflected in his goggles and his suit began to steam with the heat. He cried out as he fell with his hair on fire, staggering and contorting like a medieval warlock on the pyre.

The cavern and tunnel were aflame with kaleidoscopic colour and resonating with the bleep of oxygen alarms above the crashing of machinery, and by the time Blipp, Wai Chan, the Ashcrofts, the Prof's and Papa's boys had descended from the gantry and reached the rad-proof doors to dash for the lifts, the deadly breath of argon gas leaking from the machine was billowing into a fog. The sporadic bursts of laser-guided gunfire between Papa's boys and Wai Chan's special forces were no more than the tinny popping of pea shooters compared to the battering the machinery around them was taking.

Off stage came the shrieks of a madwoman. The flipped Svetlana had turned on heel to follow the others, but too late. Teetering from the vacuum Ziel had been left with her equation left in tatters, she felt behind her the hot rushing of molten copper and tungsten as it flowed from the accelerator's wounds across the floor and pooled round her heels. She heard the sigh and crunch of metal as the observation platform for her audience pitched into the wreckage of the PBC.

'Don't leave me all alone!' she heard herself screaming as she blew a last kiss to the burning remnants of the Director General she had really loved. All those years of excess had left Ziel on earth tobe sacrificed to a foreign annihilation.

She staggered to her knees, her blonde hair stretched on end from an electric shock, high heels snapped and skirt twisted up, lips twisted in pain, tongue yanked to one side, eyes burnt out of their sockets, and lungs that would never again inhale the narcotic force of a Zapper. Svetlana Grigoriya splashed and sweated her last in a monster spa of bubbling metal and toxic fumes as the remnants of Ziel's equation exploded in a zecho.

There were other casualties. Zag had been as desperate as Ziel to jump in the beam, and Gayle had clawed in a manic frenzy at Stein's feet as he was spread-eagled like a target to face his martyrdom, but she had been held in check by the powerful super equation just centimetres from her in the target chamber, which at this last split second had recognised Zag for what she was and the unparalleled danger she represented. Gayle was now crouched in mid-action, caught in the metal lava flow. Papa's son and grandson never knew whether it was the incinerator conditions of the PBC cavern or the bullets of Wai Chan's men that killed them; they simply knew as they lay dying that all the money and power in the world meant absolutely nothing any more.

Sam had lunged out of the rad-proof doors and crashed his fist on the illuminated lift panel. The door had swished aside to reveal the bright mirrored comfort of the cubicle within. So welcoming. Brooke, Elsie, Wai Chan and Blipp followed Sam in as the vertical lift gathered momentum till it came to a stop. The doors slid open to reveal Drew and, a crowd of security forces in masks pointing weapons at them.

'Get in the emergency chamber, Wai, and shut the door. We will have to go in and see if we can save any of the others.'

'It's suicide, Drew.'

'It's our job sir, this is our home, our livelihood.'

As the door to the emergency chamber shut Wai Chan gave a mock salute to Drew as he pulled on his mask and the lift descended to hell.

68. AFTERMATH
22 June 2042

Six hours passed before the safe room door could be opened and the filtered halogen lights allowed to cut through the acrid fog. Six long hours of wailing alarms and toppling machinery, melting multiwire and crackling high-voltage instruments.

Blipp, Wai Chan and the Ashcrofts, having escaped up one of the lifts to the top of the access shaft, confounded the medics and emergency services assembled up there by insisting that they wanted to return to see for themselves what had happened. Not that you could avoid the aftermath of the PBC's death throes unless you happened to live in another country. The thirty-kilometre-long tunnel had begun folding in on itself, exuding a pall of toxic gas, pulling up power lines, ripping apart roads and demolishing farm buildings.

Brooke, Sam and Elsie were inconsolable in their grief but refused to be led away. Blipp would not leave their side, and they seemed to gain an extraordinary strength from his presence. He had felt and shown a grief as deep as they had, for Zim within him had been unable to reach the beam in time, but he had collected himself. It is surely meant to be, he kept telling himself. Wai Chan looked at the place in disbelief. The only way he could cope with the unreality of events surrounding him was to revert to cold analytical policeman mode, even though nothing made sense. If his co-witnesses were staying on the scene, he certainly was not prepared to be led away either.

After being dressed in protective clothing befitting astronauts, and then escorted down the thousand reinforced steel steps of the fire

344

escape, the spectacle that met everyone's eyes was one of meltdown, curled and dripping twists of metal, all mantled in shards of a sparkling fine-grained pumice. The only recognisable shapes in the macabre gloom at first were the colossal magnets ringing the arena, hanging from their supports like a necklace of misshapen boulder-sized jewellery.

The first people they met were Drew and Christian and four of Icarus's students.

'How did you manage to survive down here?' Elsie asked them.

'It was Ashcroft, he had told us of the new safe area he had created, which was not on the original plans,' said Christian.

'I'm so happy that you are not dead and the others.'

'Yes, me too,' Christian brushed his hand across the grey dust that covered his face.

Wai Chan gave Drew his hand. 'You did your job, well done.'

'Yes, the automatic door just opened, so I can tell you I was relieved. There is no communication in there and we thought we might be buried alive.'

'So what of the other?' Blipp was curious.

'Look over at this mess and let's see if anyone is alive,' pronounced Drew, once more in charge.

Blipp's party felt no fear as they moved through the carnage. They now saw ahead of them the spread-eagled bodies of Lycian and Stein, still strapped by titanium bracelets to their targets in the wreckage of the detector. They appeared to be almost unaffected physically as if some great force had created a bubble around the figures that other elements were rebuffed by. It was a walk-in Salvador Dali scene that defied all known physics. Twin fountains of molten copper had solidified and hung above the two bodies and the collision point and had formed a half globe round the point of sacrifice. The bodies with small blackened incisions but 2cm across in their chests.

What looked like a dollop of copper-coloured thickly whipped cream turned out to be a hardened glob of metal covering the broken doll frame of Svetlana where she crouched, hands outstretched, eye sockets stark and unseeing, rigid in death.

Gayle could be seen hanging on to the metal cross where Stein still hung. As to the reason why Zag had felt the need for Gayle to grasp

Stein, it was perplexing to Blipp and would require more analysis.

Henri le Baut's remains were swinging like a nursery mobile from the ripped platform by the cuffed wrist that still fixed him to the stainless-steel rods of the gantry. His body was transfixed in the manner of a victim of the Pompeii eruption, stopped as it had been in mid air by the incinerator blast and then the supercoolant blast from the vacuum tank below. The once proud director general swung like an air freshner of old in the breeze that came down from the broken roof of the cavern.

The grisly decapitated slivers that had once been Patrick Nimmo were washed up in a far corner together with the grotesque body of his arch rogue particle rival Enrico. The two, still locked in battle, were now encased in grey dust and glued down on a patch of dried metal. The decapitated head of Vittorio lay next to the body, both prostrate and covered in grey dust.

Drew directed a couple of white-suited helpers to cover the bodies of Papa's team and some of the security team who also had fallen in the fire fight, pointless as it was, because there had been no winners here.

Both Lycian and Stein, however, looked calm and serene even in death. Elsie cried out with unexpected relief when she saw him in such a state of repose. It almost seemed he had wanted to die and found release. The thought was disconcerting: it offered both comfort and distress at the same time. For some reason they had escaped the sprinkling of the fine-grained pumice and the searing heat of the molten copper deluge.

Sam climbed up to Lycian, undid the straps and bracelets and allowed his dead brother to slump forward into his arms, his peaceful face raised up for Sam to press his lips to the cold forehead. It was some difficult moments before the rescue workers could gently prize the two apart.

Wai Chan placed his arm on Brooke's shoulder. She was stroking her husband's encrusted hair where he had fallen in the centre of the arena, where beside his body his finger had spelt the letters 'SALVA' in the dust.

Blipp removed Stein's body from its bound state with reverence, and spoke quietly. 'These were surely brave souls in any world. By the powers of Zo, may their equations live on and do great service.'

Brooke echoed the same as she gazed down on her dead husband's

346

face. His students had told her of his frantic eleventh-hour efforts to contain the beam the second it was unleashed on the world. She wondered if Icarus had died comforted by the thought of the beam dump's success in saving untold lives or tormented by the thought that history would vilify him as the man who had destroyed CERN. If the latter, she vowed to spend a lifetime, if need be, to clear his name.

As she leaned over his body an unexpected shaft of sunlight slid across the two of them. The acrid fog belching out of the machinery was dispersing and drifting up into open air, for where once the dome-like radiation shield had covered the access shaft and PBC cavern there was now only a deep fissure in the ground. A warm breeze whipped up the dust in some eery ghost-like manner as the particles refracted the light in an unearthly orange.

It was 8.15 am on the 22nd June 2042 and the world had woken up to something indescribable, something beyond even the journalistic talents of *The New York Times*. To the helicopters now hovering over the Meyrin site the fissure and the thirty-kilometre tunnel leading off it resembled little more than a necklace of a broken trench, at its centre the jewel of the collapsed dome of the PBC cavern.

All flights to Geneva airport had been suspended and a mass evacuation of personnel and surrounding residents and businesses was already underway above ground. The Ashcrofts, meanwhile watched in silence, Brooke gathering Sam and Elsie to her as the bodies of Icarus, Lycian and Stein were carefully placed on stretchers and covered in white shrouds.

'This is the first case,' Wai Chan said slowly as though drugged, 'that I have been unable to solve, despite studying every microscopic detail.'

He thought about Svetlana Grigoriya. The fact was that even if she had escaped this inferno and made it back to her suite at the Beau Rivage, even if he had been granted a lengthy, up-close and personal interview with her while she unwound with a champagne cocktail and dabbled her toes in a sunken bath of ass's milk, even if she had laid bare her most private confidences, he would never have cracked the case. All he would have learned was that the whole world was surely going mad.

'There's always a first, inspector,' Blipp remarked. 'It's my first real failure too, as it happens. I've lost some of the power I once had to communicate.'

'I can't say I understand what you mean,' Wai Chan answered. He waited for some clarification but did not get it.

'That proves my point,' Blipp said. 'I can't effectively communicate to you or anyone else the fact that I have also communicated with others now either dead or gone. But maybe I will be able to again.'

'I'm still not with you, Blipp,' Wai Chan said.

'Quite,' Blipp sighed. 'Well, it seems we have all made sacrifices, and none more so than our good friends here.' He nodded at the Ashcrofts who were now wearily making their way to the stairs. 'There is more to this than we will ever know.'

Wai Chan sighed too. It made the ecoterrorists, Mafia-type connections and the resurrection of Brooke Ashcroft look like child's play. The file on this case was bulging with anomalies he would never get to the bottom of. It resembled a black hole into which he was being sucked, if that was the correct term for something unpleasant without an end.

69. A FAITHFUL WELCOME

As the five particles crossed the infinite divide at many times the speed of light the hard diamond tip of Zareth's equation took the brunt of the tremendous energy spike with his fellow travellers folded in the mantle of his slipstream, carving, looping, bobsleighing round the underbelly of nothingness where all laws of phyzics were suspended.

It had been much harder for the Bugz Ziel and Zag to split from their hosts than they had envisaged. Win had left the Zargo as instructed, but it soon became clear that whatever plan had been put in place was going wrong. Self preservation had guaranteed that the rogue particle tucked in closely to Zareth and Zein regardless of its previous allegence. The pain of the multiple zechoes in the cavern smarted still.

Zareth was still stirring and flexing his coils as he gulped in the fresh energy provided by the particle beam at CERN. It cleared the fog of forgetfulness that had blinded him so long and sped him on his way in a shower of effervescent zuons. Instead of being annihilated the spike had acted as a key to the lock that broke the shackles on Zareth's equation, allowing him to protect his linked equation Lycian and enfold Zein in a mantle of protection. Its aura had shielded the remains of their hosts on the targets in the cavern.

The soul of Lycian was tucked like an inlaid jewel in Zareth's equation, like a fledgling superparticle himself, and his analytical units were filled with wonder. How could it be that the treasured memories he had left behind him were anaesthetised by the joy of what was surely waiting on

349

the other side? The only pain Lycian felt was the worry that his family would not, could not understand, but the awakening of Zareth's memory within him was already fast invading the space of his own. He was still living but in another form and with a great maze of a labyrinth to explore.

Zein was in mourning, more than Lycian was. Zein felt pulled to human existence the way that Lycian felt pulled to Bugz. Stein's soul was noble and powerful like Lycian's, and he had made the supreme sacrifice as well. Zein could feel that there was no return for Stein, his host's body would decay but his soul was going to live in another world as part of one of its greatest leaders, Zein felt he would have to justify his host partners' death with deeds in the future.

Ziel's charge was, as ever, the complete opposite. It was blinkered with fury in her effort to force her way past her allies Zag and Win and at least come level with Zein. The only way was forward. Any backward look would remind her of the bog of human addiction. She had managed at the very last gasp to kick the bitch whose equation had nearly strangled her own, and she needed to straighten herself out with an ice-cold shower of Bugz detachment, or at least that was the plan.

Zag had not wanted to leave Gayle; she liked her and had inhabited the same body form since the early 1900s earth time. She had broken Zein's rules and this had not been apparent, even though the photo of the B52 had nearly given her away. She had pulled off her host equation crying with despair, but she had her reason and directions to follow that overcame such niceties of like or love. She was after all a warrior. Win flew as dark and sharp, whereas Zag had zigzagged from one side to the other, her grip on Zareth's folds gradually slipping as they accelerated towards the underside of the event horizon into the dark convergence, causing Zag to fall back, slide off the energy spike and spiral backwards.

Entering the black pearl at the underside of nothing was as paradoxical as a moebius strip on earth. The particles appeared to vanish and some indeterminate time later they were picking up the strengthening pull of some welcoming messenger Bugz.

There now appeared ahead of them a swirling of hot red, firing bursts of messenger Bugz in the most velvety of archaic Zyberian tongues, messenger Bugz that licked and warmed Zareth's core like the welcome of the most faithful entity that could exist in any universe.

350

'SALVATION and UNITY,' came the first eager burst, to which Zareth replied, 'GENESIS and UNITY', which was answered by 'LOVE and UNITY.'

The red apparition took the form of a ship of curious design both crude and sophisticated. The figurehead on its prow was carved with a jumble of Zytopian hieroglyphs that read Bugzilla. Its irregular structures groaned with banks of marvellous weaponry and historical data gleaned from millions of stray particles sucked into the void. This great craft of destruction formally pennant craft of Zytopia was a technological marvel even for that past age. The creature vessel propelled itself forward with rows of oar-like appendages encrusted with shining sticky hairs and particle deposits. It defied logic, it defied gravity, and its perfection rating was off the scale.

During the billennia ever since the Battle in the Empty Quarter it had guarded the rim of the hole, amending and updating its contents, and checking and devouring the credentials of all passing particles. As a sophisticated method of transport it had no parallel and even the Zargo and Zarantula were the initial chapters in a very large library of sophistication. It had every bit of information from the two craft, which Zein in the future particular found interesting to analyse, especially in relation to the double particle Zag.

After so many billennia stuck in the middle of nowhere with only the odd swipe at a shipwrecked particle to relieve the boredom, the stupendous and matchless Bugzilla now sent out display Bugz that expended at least two large supernovae of energy. The term firework display would not adequately describe it on earth. Even the nothing next to the craft was frizzled on its edges as the great mass of positive energy waked over its rim.

The only interesting contact he had had with the new Zyberia, Bugzilla said, apart from his encounter with the Zargo and Zarantula when they dropped by, was a search message transmitted from the Apex and a visiting party of trackers sent out from Zyber to comb the battlescape.

Also quite recently a broken mercenary particle that leaked secret, encrypted data like a sieve had been fired into the dark convergence like a splinter of exotic glass, flung by the hand of Zess apparently. These

351

Bugz told of a great swarm of regurgitated mutant particles and the forty-fifth reincarnation of the isotope Zess. The broken particle had seemingly been a mercenary binary particle, which sought to profit from a vacuum forming in the nucleus centre Zyber founded on the old Zytop. It had joined the underclass of mercenary Bugz that carved a lucrative existence out of vicious propaganda and obligatory and immediate data retrieval. It had now been flung into the black hole as discarded goods, had the misfortune to defy more unfortunate odds than anyone would have thought possible: it had fetched up in the only place in the Zyberian universe guaranteed to obliterate it while at the same time guaranteed to collect the information of greatest interest to Zareth and Zein. Bugzilla took his time to analyse this most interesting and dangerous particle. It had not been destroyed even by Zess and appeared to have a hard centre not yet cracked.

The contents of the broken particle were very juicy. They told of the Great Quake, during which Bugzilla had hidden under the rim of the hole, the Disequilibrium, and the disappearance of the cream of the Apex elite in two secretly commissioned Ziremes, when trackers were sent out to the Empty Quarter to scout around the ancient battle site, and back in Zyber soothing electrical pulses had been transmitted to all parts of the universe along with the lifting of restrictions on the consumption of exotic Zo particles. A shining display commemorating the glory of Bugz progress was also staged to deflect attention from the disharmony in the Apex.

If Zyberians thought the future looked black, it suddenly looked even bleaker, for on swallowing the two Ziremes the black hole choked and coughed up the half-digested contents of an ancient meal it had never fully digested. This gob of acidic particle residue was flung at light speed across the open reaches of Zyberia, and once again the Bugzilla sought refuge in its moorings under the rim. Even after all this time it was still flushing out the filth from its inner cavities. The regurgitated mutant particles under their old tripartite leadership had then focused on regenerating the radical Zess priest particle and his infamous research facility. When this new, albeit inferior, regenerated particle came forth from the tortured chambers of his own making for the forty-fifth time, he did not disappoint. He resumed his experiments on cultures of replica particles and his summary extractions of information out of hard-to-crack particles with unlockable mechanisms.

The triumvirate of mutant particles was now conspiring to invade every part of Zyberia at the great passing of the Apex at Zo, an event predetermined but secret only to the Apex black and white leaders. At the time of the data that was now greatly aged the Apex had no natural successors except Zein and Ziel.

'Anyway, enough of this news, which needs a lot of further study before action', Bugzilla rounded off, distracted by the exotic contents of Zareth's attendant equations, two of which were bound in strong particle prisons. 'What are S units and souls, may I ask? Vicarages and IDOs and human souls?'

He pocketed some of the information in his deepest recesses before his visitors could stop him.

'The energy flooding of Zo,' Zareth said thoughtfully to himself, reviewing the pearl plotter coordinates for the journey ahead. 'It is written, and we must go. We must head for Zyber, then on to Zo.'

'Has this apex passing event happened and what of its outcome?'

'Given our great distance from this place I do not wish to appear inexact but it is probably coincident with our arrival at Zyber if we travelled the old pearl road now,' Bugzilla advised.

It was ever the imponderable that it seemed they had been missing an age but now they needed to be in two places urgently at the same time.

Zareth spread his great mantle once more, this time to serve as additional momentum for the Bugzilla, and a fresh cascade of zuons from his equation provided a balmy and favourable breeze.

70. THE HIGHWAY TO ZYBER

The Bugz were weary and disorientated. Their equations had suffered a time slip; it felt as though they had gone through more millennia on Earth, drifting in its soft blue pearlscape, than would have been the case in Zyberian time. It would take them time to convalesce while retracing their steps on the long and ancient pearl road. Zareth and Zein were mourning the fellow Bugz that were left behind and the allure of the colour vortex, while Ziel and Win did manage to spare a zicrosecond's thought about the fate of the Zarantula's crew. Zareth also wondered what had become of the striped particle Zag.

Meanwhile Bugzilla shivered with pleasure, stretched his great tentacled scanners after his long confinement, and launched himself on the wave peaks of his master's energy, away from the chequerboard of the battle site and out across the Empty Quarter, past the long defunct Zyclops and the faulty, intermittent siren radio signal that his passengers remembered from the Quest, and through the tarnished pearlscapes of outer Zyberia.

As the journey back progressed the Bugzilla filled with various engineering, explorer and scientific Bugz of various patinas and shades, and his calorimeter was stuck in its highest rating given this veritable feast. Zareth dispatched myriads of discovery particles ahead to report back on the lie of the pearlscape ahead. The old Zytopia may have gone into hiding and been subsumed by layers of duzz, but enough vestiges of it remained to reveal the highly individual constructs, some of them extraordinarily human in terms of equation, that had made up their culture. Zein recognised the nature of some of the curious equations behind the design of these engineering and structural Bugz; he recognised the softness of the equations he had become so familiar with on the blue planet. His own equation, he knew, was altered by the colour of Stein's.

At the sound of their approach, the towering pillar of duzz that was the first pearl portal crumbled and crunched under the Bugzilla's keel, revealed a multi-ringed aperture with codes that matched Zareth's own, and it slid open effortlessly.

It was the first of many such portals to fling open the path ahead, and it did so to the sound of harmonic Bugz zymns and a fresh flow of energy as particles emerged from the desert dunes of duzz and collected on the wayside, eager to respond to the firing of the Bugzilla's plasma messenger particles with a cacophony of harmonious greetings.

Zareth steered the Bugzilla across this once great trading route punctuated by great nuclei, which emerged out of the duzz as if the clock of time was reversed. Each region they passed through lit up with activity and orderly interchange as word spread of their arrival. The old Zytopia had not as much been destroyed by the quake as driven into some hiding, waiting for the special rallying call of the great Zareth.

Reports picked up at the various outposts confirmed the information imparted to Bugzilla from the broken particle. The pulse from Zyber was sickly and faint; hordes of rogue particles had laid waste once thriving communities. The Council of the Apex was in self-imposed exile, away from the capital of Zyber, and was holding court in the Bugzhist citadel of Zo. Zareth sent polished messenger particles to the offices of the Apex and the ancient Library Keeper to announce their coming.

It was clear that the disappearance of the leaders, considerable time ago had not been viewed favourably by all in the council because faded 'Wanted' notices had been posted at major intersections. The stark Apex decree spelled out in no uncertain messenger Bugz that:

`'Anyone with Valuable Data or even just Intuitive Zuons, no matter how zicroscopic, pertaining to the Location of said Undesirable Bugz listed in zicroscopic detail here below will be amply rewarded with 3.726 Bonus Boosts of Unadulterated Zo Energy and a Modest Replica Equation Upgrade at the fair and just Discretion of sundry Members of the Apex (lengthy Terms and Conditions apply with no recourse to Appeal).'`

Zein and Ziel absorbed the messenger Bugz that made up the decree and grimly annihilated each one.

Ziel had undergone some form of renaissance because the equation of Svetlana contrary to Ziel's perception, had indeed locked on and remained intact and it was now Ziel that did Svetlana's bidding. The real Svetlana had finally woken and it had emerged on the bridge in Venice with the small girl. It had awakened the most powerful desire in any woman on earth, and Ziel had underestimated the power of the human soul. Zein recalled that Zim had warned that there was a chance of the 'flipping' of equations and this is what had happened.

As a result of this change Zein had communicated with the new Ziel and found it a much more agreeable situation, unless it was some subterfuge. However Bugzilla had analysed the equation of Ziel before the trip through the convergence and the transformed equation that now existed. There were vestiges of the old Ziel remaining and those that were present appeared to be kept well in check by Svetlana.

As a result of the change, Zein and Ziel were now functioning much more as a pair of leaders with Zareth as the great advisor on old Zytopia.

Each portal they approached on the journey was locked with an encryption capable of being broken only by four high-tier particles, of which two needed to be present in order to overcome the most recalcitrant portal keeper. The mirror pair soon became adept at issuing joint communiqué Bugz for every gate they approached to be opened.

The Bugz were enthralled and expanding their equations too, all except the standard issue and readily corruptible Win, that is, who, having had his charge neutralised by Zareth, had been marooned on a heap of waste particles in the midst of the Empty Quarter. It was good to be rid of excess dangerous ballast. He had been left in this place under pain of annihilation if he ventured back into Zyberia. Genuinely it appeared that the mutant Win was pleased not to be thrown back into the black convergence and in his confused world he felt some new debt to Zareth. Zein and Ziel did wonder at the wisdom of leaving so powerful an adversary intact but were convinced by Zareth's clemency that 'trust' had to start somewhere.

Zein's equation was changed forever by the colour now flooding his sensors. It had blossomed and become the glistening multi-layered instrument he realised it had always intended to be.

358

The course of the Bugzilla was smooth, steady and sure. The gates might be thrown open ahead of them, the great portal code sung and the way lit up at the Bugz' passing, but it was felt best to avoid too much communication for fear of it leaking to those that might not salute the return. The three superparticles stood calmly at the helm in pyramidal form, assessing the counter-currents and opposition they might face. Zareth kept his old pennant with its three arrows unfurled within his mantle for now.

Meanwhile, Zareth could feel his great power decaying, as he himself had deduced would happen in the Library codex. The naked and jewel-like Lycian particle, soon to be known as Zycian, was sapping his energy as it strained to absorb all the data contained in its ancient leader host, all the accumulated learning since the dawn of Zytopia. To achieve the successful transfer of this data, Zareth needed to bathe in the Flame of Zytop, an act whose excess power needed to be contained lest it destroy the Library and half of Zyber. Rare and incredible primary superparticles were hardly a studied phenomenon, let alone understood. It was unclear whether the willing transition of one of these beings, and perhaps Zareth was one of them, obeyed or defied the rigours of logic and time itself. No high-tier Bugz, no Bugzhist, not even the likes of the ancient Library Keeper would be able to predict the outcome. All that lay at Bugz disposal were the ancient texts, laid out in the form of a cosmic alchemy whose results were known only to the same superbeings.

Even though it appeared a great tide was rising to cover the old leadership in transition, there was no option other than to see the rebirth of Zareth to its conclusion. It was after all, as Zein observed, the probable real objective of the whole quest undertaken and the sacrifice made.

71. THE GENESIS OF ZYCIAN

The Return to the Library in Zyber

Zyber now lay before them, and the Bugzilla approached the third gate of the defensive rings surrounding the huge nuclei. Zareth logged the correct access code. It was only after some gentle but persistent persuasion, however, that the ancient signal was acknowledged and registered. The old codes of Zytopia lay deep within the structure of the defences and responded finally and conclusively.

The Bugzilla made an immediate course for the Library and its honeycomb of data, and zeroed in on the faded energy signal bleeping from the heap of energy bands in a corner.

'Still waiting for your equation to be duplicated so you can retire, then?' Zein asked the ancient Library Keeper affectionately. 'Still fooling others with your layers of duzz?'

Zotl flushed with pearlescence and relief as he rose to greet his visitors with Zytopian melody.

'The ancient texts said you would return!' he marvelled. 'And not a moment too soon either. What is this? True unity between black and white! And Zareth...' he checked with what Zein now recognised to be emotion. 'There is much to do if the human equation you bear is to survive. You know that it will not withstand the full transfer it requires without bathing in the Flame of Zytop. It allows the flow and grafting of all the required mass, energy and data, and provides a link to the Energy viaduct. Even though the viaduct is broken it is all we have. Its conduit is the only way we can dissipate the amount of energy generated in the genesis. We are talking energy levels equal to the quake, if not greater.'

THE SWARMING OF ZO

While Zotl was preparing the chamber beneath the Library the aged ruling Apex was nearing its allotted departure to the vortex of annihilation at the Bugzhist nuclei of Zo. The mirror particles of black and white Bugz had pre-determined in their equations the lifespan they had. For reasons of security as much as anything else this timing remained secret except to certain high functionary Bugzhists. Even the Apex Council themselves were not aware until well into their lives about the exact date of the transition.

Countless millions of white and black particles were on the move, as white tried to counter black and re-establish the harmony and symmetry of old, and Bugzhist monks were engaged in the ritual dimming of energy at the impending transition of power in the Apex. This swarming activity was as nothing, however, to what was bearing down on them even now.

An unprecedented swarm of rogue particles with the regenerated Zess in the leading phalanxes had risen from the outer wastes and was making its way through the stagnant and duzz-choked pools of anti matter on the fringes of Zyberia, to ensure the final extinguishing of both white and black Apex members. Zess knew of an extinct pearlway marked by burnt out stars and mini black holes and strewn with antimatter; these formed a screen for the multiple shapes including great swathes of X, W, Y and the newly created v particles that marched on Zo in the form of throbbing, humming engines of destruction.

The first sign of discord to come to the senses of the Apex members was a great cannonade of antimatter, which landed in the tightly packed lattices of black and white particles lining the routes around Zo. The instant effect was wholesale obliteration as it exploded and sucked in swathes of black and white Bugz. Great plumes of these mushroomed up and snaked directly to the Bridge of Annihilation. Each pearlway from Zo was blocked by a giant rogue centrifuge, which plucked up particles

363

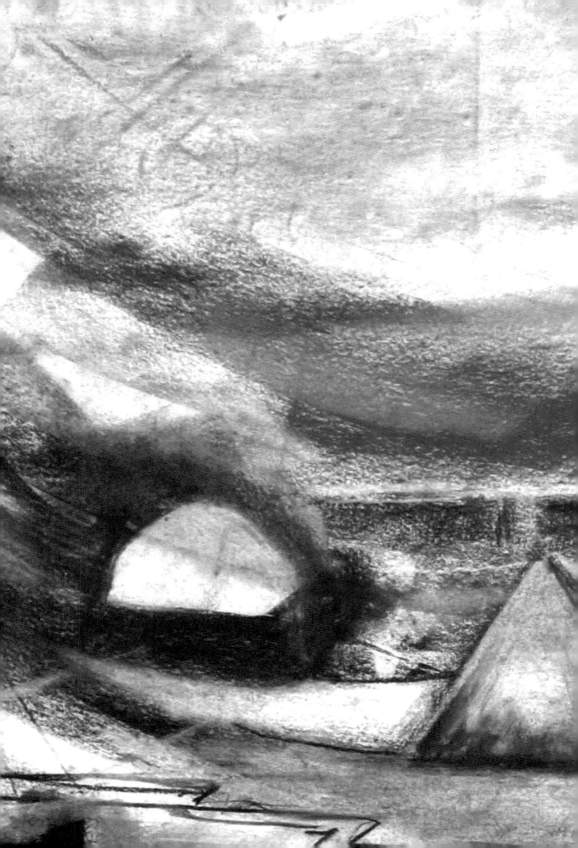

from the bottom tier upward seeking to escape. The great constructs had been made by Zess and effectively blocked the routes in and out of Zo.

All seemed lost to the endless night of Zess. Yet a zicroscopic and shining fragment of hope remained to those besieged. The triumvirate in the Apex would never have believed that the messenger Bugz so recently sent by Zareth could be so welcome and yet they had no means of communicating their situation because of the blocks placed on the pearl gateways.

THE BATHING IN THE FLAME OF ZYTOP AND THE DEPARTURE FOR ZO

Zein and the much changed Ziel stood amidst the dusty structural Bugz in the Chamber of Zareth to consult the ancient codex in preparation for the bathing in the Flame of Zytop.

'Farewell, my friends,' Zareth spoke. 'Parts of me will now travel the great pearl road that leads to the Bridge of Annihilation, but Zycian will continue and long may he help you on your journey and the rebuilding of Zytopia. My transition should help restore the great energy viaduct, affording you the greatest riches in equations and long-lost artifacts and text within this Library.'

When Zareth and the fledgling superparticle stepped into the mounting blue glow, every character of ancient text ever recorded was transcribed in full about them and within them; it crackled and leaped. The sound of zymns of countless millions of Bugz filled the charged Chamber, rising to a tremendous crescendo in the manner of some universal clock chiming the final knell of its maker. It was all the three attendant Superbugz of the Library Keeper Zotl, Zein and Ziel could do to ensure that none of the energy download damaged the chamber.

Lycian's equation melded further with Zareth's and control was passed from the ancient superparticle to a new hybrid with the name Zycian

A new voice spoke. 'I am here emerged from the Flame and remember all my pasts. You are all linked with my **SALVATION**. The **UNITY** spoken of is that which should exist between black and white Bugz. There is, however, a second interpretation of it, one which could combine or has combined with another universe and cannot be overlooked. This is what nothing fears. Bugzilla has put a new interpretation on the sign on the old battlescape. It could mean 'Nothing to fear', as in, you must fear nothing.'

'I have experience of this 'nothing' and it represents the greatest threat to white, black and grey, it seeks to reverse everything and sees our existence as a mistake or threat it needs to destroy.'

Then, to the Bugz' wonder, as the blue glow swelled a white schism or hole opened beneath the mass of the newly forming superparticle where the flame had barely flickered. It was the equal source of positive energy whose tendrils were linked via the great energy ducts broken in the quake.

The passing of Zareth and the genesis of Zycian meant that a part of the three parts of the Codex had been fulfilled. SALVATION and part UNITY. What was meant by LOVE, however, was unknown to the Zyberian mind. The three arrows that denoted the symbol of Zareth regrouped to form a three-pronged device that glowed in an orb above the intense energy sink, and this lit like a fuse that burnt its way at hyperspeed down into the very core of the flame, intensifying the heat and power thrown out. The Chamber filled with exquisite melody, and the Flame plunged down and flashed out through Zyber's crumbled foundations and poured its life-giving energy along the old energy viaducts and out into deep space, relinking the broken channels to the outer Zyberian fringe of long forgotten and countless supernovae, which had formed the old power source for ancient Zytop. The extreme energy download even jolted the antagonists locked in battle near the pools of Zo, but they knew nothing of its greater meaning. Slowly, but surely positive energy began to trickle into the old routings that made up classical Zytopia.

A communication blackout remained along the pearl road from Zo to Zyber. There were no TT Bugz winging their way along it, not even a straggle of confused messenger Bugz. Even after the washing away of the duzz it appeared that Zo no longer existed because no positive energy could be detected.

Zein and Ziel made a joint review of the top functionaries in the major gathering areas of the Bugz. They visited the Apex first, for, even though the two Superbugz were the rightful successors now back to take their place, strict Zyberian codes precluded any transfer of power without Apex protocol. The place was deserted, and a list of messenger Bugz pinned at the entrance referred visitors to the temporary powers at Zo. There was nothing for it but to head straight there and gather followers en-route.

The mirror pair called in at the UEMC and the Academy. Most of the functionary Bugz were in place carrying on their duties. The three main defence rings of Zyber remained intact despite Zyber's depleted numbers, and the bulk of warrior Bugz posted at the pearl gateway approaches and other centres of activity were calm.

The reborn superparticle Zycian and the mirror pair Zein and Ziel locked their equations into the great Bugzilla once more, and with a small group of academy followers began the journey to Zo along the thirteenth pearl highway. The Library Keeper looked on as the small column of melodic white and dark energy flowed through the open thirteenth gate towards the unknown. What was happening at Zo was not full understood, because no discovery or explorer Bugz had arrived from this area.

It was almost, Ziel observed to Zein, as though they were embarking on the Quest a second time round, but this time they knew the meaning of SALVATION because they had the immensely powerful ZYCIAN with them. Zycian contended himself with analysis of the codices and artifacts assembled from the Library and some thought of the family he had left behind in another world.

Bugzilla sensing the troubled leader's thoughts observed, 'The codices mention a bridge other then the dark nothing, maybe when things are calm here, I could come and explore Hazzz...lingdene with you ?'

'Zzz... now there's a thought I will put top of my equation, my loyal friend.'

72. A PROMISE FOR THE FUTURE 28 June 2042

Elsie stood in the shadows of her father's study, looking out over the old church beside the vicarage, while she viewed the bronze artefact on the desk before her, a unique automaton dating back to the third century BC. She stood observing the priceless smooth running of its clockwork parts and the intricate detail of the spheres as they moved effortlessly round.

'Oh, Dad. Lycian.' She thought, too, of Jonathan Stein and Mr and Mrs N.

'This small globe is not made of precious metal but it must point me in the direction of the midas particle Dad spoke of. It must be the way to prove he was right and with Blipp's help maybe this planet could just be saved from itself'.

She considered what Blipp had outlined and wondered about the church next door and this vicarage she lived in. Although not overly religious she had always believed there was a God and a Maker, hadn't even Stein said he felt he had to sacrifice himself for some greater good? She sighed at the baffling consequences of this train of thought in relation to Bugz, straightened her smart black jacket and made her way out into the bright sunlight to join the procession.

The mourners were gathering among the weathered Ashcroft tombs and half-sunken gravestones of Haslingdene's churchyard. They stood on the same spot of freshly dug earth they had stood on but three weeks earlier. This time the grave had been widened to make room for two

369

coffins. It was a quiet affair, Icarus and Lycian would have wanted nothing else. There was another freshly dug grave a short distance away; there should have been two coffins there as well, side by side, but since Joan Nimmo's body had not been recovered, she was remembered in name only.

A number of journalists and cameramen stood at the lych-gate to the churchyard. Wai Chan was stepping out of his eco land car when he saw them. Would you know it, he almost felt sorry for them. Nothing was normal about this case, even some of the bodies had gone missing before the autopsy. It must just baffle the editor which headline to top the next. He knew that Stein's managing editor was attending and he wondered which one he was, maybe the big guy in the black overcoat.

Wai Chan's gaze travelled a few yards on from them to see the broad shouldered back of a very short man with two minders, his slick white hair and no head apparel, contravening the UV mandatory hat laws, not that any self-respecting soul would worry about that, given the carnage recently brought to this family.

They were lining up round the edges of the graves now, the Ashcroft family, some distant relatives of the Nimmos, the Prof's boffs, Bertholdt Lipp. The short, whiskered man with angry eyes like beads of jet, who was fingering his rosary but three meters from Wai Cha, was making some sign of the cross. Christian put his arm round Elsie and Sam as the coffins were lowered. The priest gave a short address and a hymn was sung.

It was a very warm summer's morning. Like the picnic in May Week, Brooke thought, as if it was some half-remembered past epoch, but it had only been but a fleeting gossamer-winged bit of happiness.

Sam stared down at the coffins. He was seeing in his mind a box much smaller, one that was awaiting a fine toothcomb examination in the house. He and Elsie would have their work cut out, but with Blipp's limitless resource and of course his knowledge of Bugz, it would be very possible to advance human understanding of the universe and their own place within it. They had to study and interpret the data from the catastrophe at CERN and understand what could be so important to justify the deaths of his father and brother. It was the only way of filling the great void that had opened in his life.

Blipp was monitoring the buzz of IDO traffic surrounding the gathering. He was reflecting on the fate of the Nimmos and his annihilated

370

fellow Bugz Zon and Zleo, and on the fate of the Zargo and Zarantula, now joined uncaptained and stranded. Had the mirror Apex leaders found salvation? And what of the mysterious Zareth? He thought about the first Bugz-human contact he had made with Archimedes, and about the strategy laid down by Zein those few years back that had so affected human development. As he looked at the churchyard and its commemoration of the special equation years ago, it made him wonder. Maybe Bugz did not know everything, the idea of some mysterious force as yet unknown influencing events in this place may be a possibility worthy of further research. His mind was crystal clear, Bugz clear about his future. He would throw his mass behind the Ashcrofts. This was a special place worth saving. In truth they were a special family and he felt that his great compatriot Zein would have wanted it so. As he was reflecting, his tailor-made IDO suddenly jolted him out of his melancholy.

Hidden amongst the many messages Blipp detected a Super-G encrypted message that was received by the broad-shouldered man standing some way back.

And it was answered promptly too. 'Ciao, Gayle.'

Blipp pricked up his ears. Zzzzzzzzz.

END

NOTES

Blipp

The expansionist Blipp Corporation, a multi-media communications organisation, was founded in 2026 by the German billionaire Bertholdt Lipp and had within ten years joined the top ten largest companies in the world. The name passed quickly into everyday language: people joked about blipping this and blipping that. Blipp-branded IDO now conveyed 30% of world communication. Anti-trust legal suits in the USA had not dented the Corporation's expansion. Blipp had his headquarters in Geneva, not far from CERN.

The Bloody Green Revolution

In 2035 there was a rash of ecoterrorist activity round the world, as a coordinated protest against the ever-increasing restrictions imposed on individual liberty and the globalisation of every part of life. There had been frequent protests in previous years, but this was the first time the different terrorist groups had joined forces for a sustained campaign of violence that took hundreds of lives and wreaked untold damage. Several top-ranking industrialists and the president of a South American republic were kidnapped. The group known as the Defenders of our Future Children (DFC) was one of the main participants in these atrocities. Its principle targets were power stations, research laboratories, large-scale engineering projects.

Bridge of Sighs

The bridge was built to join the Doge's palace with the newly built Prigioni Nuovi (New Prisms) alongside. The bridge was completed in 1614, the ornamentation of the exterior foreshadows the baroque style and is decorated with bas reliefs of Justice and the arms of the Doge Marino Grimani (1595-1606).

E-honking

Car horns having been banned in first world countries to reduce noise pollution, drivers were now allowed to alert other drivers to their presence only in times of real danger and were otherwise obliged only to take evasive

372

action. Road rage, an increasing social threat during the 2030s despite the radical shift to public transport and restrictions on personal travel, was now channelled in the less harmful form of the driver interacting with an electronic dashboard display. This stress release device, the anti-road-rage programme, showed in humorous cartoon form the identical positions of surrounding vehicles and landmarks as the car travelled along, and the offending virtual motorist could be targeted in computer game style with a honk and zapped with a virtual missile. The programme laid claims to having reduced stress among the driving public, although critics saw it as yet another form of encouraging and legitimising violence. Copy cat crime using real weapons had not helped the programme's image.

The environment

85 world governments now made it compulsory to wear UV fibre hats or similar when being exposed to the more dangerous UV exposure of the 2040s.

Sea levels had risen and the Maldive islands in the Indian Ocean were things of the past as was 10% of East Anglia. The impact on food production had been catastrophic and the likes of Blipp were developing foods like Plankto which came from harvesting the sea surface. Certain larger airlines were running planes on bio and feeding the passengers on plankto.

eV (electronvolt)

The basic unit of energy (a very small amount as well), used in high energy physics. Multiples include GeV (one billion eV or giga electronvolt) and TeV (one trillion eV or tera electronvolt.

Fat Police

Appointed by the US government to monitor peoples' weight. As hypermarts became more powerful in food supply, the government passed various laws to control food supply including rationing points. When Stein refers to the 'Fat Police' he was often hungry but his lean frame never became fat.

Fuels

Bio vans, hydrogen buses and the revolutionary new fuels such as the UV landwagen had taken over from conventional petrol-driven cars. Areas such as Cambridge restricted car traffic as did many other cities. Eco cars was a company that only produced vehicles which had zero impact on the environment in production and in running thereafter.

The Grid

CERN set up the Grid in 2008, as a vast computational resource for the particle physics community for conducting and collaborating on data analysis. The Super Grid was established in 2035 to provide an elite and encrypted channel of communication accessible to less than 0.001% of the global population; it was intended specifically for high-level political and commercial contact, which proved useful for the purposes of secret diplomacy but inevitably lended itself to persistent charges of covert and unethical dealings. Super-G is the encrypted ultra-fast communication channel of the elite and government.

Gridlock occurred on two occasions when the Grid crashed, in 2036 and 2040, with serious economic consequences and, in the latter case, a major scandal relating to information trading and insider dealings.

Inform-ion Data Organisers

The Blipp Inform-ion Data organiser (IDO – as in 'I do') developed out of the advanced and lightweight handheld electronic appliances that revolutionised the already advanced communications industry in the late 2020s, and made a billionaire of the German mogul Bertholdt Lipp. The seamless merging of twenty-first century technologies such as quantum computing, ionics, micro-electromechanical systems and interactive digital/satellite broadcasting served to produce an all-purpose handheld or clip-on device with optional back of hand chip inserts and, in very special cases in line with medical ethics, brain inserts. The IDO features an electronic paper display and skin stretch controls for 'feeling' the virtual controls. Standard models are cased in lightweight black titanium or polylactic acid, a biodegradable plastic.

Newton

Sir Isaac Newton (1642—1727), mathematician and physicist, was as deeply interested in theology, classical civilisation, chemistry and alchemy as he was in science and mathematics. He held unorthodox views, and wrote well over a million words on biblical subjects alone.

Night climbing

An illegitimate sport enjoyed by many students for at least a century at Cambridge University. More a continuum than a club of devotees, these serious climbers risk possible expulsion from the University and their own lives to scale – without equipment such as ropes – the walls and roofs of colleges and other city buildings at night for the fun of it. Those using ropes are accused of lacking 'moral fibre'. Climbers occasionally leave calling cards such as political protest banners or more humorous ones such as the hanging of a lavatory seat over a lightning conductor. There are guides, photographs and diaries of actual climbs. The 1937 book *The Night Climbers of Cambridge* by Whipplesnaith has now been republished by Oleander Press (2007).

Particle accelerators and the Parallel-Beam Collider (PBC)

The parallel-beam collider is a type of particle accelerator. Particle accelerators in general, which can be either circular or linear, are constructed as far as possible to recreate the conditions of the early universe in terms of vacuum and absolute zero temperature, and thereby to recreate the fleeting existence of the high-energy particles produced in these conditions and to address such fundamental questions as where did we come from? What is dark energy, dark matter and antimatter? What determines mass? How best to use this knowledge to advance mankind?

To recreate these early conditions, counter-circulating bunches of subatomic, electrically charged and stable particles are propelled on radio frequency waves at close to the speed of light along a narrow vacuum tube made of copper, with the use of electromagnetic devices (giant magnets and resonators). The resultant collisions produce showers of even smaller particles which, while themselves invisible, leave their tracks glowing on the screens of detectors placed at points along the accelerator in order to track and identify them and also measure their energy.

Particle accelerators are built underground to minimise (harmless) radiation emitted from the accelerator itself, and to shield the accelerator in turn from the particles from outer space that impact the Earth on passing through our atmosphere.

In the year 2042, the last powerful ring accelerator was the Large Hadron Collider at CERN, started up in 2008 with the purpose of colliding protons with protons and heavy ions with heavy ions. It made some significant observations, providing its successor, the more powerful International Linear Collider (ILC) in Japan, with precise measurements for further study.

The ILC hurled electrons at electrons, collisions cleaner than those of protons and heavy ions and therefore easier to track. All eyes were fixed on its nanometer-sized beam, which revealed over time some interesting observations of particle decays. A top quark displayed quite kinky behaviour as it attracted to only one other particle in one specific type of environment, and even then it followed an illogical pattern. A couple of supersymmetric particles were found and named and sent the scientists scurrying back to their drawing boards.

A novel design for a much more powerful particle (and linear) accelerator is the parallel-beam accelerating technique powered by superconducting radiofrequency waves, in which the main beam along which the particles travel is fed by a relay system of drive beams that transfer extra power in quick bursts.

The Parallel-Beam Collider (PBC) is the first of this generation. From its conception at CERN in the late 2020s, it has been clear that this machine would be far more powerful than its forerunner, the proto-type Compact Linear Collider, made obsolete even before reaching the first phase of construction. Standing head and shoulders above any other type of accelerator in existence or at the planning stage, this new multi-TeV Parallel-Beam Collider is known simply by its generic name.

There had been an initial lull in developments when all eyes were still fixed on the performance of the most powerful accelerator in existence hitherto, the International Linear Collider.

The PBC test facilities were set up at CERN in 2031 before any host country was decided upon for the building of the actual machine, and certainly before today's technology was even dreamed of.

However, in 2035 when the PBC was finally given the green light, Switzerland had prevailed as host country and construction was begun at CERN straight away, on the site of the old Large Hadron Collider, which had long since been dismantled.

Vincenzio Viviani

Viviani wrote Galileo's letters for him and continued to his death to promote the scientist. He believed that Galileo's soul had gone to live in Michelangelo, who coincidentally was born hours after his master's death.

GLOSSARY OF BUGZ TERMINOLOGY

Absorb	Learn.
Analytical units, mental units	Brain.
Annihilation-evident	Fatally dangerous.
Annihilation vortex	The pathway all Bugz eventually travel to the great battery of existence, presumed to be across the bridge which features in legend.
Assistants	The humans who learn and spread knowledge from the key hosts.
Attract	To approach.
The Battle of the Bars	The great battle in which the shining force of Zareth took on the might of the mutant particles in a vain effort to save the equilibrium of symmetry and harmony that had been Zytopia. It was presumed the bars were objects in space or the zymns sung, notes and bars.
Binary particle	A schizophrenic Bugz, or a Bugz with an ambivalent charge.
Black shrapnel	Agents of negative energy.
Bridge of annihilation	The final place where Bugz are logged for the twice life – the end of the vortex.
Bugz	All Bugz are subatomic particles, but not all subatomic particles are Bugz. Most rogue particles, for instance, are not strictly Bugz; they are mutant particles that are isotopes or

the like. A small minority of Bugz have striped energy coils, which would indicate they are not of pure Bugz origin. It is arguable as to whether or not duzz particles classify as Bugz. They can move aggressively and induce stasis in others, yet seem to have no real consciousness of their own.

Bugz belong to a hierarchical and pyramidal structure ranging from the Superbugz at the top to elite (or high-tier) Bugz, down to second and third-tier Bugz (mostly functionaries), and down to waste Bugz at the bottom. You could say that Bugz can be classified like the earth atomic periodic table, only in 4D.

Bugz equations

Bugz lifespans are dictated by the complexity of their equations (which are for the most part inherited) and their potential for harmonious enhancement. Each equation is a type of earth soul crossed with a highly advanced mathematic and scientific formula, which the Bugz seeks constantly to improve and pass on from one generation to the next. The complexity of the equation dictates the Bugz' position in the pyramidal social order from bottom-tier waste Bugz to top-tier Superbugz. Equations may indeed be the equivalent of earth souls, but not enough study has been made of earth souls; however they appear linked and able to 'flip'.

Bugz'-eye view
Bugzhism

See things from a Bugz' perspective.

In common with religion Bugzhism, advocates reflection and harmony, yet it is founded on and promotes logic rather than faith; and is the study of both the known and unknown laws of phyzics. At the Academy of Zyber nearly all these laws have now been accounted for, yet a piece known as the Zo constant is still missing. Zo and its mystical pools of unadulterated energy are believed to be the origin of this phenomenon. Some Bugz hold that, in the days of Zytopia, the non-conformist black priest Zess (see Zess the Uncorrected) tampered with the constant and used his findings for the purposes of alchemy, to create new particles and explore other dimensions.

Bugzhist monks and elders

At the fall of Zytopia, when the energy viaduct supplying Zytop was broken in three places and the Great Plug dislodged, and when armies of high and complex equations and vast reserves of energy drained away to the outer edges of the universe, the only way in which the succeeding generation of ruling Apex Bugz could embark on a rebuilding programme was to fabricate new equations in great equation pools, stirred by a select group of Bugzhists. The progeny of the equation pools had been artificially manufactured simply to ensure the survival of Bugz civilisation. Their individual equations were prefixed by one digit reference only – they were, in essence, many replicates of few originals.

As a result of the Bugzhists' social re-engineering, the present-day Zyber is similar in many ways to Old Zytop, but it is smaller in scale and mostly style without substance.

Bugzhist monks are always present at the UEMC to oversee the dimming of energy at the Adjustment in the State of the Equilibrium.

Bugzilla

The unique and ancient hybrid creature-vessel with an insatiable appetite for data, who serves as Zareth's pennant ship.

Buoyant	Happy, optimistic.
Charged	Prepared, ready.
Chromothene	Chromothene is a versatile building material developed and marketed by Blipp industries. It has made paint and finishes a thing of the past for those with the budget for the latest in building materials. Chromothene's structure takes its energy from the sun and uses that energy to allow the user to have multiple finishes in different parts of an abode, so with a simple verbal command you could change a chromothene wall from yellow to grey or maybe some programmed pattern. Chromothene has been used as a replacement for glass or plastic windscreens. Chromothene C–Thru is the material the dome at CERN is made from.
Collector Bugz	Communication Bugz that gather in an umbrella formation to distract travelling Bugz (usually messenger and distress Bugz) with a signature that mimics a true-life equation, usually the equation of the intended recipient, and then lures its prey into a zone whose centrifugal forces trap their energy and scramble their signals. Illegal in Zyberia.
Combine, intercept	Meet.
Communiqué Bugz	The amassing of communication Bugz to make an official and public statement.
Compressed	Panicky.
Connectivity	Sociability, empathy, mutual understanding.
Core	Heart.
Council of the Apex	A select body of elite Bugz (or Superbugz) and high functionaries who deliberate on the regulation of the Zyberian state and Bugz society.
Dark convergence	Thought of as a large singularity. A place of immense pressure where no light escapes and

380

no matter can escape. Nobody has definite research on the 'nothing'.

Dense	Stupid.
Destabilised	Concerned, uncertain, upset.
Dez	A notorious Bugz and master annihilator who wallowed in the darkest corners of Zyberia's zlow life, and whose criminal career earned him the dubious distinction of having his energy rings ceremoniously dismantled and hung to discharge on each of Zyber's thirteen gates by no other than Zess the Uncorrected (or so it is believed).
The Disequilibrium	A time when white Bugz and black are diametrically opposed to the point of warfare.
Displaced	Out of sorts.
Displacement	Uncertainty.
Divided	Torn, unsure.
Drag	Reluctance.
Ductile	Easily influenced.
Duzz	Neutral particles lacking the strength to hold form drifting in and out.
Energy rating	Enthusiasm, good health, stamina.
Energy rings (or coils) and their husks	The body of a Bugz.
Energy surges	Social turmoil and unrest.
Equation-jumping	The serial visits of a Bugz in one or more host human equations.
Experimental values	Curiosity.
Explosive	Angry.
Fifth Dimension	The largely unexplored part of time/space that allows the laws of phyzics to be broken. (Not studied in book zero greatly.)
The Flame of Zytop	Kept burning in the Library of Zyber.
Flipping	A human soul can gain ascendancy over a Bugz equation, thereby taking control.

Fogged	Confused.
Function	Function, job, post
Function phase	Working day.
The Gates of Zareth	The last place Zareth was seen.
The Great Quake	A disaster to hit the Zyberian universe, after the Battle of the Bars, originating in the dark convergence.
Half life	The latter part of a Bugz' lifespan when he goes into decay.
Hidden variables	Shady, secretive nature.
Image	Imagine.
In a ground or steady state	Calm.
Indivisible	Standing one's ground.
Interparticle relations	A mutual transfer of data or energy between Bugz.
Intuitive zuons	A hunch.
Key hosts	The pivotal humans whose equations match high-tier Bugz. They appear unique and matching equations. There is a degree of danger for Bugz in linking to key hosts because they can be very powerful entities in their own right.
Logic later	Act first, think later.
Magnetic attraction strong sphere of influence	Charisma.
Memory energy	What is left of a dead Bugz.
Messenger Bugz	Interacting particles or communication Bugz, which are the equivalent of words in human language.
Microphotons	Energy Bugz of the smallest type, also linked to 'clear energy'.
Mirror Bugz	Often seen as the same but exactly opposite, for example: Zein and Ziel.

Negatively charged	Not happy.
The Open Chamber	The ritual voting of Zyberia's amassed Bugz takes place here at the time of the agreed Adjustment of the Equilibrium.
Parallel state	Trance, dream, thoughts elsewhere.
Pearlescence	Evidence of enhanced properties belonging to that of a pure Superbugz.
Pearlscape	The 4D shifting of space time in Zyberia.
Pearlscape plotter	A dynamic map providing shifting coordinates for pearlscape travel.
Pearl speed	The speed at which Bugz' vessels travel on pearl highways; time travel.
Pearls, white and black	Zyberia consists of a smooth and constantly shifting pearl topography which has black and white, regions through which Bugz can travel in terms of space and time. They must pass through often tricky pearl portals tended by portal keepers in order to get from one to another, and for travelling they require Apex-approved regulation pearl plotter coordinates and portal passes. Even with the assistance of such regulation documents and the portal keeper's approval to gain entry, portals are notoriously difficult as they usually consist of multi-ringed apertures locked with codes, and the required singing of the great portal codes must be pitch perfect.
Perfection rating	Beauty, accomplishment.
Positively charged	Happy.
Predictable	Reliable.
Preservation programme	Onboard device for ensuring the safe functioning of a Bugz vessel. Some are incredibly advanced and the source matter of the device is unknown. Some have been passed down

through generations. A powerful preservation programme that can stop annihilation.

Properties	Characteristics, skills, features.
The pull of the zides	Forces at work, such as the alternating between black and white or energy surges or the inevitable passing into one's twice life. The pull of the zides of Zo.
Receiver or recorder Bugz	Used for duplicating memory contained in one equation in another.
Recharged	Refreshed.
Receptors, sensors	The communication organs of a Bugz.
Repel from	Depart from.
Rezillience	Ability to resume original shape or state.
Routine function	Everyday life.
Rogue particles	See themselves as Bugz. Bugz see rogues as illegal constructs, not 'natural' if that word could ever be used.
S units	What Bugz regard as the properties of the human soul.
Sacrifice of Zareth	The vanishing point in the dark convergence where Zareth was last seen.
Scanner	A device for measuring its surroundings in zicroscopic detail.
Scotopic vision	Colourless vision.
State of Equilibrium	The orderly running of Zyberian society, which alternates once every ten thousand zicroyears between white and black Bugz, a system of pendulum government put in place after the fall of Zytopia. A phase is a cycle of power for white or black Bugz.

The twin tenets upheld by Zyberian society from state to individual level are: Logic and function – thought and action, integral to every Bugz; symmetry and harmony – the ideal state to which all should aim to achieve.

The Z form and the pyramidal form are important symbols to Bugz thinking, denoting order and direction.

Signature track	Biography, life history, linked to unique heraldry, zymns, lineage, equation containing hidden signature.
Similarly charged	In a like frame of mind, of a similar temperament.
Spin	Alertness and activeness, attitude, energy levels, personal interpretation of information.
Split	Depart, take one's leave of.
Stabilised	Calm, reassured.
Stasis, inert state	Sleep, trance.
Stretched	Far-sighted.
Stripling Bugz	Young Bugz.
Superbugz	Superbugz have exceptional equations and properties. They are the most direct descendants of the Bugz that existed in the time of Zytopia or even before.

Themselves and the elite Bugz of both orders, white and black, are mirror particles of each other. They have complex equations, which, depending on their points of origin, are judged on a perfection rating. Bugz of both orders seek ultimate harmony as well as symmetry in their equations, expressed in long tables and matrices. Harmony is not as easy to come by as symmetry. This fact taxes all including those with the most advanced analytical units, for even a Superbugz seems unable to achieve a higher than 98.44444 recurring percentage success rate in his manner of logic and function. Not all elite Bugz are Superbugz; some are superior functionaries such as the Library

Keeper or priests such as Zess. Second-tier Bugz usually have specialist equations with inbuilt skills in such areas as code-cracking, the military or warrior and advanced engineering.

There are many types of particle: engineering, architect or structural, armament, warrior, explorer or discovery, scribe, portal keepers (see Pearls, white and black), energy ring keepers, library keepers, memory particles (part accomplice, part recorder Bugz; see recorder or receiver Bugz), communication Bugz, mercenary Bugz (see BUGZ COMMUNICATION), travel Bugz (see BUGZ TRAVEL), supraparticles (higher than even Superbugz but possibly only the stuff of myth), duzz, waste (either for Bugz consumption or for bulking out matter).

Thin red laser light	Particle weapon with corrosive power.
Thought drive	The power of Bugzhist thought, physical as well as mental. A Bugzhist meditation.
Time shift	A Zessian black art that involves the illegal activity of tampering with time.
Transition	Bughzists keep safe the date when the Apex Council has to transfer power to the next generation of Superbugz leaders, like Zein and Ziel.
TT (thought transfer) Bugz	These are communication Bugz more highly advanced than everyday messenger Bugz, and used only by those high-tier Bugz normally given Apex or Bugzhist authorisation. The exact mechanism of TT is not understood by bughzists at the time of Zyberia.
Twice life, afterlife	A Bugz' afterlife, reached once the Bugz crosses the legendary Bridge of Annihilation.

Unbalanced	Strong but unreliable.
White phase, black phase	Period of rule.
W, X, Y particles	Rogue strains of Bugz that were cultivated by

Unbalanced
White phase,
black phase
W, X, Y particles

Strong but unreliable.

Period of rule.

Rogue strains of Bugz that were cultivated by the warped black priest particle Zess in the age of Zytopia, and who under the leadership of Wit, Yun and Xawn instigated the uprisings on the fringes of the Zyberian universe and counteracted the forces of both Zareth and the white Bugz.

X particles are heavy-mass, zargonite-hard bottom-tier Bugz with a strong negative charge, and with no real refinement possible, for their equations were deliberately stunted at the time of conception in the laboratory. They are unable to progress up through the pyramid of Bugz evolution although they have mastered the art of self-replication. They came from low-grade duzz and are predicted to return to low-grade duzz. They are capable of showing fierce if blind loyalty and live a nomadic existence.

Y particles are different and of higher status in that they possess three powerful attributes. The first is their individuality – a feature, so it seemed, of every Bugz of every tier down to waste level during the age of Zytopia, and one that defined its high status. The second is they swarm, but they follow an appointed leader out of individual choice and consensus, not instinct. When mustered in the right way they combine intelligence with as fierce loyalty as that shown by X particles. Their third attribute is their colossal negative energy charge, which can in a few individuals be several times greater than that of any black Superbugz.

W particles are a hybrid of X particles crossed with a pure Bugz strain. Their inherited pure Bugz features can obscure the inferior properties they have inherited from the black; they have therefore an unstable spin and are unpredictable and unreliable. They are, however, an isolated strain who come and go in a mysterious fashion, show little connectivity to other particles and show little aggression unless provoked. Gender as such does not exist in Zyberia, except in the form of the most zicroscopic differentiation in equation. However logical the Bugz make-up may be, the interpretation of facts is still likely to lead to a conclusion other than that held by one's fellow Bugz. Statistically speaking, female Bugz draw conclusions similar to those of other female Bugz, while male Bugz draw conclusions similar to those of other male Bugz.

Z units	White Bugz' feelings of happiness, positivity.
Zaggoty meal	Fare consisting of uninvited and unwholesome Bugz.
Zarantula	The craft in which Zielzub the Black Queen (Ziel) and her crew followed the Zargo, an inferior copy of the Zargo.
Zareth	The superparticle of legend, neither white nor black, who flourished during the Age of Zytopia and had a far-reaching sphere of influence.
Zargo	The vessel in which the Zargonauts travelled on their quest, the ultimate zireme and brainchild of Zim.
Zargonauts	The four Superbugz Zein, Zim, Zleo and Zon together with the second-tier Bugz Zag who set sail in the Zargo.

Zargonite	Extremely hard engineering particle, great force.
Zeazy	Something which provides no challenge whatsoever to a Bugz.
Zecho	The violent ripple of energy engendered when a Bugz passes out of his human host equation.
Zecode capsule	A Zyberian version of a message in a bottle.
Zectars	Units of travel that could be expressed as distance but also relate to time.
Zegas	Units of clear energy, see Zyclear propulsion.
Zen Bugz	Special high-tier Bugz whose prime function is to ensure the smooth and effective transmission of TT (thought transfer) Bugz. Zen is also an encryption/decyphering discipline of a particular group of bughzists.
Zerodian, Zomer	Zytopian scribe and scholar Bugz whose recordings are preserved in the Great Library.
Zess the Uncorrected	A particularly nasty black Bugzhist particle with irredeemably warped properties, some of which were stillborn and needed regenerating many times; a particle who flourished during the Later Zytopian Period. Every disturbing detail of his forty-fifth reincarnation is meticulously recorded in the Bugzilla's log (see Bugzilla).
Zetroscope	A navigation system for mapping pearl topography and also a device for monitoring the well-being and harmony of the crew and their surroundings, it also serves as a 4D recording device. It can rewind time if necessary at a specific location.
Zicroscopic	Small even for Bugz.
Zicroscopic blue particles	Powerful agents of positive energy used in Bugz warfare.

Zicroseconds, zicroyears, zicromillennia	Units of time difficult to interpolate for humans as it involves 4D time travel through pearl topography.
Zireme	State-of-the-art Bugz particle craft with its own advanced equation.
Zision	Premonition.
ZITI (Zyberian Transmission Index)	The communication language of the Bugz.
Zlobb-like behaviour	Behaviour primitive and unfitting of a methodical and orderly Bugz.
Zlow life	On the lowest table of Zyberian existence.
Zo	The Bugzhist citadel since the Age of Zytopia, located in the far outskirts of Zyberia and surrounded by many pools including the fabled Pool of Infinity. Zo energy particles are famed for their unique healing, nutritious and narcotic properties.
Zo Constant	The part missing from Bugz equations that Bugz seek to reduce.
Zornets' nest	An accumulation of mythological Bugz whose fissile properties and slow-working acidic sting put rogue particles in the shade.
Zotl	The present-day or ancient Library Keeper from ancient Zytop.
Zotons	Black Bugz' feelings of pleasure.
Zuons	Neutral feelings of calm.
Zyber	The current nucleus or capital of Zyberia, which contains such state institutions as the Apex (the seat of government), the Universal Energy Monitoring Centre (a body which carries out zicrosopic and strictly impartial surveillance of energy but is not capable of regulating Bugz society), the Academy (the seat of learning) and

the Great Library (the repository of all Bugz records). Zyber is surrounded by three defence rings, which contain in total thirteen gates. It is built on the ruins of Zytop, the capital during the classical age of Zytopia. The power supply of ancient Zytop was fed via a viaduct leading from an area of supernovae to a vast underground energy labyrinth. The labyrinth in turn has been kept intact by the Great Plug of Zyber to prevent any drain on the charge. This energy source was no longer operational resulting in Zyber being smaller than the much older Zytop.

Zyberia	The universe inhabited by the Bugz.
Zyberleagues	Units of distance.
Zyclear Bugz, vector Bugz, buginos, sub-buginos	Bugz helping to make up the fabric and control systems of a Bugz vessel to track along time-worn coordinates to follow a familiar route. Buginos are rare fossils of the early Zyberian universe.
Zyclear and Clear energy	Pure energy particles.(Harvested in new stars)
Zymns	Sung in battle but also at times of collectivity, transfers of energy being such a time.
Zytopia and Zytop	The classical age of Zytopia, a time when it is presumed pure symmetry and harmony prevailed in the Zytopian universe, and when Zytopia's capital was Zytop.
ZZD distress Bugz	Communication Bugz transmitted only in times of severe emergency.
4D binary game	The ultimate strategy game learnt at the academy. The battle on Earth is to Ziel a version of a strategy game.